“This is the third killing in three days.”

“All the victims are vampires, which on the surface at least leads to the conclusion that someone is targeting us.” Tobias peeled off his latex gloves and walked to the perimeter of the scene.

“That has to mean something.” Staring up at him, Nix saw the anguish he couldn’t hide. Without thinking she put her hand on his forearm.

Muscles bunched beneath her fingers. He looked down at her. His tongue swept out, leaving his lips moist and inviting. Even the hint of fangs peeping over his bottom lip was sexy. Memories of their time together, of the joining of their bodies twisting on soft, silky sheets swirled in his darkened eyes. Memories she shared. He bent toward her.

“Don’t,” she whispered, putting her other hand against his chest. She wished she’d sounded more sincere. Wished the hand against his chest was firm and determined instead of soft and giving.

“I have to.” He brushed his lips over hers…

Kiss of the Vampire

Cynthia Garner

FOREVER

NEW YORK BOSTON

Forever
Hachette Book Group
237 Park Avenue
New York, NY 10017

www.HachetteBookGroup.com

Forever is an imprint of Grand Central Publishing.
The Forever name and logo is a trademark of Hachette Book Group, Inc.

Printed in the United States of America

First Edition: February 2012

10 9 8 7 6 5 4 3 2 1

Acknowledgments

To my family: You may not have always understood this need I have to write but you've always supported me as I do it and I thank you with all my heart; thanks especially to my sister for being my number one fan.

To my fabulous critique partners Suzanne Moore, Alison Hentges, Sara Creasy, and Roz Denny Fox: Thank you for your invaluable input and unflagging support.

Special thanks to Susan Ginsburg for being an amazing agent and believing in my writing, and to Latoya Smith and Selina McLemore for being incredibly helpful and enthusiastic about this project.

Kiss of the Vampire

Chapter One

***Arizona Daily News*, February 13, 2012**

From the Editor

By Simon Tripp

In just under two years this planet will see another Influx of incorporeal beings. Most of them will be criminals, but some will be political dissidents or religious prisoners. The dimensional rift itself is caused by the return of the Moore-Creasy-Devon comet making its 73-year journey through the solar system. Beings from the other dimension have been using Earth as their own Botany Bay for millennia, and as of yet our scientists have been unable to find a way to stop it. These inter-dimensional marauders will stream through the rift like Vikings of old riding the rough waves of the sea to take possession of human bodies without any regard for those they displace. Or, more accurately, suppress.

We know little more about them now than we did when we first became aware that vampires and werewolves and all those other creatures of myth were, in fact, real. According to Dr. Nandi Wesley of NASA, an Extra-Dimensional (ED) takes possession of a human and the combination of their otherworldly essence with that of their host determines just what creature they become. How that happens still remains a mystery. No one in this world can explain on a genetic level what makes one a vampire, another a werewolf, still another a pixie, not even the renowned Dr. Wesley. As well, governments around the globe are as unprepared now as they were three years ago when word of this rift became public knowledge. Following the hysteria that caused families to turn on each other because they suspected their loved ones had become EDs, the United States passed a law that protects EDs from discrimination in housing, employment, and other aspects of life. The Preternatural Protection Act (PPA) also includes strict penalties for hate crimes directed toward EDs.

I've always pretty much been a live and let live sort of guy, but I'll admit I'm troubled by this laissez-faire attitude we have toward the monsters in our midst. Just because they say they'll police themselves doesn't mean they will. It's up to the everyday citizen to protect him- or herself, since our government won't, because in less than twenty-four months we'll have even more EDs to contend with, vampires being the worst of them.

Everyone knows these beings have been preying on humans for centuries. Just last month a woman was brutally attacked and died while her two small children looked on in terror. The vampire who was responsible has yet to be brought up on charges. More accurately, he or she has not been found. I don't know about you, but it seems to me that more often than not preternaturals literally get away with murder. Maybe some of these anti-preternatural groups that have sprung up over the last few years aren't all wrong. Maybe, just maybe, the people who killed that vamp in Scottsdale yesterday had the right idea.

I'm not satisfied to leave things as they are. Are you?

* * *

Nix de la Fuente scowled at the editorial as she made her way from her car to the latest crime scene. She folded the newspaper and stuffed it into her oversized bag. It was garbage like this in the media that kept people stirred up. At least the guy hadn't mentioned demons at all. She supposed she should be grateful for that. Thousands of years of propaganda foisted on humans by various religious establishments had definitely made demons out to be the bad guys. Some of that negative press wasn't wrong. Okay, most of it was pretty accurate.

Since she was only half demon, though, she considered herself one of the good guys. Most of the time, anyway. And it was her somewhat unique heritage that had landed her the job as one of the liaisons between the region's Council of Preternaturals and the local authorities. That hadn't earned her many friends on her mother's side of the family, because most demons wanted nothing to do with the council. They figured it was their right to live and kill others as they pleased. Her mother had been downright pissy about Nix taking a job with the council, but Nix didn't see any reason to placate a mother who'd been mostly absent from her life, letting Nix's paternal grandmother raise a child she'd resented and sometimes had even seemed to hate.

As Nix neared the crime scene, she paused outside the taped-off area and grabbed a pair of shoe covers to put over her boots. In between two tall saguaro cacti, she braced herself against the wall of the building and slipped on the covers. Flashing her ID at the uniformed Scottsdale police officer, she ducked under the yellow crime scene tape he held up for her. Taking care where she placed her feet, she walked several yards to where a corpse was covered with a black tarp. She pulled a pair of latex gloves out of her purse and with a sigh squatted down, slipped them on, then folded back the plastic sheeting.

Under the setting sun the blood appeared dark and dull on the victim's face and streaked the once beautiful but now grimy blond hair. Vacant blue eyes, clouded over, still held a look of surprise in their depths. In death her fangs hadn't retracted, the tips resting against her lower lip.

Nix's heart gave a thump. She knew this victim. Amarinda Novellus. Nix would never have thought she would see her like *this*. She blew out a breath and lifted the tarp higher to see more of the body. What was once designer clothing hung in bloody tatters. The rib cage gaped open, some of the bones broken. Most of the victim's internal organs were gone. One leg lay bent beneath her at an unnatural angle. Her right arm was at her side, palm down, while the left one was bent above her head. All of her fingers were gone; no doubt her attackers had removed them to hide the bits of flesh and blood Amarinda had gouged out of them with her nails. Deep slashes scored her forearms, her thighs. She hadn't gone down easily.

There were any number of preternaturals with the capacity and the desire to do this sort of thing, but the suspects greatly decreased when victimology was taken into account. Vamps were strong. Really strong. And fast. Even alone, this one should have been able to defend herself against almost anything.

Except there'd obviously been no defense against whatever had done this to her. At this point it was difficult to tell whether she'd been gutted by claws or knives.

A pair of men's scuffed brown shoes moved into Nix's field of vision. She glanced up past a potbelly to the ruddy face of one of the assistant medical examiners. "George. How're you doing?"

The porcine shifter scratched the side of his nose with a stubby finger. "Can't complain. Wouldn't do any good if I did."

"Family all right?" she asked. "Your youngest just went off to college, right? How does she like it so far?"

A broad grin creased his face. "Family's fine, and my baby's lovin' the college life. Worries me a little," he muttered, his smile losing some of its brightness. Knees cracked as he squatted next to her. "Helluva thing," he said with a slight gesture toward the body.

"Yeah." Nix sighed. "What d'ya got?"

"Murder by person or persons unknown. Just like the one yesterday." At her exasperated look he shrugged. "What do you want from me?" He gestured the length of the body. "She's been cut open and disemboweled. The how of it I'll know once I get her on the table. The why of it's your job. I can tell you she fed within the last twenty-four hours. That's determined by how soft and pink her skin is." He reached out and lifted her upper lip. "See how red her gums are? That shows she's fed recently, too." He let her lip fall back into place. "'Course, it could be that she took a long draw from the bastards that did this to her. I can't say for certain." He paused, shaking his head, then blew out a sigh. "It's a damned shame." He stood with a groan and stretched his back. "The boys should be here shortly to collect her. I'll let you know what I find out from the autopsy."

Nix watched him amble off and then looked back

down at Amarinda. As with the earlier victim, there weren't any visual clues that she could see on the body, but maybe there was some scent left. Nix leaned forward slightly. Just as she started to draw a breath to focus on the various odors from the body, a spicy, woodsy scent tickled her nostrils. A man moved into her peripheral vision and hitched up his black slacks to hunker down beside her.

"Nice of you to come," Detective Dante MacMillan murmured, shooting her a sidelong glance. Dante had been assigned to the Special Case Squad only a month ago. Even though it usually took her a while to warm up to people enough to call them friends, she and Dante had been on several cases together already and she knew he was a man of deep integrity and an abiding sense of justice. Plus he made her laugh. Nix wouldn't hesitate to name him as a friend, even after such a short amount of time.

She grimaced. "I came as soon as I got the call." Damned werebear dispatcher had a thing about demons, and he always waited until the very last minute to call her about a new case, making sure she strolled on to the scene later than everyone else. She'd probably hear about it from her bosses afterward.

"I've been here ten minutes. First officer on scene secured the site and started jotting down makes, models, and license plate numbers of cars on the street." He clasped his hands between his knees. "I have uniforms doing a canvas of the area. So far no witnesses. At least none that want to tell us what they know."

She looked down at the body. "I know her. Her name is Amarinda Novellus."

"How do you know her?" Dante's voice was hushed, his tone compassionate. Finding out that you knew a victim was never easy. It brought the violence of the murder all that closer to home.

"She was a friend." Nix clenched her jaw against the pain of her loss. She and Amarinda had drifted apart over the last five years because being around the female vampire had dredged up too many memories Nix hadn't wanted to deal with. Now she'd never have the chance to renew their friendship. Her emotions rose, her gut churning with demon fire as if the beast inside was trying to burn its way out.

Nix stared at what was left of her friend and pushed the guilt and grief aside. She had a job to do. Had to focus and get it done. She could grieve and wallow in regrets later. After she found Amarinda's killer.

Dante glanced at the victim, his face drawn and taut. A heavy sigh left him. "The second dead ED in as many days. God, I thought humans could be vicious to one another, but what EDs can do to each other..." He gave a slight shake of his head and gestured toward the gaping rib cage. "I mean, an ED had to have done this kind of damage, right?"

"Could have been a pret." Nix refused to call them EDs. It wasn't that there was anything technically wrong with the term, "extra-dimensional" really was quite accurate. But most humans said it with such disdain in their voices that it had become an insult and wasn't used by most preternaturals. She replaced the tarp and rose to her feet, removing her latex gloves and tugging the back of her short leather jacket down over the knife scabbard at the small of her back. She might possess more strength than an average human female, but it never hurt to have actual weapons at your disposal. Like a blade made of silver at her back and the Glock 9 mm at her waist.

Dante stood as well, towering over her. Of course, most men did, since her human DNA contributed to the fact that she was only five four in her stocking feet. Good thing she had on her three-inch-heel boots tonight. That way, at least, her eyes were level with his chin instead of his Adam's apple. She met his gaze. "There don't seem to be any bite marks that could make it a vampire kill, and I don't see any bites or scratches or tufts of fur on Rinda that would suggest a shape-shifter. Until the coroner can take a closer look, we won't know if the damage was done by humans with knives or prets with claws and teeth."

He cocked an eyebrow. "You really think humans could've done this?" He gestured toward the covered body.

"Maybe." The editorial she'd read just before she'd entered the taped-off scene came to mind. "Some of the anti-pret groups might have moved from rhetoric to rampage." She shrugged. "I've met some pretty violent humans, especially on this job."

"Yeah, me, too." He paused. She could tell by the look on his face he was really hoping humans hadn't been involved. Of course, if they weren't, that would mean that both of them would no longer be involved on this case. If this incident were pret against pret, human authorities would back off and allow the preternatural council to resolve the issue. Dante added, "This didn't happen here. Not enough blood." He gestured around the site. Criminalists were busy doing their jobs, from those taking photographs and placing evidence in paper bags to the one at the edge of the scene making a video recording. "There should be spatter everywhere, but there's only what's on and under her body."

Nix agreed. "This is definitely a dump site. She was killed somewhere else." The killing hadn't taken place that long ago, either. What blood was there was still fresh. One of the human techs walked by, the air disturbed by his movements wafting the rich smell of blood toward her. She could almost taste the coppery tang on the back of her tongue, making her stomach knot even more.

Demons didn't ingest blood like vampires did, but the smell of the stuff still brought out a primal response. A dull throb set up in her forehead and she brought one hand up to rub under her bangs, willing her horn buds to stay hidden. The last thing she needed was to start showing her demon at a crime scene. None of her human colleagues except Dante knew she was anything but 100 percent bona fide human being. She planned to keep it that way. While most people had settled down fairly well after finding out that vampires, werewolves, and the various fairy folk were real, they were downright hostile about demons. She didn't need the prejudices of the cops and the crowd gathered on the other side of the yellow tape hindering her work.

"George says based on rigor mortis she's been dead about an hour. No more than two." Dante rubbed his jaw. "He went into some mumbo jumbo about how it's different with a vampire 'cause they're technically already dead. My eyes glazed over after about the fifth time he said 'Adenosine Triphosphate.' "

Nix shot him a look of commiseration. The assistant

ME was a verbose little shape-shifter who loved the sound of his own voice. Especially when he was able to trot out long, complicated words. She was amazed he hadn't gone into more detail with her, but maybe he figured he'd already given the information to Dante, so why bother? "So once we have a suspect list we'll want to check alibis between the hours of two thirty and five thirty, just to be sure."

Dante nodded. "Hey, can you..." He looked around and lowered his voice. "Can you smell anything?"

Dante was always discreet, and Nix was forever grateful. She took a deep breath and held it, pushing past the scent of blood for other odors. The sounds around her faded as she focused on her olfactory sense. There was a light smell of vamp, some lingering aroma of shape-shifter, but nothing recent enough to support or discount their involvement. There was something else there, though, a smoky odor lingering just beneath everything else, something...like demon.

Nix stilled. Why in the hell would demons have attacked a lone vampire? As far as she knew there had been no blood feuds called. And most demons wouldn't dare strike out on their own without sanction from their leader. Of course, there was always a possibility that a few had gone rogue and were having fun like in the old days, ganging up on a vampire who'd been foolish enough to venture out on his or her own—but she didn't think that was what was going on. The scent of demon would be a lot stronger if that were the case.

She drew another breath. While her sense of smell was better than a full-blooded human's, it wasn't as good as a full-blooded demon's. And nowhere near as good as a vamp's or any of the shape-shifters. But even she could tell there was something wrong here. The demon scent was too faint. If actual demons had been here, the odor would be much stronger. Maybe it was residual from earlier in the day. But still, it troubled her. It wasn't enough to definitely say demons were involved, but it was too much to rule them out.

"The strongest smell is of humans," she murmured. "I'm no bloodhound, though, and I can't tell older scents from the current ones," she added with a glance at the technicians working the scene. She kept her voice low. "All of the pret scents are so faint, my first assumption is that the attackers were human. It's just too difficult to sort out all the other smells." Plus if vamps fed on humans just prior to the attack, they'd have an overriding odor of human on them. She said as much to Dante.

His low sigh drew her attention back to him. His eyes looked tired and soul weary, like most of the other human cops she knew. Poor guy. He looked a little pale, the lines around his mouth testament to the strain he was under and the confusion he was trying to sort through.

"What is it?" she asked.

He scrubbed the back of his neck with a big hand. "It's just...all this." He drew a deep breath. "Here we were, going along for thousands of years thinking we were at the top of the food chain. We gave names to things we didn't understand, like vampires or werewolves or goblins. And then to find out we weren't kings of all we surveyed, that these things were real, just not in the way we'd imagined them."

"What do you mean?" Nix crossed her arms and stared at him.

"Vampires aren't vampires, shape-shifters aren't shape-shifters. They're all just a bunch of interdimensional squatters."

She grinned. His metaphor was accurate. "Technically they *are* vampires. They have fangs. They don't eat, they drink blood."

"But they're not reanimated corpses like in the legends. That's what I mean." When she started to correct him, Dante waved her off. "Okay, okay, I realize that the entities that turn into what we call vampires can only take over dying or newly dead bodies, so I suppose that makes them reanimated corpses. But...you know what I mean." Frustration colored his deep voice. He gestured toward Amarinda. "She's not human. Not really. She's an alien possessing a human body. And in just under two years even more entities will come through the rift and nobody knows how to stop them."

"It's not like it's going to be the end of the world," Nix said slowly. She wasn't sure how she felt about the next Influx. She was part demon, so the fact that more prets were going to come through the rift didn't frighten her. If anything, she felt a little sad for all the humans who were going to be possessed by strangers, completely unable to do anything to prevent or avoid it. Thousands of families would become dysfunctional overnight. "We'll adapt." She hoped that was true.

"Yeah, I suppose." He took a few steps away from the body and began moving around the crime scene, following in the footsteps the criminalists had already taken.

Nix pulled a small but powerful flashlight out of her purse and followed him, looking closely at the ground, at the adobe walls of the nearby building. Except for the body, there didn't seem to be any other evidence of a crime, which supported their conclusion that Amarinda had been dumped here.

"Something this brutal tells me it was personal." Dante circled back toward the body. "You just don't do this kind of damage to someone you don't know."

"You don't think so? Remember, if it was prets that killed her..." Nix gave a quick shrug. At his questioning glance, she reminded him, "Werewolves eat people. And the internal organs are the yummiest."

"Oh, hell." He grimaced. "I really didn't need to be reminded of that. I don't think I'll ever get used to seeing stuff like this." He hooked his thumbs in his belt, fingers framing the large silver buckle. "I wonder what's keeping Knox?"

"I don't know." Nix looked around the crime scene for any sight of the quadrant vampire liaison. It was unusual that he wasn't here yet. She stared down at the tarp, her heart beating like bongo drums in her chest. Amarinda was the second vamp to be killed, and Knox was late. What if... She drew in a breath and held it, trying to calm her fears. She hoped he was all right.

Dante gazed toward the edge of the scene where the techs were beginning to pack up their cases. "Hey, Marks!" When the man looked up from the computer tablet he was jotting notes on, Dante asked, "Did you get word to the council dispatch that the vic is a vamp?"

The man nodded.

Dante glanced at Nix. "Then they should've called him by now." He brought up his wrist to look at his watch. "Wonder what's keeping him." He dropped his hand, hooking his thumb over his belt again. "So, what can you tell me about your friend here?" He gave a quick nod toward Amarinda's tarp-covered body.

Nix wet her lips. She realized she was thirsty and reached into her bag for a bottle of water. She usually carried at least one bottle with her because in the low humidity of the desert it was easy to become dehydrated. "She came through the rift somewhere around 330 BC, give or take. There are vamps older than her, but not many." Being immortal, like a vampire, didn't mean you couldn't be killed. It just meant it took a lot to do it, especially the older a vampire was. "She works…" Nix broke off and swallowed, surprised at how much this hurt. She twisted off the cap of the bottle and took a swig of water, using the few seconds to recap and replace the bottle to get her emotions under control. "*Worked* with Maldonado."

"The quadrant's vamp leader?" Dante gave a low whistle. "Someone must have a death wish, to take out one of Byron Maldonado's people."

"They may not have known. Or cared," Nix said.

"Who didn't know or care about what?" The raspy bass voice with a flavor of South Carolina came from behind her.

That deep voice stopped her heart. She turned, and when she saw Tobias Caine duck under the crime scene tape her stomach lurched. He was pulling on latex gloves as he walked. His thick black hair was in its usual rakish mess with a few strands falling over his forehead. He straightened and loped toward them with an easy long-legged stride that belied his underlying intensity.

Five years. It had been five years since he'd walked out on her. Five years since he'd thrown away her love.

It was like a dagger to the heart, seeing him again. He

looked the same as ever, tall, lean, handsome as sin. His gray shirt matched his eyes and his leather coat fell to midthigh, drawing attention to those long legs encased in dark blue denim. He looked damned fine. His presence revved up her pulse and that made her mad. There should have been some sort of sign that he'd suffered as much as she had, the bastard.

Nix stiffened her legs, telling herself it wasn't seeing him again that made her weak in the knees. There was no denying that lust surged through her body in tune to her quickened heartbeat. It didn't seem to matter he wasn't hers anymore.

Some people used meth. Others drank themselves into a stupor. Her drug of choice was Tobias Caine. And it seemed that even after five years of sobriety, she was still as addicted as ever. Her eyes began to burn, signaling the rise of her demon. Tobias had always had that effect on her, as if his darkness called to her own. When they'd been in the middle of making love it hadn't been a problem, it had even enhanced the experience. But now, while she was on the job... She gritted her teeth and forced the demon back.

Dante shifted, his right hand sliding over to unsnap the safety strap on his gun holster. He let his hand rest on the butt of his weapon. She could see how tense he was, his shoulders taut, hand ready to draw his pistol.

Nix didn't blame him. She was tempted to draw her gun, too, but for an entirely different reason. Battling back the urge to tear into Tobias, she asked him, "What're you doing here?"

His hard, stormy gaze locked on hers. "Nix. It's good to see you."

She ignored the throb between her thighs as her body reacted to his voice and those damned pheromones that spilled from him. Vampires had the ability to influence the behavior of others through these pheromones, excreted colorless chemicals that human senses were too dull to detect but pret senses could identify just fine. Some vamps were better at using them than others. Tobias was one of the best she'd seen. Or, more accurately, felt. "I asked you a question," she stated with a glare.

Tobias reached into the inner pocket of his leather jacket and pulled out a wallet. He flipped it open and showed ID that looked suspiciously like hers—that of a council liaison. "I'm your vampire liaison."

"You're not my anything." She folded her arms over her breasts. "What happened to Knox?"

Tobias shrugged. "He's been temporarily reassigned."

"Mr. Caine." Nix heard Dante's hard swallow but his voice held steady as he said, "I'm Detective MacMillan."

"No need for formality. Call me Tobias." Tobias reached out and the two men shook hands in greeting. Tobias tucked his ID away. "It's Dante, right?" Upon receiving a nod of affirmation from Dante, Tobias looked at Nix again.

As he took a step forward, she raised a hand to ward him off before he thought to come any closer. The pheromones still rolled off him in a steady stream, making it hard to breathe through the sensual fog they created. She ground her teeth to keep from leaping into his arms. Or baring her throat. Or both. "You need to ramp it down, Caine," she muttered.

"Don't know what you're talking about," he returned blandly.

She glanced at Dante. His hand rested once again on the butt of his gun but he didn't seem to be overly affected by the pheromones. While it was true he wouldn't sense them, he would still be influenced by them if that was what Tobias wanted. Since he wasn't, that meant Tobias was deliberately directing them her way. Her human DNA made her more susceptible to the effects than a full-blooded demon would be, and he knew it.

"Caine!" she bit out, taking a step backward, putting more distance between them and ignoring the confused look Dante sent her way. "Just what the hell are you doing here? Since when are you a council liaison? And why was Knox reassigned?"

Tobias gave her a cocky grin, making her heart flutter in unwanted longing, though his stare remained as penetrating as ever. "I arrived in town early this morning. As soon as word of this came to the council, they asked me to be a special liaison because of my background and the spate of murders that's happened recently."

She scowled and ignored, for the moment, the fact that they'd be working together. "Since when are two deaths a 'spate'?"

"Since today." His gaze snagged on the body. "Let me take a look at the victim."

Oh, crap. Amarinda and Tobias went way back. She was the one who had introduced Tobias and Nix. When he had left town, Nix had gone out of her way to avoid Amarinda after that, effectively ending their relationship. Something she would never be able to fix.

As he started forward, she put her hand on his arm. "Tobias..." There was no easy way to say it. "It's Rinda."

Tobias's face became drawn and the spill of vamp

pheromones increased, though now they vibrated with building rage and sorrow. "Damn it." He breathed out a sigh and crouched beside the body. He folded back the tarp to reveal her face.

Nix noticed a slight tremble in those long fingers and couldn't deny the sympathy she felt for him. Despite his meeting Amarinda more than a hundred years ago, the two had managed to maintain a close friendship. Before he'd left Scottsdale, they'd both worked for Maldonado—Tobias as one of Maldonado's enforcers and Rinda as a kind of jill-of-all-trades. Nix had never really been sure exactly what the female vampire's job had been.

Nix moved to the other side of the body so she could see Tobias's face better. His expression was controlled, placid even, but she could detect the stirrings of rage in the way his pupils dilated until there was only the smallest circle of gray rimming them.

She pushed aside the feelings Tobias's reappearance in her life engendered and focused on the job. She could get through anything if she just kept things on an impersonal level. *Just forget you know what he tastes like, how his skin feels against yours, how full you feel when he's deep inside you.* She tried to ignore the eager thump her clit gave and drew in a steadying breath. "Can you smell anything?"

He closed his eyes and inhaled. After a few seconds he grimaced and opened his eyes. "There's a little bit of shape-shifter and some vamp other than Rinda's scent. That could be odors here at the scene and not necessarily on her body. And then, there's you." The look he gave her suggested he could sense her physical reaction to his presence, probably even smell the involuntary stirring of arousal within her. "But there's something more, something beyond this overpowering odor of all these humans." He glanced at Dante with a mumbled, "No offense."

Dante scowled. "Offense taken."

Nix pressed her lips together while the two men sized each other up. Even as alpha as he could be, Dante was one of the most easygoing guys she knew, yet she wouldn't be surprised if Tobias managed to rub him the wrong way. When he wanted to be, Tobias could be a real charmer. Most of the time he didn't bother to put forth the effort.

Tobias cocked an eyebrow but didn't respond. With slow deliberateness, almost as if he were taking the time to say good-bye, he drew the tarp back over Amarinda's face and stood. He shoved his hands into the front pockets of his jeans, drawing Nix's gaze there. The material pulled taut across his groin, showing the outline of his cock. She jerked her gaze away and glanced at his face. Thankfully he hadn't seemed to notice where she'd just been looking.

"There is something... It's familiar, yet not. I don't know what it is." Frustration colored his voice, made the low tones tight and even raspier. "Who the hell did this?" His gaze caught Nix's. "Humans? Or someone trying to make it look like humans?"

She didn't have an answer. Not yet. "Since she wasn't killed here, it's hard to say. But the strongest scent is human, not pret."

"That might be technically accurate," Tobias murmured. He pressed his lips together and drew in another slow, deep breath. "That other smell. It smells like... demon." All demons had an underlying scent of burned wood or paper that was undetectable to humans. From the scent you couldn't tell one demon from another, but you could separate demons from other prets. Vamps and shape-shifters had no trouble picking it up. He looked at her, a hint of accusation in his eyes that immediately made her mad.

Not back in her life five minutes and already he was pointing fingers. She couldn't help being part demon, damn it. "Not every unexplained murder has a demon behind it, you know." She darted a glance around, making sure the police officers and assorted crime scene specialists weren't within earshot, then looked back at Tobias in silent warning. He should know better than to bait her about her lineage in front of the cops.

Of course, he probably figured there wasn't a whole hell of a lot she could, or would, do about it. And he'd be right. If he really did want to "out" her, he could. But she didn't think that was what he was after.

"It's not demons," Nix muttered, glaring at him. So, yeah, she'd caught a whiff of the same scent, but it was too faint to mean anything. She was about to say more when activity from beyond the yellow crime scene tape caught her attention. Two tall, slender men in dark blue one-piece uniforms stood on either side of a gurney upon which lay a folded crimson body bag. Council-appointed corpse retrievers, though they generally called themselves body snatchers, were there to collect Amarinda's body.

Tobias waved his hand at the cop at the perimeter. "Let them in." Since the victim was a vampire, authority in this case fell to Tobias. He took a few steps back from the body, making room for the two men.

Nix stepped back, too, and watched in silence as they

unfolded the body bag and stretched it on the ground next to Amarinda. They picked her up and placed her with great care in the open bag, then pulled the top portion over her, zipping it until she was completely covered.

It wasn't until the men had wheeled the laden gurney to the other side of the yellow tape that Tobias, his gaze on the departing body of his friend, said, "There's really not much else you can do, Nix. The crime scene techs will gather enough evidence so that equal measure can be tested by human forensics as well as turned over to the council for testing by our lab. You don't need to stay."

Chapter Two

Tobias saw anger flare in Nix's eyes. Before she could respond, he started to move away from her. She touched his arm to stop him. Just the weight of her slender hand on his sleeve sent a shockwave through him. Damn, but he'd missed her. He hadn't allowed himself to think about how much until now. The only reason he was back in town was because Amarinda had needed him. Otherwise he wouldn't have been within a hundred miles of here.

He stared down at Nix and resisted the urge to comb his fingers through her short black curls, slide his palm down her soft olive-complexioned cheek. Take those sexy courtesan lips with his own. Sympathy swirled in her dark eyes. That had been one of the first things that had struck him about her, those gorgeous brown eyes that so clearly communicated what she felt. He was humbled that she possessed such an amazing capability for empathy. No matter how much she might hate him now, she could still be sorry for his loss of a friend.

She dropped her hand and took a step back, going still like prey in the presence of a predator. Her small fists clenched at her sides and that stubborn chin of hers went up. Intelligence and good sense were qualities about her he admired. She knew better than to show fear in the face of his thin control. From the change in his vision he knew his pupils had expanded to obliterate his irises, and from the wary way she watched him he suspected the whites of his eyes had been taken over by crimson. His fangs were down and the bones in his face had hardened. Nix's step back had been her humanity reacting to the changes in him. His race was a race of hunters, regardless of which dimension they were in, and she knew it.

When she'd stiffened to stand her ground, well, that was the demon in her taking up the challenge. And there was the danger, that attraction of pret to pret, regardless that most demons and vampires barely tolerated each other. That was why he'd left. For her. To make sure she didn't lose her grip on everything that made her human.

Nix cleared her throat. To his surprise, instead of arguing that she should stay, she said, "I'm sorry. I know she was your friend."

He appreciated her sympathy even as he held himself rigid against the urge to yank her into his arms. "She was your friend, too."

Sadness and regret passed through her eyes, small specks of yellow mixing with the brown of her irises. Her emotions were cutting away at her ability to control her demon, but she didn't seem to be in any danger of losing control. He was impressed. But it still didn't change the fact that they'd been together all of five minutes and her demon had surfaced. Which meant he still had the ability to drive her insane and he couldn't—*wouldn't*—do that to her.

"Yes, she was. Once." Nix paused then repeated, "I'm sorry." Turning, she walked away.

Watching her ass sway as she moved away from him made him hard. He ground his jaw. His big head might know he was bad for her but his little head sure didn't give a damn.

He watched her duck beneath the crime scene tape and his jeans pulled even tauter across his groin. She paused and pulled off the booties, dropping them into a box set aside specifically for used protective gear. She gave a small wave to MacMillan and called out, "See you later, Dante."

The detective held up one finger, silently asking her to wait, and called out to Tobias, "When can we get together to compare notes?"

Tobias checked his watch and responded, "Why don't we get together first thing in the morning? We can discuss it over coffee."

"Coffee for you, maybe. Breakfast for me." MacMillan murmured something to the tech next to him and then said to Tobias, "Seven a.m. at IHOP all right with you? Nix?"

Tobias gave a nod. He really didn't care where they met.

"Oh, wait, that's daytime hours..." MacMillan grimaced, then shook his head.

"Newly turned vampires are the only ones who can't abide sunlight," Tobias said, "but after twenty-five years or so it's not a big problem. Sunglasses help."

"Oh, never mind, then. There goes that whole 'creatures of the night' mystique thing you had going on, though," Dante taunted.

Tobias caught the glance MacMillan sent his way before the detective asked Nix, "Can I talk to you for a minute? In private." She smiled and they walked several yards down the street, well away from the crime scene. "Can he hear us from here?" MacMillan asked.

Yes, he can. Tobias scowled. What was so damned important that the cop had to talk to her alone?

The detective leaned toward Nix, one arm braced against the wall of the building they stood by. It was clear from his stance that he was interested in her. With a snarl Tobias turned back toward the crime scene. Nix's private life was none of his business, not anymore. Resisting the urge to turn back to watch the two of them, he caught the attention of one of the techs and motioned him over. "What have you recovered so far?"

The man shook his head. "Not much of anything. This was a body dump, all right. She was killed some place else." At Tobias's grunt of impatience, he added, "We have blood and tissue samples, probably all the victim's, but that's it, man. There's nothing else here."

"Okay, thanks." Tobias stood still, staring at the ground, at the blood staining the dirt. Rinda's blood. She was his friend. Had always been a kindred spirit. It was a disconcerting thing, waking up in someone else's body. But when you found someone who'd gone through the same thing, you right off the bat had something in common. Sometimes that translated to friendship or something more. She'd been like family to him.

Tension rode high down his neck and into the rest of his muscles. He rotated his shoulders, working out the kinks. Who would have done this? And why? He ground his jaw. She'd had something to talk to him about and he'd gotten back to town as quickly as possible, but he'd been too late. He'd failed her.

Tobias tightened his jaw even more. It wasn't his first failure. He still hadn't found the quarry he'd followed through the rift. But he would. As soon as he found Rinda's killer, he'd get back on the bastard's trail.

Tobias went over to the medical examiner's van, taking off his booties and gloves and dropping them in the disposal box on the way. "Hang on a second there, boys," he said before the body snatchers could close the back door of the van. "I need the autopsy report as soon as possible. When can I expect it?"

The lead tech, a werewolf, didn't look up from his clipboard. "I'll be assisting the doc with whatever's left of the old gal. Report should be ready by tomorrow or next day at the latest."

Son of a...With speed fueled by rage Tobias grabbed the man by the front of his coveralls. Lifting him off his feet, he slammed him into the door of the van, rocking the vehicle. The werewolf looked up from his clipboard, his startled gaze fixing on Tobias's. Tobias snarled, "You treat her with respect or they'll be picking what's left of *you* up off the street. Understood?"

The werewolf's throat moved with his hard swallow. "Yes, sir. I meant no disrespect."

"Uh-huh." Tobias let him down slowly. With his face just inches from the tech's, he whispered, "Victims should not be victimized again by your indifference. Show a little compassion."

The tech pressed his lips together and nodded. "Got it. Won't happen again."

Tobias smoothed the material where he'd bunched it,

holding the werewolf's gaze a moment longer, and then turned away. He stopped, his eye caught by Nix and MacMillan still talking. He wondered what the hell they could be talking about so long and then reminded himself it was none of his business. He was here to do a job, and once it was done he'd leave again. Get back to tracking down the man who'd assassinated the leader of Tobias's people, the reason Tobias had come through the rift to begin with.

The only reason he had to keep going, now that he no longer had Nix.

* * *

"...and that's how he and I met," Nix finished. She looked back at the crime scene to see Tobias standing tall and strong. She was struck by the lonely picture he made. Surrounded by people and yet all alone. It was almost enough to make her want to go back to him, offer him companionship.

Almost. The pangs of hurt vibrating inside kept her feet planted right where they were.

Dante nodded. "Well, again, I'm sorry about your friend."

"Thanks."

"So..." He paused and looked at her. She could almost see the wheels turning inside his head. He said, "You seem to understand the different factions."

She had a feeling that wasn't what he'd originally meant to say. "Yeah," she said slowly, wondering where this was going.

"How did you get involved with EDs? I mean, I'm in this because of my job. Special Case Squads were set up pretty quickly as soon as we humans realized EDs were real, and once I'd gotten the requisite amount of detective hours under my belt, I signed on for this quadrant. But you...How did you get mixed up in all this?"

"You mean what's a nice girl like me *etcetera, etcetera*?" She raised her eyebrows, smiling a little when he shrugged and looked like a sheepish little boy. All he needed to do was scuff one foot back and forth and the picture would be complete.

"Yeah, I guess." His stare sharpened, reminding her there really was nothing boyish about him at all. He was a tough cop. He used humor to deal with the horrible things he saw every day, but when it came down to it he was a hardened warrior. "There has to be more to it than that you're part demon."

She gave a short laugh. "No, no, that's pretty much it. My demon half gives me certain...advantages over full-blooded humans. I can smell better, my sense of taste is stronger, and I'm physically stronger than a normal human woman. Or human man, for that matter." She grimaced. "Of course, there are definite disadvantages, too."

He didn't take his gaze off her. "Like what? Seems to me being stronger than most others around you and having more acute senses would outweigh any disadvantages."

"You don't know what it's like..." Nix shook her head. "You've never seen me go demon."

He frowned. "I've seen your eyes go from brown to yellow. Which, by the way, they are a little right now and it's kinda creepy. Just sayin'."

She rolled those eyes. "That's just the tip of the horn, my friend."

"Meaning...?"

Maybe it was because she was a little off her beat due to seeing Tobias again. Maybe it was because she had no problem trusting Dante with something so personal. Maybe it was because she was just so tired of always hiding part of herself. Whatever the reason, she looked him in the eyes and said, "I sprout horns. Literally." At his look of surprise she qualified, "They're really horn buds, but they pop up from under my skin just beneath my hairline. But that's not the worst of it."

Dante leaned closer, one shoulder against the wall, his entire stance one of protection as if to shield her from prying eyes. "What's the worst of it?" His deep tones were hushed, eyes conveying concern and compassion.

Could she adequately describe the raging needs that came with being a demon? "Since it usually only happens when I'm angry or upset, those emotions are intensified. If I was angry before the demon came out, then afterward I'm enraged. I see everything with a tint of yellow. The only thing I can think about is violence. And sex," she added as an afterthought. When his eyes widened slightly, she said, "It isn't only men who think about sex a lot."

"So, when you get mad you want to rip a guy's head off or maybe do a little somethin' else with his other head?" He waggled his brows.

She didn't laugh. Dante didn't understand exactly what could happen. "My mother is from a clan of demons that drain the life force from their mating partners. If they're not careful they do it all at once and kill the man they're having sex with. Sometimes that's the way they want it, to orgasm while their mate is dying." She pressed her lips together and looked down at the sidewalk. "That's what my mom eventually did to my dad. I was just a baby, and she killed him."

He gave a low whistle. "So your mom is a praying mantis of the demon world, eh?"

"Something like that." It was why her grandmother had resented, even hated, Nix so much. After her mother had dumped her with the old woman to raise, Grandma had provided a roof over her head, food to eat, and clothing to wear, but not much love or acceptance. Nix had thought that was normal because she hadn't gotten much love from her mother, either. Then her grandmother died, and, at sixteen, Nix became a ward of the state and was placed in a foster home. She'd never really fit in, and seeing firsthand what a loving relationship between parents and children was supposed to be like had been too much for her. She'd run, living on the streets, getting into trouble, learning how to survive.

She shook herself free of the past and said to Dante, "It's her kind of demon—*my* kind of demon—that gave rise to stories about succubi and incubi."

His eyes widened again. "Are all demons like that?"

Nix shook her head. "There are different clans with different... abilities. Some are assassins and have the requisite abilities to be damned good ones, some can induce fear and panic in others, some are empathic. It's quite varied. But one thing all the clans share in common is that they're considered the lowest of all preternaturals." She tamped back the natural outrage she always felt whenever she thought of the way demons were looked upon by other prets. "As far as the rest of the pret community is concerned they're bottom feeders."

Continuing to talk about it dredged up old memories that brought anguished emotions rushing to the surface. Nix felt pain skittle below her hairline and brought up one hand to rub her forehead. She looked at Dante. "Anyway, the more I lose control of the demon the more I lose my humanity. There haven't been that many, but most hybrids like me, children born of a pret and a human, go insane by their early twenties. It's too much for their human brain to handle the violent and sometimes sexual demands of their inner preternatural. If I can keep the demon at bay I can keep my mind intact." She crossed her fingers behind her back. Unwillingly she glanced past his shoulder and watched Tobias for a few seconds. God, she'd missed him. She'd loved him. Hated him. And now her emotions were so conflicted she wasn't sure what she was feeling. Her head ached beneath her bangs, like a sinus headache only focused higher, and her eyes burned as the demon used her emotional upheaval to make itself known.

"And now your eyes are yellow rimmed with red." He straightened. "Should I, ah, be concerned here?"

She dragged her gaze back to Dante. "It takes more than a few sad memories to make me go demon." That control had been hard won and found largely through trial and error. If nothing else, Tobias's leaving her had shown her how close she'd been to giving over to her demon. She patted Dante on the arm. "I'm okay. You don't have to worry about me going demon on your ass, especially not in front of all our colleagues." She took a few deep breaths to refocus her control and felt the burn leave her eyes. She knew Dante was aware of how she always fought to keep her demon under control. Now he knew why.

He lifted his chin in acknowledgment. "So... the factions?" he asked, bringing them back to his original question. He hooked his thumbs over his belt, his fingers framing the large cowboy belt buckle he always wore.

"They're not factions per se, Dante. All preternaturals were corporeal, mostly humanoid beings in the other dimension. And, unfortunately, just about all of them were criminals." She crossed her arms and leaned back against the wall of the building. She glanced at the scene behind him again and noticed that most of the technicians were starting to pack up their things. That spoke volumes to just how little evidence was at the scene. "Some were political prisoners, persecuted for their stand against the authorities on their various worlds, or were denounced as religious heretics. But most of them were undesirables." She paused, waiting for Dante to process what she'd told him so far. At his nod, she went on. "Tobias is one of the few exceptions. He was kinda like a Secret Service agent and U.S. marshal rolled into one. He came through the rift chasing a criminal who'd assassinated their leader. The assassin was tried and found guilty and was supposed to be executed. But he bribed a few officials and escaped through the rift instead."

Dante's eyebrows went up. "I didn't know that. I just assumed..." He turned to look at Tobias. "I figured he'd been a criminal like the others." He looked at Nix. "Though I'll admit, most of the EDs I've come into contact with have seemed law abiding for the most part."

Nix watched Tobias, too. He was talking to one of the criminalists, most likely telling him how to do his job if the way he was pointing toward the scene was anything to go by. She brought her attention back to Dante and nodded. “Many of them see this as a second chance. Most of the worlds they come from don’t practice capital punishment, which is why when the rift was discovered it seemed like an ideal solution. I suppose once the initial outlay of capital for the technology was recouped, they actually save money. No housing prisoners in jails, giving them three squares and time in the library every day.”

“Yeah, the grand solution was to send their criminals to us.” He scowled and hunched his shoulders. “Out of sight, out of mind, right?”

“Well, to be fair, I don’t think they know exactly what’s on the other side. They probably think the incorporeal entities they send through the rift are just...I dunno. Floating around.” She made a vague gesture with one hand. “I’d hate to think they know that the people they exile are, as you say, squatting in other people’s bodies and they just keep right on sending them through anyway.”

“Yeah, well, I wouldn’t put it past ’em to do just that. As long as they get rid of their problems, why should they care what it does to people they don’t even know?” Dante leaned one shoulder against the wall and stared down at her. His dark eyes narrowed a bit. “This is really hard for me to get my head around, you know?”

“I understand.” She shifted her stance to face him. “If I hadn’t grown up around them I’m sure I wouldn’t be so matter-of-fact about it. I mean, when something that only existed in myths and legends is suddenly living right next door, it’s only natural to freak out a little.”

“A little?” He snorted. “People were dousing family members with gasoline and setting them on fire, trying to ‘kill the beast.’ ” His face hardened with the memories of those early days. “I had to start watching my back because of the witch hunts going on in the department. It's settled down now, but I don't think it would take much to make things flare up again. Especially the closer we get to the next Influx."

"Well, maybe Congress will sign that funding bill."

"Don't hold your breath." Dante scuffed one booted heel against the dirt. "Even if they do free up billions of dollars for research, no one that I've heard of has the remotest idea how to stop the rift from happening. We don't have enough time. Or the right technology." He paused and blew out a breath. "So, look, about what I didn't want Tobias to overhear..." He jerked his head toward the vampire and looked at Nix. "I was wondering...that is, I was hoping we could go get a couple of drinks." When she didn't respond, he sighed and started to turn away. "Not a good idea, huh? I know you said early on that we should keep things strictly professional, and you've turned me down other times I've asked, but I'd hoped maybe you'd change your mind." He glanced at her, disappointment reflected on his face. "Let's just drop it."

"Dante..." Nix would like to have drinks with Dante, but only as a friend. She didn't want to send him mixed signals, though, so she shook her head in refusal even as the fleeting thought of using Dante to make Tobias jealous flitted through her mind. It would be a waste of time, because she knew Tobias wouldn't care one way or another. After all, *he'd* been the one to leave *her*. Plus it would hardly be fair to Dante to use him like that. "I can't," she told Dante. "We're friends. I don't want to mess that up."

He blew out a sigh. "I figured you'd tell me no again. Can't blame a guy for trying though, right?"

She touched him briefly on the arm. "No, I can't." Not knowing what else to say, she glanced at her watch and murmured, "I have to make my report to the council."

"Sure." He gave an easy shrug and started back toward the crime scene. Nix fell into step beside him. As they walked, Dante said, "I've been thinking about trying out a new place. Well, new to me anyway. You ever been to the Devil's Domain?"

"It's only the hottest, trendiest place to hit town in the last twenty years." She stared at him, grateful he'd so easily changed the subject, and seemed to not be bothered by her refusal to go out with him, but she was a little concerned about his choice of bars. "You do realize it's owned by Maldonado, right? And that prets hang out there? A lot of them." Most nights it was packed to capacity and looked like the United Nations of the fanged and furry.

"Oh, yeah, I know. I just..." Dante gave a lopsided grin. "Lately it seems the only time I see EDs is when they're dead. Or killing someone. I guess I'd just rather see them in more normal circumstances."

Nix slid a sidelong glance at him. While his attitude was commendable, he obviously still had a lot to learn about the preternatural community. Most of them had a bit of nasty worked into their DNA, which meant they could get really cranky really fast. Even cute, flirty little pixies could be deadly when riled or drunk. There was no such thing as "normal" when you were talking about prets.

Not sure she wanted to dispel his hopeful outlook, she still felt the need to warn him. "You're not likely to see prets at their best when they've had a few too many drinks, you know."

He grinned and patted his gun. "I can handle myself."

Nix bit back a sigh. Dante was still so naive about prets. A vampire could stand motionless ten feet away and then be at his throat before he ever had time to draw his weapon. Werewolves and the cat shifters were almost as fast. The only consolation with Dante going to the Devil's Domain was that security was high and the bouncers would protect humans as well as prets who might be under threat from someone else.

They stopped a few feet away from Tobias, who she knew had heard the last of their exchange. She waited for him to make some sarcastic remark, but, with his gaze on Dante, all he said was "One of your techs wants a word with you." With a lift of his chin he motioned toward one of the men standing at the opposite side of the crime scene.

Dante glanced down at Nix. "I'll see you in the morning." He walked away to talk to the man in blue coveralls.

In the silence that remained, Nix shifted air from one cheek to another and then blurted, "He asked me out." Some small measure of satisfaction filled her in imparting the information. She couldn't help it. At least Tobias would know someone was interested in her even if he wasn't.

"I didn't ask."

Nix stiffened at the complete unconcern and lack of interest in his voice. Hurt shafted through her again, then she got angry at herself. She shouldn't care that he wasn't bothered that Dante had asked her on a date. At least now she knew when he was tossing those damned pheromones her way he was only being a jerk. She propped her hands on her hips. "You're a real piece of work, you know that? Just how long did you say you've been back in town?"

"Got in this morning. And since I was here, like I said, the council asked me to look into these murders." He stared at the blood on the pavement where Amarinda's body had lain. "I wouldn't be back now, except she called me." His voice was soft and full of regret.

Nix focused on his last statement. "She called you? About what?"

"She wouldn't say." His lips firmed. "All she told me was that she had something she wanted to talk to me about, but she didn't want to do it over the phone." His steely gaze cut back to Nix. "Guess now I'll never know."

"Unless it ends up being the reason she died." Still fighting back outraged anger, Nix was proud of the noncommittal tone of her voice. Looking around the crime scene, she added, "I don't care what you say, demons didn't do this."

He stared at her a moment, then gave an abrupt nod. "Tell you what. I won't include it in my report, for now." His eyes narrowed. "But you have to come back with solid evidence that rules them out, not just a gut feeling. Or I *will* have to let the council know."

She blinked. Tobias Caine, the original Mr. By the Book, was actually going to let her skate on this one? Against her better judgment she found herself cutting him some slack. If he could relax his vigil on the rules, maybe he had changed a little in the years they'd been apart.

Tobias glanced at his watch. "Speaking of the council, I'm surprised we haven't gotten a call yet."

Nix's phone rang. She pulled it out of her pocket and glanced at the number. "Yeah, speak of the devils," she said.

"That's them?" He seemed genuinely surprised.

She looked at him. "What did you do, page them when I wasn't looking?" She wouldn't put it past him.

"No." He shoved his hands into his pockets. "It's coincidence."

"Uh-huh. Someone told me a long time ago that when you're dealing with murder there's no such thing as coincidence." She shot him a pointed look.

"That hardly applies to a phone call," he said, the look on his face showing he remembered that he'd been the one to tell her that.

She huffed out a sigh and answered the phone.

"They want you here, pronto," one of the dispatchers told her.

Nix frowned at his abrupt tone. "I'm doing well, thanks for asking," she replied. As he started to respond, she cut him off. "We're just about finished up here—"

"They said now. Just you. Since the vic is a vamp, Caine's lead on the case. He can finish up at the scene."

There wasn't any point in saying anything other than, "I'm on my way." She disconnected the call and looked at Tobias. "They want me."

The look that flashed through his eyes sent a shiver snaking down her spine. At one time that look had been much less fleeting and had been the start of hot, intense sex.

Nix drew in a breath and held it for a five count. The council was waiting and she'd better be on her way. To cover her reaction to the banked need in his eyes, she gave Tobias a mocking salute and turned toward her car, waving to Dante. As she drove away she glanced in her rearview mirror, watching the vampire standing so tall and straight, surrounded by activity yet so alone, the man who always managed to entice her inner demon to the surface.

Chapter Three

The Council of Preternaturals, made up of thirteen representatives from most of the major groups of preternaturals, tried to keep peace among prets as well as between prets and humans. They were not always successful, especially recently with tensions rising because of the upcoming rift. There was always some uproar or another needing their attention. They were overworked and under a lot of stress, which made for some interesting and not-so-pleasant interactions. Whenever things rolled downhill, the liaisons were the ones to catch all the crap. At least that's how Nix saw it.

She was kept waiting for almost two hours. Her emotions were already topsy-turvy, first from seeing Amarinda's body and then Tobias at the crime scene, and this delay certainly hadn't made her any more even-tempered. As it was, it probably wouldn't take much more to make her go off. Standing at the end of the hallway, several yards away from the doors of the main chamber, she tried some deep breathing to stave off her nerves. It helped, but not a lot. Not as much as a tai chi workout would have, but she couldn't just break into her routine outside the council chambers. She wouldn't give them any reason to doubt her ability to do her job.

Once they finally did deign to see her, she was hard pressed to keep the irritation from shining through. But while most demons she knew would just as soon spoon someone's brains out through their nose, she was determined to follow a more human path and kept a pleasant expression pasted on her face. No matter that her skull felt like it was about to split open, a sure sign that it wouldn't take much for her horn buds, usually recessed in her forehead, to pop out. Then it was anyone's guess as to what would happen. But she'd do her best to hold it together, because the people in this room were very powerful.

The room in which she stood was dimly lit. Roughly the size of a high school auditorium, it held a long semicircular mahogany table at the far end where the council members sat. There were a few chairs in front of the table, ostensibly for liaisons to use while making their reports, the wooden folding kind that were hell on the butt. Nix usually stayed on her feet mostly because of that, but also because the council was big on formality, and it seemed much too informal to sit in their presence.

When the full council met, thirteen people sat at the table. Which meant when she spoke before all the members, her nerves increased tenfold. Today, thankfully it was only a tribunal of three, though they were not always on her side. "We'll know more after the autopsy, I'm sure," she said as she wrapped up her report. She looked at the members of the tribunal and tried to gauge their reaction to this latest news. That they were disturbed was obvious, yet she could sense something else. Some other disquiet.

"Is there any significance to the fact that this victim is also a vampire, other than the obvious hate crime scenario?" Deoul Arias, a high elf and president of the council, leaned forward, elbows resting on the table top, chin resting on his fingertips. The flowing white sleeves of his formal council robe fell away from his forearms. His skin had the translucent quality that all older elves possessed, and he wore his long black hair loose except for two thin braids at either side of his face. His pale blue eyes seared Nix, skewering her into place like a bug pinned to a display board.

"We're not quite sure yet." She glanced at the other members of the tribunal—William Braithwaite, a vampire who'd come through the rift at the same time as Tobias, and Caladh MacLoch, a shape-shifting seal commonly called a selkie in his native Scotland. Even as she looked at him, he picked up a small spray bottle and spritzed his face with water. He had to keep his skin cool and wet or the resulting dryness made his skin crack in long, deep furrows that were excruciatingly painful. Knowing that Deoul waited for an answer, she moved her gaze back to him and added, "It's really too early to tell."

Deoul heaved a sigh laden with irritation and impatience. He folded his arms and narrowed his eyes. "Isn't it your job, as a quadrant liaison to humankind, to know the answers to these questions and to show up at the crime scene on time?" His voice was cultured, holding disdain and the hint of an accent so ancient it spoke volumes about the kind of power he possessed.

Anger at his attitude, at his continued questioning of her abilities, because this certainly wasn't the first time, rose within her. And, as usual, she tamped it down even as the patches of skin covering her horn buds started to itch. It wouldn't do any good to lose her temper. She wondered if he did it on purpose, trying to teach her patience or some other fey nonsense. Or maybe he just liked pushing her buttons. Seeing the derision in his eyes, she decided he did it because he didn't like her.

The feeling was mutual.

"I showed up within a reasonable time of when I got the call from dispatch." Nix kept her voice steady and calm, and hopefully respectful enough to pass muster. Damn that werebear dispatcher. She knew he'd deliberately waited to call her, and now Deoul was taking it out on her hide. She drew a breath and went on to answer the first part of the derisive question. "It's my job to find the answers to your questions. Which I will do as quickly as possible, I assure you."

Deoul's lips pursed, disappointment flashing across his face. He *had* wanted to get a rise out of her. Bastard. It made her doubly glad she hadn't given him the satisfaction. If it killed her she'd hold on to her composure, just to spoil Deoul's mood. Her grandma used to quote Scripture at her, obviously trying to subjugate the demon, and mostly Nix hadn't listened. But one particular quote had stuck with her. *Therefore if thine enemy hunger, feed him; if he thirst, give him drink; for in so doing thou shalt heap coals of fire on his head.*

Damn, she'd wished her grandmother had practiced what she'd preached with that particular passage. But for now Nix would reflect on those words as it related to Deoul. Heaping figurative coals of fire on his head might be just what she needed to maintain her control around him.

Deoul leaned back in his chair. His icy eyes glittered but he remained silent. She glanced at Caladh and Braithwaite and saw varying amounts of displeasure on their faces. Her heart pounded a little harder as her anxiety increased. She was doing the best she could, but this might just be the excuse they needed to get rid of her. She knew the reason they'd chosen her to begin with was because she was so familiar with prets. They'd pushed aside their aversion for everything demon and had focused on her humanity.

At least she'd thought they had. Now she wasn't so sure. It seemed the longer she served as a liaison the more contemptuous the council became. Maybe one day she'd find a sense of self-worth not attached to the job and tell them all where they could shove their biases. For now, though, she had something to prove to them. To herself. She drew in a breath and held it, counting to five. Then she exhaled. "Look, I'm not a medical examiner or a forensics expert. You didn't hire me to be either of those. What you *did* hire me to do is act as a go-between, to gather information and sift through it to get to the truth." She made eye contact with each of them. "And that is exactly what I will do. But you have to give me time."

"Two murders in two days would suggest we don't have a lot of time to give." Deoul rested one hand on the table and began drumming his fingers on the dark wood surface. "Just how many more bodies will we go through for you to get to the truth?"

She'd like to see him go out and do what she did. See how fast he came up with information. "I promise you'll have answers sooner than you expect."

"How can it be sooner than I expect when it's already later than I'd thought?" He lifted a dark eyebrow and turned his head to one side to glance at his colleagues.

The upper curve of his ear peeped out from his long hair, and Nix had the sudden urge to lean over the table and yank on it. Elves had very sensitive ears. She knew his yelp of pain would be very satisfying for her.

She restrained her mischievous urge and clenched her jaws against a scathing response. "I'll have answers as soon as possible."

"See that you do." Deoul gazed toward the back of the room and gave a nod.

Nix heard the doors open and turned sideways so she could see what was going on yet still keep an eye on the council members. Not that she didn't trust them, but…

Hell. She *didn't* trust them. None of them had gotten to the powerful positions they were in by being nice. While it was true they were intelligent and generally made positive decisions that benefited the pret community as a whole, it was equally true that most of them had had to be ruthless, conniving and downright mean to get a seat at this table.

Tobias and a slender woman in a flowered skirt and white blouse—Victoria Joseph, werewolf and liaison to the shape-shifter community in Nix's quadrant—walked in. Well, Victoria walked. Tobias sauntered.

And looked damned fine doing it.

Nix scowled. This was so far away from being good. The fact that they were calling in two other liaisons, especially Victoria, who shouldn't even be involved, didn't bode well for Nix.

When the two reached the table, they both bowed to the council. "*Ati me peta babka?*" they asked in unison in the common language from the other dimension. *How may I serve?*

Deoul's gaze cut to Nix as if to say, *See? This is how it's done.*

She scowled. So she hadn't given a damn bow. She'd said the frickin' words, hadn't she?

"Thank you both for coming on such short notice." Caladh spritzed his face again and gave a soft sigh of relief. "Victoria, my dear, it is agreeable to see you again." Pleasure turned his dark eyes liquid.

The werewolf's smile was slow and sultry. "It's good to see you, too."

Nix looked from one to the other. She wasn't always the quickest match to light, but there were definite undercurrents between these two. Interesting.

Caladh's gaze lingered on Victoria a moment before he turned his attention to Tobias, signaling that it was now Tobias's turn.

Tobias clasped his hands behind him and rocked back slightly on his heels. "I await the pleasure of the council."

"We would like to know your opinion on the current spate of murders," Deoul said.

Again with the "spate." Nix shot a glance at Tobias, who only shrugged. She wasn't stupid. *This* was why the council had kept her waiting. They'd snuck Tobias in around her and had already heard his report. Now they wanted him to trot out everything again for her benefit.

Shit. If he'd told them about smelling demon at the scene, even though he'd promised her he wouldn't, she was SOL because she'd kept it out of her report. She ground her jaws together and focused on keeping a placid expression on her face. By the way her eyes had begun to burn she knew the demon yellow in her irises was shining, spurred by her bubbling but as of yet not boiling over temper.

Tobias answered Deoul. "There is no conclusive evidence to point to a specific preternatural. The predominant scent was that of human."

There was silence, as if the council waited for him to say more. Nix shot him another glance but he didn't look her way. His steady gaze remained on the three on the other side of the large table.

Finally Deoul looked at Victoria and asked, "Have you heard anything from the shape-shifter community?"

"There have been murmurings, of course. Where there's a lack of truth, rumor runs wild." Her voice was melodious, as calming as wind chimes on a summer breeze. Quite at odds for someone who went furry once a month, oftentimes more, and would just as soon rip your lungs out as look at you. "Nothing substantive, though."

"So we don't know if humans did it or prets?" Caladh sat forward and reached for the spray bottle again. His eyes glittered and a scowl darkened his face. "That's quite helpful." Before Nix could respond to the sarcasm, he said, "There has been some unrest as of late. Prets have become targets of human prejudice and I've heard of escalating tensions between prets, especially between vampires and demons. Perhaps demons have called a blood feud?" he said with a glance at Nix.

Nix's heart stuttered. Was it possible? Could demons have officially been on a vampire hunt? No. She hadn't heard anything, and she would have been informed if a blood feud had been called. Plus the scent of demon would have been much stronger at the scene. With a quick glance at the faces of the council members, she still couldn't tell if they knew about that or not. For now, she'd take Tobias at his word and proceed as if the council was in the dark. She shook her head. "It wasn't demons." At their skeptical looks, she said, "If it had been a demon, we wouldn't be standing around asking if it could have been one. The scent would have been unmistakable."

Braithwaite finally entered the conversation. "Unless, perhaps, the suspect has learned how to mask its scent from other preternaturals."

Nix wished he'd kept his mouth shut. He was just making her mad. "I don't see how. Besides, it isn't likely." At the questioning looks sent her way, she added, "It's not their nature."

"Not their nature?" Deoul drummed his fingers on the table. "The nature of demons is to be deceptive, devious, and untrustworthy," he said as he ticked off the list on his fingers. "This, it would seem to me, would be exactly the sort of thing a demon would do."

"There has been no evidence at either scene to support your supposition that demons are behind this." It wasn't a lie, not exactly. A scent at the scene that might have been demon wasn't *evidence*. "Demons see no need to disguise themselves from anyone, let alone other prets. They don't care what anyone thinks of them. They're like the British Redcoats during the Revolutionary War, loud, proud, and obvious," Nix defended. That at least got a snort of amusement from Caladh. She went on, "Why else haven't they protested the fact that there's no representation of their sect on the council?"

More skepticism from the council members. Braithwaite flashed his fangs as his lip lifted in a sneer. He leaned back in his chair, eyes hard and glittering.

Maintaining her composure by the thinnest of threads, she ground out, "What exactly is it that I've done, or not done, to earn your distrust?"

"You're part demon, girl." Deoul's voice was as flinty and unforgiving as the expression on his face. "The only reason we appointed you as liaison to the human community was because of your ties to the preternatural community and your partial humanity. But I'm afraid it's only a matter of time before the demon in you overrides your humanity and you go mad." His voice lowered. "You can't deny your heritage."

Nix couldn't deny that her mother was a succubus. She couldn't deny that being part demon enhanced every violent tendency she tried to keep hidden. She couldn't deny that sometimes she herself thought if she didn't have sex she'd die, and while a focused tai chi workout wasn't nearly the same as an intense round of sex, it was safer and it worked.

She *could* deny that she was merely the sum of her parts. "I'm more than my genetics."

"It's in your blood." Deep in those pale elvish eyes lurked a hatred of her kind. Of *her*.

She swallowed. Her brow puckered. How had she not seen that before?

Blowing out a breath, she tried to calm her thudding heart. "I've been doing my job to the best of my abilities for two years now. I'm damn good, you know that." She stared at Deoul, hoping her anger was still hidden, and resisted the urge to scratch that itch beneath her bangs. If he saw her rubbing over her hidden horn buds, he'd know for sure he was getting to her. "If there's something I can do differently, anything I can do to convince you that I'm more than, *better* than, a demon, that my humanity is still very much in control...please, let me know." God, she was buying into the entire bias against demons, that somehow she should be better than a demon. Before she could retract her last statement, the council president leaned forward and put one fingertip on the table.

Deoul narrowed his eyes. "Watch your tone, Ms. de la Fuente."

Tobias took a step forward. "Her tone was quite respectful, Deoul, and she asked a valid question. An answer I'm interested in hearing, too."

Nix tried to ignore the surprise that went through her at him standing up for her.

She was stunned when Victoria piped up as well. "As would I."

Braithwaite shot to his feet, hands on hips, and glared at all three liaisons. "We're not required to explain ourselves to any of you." He pointed at them. "You work for us, not the other way around."

"Of course we do," Tobias replied, unfazed by the other vampire's outburst. "But when I see a colleague of mine being treated with disrespect for no apparent reason, or strictly because of her bloodlines in which she had no choice, I have to wonder why. I also have to wonder how long it'll be before I'm treated with the same discourtesy." He folded his arms over his muscular chest.

Nix envied his ability to stay cool. Her emotions were pinging all over the place, partly because of the way the council had been acting toward her, but mostly because of Tobias and the confusing mix of feelings he wrought in her. The itching sensation on her forehead had increasingly become more and more uncomfortable and now bordered on pain. She had a feeling it wouldn't take much more for her to pop her horn buds. While she knew she couldn't overcome all of the people in the room, they were a hell of a lot stronger than she was, she could still do a lot of damage. Going demon not only gave her additional strength and agility, it also let loose an unholy rage that lurked deep within her like a hidden river of bubbling lava. Only the calming influence of her daily tai chi workout kept a lid on it. That and the fact that Tobias had been so willing to stand up to the council in her defense lent a level of shock that somewhat quelled the other emotions.

Tobias murmured, "I'm well aware of how other preternaturals look upon vampires. You call us *akĥ khantu*, carrion feeders. Partly because we can only take over a dying or recently deceased body, and partly because in order to make another vampire we must drain the person of almost all their blood." He glanced at Nix, his gaze unreadable. "I would like to believe we've all grown beyond that attitude; that we look at people for their individual worth. It's no less than I deserve. It's no less than *any* of us deserve, including Nix."

Nix released the breath she hadn't realized she was holding. It was nice to have someone on her side in such an obvious way. She didn't get that support often. She barely ever saw her mother and when she did it was like two strangers getting together. She'd never known her father, and her paternal grandmother had passed on almost ten years ago. Nix had gone to the streets, supporting herself by petty thievery and a few bigger jobs. She wanted to stay mad at Tobias, keep the hurt close to the surface, but right now she was just damn grateful for his support.

Deoul turned his glare solely on Nix. "She is a halfbreed," he spat. "An abomination."

Here we go. More of the "purebreds are better" bull

Deoul dished out as often as he could. Unable to help herself, Nix whispered, "I believe the politically correct term is hybrid." Before Deoul could deliver what no doubt would have been a scathing response, she continued in a louder tone. "You knew when you hired me that I was part demon." She glanced at the other two councilors and then back at Deoul. "I was told at the time that my hiring was a unanimous decision, so what's changed?"

The elf's chin lifted. "Some of us were lobbied quite extensively on your behalf. It by no means began as a unanimous decision." He glanced at Caladh with a frown. The selkie must have been one of the members originally in favor of hiring her. Deoul went on, "While we understand you are also human, and it cannot be denied that you've done an acceptable job for us, it still remains that your humanity is twisted with that of demon. It is, without a doubt, only a matter of time before your inner demon comes out to play. Literally. And what then?"

What then indeed. Nix wanted to say that when she did start going demon, Deoul would be the first one on her list, but she restrained herself. "I disagree. I'm twenty-eight years old. If I was able to maintain control over my demon during puberty—a time during which many human parents believe their children are demons—and didn't fall prey to madness in my early twenties, I'm confident I'll be fine." She made eye contact with Deoul, holding his gaze for several moments, then did the same with Caladh and Braithwaite. They could never know how many self-doubts she had about her ability to stay in control. The tai chi worked, but would it always? "I'm already five years, almost six, beyond the time when most other hybrids have lost the battle. Have I given you reason to believe I'm about to lose it? Or are you just speaking out of fear?"

All three of them stiffened, as did Tobias and Victoria, and, as Nix's heart rate tripled its beat, she thought she'd finally gone too far.

Braithwaite opened his mouth, probably ready to give her a scathing put down, but Caladh slammed his palm on the table. "Enough!" Looking at Braithwaite, he muttered, "Sit down." When the vampire didn't move, Caladh bared his teeth, showing a set of pearly whites that were starting to sharpen into neat points. "Sit. Down."

A muscle twitched in Braithwaite's pale jaw. He looked at Nix, his pupils dilated, swallowing up any trace of brown. Pressing his lips together, he sat, though Nix could tell it was done with reluctance. He glanced at Caladh, his expression a mixture of subservience and irritation. The selkie was a longtime member of the council, and a powerful man in his own right. It wasn't smart to get on his bad side. When Caladh spoke, the younger councilors listened. Unless they were stupid, and Braithwaite was, if nothing else, not stupid.

"Thank you." Caladh looked at Nix with sympathy in his eyes. "Nix, I realize you're in a sometimes untenable position. Due to your work with us you've become something of a target among demonkind, yet you rarely receive any sort of acclaim." He sent a pointed glance his colleagues' way. "Let me say, for the record, that you do an admirable job under very difficult circumstances. I, for one, appreciate the fact that you're on our team."

Nix blinked. While it had been obvious to her that Caladh was the least judgmental of the three, it had seemed that he did, indeed, disapprove of her. But if he said he appreciated her, she'd take it, even if he was lying through those oh-so-white teeth. "Thank you, my lord Caladh." See? She could be just as gracious as the next person.

A small smile curved one side of his mouth. "I think we can call this meeting adjourned, don't you, Deoul? There's nothing more to be discussed at this stage." He winked at her and turned a solemn face toward the other members of the council. "As our human liaison has stated, it's too early to tell."

Deoul gave an abrupt nod. "I agree. I expect an update, in person, the second you have more information," he stated, looking at Nix.

She nodded.

"We're adjourned." Deoul stood and walked away from the table, Caladh and Braithwaite following him.

As soon as the doors closed behind them, Nix turned to Tobias and Victoria with a sigh. "Thank you both for coming to my defense. I thought I was about to be put on a spit and roasted."

"It could still happen," Victoria said with a wink of her own. Her usually somber face lit with a rare smile. "Deoul, I'm told, has a fondness for rump roasts." She glanced at Nix's rear, then gave a small wave and walked out of the room.

That left Tobias. "I thought there for a while that you'd told them about the you-know-what at the scene." Nix didn't want to talk too loudly, because with a building full of shape-shifters, vampires, and other sundry preternaturals, she never knew who was listening.

His expression didn't change from the polite, bland facade he'd presented to the council. "I told you I wouldn't say anything. For now." His gaze held hers. "But you'll need to provide evidence to the contrary."

Vampire pheromones wafted her way. She swayed, her body tightening with the beginnings of arousal. She drew in a shaky breath, slipping out her tongue to wet her dry lips. Staring at his mouth, she wanted to feel it against hers again. Against her breasts. Against her throat...

As soon as she realized her head was beginning to tilt to one side she drew herself up and glared at him with stiff outrage. "Caine! Keep your damned pheromones to yourself."

He met her scowl. "Can I help it if I know you're such a tasty morsel?" He fixed his eyes on her throat. His pupils dilated, and she caught a glimpse of fangs. Lust darkened his face. He always used to look at her like that, but five years ago the lust had been tempered with love. Or so she'd thought. Now, though, there were no tender emotions reflected in his eyes. Now it was only hunger. Physical and sexual.

She tightened her lips. Bastard. She wasn't good enough or was too demon or something for him to love, but he was making it pretty obvious that he'd be willing to pierce her with fangs and cock again.

Nix fisted her hands and fought back anger at his callousness. He had never been so cold. He used to care about his sexual partner's feelings, didn't just use people for blood and sex. But now he seemed indifferent. To her, at least. She turned on her heel and strode away.

She didn't know whether to be happy or sad when he didn't come after her.

Chapter Four

Half an hour later Nix unlocked her front door and pushed her way past an excited, full-bladdered dog. One of her neighbors routinely took the mutt out for an afternoon walk around three p.m. and fed him, but it was now almost ten and she knew he needed to go again.

He circled around her feet, his shoulder butting her thighs, a *woof* of impatience leaving him when she dropped her shoulder bag on the floor. "I know, sweetie." She ruffled the top of his head and toed off her boots. If they could have, her feet would have breathed a sigh of relief. "Just let me change shoes, all right?"

She headed into her bedroom, Rufus at her heels. As she went through the living room she noticed the book she'd been reading was on the floor. It didn't look too worse for wear, but she could see it was a little mangled around the edges. "Have you been nibbling on my book?" she asked the dog. A stray that had started hanging around the apartment complex, he'd adopted her a couple of years ago. Every time he'd seen her he'd immediately rolled onto his back for his belly to be scratched. Nix had managed to ignore him the first few times, but the dog had been persistent.

Now he was her constant companion. She sat on the edge of her queen-size bed and shoved her feet into her old-fashioned sneakers, pulling the laces tight. "Don't you know dogs don't like demons?" she asked him for the umpteenth time. He gave her a doggy grin and wagged his tail.

She supposed it was the human in her that the dog was drawn to. Or, as she had long suspected, he was just a little on the nutty side.

As she was tying the shoestrings, Rufus yipped at her. She finished and stood. "All right, already." She walked back to the entryway and grabbed his leash. He started prancing around, making it difficult to get the leash clipped to his collar. She finally did, though, got the door opened, and pulled it closed behind her as Rufus yanked her out onto the sidewalk. As soon as they were outside, he took off for the grassy area between the building and the parking lot, Nix jogging to keep up with him.

"You poor baby."

Rufus sent her a look she could only interpret as gleeful canine relief and shortly began walking her the length of the parking lot, dodging around stately saguaros and clusters of purple-tinged prickly pear cacti. As the dog stopped and sniffed everything in sight, he ignored the sound of traffic from the street and the loud music coming from the apartment on the corner. Usually Nix had patience with him and let him do his doggy thing, but tonight…

Between seeing Tobias again and the nonsense the council had put her through, her inner demon was pretty ramped up. She needed to get back inside and calm it down with tai chi.

She got Rufus inside and gave him half a cup of dog food as a treat for not ruining the apartment in her absence—she wouldn't count the gnawed-on book against him—then changed into a loose pair of cotton shorts and a tank top. Going back into the living room, she dimmed the lights and began her tai chi routine by raising her hands above her head on an inhale, and then bringing them down and in front of her while exhaling. One form flowed slowly into another, from Embrace the Tiger to Return to Mountain. Arms and legs worked in controlled harmony. Her breathing evened out, her soul centered and became calm.

Waving Hands in Clouds was followed by Golden Pheasant Stands on One Leg. She remembered when she first began doing tai chi and tried this move, she'd wobbled back and forth like a bobblehead. Now she was steadfast, her balance true. A few more moves, a cross of her hands in front of her, a final exhale, and her routine was complete. She felt relaxed and in a much calmer frame of mind. She went through her nightly bedtime preparations, and, with her favorite penguin pajamas on, she turned off the light and climbed into bed. She heard the clatter of Rufus's claws on the hardwood floor. They stopped and in the dark she could feel him staring at her. She gave him a firm no. He huffed a sigh and padded over to his thick dog bed. It was a routine he followed every night. Standing by her bed making doggy eyes at her, hoping to get to sleep up in the big bed with her. And every night she told him no. She had a hard enough time sleeping as it was. She wasn't about to let him spread out and take up most of the room.

Nix bent one leg and stretched her arms out. The tai

chi had done what it was supposed to, relax her body and calm her mind, but she could already feel her thoughts beginning to race, drawing her back to when she'd first seen Tobias again. It had been so long since they'd seen each other, but in those first few seconds it had been like no time at all had passed. It would have been the most natural thing in the world to walk right back into his arms.

She couldn't stop her mind from taking her to a time when she and Tobias had been happy together. They'd gone out to celebrate her twenty-third birthday. A night out at one of Maldonado's clubs, then home to bed. But not to sleep.

Nix shivered and rolled onto her side. The year that she and Tobias were together would be ingrained in her memory until the day she died, but that night...the details of that night were as fresh as if it were just yesterday. There'd been the slow walk across the bedroom floor, him guiding her backward as his mouth never left hers. When the mattress had hit the back of her thighs Tobias had steadied her.

He'd gone down on one knee and slipped off her shoes, gentle hands cool against her ankles. He'd kissed his way up her leg until he reached the hem of her short skirt. He'd paused and looked up at her then, eyes completely black and pheromones rolling off him in undulating waves.

Back then she hadn't minded the pheromones. They'd increased her arousal, as they were meant to, but more important they had been evidence of *his* arousal.

Nix turned onto her back. Closing her eyes, she lost herself in the memory of that night. Tobias slid the zipper of her skirt down, each click of the tab against the metal teeth sounding loud in the silence of the room. The only other sound was her ever quickening breathing and his low murmurs of encouragement. Her frilly red blouse was next to go, leaving her standing next to the bed clad in only a skimpy pair of black silk panties.

Tobias rested his cheek against the slight mound of her belly, his dark hair tickling her skin. She combed her fingers through his hair and then gripped his shoulders. "Come up here," she whispered, tugging at him.

"Not yet." His deep voice rasped across her eardrums, ramping her arousal even higher. "Got some territory to explore right here." Warm breath puffed against the juncture of her thighs. His lips pressed a slow, open-mouthed kiss high up on her inner thigh. She caught her breath. When his tongue dipped under the elastic leg of her panties and traced against the fleshy lips of her sex, she moaned and leaned into his touch.

He abruptly stood, mouth crushing hers, tongue thrusting inside in primal possession. She moaned and met him, her tongue parrying his every move while her fingers dug into his shoulders, his back, slid down to grab his lovely, firm ass and pull him against her.

He groaned and rocked against her, his erection hard against the fly of his pants. With a soft oath he tore away and stripped off his clothes, his lean, muscular body bared to her ravenous stare. In the soft moonlight streaming through the window, his fangs glinted, his eyes black holes surrounded by crimson. Muscles bunched and rippled from his neck to his shoulders, to his abdomen where a treasure trail of dark hair drew her gaze lower. His cock was so rigid it curved up against his belly. The veins pulsed, powered by a heart that beat only after he had fed.

She swallowed as she remembered when he'd fed last.

At the club, their bodies entwined on the dance floor. He'd kissed her neck and then fangs had slid into her throat so gently she almost hadn't felt it.

Almost. But the sensual onslaught that came with his bite had been impossible to ignore. Her body had ignited, her core softening and becoming slick with arousal, preparing itself for his possession. His groan against her throat had told her he'd smelled her desire. Hands hard against her hips, he'd pulled her lower body closer to his.

Now, as then, his need was tempered by tenderness. He looked like a wild thing ready to rip into her with fangs and cock, but Nix didn't fear for her safety. As long as Tobias was around, she would never be in danger.

She'd felt just as wild. The pheromones coming from him had called to her demon. She'd felt her eyes flame, her strength increasing as the demon came to the surface. She'd moaned as her horn buds had popped through her skin. She'd tried to force him higher, but he'd resisted and she'd let him have his way.

Long fingers slipped her silky panties down her legs and a gentle push tumbled her back onto the bed. Tobias pulled her forward, big hands lifting her rump as he moved between her legs. His breath came hot against her sex, and then his tongue flicked against her swollen clit. She jerked and cried out, her hands coming down to grip his hair.

Another flick, then his tongue slid down to delve into her slick heat. She shuddered at each caress, each flutter, each thrust. When he withdrew she moaned in protest, only to lose her breath when two long fingers stroked into her core. "Don't worry, honey, I'm not going anywhere," he said, his voice vibrating against her sensitive flesh just before his mouth latched onto her clit. He sucked hard, tongue circling and flicking as those fingers thrust in and out, slowly at first then with increasing speed until she rocked against the bed with the force of his movement.

She screamed as she came, over and over, her body bowing and bucking, all the while he worked at her sex, mouth and hand driving her from one orgasm to another until he finally stopped. She sighed and opened her eyes, gaze centered on his cock as he got to his feet. She spread her legs farther apart, opening herself in invitation. He sank between her thighs, sliding his shaft between her swollen folds, coating it with the slick cream of her arousal.

Nix wrapped her legs around his lean hips. "I want you inside me. Now."

The tenderness in his face mixed with lust, hardening his features. He drove into her, seating himself to the hilt with one thrust that wrung another cry of ecstasy from her. He pulled back, his strokes gentling.

She wanted more. "Harder," she directed him, watching him as she dug her fingers into his taut buttocks. "Faster."

His big body shuddered but he complied, his hard thrusts driving her into the mattress. She lifted her hips to meet each ferocious jab, her body clamping down around him. Another orgasm shattered her into a million pieces and she heard his roar, felt the jet of his release as he came deep within her. His fangs sliced into her throat, and the drawing of her blood threw her headlong into another climax. She'd dug her nails into his skin, the inner fire had burst free in the form of horn buds and burning eyes. Her demon had feasted on him, drawing on his life force.

Sexual energy flooded her, filling her with a euphoria that was indescribable.

Finally he collapsed against her. He rolled to one side, holding her close, cock still snuggled inside her. They'd gone to sleep like that, arms around each other, the smell of sex heavy in the air.

Nix dragged herself away from the memory of that night, drawing in a shaky breath. She flopped onto her stomach and punched her pillow, bunching it beneath her head. A string of expletives burst from her before she tightened her lips and bottled the rest of it up. They'd been so good together, she and Tobias, and it had all gone so wrong after that night.

She had to stop this, now. What was between them was gone. Never to return. She'd have to be insane to get mixed up with him again. Going crazy was just what she was trying to avoid.

After that volatile memory she was unsettled again. Pain rolled across her forehead, her gut churned with demon fire. "Shit." She sighed and climbed out of bed. She could tell she was going to be doing a lot of tai chi while Tobias was around. She got in the opening posture and drew in a breath. *Here we go again.*

* * *

Tobias took a final look around Rinda's apartment, hands thrust deep into his pockets. Crime scene techs had been through here already and they'd found nothing out of place. Neither had he. But he'd had to look for himself, just in case they'd missed something.

They hadn't. Damn it. The more time that passed the less chance he had of catching Rinda's killer. The first twenty-four hours were critical, and he was getting nowhere fast. Her kitchen was meticulous, her bedroom less so. The comforter was half off the bed, the pillows askew. A pair of tennis shoes lay on their sides next to her closet, and a bra hung from the doorknob. Lingering odors in the air told him she'd had a male visitor, a human, recently. Perhaps even the night she'd died. The scent was too faint for him to be able to sniff out who it belonged to. Tobias needed to find out who she'd been seeing, and he'd have to do it through old-fashioned detective work, not by using his preternatural sense of smell. Since most murders were committed by someone the victim knew, the boyfriend could have something to do with Rinda's death.

Tobias needed to go talk to Byron Maldonado. Rinda had been working for the quadrant vamp leader for the past few decades, had known Maldonado long before Tobias had met him. Maldonado needed to know she was dead.

More than that, he needed to know that someone was apparently targeting vamps in his jurisdiction. At the very least he might have an idea why. Tobias figured it was too much to hope that Maldonado could actually stop it. And he was pretty sure the vamp leader had nothing to do with it, because he wouldn't be so sloppy as to leave his kills lying around to be found.

Tobias decided to take Nix with him when he went to see Maldonado, even though it would make his job more difficult, having to contend with trying to ignore her sexy allure. But she and Maldonado had gotten along well enough before, and she read people well. Maldonado had a certain charm that Nix had been able to ignore. Tobias had to think she could still see through Maldonado's bull to get to the truth.

He pulled out his phone and dialed her number. Though he needed to speak with her he was silently hoping the call would go straight to her voice mail. No such luck. Her sleepy voice came on the line after the second ring. Tobias glanced at his watch, wincing when he saw exactly how late it was. "Nix, honey, I'm sorry to call so late."

"Tobias?"

He heard the rustle of sheets and pictured her sitting up. Which meant she'd been lying down, and that brought all sorts of carnal thoughts streaming through his mind. "Yeah, sorry." He cleared his throat and tried to clear his head as well. "I need to go see Byron, let him know what's going on." He paused. "You haven't already talked to him, have you? After the first murder?"

"No." She sighed. "The first murder just happened yesterday, and there were lots of people we had to see. Maldonado was on my list, but not at the top." Her yawn came through loud and clear. Mostly loud. "What time do you want to go see him?"

"You know what? Never mind. I'll go see him by myself."

"No! I'd like to go with you." She yawned again. "Just tell me when."

"I'll pick you up at five thirty. That should give us plenty of time to still meet MacMillan at seven."

"Okay," Nix said sleepily before hanging up sans a good-bye.

Tobias grinned and disconnected the call. He was happy to have that moment to talk to her and hoped she could get back to sleep. A sleepy Nix was a cranky Nix, and she was bad-tempered enough just being around him.

On his way out of the apartment he paused by the desk at the edge of the living room. He was surprised to not find a computer anywhere in the apartment. He took a closer look at the desk and saw there was a dead spot that didn't have as much dust on it as the rest of the desk. The dead space was the size of a laptop, yet there was no laptop in the place. Had Rinda taken it somewhere? Or had someone else been here and removed it to conceal whatever evidence it might contain?

A couple of books on astronomy sat at one edge of the desk, and some scribbled notes on the top page of a yellow legal pad. He flipped through the pages, again, still seeing nothing of interest. With one finger he traced along the handwriting. Rinda had learned to write some time back in the Middle Ages, taught by a kindly monk who was ahead of the times when it came to educating those of the female persuasion. Plus she was, *had been*, relentless when she wanted something.

Unfortunately, in most cases as soon as she got what she wanted she became bored and ready to move on. When first turned, he'd felt the same way as she. Neither one of them had been able to invest their hearts in a relationship. That is... until he'd met Nix. Things had always been different with her.

Tobias swayed, caught off guard by a wave of lightheadedness. Between being focused on leads to find Natchook, the person responsible for murdering his leader, traveling back to Scottsdale from Fairbanks, and jumping right into this case, he hadn't fed in close to four days. Before he did anything else, he needed sustenance.

Twenty minutes later, he leaned one hip against his kitchen counter as he waited for the microwave to complete its cycle. While blood drawn fresh from a willing victim was always the optimal choice of nourishment, this was an acceptable second best. The anticoagulant it was treated with gave the blood a slight piquant bouquet. Drinking any more than a pint was gluttonous; it didn't take much to provide appropriate nourishment. All in all, this wasn't a bad substitute.

At least, that's what he told himself. But truthfully, once he'd had Nix there was nothing else that could compare. So in his travels he'd taken blood from various blood banks or the wrist of an occasional willing donor. Now he made do with blood provided by an entrepreneurial college student who was making a lot of money with his home delivery service. Rather like the milkmen of fifty years ago, the young man had lined up donors and made deliveries once a week, leaving the sealed glass bottles in insulated coolers on his customers' doorsteps. Some vampires merely took off the caps and drank the blood directly from the bottle. Tobias didn't care for his meals cold, so when he could he poured the blood into a coffee mug and heated it up to body temperature or above.

The microwave dinged. He pulled out the ceramic mug and brought it to his lips. The first sip singed his tongue, a pain that quickly faded as the liquid nourishment slid down his throat. As it hit his stomach and was quickly absorbed by his system, he closed his eyes to savor the feel of his body warming, his heart picking up a dull beat, the tingle along the tips of his fingers and toes.

He'd much rather take blood from Nix. God, he hadn't

realized how much he'd missed her until he'd seen her again. No, that wasn't quite true. He hadn't let himself dwell on how much he'd missed her, that pixie face, the stubborn way she'd tilt her chin when she got mad at him, the fire in her eyes when they made love. Not that he was going to get back with her. She needed more than he could give her. She needed humanity, something he no longer had, to help her keep her own in charge. When they'd been together all those years before, he'd become more and more concerned at how less and less she'd been able to control her demon tendencies. Finally he'd walked away for her own good.

He'd seen tonight how well she'd maintained her control. Perhaps partly because she was on the job, but he hoped mainly because she'd matured a bit and had found something that worked. Or it could be as simple as the fact that she wasn't routinely shtupping a vampire.

He walked to the sink and rinsed his mug. He put it on the top rack of the dishwasher and paused. It was astonishing how easily he'd slipped back into his old routine. He'd been back in town, back in this house that he'd maintained during his absence, less than twenty-four hours, yet in many ways it felt like he'd never been gone.

Except for the empty place next to him in his bed, things seemed much as he'd left them.

* * *

Nix stifled a yawn and glanced at her watch again. It was just after six o'clock in the morning and because of her tumbled thoughts she hadn't gotten a lot of sleep last night. The sofa on which she sat was the most comfortable she'd ever parked her rear on. She held back another yawn and resisted the urge to get even more comfortable. She'd fall asleep if she did. She should never have sat down to begin with, but it would have been rude to refuse.

She looked at Byron Maldonado sitting in his big leather armchair next to a crackling fireplace. Legs crossed, he was the picture of elegant grace. Yet she was all too aware of the dark danger that lay beneath the surface.

Tobias had broken the news about Amarinda to him, and now the other vampire's eyes were black rage surrounded by crimson sorrow. The look in his eyes reminded Nix of a wounded animal.

"What happened?" Maldonado asked, his gaze flicking from Tobias to her and back again.

When Tobias seemed unable to share the details of the grisly death, Nix said as gently as she could, "There's no easy way to say this. She was eviscerated."

Maldonado's lips thinned. "Bastards," he muttered. His eyes grew wilder. "Why?"

"We were hoping you could help us on that one." Tobias leaned forward and rested his elbows on his knees. His voice was low, calming. "What had she gotten herself into, Byron? She called me in Alaska, asked me to come home. Do you have any idea what she wanted to talk to me about?"

Maldonado closed his eyes and pinched the bridge of his nose. "No, not really." He looked at Tobias, the fine lines at the corners of his eyes deepening. "She changed, Tobias. Over the last several months I noticed a shift in her personality and it was not for the better. She was . . . jaded. Bored. But when she talked about the stars, about space . . ." Sadness flickered over his face. "She was more animated than I had seen her in years. Centuries."

"Was that what she wanted to talk to me about? Space?" Tobias looked as lost as Nix felt.

Maldonado lifted one shoulder. "I honestly don't know. She had taken a leave of absence from... my organization while she attended school." He leaned his head against the back of the chair. "But I never thought she would end up..." With a speed as violent as it was unexpected, he surged to his feet and slammed his fist into the mantle. The wood fractured and splintered, the end falling loose from the river rock it had been embedded in. "Damn it to hell." He bent his head and stared into the hearth. After several seconds he turned back to them. Nix noticed his eyes had returned to their normal rich hazel. Good thing he'd gotten control of himself. Though Nix and Tobias were trained and could take care of themselves, Maldonado was... Maldonado. He'd come through the rift at the same time as Deoul, which made him the oldest vampire around. At least if there were any older she'd never heard of them.

"Rinda was the second victim, Byron." Tobias stood, too, though he didn't move any closer to the other vampire. Maybe he didn't trust that Maldonado's control was as strong as he'd like it to be. "The first was Johnson Pickett. Know him?"

Maldonado shook his head. He leaned his shoulder against the river rock of the fireplace. "No. I'd heard of him, of course. But I never had any reason to look him up. He was harmless, as far as I know."

"That's pretty much what I've been told," Nix said. Even knowing how ruthless the vampire leader could be, she found herself feeling sorry for him. "So he had no dealings with any of your companies?"

"I just said no." He shot her an arch look. "And as far as I know Pickett and Rinda were not involved in anything together."

"But you just said she'd changed," Nix said. "Is it possible she kept things from you?"

He straightened from the fireplace. "As much as I'd like to deny that, with the way she'd been acting these last few months, I can't answer in the affirmative."

"You just can't help yourself, can you?" Nix murmured.

"Nix." Tobias's voice held a deep note of caution.

"Can't help what?" Maldonado asked, folding his arms lazily over his chest.

"Couldn't you just have said, 'Yes, it's possible she kept things from me'?" Nix rolled her eyes. "Good grief, Byron. You certainly haven't changed."

He stared at her, his expression stern, then a wide grin split his face. "And you haven't changed that much, either. Still calling people on their bull."

"That's me. A regular bull caller." She turned the conversation back on topic. "Is there anything else we should know about Rinda?"

"Not at the moment, but I'll let you know if something comes up."

Tobias stepped forward and held out his hand. "Byron."

Maldonado clasped his hand and the two men hugged, pounding each other on the shoulder a few times before pulling away. "Tobias, it's good to see you. You've been gone too long."

Tobias glanced at Nix and didn't comment.

When Maldonado reached out a hand toward her, Nix let him clasp her fingers in his. "Nix, as always, it's nice to see you, too. You should come by my clubs more often." He lifted her hand and pressed a kiss against her knuckles.

"Maybe I'll do that," she said.

He dropped her hand and looked at Tobias. "I expect you to keep me informed, old friend. I have to protect my own."

Tobias lifted his chin in acknowledgment. Nix gave Maldonado a sympathetic glance and turned to leave. She and Tobias said their good-byes and left Maldonado's suite of rooms. The big vampire bodyguard who'd escorted them in waited for them at the elevator and the ride down to the ground floor was accomplished in silence. She believed Maldonado hadn't known what was going on, and he seemed righteously angry over the killings.

As soon as they were outside, Nix let out a breath. "Why does it seem like this investigation is going exactly nowhere?" She was so frustrated she felt like screaming.

"Probably because it's going exactly nowhere." Tobias unlocked his black Jaguar and opened the door for her. He didn't seem to notice the frown she shot him as he said, "Just the fact that Rinda had distanced herself from Byron, that she was keeping secrets from him, tells me there's a lot more to this."

Nix slid into the low-slung vehicle and he closed the door behind her. He walked around the vehicle and climbed behind the wheel. Hand on the ignition he said, "She was mixed up in something that made her keep secrets. Made her pull away from her closest friends." His stormy eyes cut her way. "Whatever caused that can't be good."

"I agree." Nix fastened her seat belt and then stared out

the windshield, her thoughts tumbling over each other as she tried to make sense of everything.

"She didn't say anything to you?" he asked.

Nix swallowed back regret. "We hadn't..." She cleared her throat. "I hadn't talked to her in a while." When Tobias seemed about to question her further, she slashed one hand through the air. "Just leave it alone, all right? Please."

"All right," he said slowly. He twisted the key in the ignition and put the vehicle in gear.

Nix turned her head and looked through the side window. If she'd kept up her friendship with Amarinda, would the vampire have let her know what was going on? Or would she have kept her as in the dark as she'd kept Maldonado, a man she'd known for centuries? Nix was saddened at the thought that she would never know the answer.

Chapter Five

Apparently Detective MacMillan had been in the mood for pancakes, as Tobias found out an hour later. The man shoveled the last of his short stack into his mouth and leaned back with a sigh, one hand on his flat belly. Which wouldn't remain flat for very long if he kept eating like that.

"I don't know where you put it all," Nix muttered from where she sat next to MacMillan. Tobias had hoped she would sit next to him. Not only had she insisted he take her home so she could get her own car, when they both arrived at the restaurant and had been led to their booth, she hadn't even looked his way as she slid in next to the detective.

"Hollow legs." MacMillan took a sip of coffee. "That's what my mom always used to say, at any rate. Man, that hit the spot. Whoever suggested we meet here had a damn good idea." At Nix's snort, he shrugged. "I'm just sayin'." He stretched out his legs under the table and murmured an apology when he bumped Tobias's foot.

"No problem." Leaning forward, Tobias clasped his hands around his coffee cup and rested his elbows on the table.

MacMillan smiled at the waitress as she began clearing the table. "Thanks, sweetheart," he said softly as she left.

Nix heaved a sigh. "You flirt with every woman you see, don't you?" She sounded more aggrieved than jealous. Somehow that made Tobias feel better.

"I like women. You're my favorite though," the detective added with a slight smile.

"Oh, give me a break." She stared at him, lips twitching, and Tobias knew she fought a grin. She couldn't win the battle, though, and let out a laugh, leaning sideways to bump MacMillan with her shoulder. He wrapped an arm around her shoulder and hugged her to his side.

Tobias stared down into his coffee cup for a second. Once upon a time, he and Nix had been affectionate like that. More than just being in love, they'd genuinely liked each other. Now he supposed, at least on her side of things, that was gone. He tightened his lips. He couldn't exactly begrudge her easy friendship with the detective, especially since it was more like brother and sister than anything romantic, but it rankled just the same. He looked across the table at his colleagues. "Can we talk about the case?"

"So what's the plan, chief?" MacMillan took his arm off Nix's shoulders and stretched it along the back of the booth bench.

"We should get started on interviews with Rinda's friends." Tobias paused. "You've already talked with the first victim's friends and co-workers?"

Nix nodded. "The body was discovered early yesterday morning, but the ME says TOD was probably somewhere between ten and midnight the night before. From the time I left the crime scene up until I got the call about Rinda last night we were interviewing the friends we knew of. We still need to talk to his business partner, but other than that, we didn't turn up much." She leaned back against her seat and crossed her arms. "All of that should be in the report. Didn't the council give you a copy?"

"They did." He shrugged. "I'd like to hear it from you, though. Get your impressions."

"Okay. His name is Johnson Pickett, and he came through the rift in 1136 AD. According to everyone we talked to in the pret community, he was held in good regard. No enemies that anyone was aware of." Her voice was matter-of-fact. She recited dry facts, which wasn't what Tobias had been looking for.

"He was a vampire," MacMillan chimed in before Tobias could say anything to Nix. "It wouldn't be much of a leap to assume he had enemies."

"You're right." Tobias lifted his coffee cup and took a sip. He'd long ago lost the capacity to taste anything sweet, but he could still savor bitter and tart. "There's no such thing as a vampire without enemies. Some of us just have more than others."

"No big surprise there," Nix stated with an arch look across the table at him. Before he could respond, she cleared her throat and went on. "Pickett's business partner—and from what we've heard his sexual partner, since they lived together—was supposed to be back in town as of last night. We should be able to talk to him today. Once we've talked to Amarinda's friends, too, we should have a clearer idea, don't you think?" Her voice lost some of the recitation tone of earlier.

"This all needs to happen sooner rather than later.

We need to go talk to the business partner now." Tobias signaled to the waitress. "I don't want any more killings."

"Yeah, let's not add to the spate." Nix picked up her diet cola and took a long sip from the straw.

MacMillan grabbed the check from the waitress and fished in the rear pocket of his jeans for his wallet. "Am I missing something?" His gaze went from Nix to Tobias and back again.

Ignoring the detective for the moment, Tobias advised Nix, "Let it go. You can appreciate the council's stance. We have two murdered vamps on our hands and not one clue as to why they're dead or who killed them."

MacMillan pulled a few bills out of his wallet. "Oh, I got it." He looked at Nix. "Council's been giving you a hard time again, have they?"

Tobias didn't like the implication of that statement. From what he'd been told, Dante MacMillan had been on the Special Case Squad for only a month, yet the detective already knew that Nix and the council were at odds? Just how close were these two?

She rolled her eyes. "Apparently two deaths is now a 'spate.'" Her brows dipped. "Not that I don't understand why they're upset. But I'm working as fast as I can." She grabbed her wallet and dropped a five-dollar bill on the table to pay for her cola and oatmeal. She scooted off the seat to let MacMillan out.

He eased out of the booth. Picking up the check and Nix's fiver, he added his money, then snatched his suit coat from the edge where he'd draped it. "I got you covered there, chief," he said with a nod toward Tobias. The detective shrugged into his jacket and said, "I'll meet up with you outside." He walked toward the cash register at the front of the restaurant.

Tobias stood. "You and MacMillan seem close."

Nix slipped the strap of her purse over her shoulder. "Yeah, well, when you see what we see on an almost daily basis, you tend to establish a rapport pretty quickly."

"You took longer than a month to warm up to me," he replied as he followed Nix out of the restaurant. The bright sunlight hit his eyes like knives. With a low oath he slipped on his sunglasses.

"Yeah, well, Dante's not a pret." She put on her own sunglasses, small rectangular ones with purple lenses that made her look damned adorable.

To give his hands something to do because otherwise he might just haul her in for a kiss, Tobias fished his car keys out of his jeans and began flicking them back and forth. "What's that supposed to mean?"

"Just about every pret out there looks down on demons. Especially vampires." She pushed her glasses down her nose and stared at him over the rim, her head slightly tilted to one side. Little yellow flecks danced in her eyes, showing him again just how easily his presence brought out the demon in her. "Looking back on it, I'm amazed you and I ended up being together as long as we did." Her voice held a note of the surprise she claimed to feel. She pushed the glasses back up. "We should have known it wouldn't last."

Tobias scowled. She didn't have to sound so perky about it. "And you think something with a human like MacMillan would last longer?"

"I didn't say that." She frowned and looked toward the building, muttering something about someone getting up on the wrong side of the coffin. "It's not like it's any of your business, anyway," she said in a louder voice. MacMillan walked toward them, shoving his wallet into his back pocket as he came. "You ready to go?" she asked him.

He gave a nod. "You wanna ride with me?"

"Why don't we all just go in my car?" Tobias flipped his keys faster.

Nix glanced at him. "In your Jag." Her voice held sarcastic disbelief. "With someone, probably me, climbing in and out of the backseat?" She shook her head. "No, thanks."

MacMillan looked disappointed.

"You want to hitch a ride with me?" Tobias asked him.

"Sure." He gave Nix a grin. "I've never ridden in a Jag before."

"Boys and their toys." She grimaced. "Fine. I'll meet you at Pickett's."

The detective pulled out his small notebook. "Just need to check..." He thumbed through a few pages. "Ah. Okay." He looked up and slipped the notebook back in the inside pocket of his suit coat. "I've got the address. We'll see you there."

Tobias hesitated. "You sure you don't want to ride with us?"

"I'm positive." Her smile looked forced. "You boys have fun." She waved and walked off toward her car, hips swaying, sun glinting off her dark curls.

"I'm this way," Tobias told MacMillan, tearing his gaze away from Nix and heading toward his low-slung limited edition sports car.

The detective gave a low whistle when he saw the sleek black vehicle. He ran his palm over the fender as he walked along the side of the car. "Nice." When Tobias unlocked the doors, MacMillan got in. "How in the hell'd you manage to get your hands on one of these? They made less than two hundred."

Tobias grinned. "A hundred seventy-five for their seventy-fifth anniversary. I know a guy who knows a guy."

MacMillan fastened his seat belt and settled back in the leather seat. "Sure beats the hell outta my four-by-four. Make a right onto Mountain View and take it to Gainey Ranch."

Tobias pulled smoothly out of the parking lot. He saw Nix's small red Prius already half a mile down the road. Little spitfire, she always had had a lead foot. He wondered how many points she had accrued on her driving record now. "What do you drive?" he asked MacMillan.

"Heavy-duty pickup truck." MacMillan twisted to look at the backseat, then faced forward again and stared at the dash. He looked at Tobias. "I need the torque for hauling my horses."

"Oh? What kind?"

"An Appaloosa and a quarter horse." He grinned. "And a burro. He's kind of the stable mascot. Keeps the horses calm."

Tobias smiled. "I had a cat that did that."

"You have horses?"

"Used to, long time ago." Tobias stopped at a red light and glanced at the detective. "When I first moved to Arizona."

"Just how long ago was that?"

"'Bout a hundred and fifty years ago." The light turned green and Tobias eased the car forward. "I owned a ranch for a time, but up until our existence became well known, I had to move on after about twenty years or so." He shot a look at MacMillan. "Once people began to notice I didn't age, they started asking questions I couldn't answer."

"Right. Well, that has to be a plus to being outed, right?" MacMillan shifted to rest one shoulder against the door. "You can stay put in one place."

"Yes." Except for now. He was here to do a job, which he would do. But once the job was done, to preserve Nix's sanity he had to leave again.

MacMillan's phone rang, some country western tune, and the detective pulled it out and looked at it. "Excuse me," he said, and answered. "Lily? What's wrong?" He kept his voice low. The tenderness in his tone told Tobias this was someone important to the detective.

Tobias did his best to not eavesdrop, but it was impossible not to in the confines of his car. When MacMillan ended his call, Tobias asked, "Everything all right?"

"Yeah. That was my sister. It's nothing." MacMillan turned his head to look out the window. "She's just having a tough day."

Tobias understood the desire to keep his personal life separate from work, so he didn't press the issue. Instead he commented, "Sweet phone."

MacMillan looked at him with a grin and pulled the phone out of his pocket again. "Isn't it? I'm kind of a gadget guy." He pushed a couple of buttons and showed Tobias the screen. "Google maps. I can check my Facebook account, even surf the Web while I talk." He pressed another button and showed the screen again. "Twitter. In case you want to, you know, tweet."

Tobias gave a little growl. “I hate this decade.”

MacMillan snorted and tucked his phone away again. “The guys at the station razz me about not using my phone to take notes, but I know how easy they are to drop and then I’d lose everything.” He glanced out the side window. “Our turnoff’s just up to the right.”

Tobias made the turn onto Gainey Ranch. “Where from here?”

“Third subdivision on the right.”

Tobias pulled into the upscale neighborhood and followed the detective’s directions until he saw Nix’s little Prius parked on the street in front of a sprawling Santa Fe-style house. Nix got out of her car as he stopped the Jag behind her.

“This is one sweet ride,” MacMillan said as he opened his door.

Tobias smiled. “I thought you’d like it.”

“Man, if I had money to throw away on a car, this would be it.”

Tobias gave a quick laugh. Once upon a time he hadn’t had much money, and he remembered how it felt to have to scrimp and save every penny to buy the necessities, let alone a luxury item. He appreciated how the other man felt.

* * *

Nix stared at the two men as they got out of the luxury car, both grinning and acting like best buds. She scowled. Men. “If you two are done with your bromance, can we maybe get some work done?” She looked at Dante. “I thought it was women who were supposed to be turned on by a guy’s car?”

Dante's grin widened. "Oh, you know me, hon. I'm easy."

Tobias's gaze darkened as if he remembered just what did turn her on, and her heart thudded a little faster in her chest. To try to cover her reaction to him, she cleared her throat and started toward the house. The two men fell into step behind her.

"Just what's the game plan?" Dante asked.

"I'll do the talking." Tobias stood beside Nix at the door and waited while she knocked. "Vampire to vampire should go better," he added.

A slender man in a crisp black suit showed them into a home office at the front of the house. Before she went into the room, Nix looked down the hallway and saw glass-paned doors open on to a courtyard complete with a large infinity pool and spa. Polished concrete with tile inlay covered the floors of the hallway and the room she now stood in. A large painted portrait of a Native American chief hung above the gas fireplace, next to which were two wingback chairs. A dark wood desk sat near the large window overlooking the front yard. Two leather armchairs perched in front of the desk, a small table with a kachina doll on it nestled between them. "Mr. Loren will be with you in a moment," the black-suited man told them. "May I offer you some refreshments? Water, perhaps? Or lemonade?" He looked at Tobias. "I can give you a glass from Mr. Loren's personal stock. It's fresh."

"No, thanks," Tobias said. "Just let him know we're here."

Nix and Dante also turned down his offer.

Within a few minutes a short, bald man walked into the room. He wore shorts and a red T-shirt with the words

"Kiss me, I'm a vampire" emblazoned across the front. "I'm Carson Loren. My man said you're from the council?" He seemed soft, more like a mouse than a fearsome predator. Unusual but not unheard of for a vampire. If Nix had to guess, she'd say he'd come through the last Influx, though with his timid manner she was amazed he'd lasted this long.

Tobias went through the introductions. "We'd like to talk to you about Johnson Pickett."

The vampire spread his hands. "We split up the partnership a few months ago, though he still lived here. We led separate lives, so I don't know what I can tell you." He sat down in the chair behind the desk and motioned for them to sit.

"What sort of business did you have?" Tobias asked as he took a seat in front of the desk. Dante glanced at Nix and she waved him toward the other chair. Tobias wanted to do all the talking and she was fine with that. She knew from her notes and from talking to other acquaintances of Pickett's the day of his murder that he and Loren had owned an import-export company. Tobias probably knew that, too, since he'd read the report, but most likely he wanted to see if Loren would lie about anything.

"International trade." Loren shifted his feet. A tic started up beside his left eye. "We would purchase goods, usually from a foreign country, import them into the U.S., and resell them. It was quite lucrative for several years."

"And?" Tobias prompted when Loren faltered.

The other vampire shrugged. "The economy went down the toilet here and in just about every country around the globe. We were having a much harder time making a profit. Some months we lost money. A lot of it. So we closed up shop and disbanded the partnership." He rubbed one hand over his scalp. His gaze darted from Tobias to Dante to her and back to Tobias. "That's all. Nothing more sinister than a failing economy."

Nix leaned her shoulder against the door frame and watched the exchange. Loren was twitchy, and it was more than the fact he had three investigators sitting in his office. If he were human, he'd be sweating buckets right now.

"Do you know of any reason someone would want him dead?" Tobias crossed one leg over the other, his demeanor relaxed but Nix knew he watched Loren closely.

"No. Of course not. Johnson is... was... harmless." He clasped his hands on top of the desk and started to pick at his cuticles. A nervous habit left over from his days as a human, and one he hadn't yet gotten rid of.

"He was a vampire," Dante said in a dry tone. "Hardly someone I'd call harmless."

Loren barely spared him a glance. "I don't know anything about what Pickett got himself into, or why he was killed." He rubbed his head again. "I'm sorry." He abruptly stood. "I just don't know anything that can help you."

"We're not finished." Tobias didn't move physically, but his entire being radiated danger. "Sit." When Loren remained on his feet, Tobias said, "Don't make me repeat myself."

The other vampire slowly took his seat once more. He kept his eyes glued to Tobias. "You used to work for Maldonado, didn't you?" The look on his face suggested he'd just made the connection.

"Yes." Tobias uncrossed his legs and leaned forward

slightly. "Where were you the day before yesterday?"

"You want an accounting of my whole day?"

"Since you were unavailable for questioning at the time, yes, I want an accounting of your whole day." Tobias tapped his fingers on the arm of the chair. "Starting with the morning and going through till midnight when your former partner was killed."

Loren sputtered and stammered, but he finally trotted out his itinerary.

Dante pulled out his phone and started playing with it. Nix saw his eyebrows shoot up and he looked like he was suppressing a grin.

After a few minutes, Loren petered to a stop. "I had nothing to do with any of it, I swear."

"We'll see about that." Tobias got to his feet. He pulled out a business card and jotted something down on it. "That's my cell number," he said. "In case you think of something."

Loren's eyes flickered but he took the card Tobias handed him. "I don't know anything," he repeated. When Tobias merely stood there, staring at him, Loren lifted the card and with a trembling smile tucked it into the front pocket of his shorts. "If I think of anything, I'll call you." His tone was largely unconvincing.

A minute later, they left the home of the late Mr. Pickett's business partner and walked back to their cars.

"Well, that was fun." Dante tucked his notebook away. "And unproductive. What happened to 'vampire to vampire should go better'?"

Tobias frowned. "He's scared."

"Yeah, obviously." Nix stopped behind her car and looked at her colleagues. Both men had slipped on sunglasses, both wore jeans with suit coats, both had on button-down shirts with no ties. Both were tall, dark, and handsome. And while she had no doubt that Dante was formidable in a fight, Tobias was dangerous. You could feel it, perhaps partly from the pheromones that all vampires released to help subdue their prey. Whatever it was, Tobias had mastered it.

"I don't think he knew a thing," Dante murmured. "He was too nervous to lie convincingly." He gave a one-shouldered shrug. "I got online while we were in there and was able to verify his alibi at the time of Pickett's death, though. Loren was at a party that got kind of wild. It was caught on tape and posted online. I saw him. It wasn't pretty." He pulled his phone out and punched a few buttons, then turned the phone around to show them the video. When it ended he sighed and shook his head. "Chances are he wasn't involved with Amarinda's death, either."

Pickett's business partner hadn't turned his back on them once, and, if he'd been human, he'd have been sweating like a horse. Nix agreed with Dante. The vamp hadn't known anything, and maybe that was what scared him the most because for all he knew he could be next.

"From a purely materialistic point of view, it sure pays to be a vampire," Dante added dryly as he replaced his phone in its holder on his belt.

Nix glanced back at the multimillion-dollar home they'd just exited. The house had to be at least ten thousand square feet, with lots of glass. "You can accumulate a lot of wealth over several centuries. It's easy to save money when you don't have to buy food, right, Tobias?"

He shrugged. Nix could see the lines fanning out from

the corners of his eyes and knew he was squinting behind the sunglasses. Like most vamps his age, Tobias could spend time outside during daylight hours without any damage, but his eyes were still very sensitive to bright light. “Don’t look at me,” he said as he pressed the remote to unlock his Jag. “I’m not into material things.”

“Uh-huh.” Nix opened her car door. “Just how many cars do you have?”

His brows dipped. “Just this one and the SUV.”

She shared a wry glance with Dante. Leaving it alone for the moment, she asked, “So, where do we go from here?”

“There’s a woman who went to school with Amarinda, a fellow astronomical sciences student...” Dante skimmed through his notes, his index finger tracking along his writing. “Samantha Smith.” He looked up, his gaze going from Nix to Tobias. “She’s up from Tucson for a long weekend with her family in Chandler.”

“All right, let’s do this.” Tobias opened his car door and rested one arm along the roof of the low-slung auto. “Nix, you go on home. I’ll stop at my house and get the SUV, and then we’ll swing by and pick you up. It doesn’t make sense for us to be driving different vehicles.”

Nix didn’t want to spend any time cooped up with Tobias, even if Dante were going to be there. She was already feeling jittery and knew it was just going to get worse the longer she was exposed to him. And those damned pheromones he just kept spewing her way. She opened her mouth to argue but Dante cut her off with “Good idea. My truck will be fine at the restaurant.”

She’d just look silly arguing the point, so she mumbled, “Whatever,” and got into her car. She started it up and pulled away from the curb, making a U-turn to head back the way she'd come. Stopping next to Tobias, she rolled down her window. Figuring it would take him ten minutes to get back to his house, and at least another ten to get to hers once he switched cars, she said, "I'll see you in about twenty minutes." Without waiting for him to respond, she drove away. Maybe if she got home quickly enough she could take a few minutes to do an abbreviated tai chi workout. It certainly wouldn't hurt, anyway.

Eight minutes and probably at least one land speed record later, she screeched into her parking spot and jumped out of the car. If she went inside Rufus would demand to be taken out and she didn't have time for that. But she didn't want Tobias or Dante catching her doing a workout, either. As a compromise, she went around the corner of the building and stood on a patch of grass in the landscaped portion in the middle of the apartment complex. She brought her hands slowly down and to the side, waving them back and forth and focusing on her breathing. Inhale. Exhale. Slow, steady. In, out. Even movements, even breaths.

She transitioned into a slow lunge to the left, then to the right, always moving her arms. The jittery feeling dissipated, leaving her once more feeling if not exactly serene, at least calm enough to continue dealing with Tobias and the emotions she'd thought long gone.

Nix heard a car engine then two doors slammed. She headed back to the parking lot, rounding the corner of the building in time to see Tobias and Dante heading her way. "You didn't need to get out," she said.

"It's no trouble," Tobias replied. He sent her a look, his expression a little bemused. He probably could sense she was calmer than she had been and wondered how she'd gotten control of herself so quickly. Well, she wasn't the same girl he'd known before. A lot had changed in the last five years.

She unlocked her car and grabbed her purse, then joined the two men at the SUV. "It's a Porsche," she stated, staring at the dark blue vehicle.

"So?" Tobias's dark brows drew down in a frown.

"I thought you weren't into material things." At his confused look, she rolled her eyes. "Never mind." She opened the back passenger door of his expensive SUV and hopped in.

Dante wrapped a broad hand around the edge of the door before she could close it. "Why don't you sit up front? You can ride shotgun."

"That's all right." Nix pulled her notebook out of her bag and tapped it. "I can add to my notes and review them better back here." Plus she wouldn't be as close to Tobias. Sitting in the front seat with him would feel too intimate even with Dante in the vehicle with them. Being with him in the Jag had been bad enough. She didn't want to do it again.

Dante didn't appear to buy her explanation, but he closed her door without another word. Both men got in the front of the vehicle, buckling their seat belts with moves that mirrored each other exactly.

"You two should try out for synchronized swimming," she quipped.

"I don't think I'd look good in one of those flowered swim caps." Dante sent her a look from the corner of his eye, one side of his mouth twitching.

"Oh, I don't know." Tobias started the car but didn't

take it out of park. Without looking at Dante, he mused, "Get a blue-and-white one. You'd look fabulous."

Nix rolled her eyes. She didn't get how men could go from being rivals to acting like best buds in a heartbeat. Making good on her excuse, she flipped open her notebook. She read through the notes she'd taken inside the house, then jotted a few more thoughts. Sticking the capped end of the pen in her mouth, she chewed on it and then said, "I don't think Pickett's former business partner had anything to do with either of their deaths based on his alibi. It was pretty solid." She looked at the men in the front seat. "And there's a lack of motive, on the surface anyway."

Dante thumbed through his own small notebook. "The sooner we talk to this friend of the second vic the better."

"Her name is Amarinda." Tobias's tone was biting.

"Sorry?" Dante's brows quirked as he glanced at the other man.

"The second *vic*. Her name is Amarinda." He turned his head to look at the detective.

Dante gave a nod. "Sorry. I'd forgotten she was a friend of yours."

"We hadn't seen each other in a while." Tobias's head turned slightly and Nix knew he was looking at her in the rearview mirror, though she couldn't see his eyes through the reflective lenses of his sunglasses. "I have no idea what she was mixed up in or if that might have had anything to do with her murder. It's possible that she was simply in the wrong place at the wrong time."

Dante murmured, "Hopefully some of her other friends can shed some light on that." When Tobias shot him a glance, Dante held up one hand. "Didn't mean anything by it, chief. It was just a comment."

Nix glanced back down at her notes. "So let's go talk to Samantha Smith." She looked up, her gaze going from one man to the other.

"Yes, let's." Tobias backed out of the parking space and stopped at the roadway. When traffic cleared he pulled out onto the road. He put the vehicle in drive and pulled out into traffic. "Where does she live?"

Nix gave him the address and the main crossroads, then sat back in her seat.

"So, Amarinda was a student?" Dante twisted in his seat to look at Nix over his shoulder.

She nodded. "A perpetual student. She loved to learn." Nix rested her arm along the edge of the car door and stared out at the houses going by. "That's one reason she was so happy when prets were outed. She could go to school without trying to hide what she was."

Tobias stopped the car at a traffic light. "Rinda has..." He shook his head. "Had. She had six undergrad degrees. This program in astronomical sciences would have been her third master's degree." Sadness colored his voice. The light turned green and he drove through the intersection.

"She loved to learn," Nix whispered again, mostly to herself. She hadn't really allowed herself to think of her friend as a friend, only as a victim. She'd been too focused on fighting her resurging feelings for Tobias to let herself feel her own loss. As tears welled, she bit the inside of her cheek and stared blindly out the window, trying to get control. She didn't want to break down now. Not on the job. Not in front of Dante and especially not in front of Tobias.

The SUV turned onto a narrower side street and slowed. Then it stopped in front of a ranch-style brick house, and Tobias shoved the gear lever into park. "We're here."

Nix climbed out of the backseat and stared at the house as she shut the door. It was a nice, normal-looking house with a nice, normal-looking minivan parked in the driveway. It looked the same as all the other nice, normal-looking houses on the street.

Perfect for the nice, normal human family that no doubt lived inside. Part of her wondered what that was like. Being normal. She'd never known that, simply because of the demon twisted in her DNA. She'd given up on the idea a long time ago, but every once in a while she felt a twinge of envy for everyday people who only had to worry about being embarrassed by their relatives at the family reunion, not about Uncle Harry trying to eat them for dinner.

For the first two years of her life, most of which she had no memory of, Nix had lived a somewhat normal life. She'd had a loving father who had spoiled her rotten even while his addiction to her mother was draining his life away. And once he was gone, her mother, who'd at best been indifferent to the child she'd birthed, had walked away, leaving her little girl with a woman who'd resented her, even hated her, though duty had dictated she care for her granddaughter.

And she'd never let Nix forget she was demon-spawn. Never let her be more than her genetics. After a while, Nix had decided to prove her grandmother right and started living down to the old woman's expectations. As a young teenager she ran with the wrong crowd, learning how to pick pockets, escalating to breaking and entering. By her fourteenth birthday her demon tendencies had begun to manifest. When she was fifteen her grandmother's health had begun to deteriorate, and, by the time Nix turned sixteen, the old lady was dead.

Nix had wanted to feel sad, but really all she'd felt was relief. No more haranguing, no more being told she was worthless. No more feeling like she didn't deserve to live.

The day of her grandmother's funeral, Nix took what little belongings she could carry with her and went into the foster care system. Being around people who loved their children, people who had tried to love her, had been more than she could bear. At that age she hadn't felt lovable. After all, her mother hadn't wanted her, her grandmother hadn't wanted her. So she'd run. She lied about her age, took what paying jobs she could get, and stole or scrounged for whatever else she needed.

"Nix?"

She dragged herself away from her memories to see Tobias and Dante staring at her. She cleared her throat. "Yeah. Sorry. Are we ready?"

Thankfully both men kept their thoughts to themselves.

"Let's go." Tobias started up the walk.

When Dante raised a brow but dutifully followed, Nix fell into step beside him. "Of this team, Tobias is lead, you know that."

"Because all the vics are vamps. Yeah, I know," Dante said. They stopped in front of the stoop and watched Tobias knock on the door.

Nix looked around. Fuchsia bougainvilleas rode up a trellis on one side of the house while white oleanders, kept short in bush formations, squatted beneath the windows. Various potted plants sat on either side of the small porch. The clean floral scent of the flowers helped mask vampire pheromones that Nix still fought so hard to ignore.

Dante leaned sideways. "It wouldn't hurt him to say 'please' and 'thank you' every now and again."

Tobias shot a sharp glance over his shoulder.

Dante grinned. "No need to get your shorts in a twist, Tobemeister."

Oh, boy. Nix watched as Tobias stiffened and began to turn around. "Tobemeister. Seriously?" Nix elbowed Dante.

Before Tobias could say anything, the front door opened. A middle-aged woman stood there, a polite smile on her face. "Yes?"

Tobias pulled out his ID and showed it to her. "I'm Tobias Caine of the Council of Preternaturals. These are my colleagues, Nix de la Fuente and Detective Dante MacMillan." He slipped his ID back into his pocket. "We'd like to speak with Samantha."

The woman stared at him for a few seconds. Then she asked, "Does this have to do with her friend who was killed?"

"Yes." Tobias took off his sunglasses and tucked them into the front pocket of his white button-down shirt. "Samantha may know something that can help us find out who murdered Amarinda."

She nodded and stepped back, opening the door wider. "Please, come in."

As she walked into the house, Nix took in her surroundings, assessing any potential threat, and she knew both men were doing the same thing. It only took a few seconds. The decor was typical Southwest style. A large fireplace took central stage in the outside wall of the living room. A hallway leading presumably to the bedrooms ran along the wall to the left of the foyer.

Nix took a breath and held it a moment, then slowly exhaled. Other than her and Tobias, she couldn't smell anything here except humans. It appeared that it was as normal on the inside as it looked on the outside.

"I'll just go get my daughter." Mrs. Smith closed the door and motioned toward the living room. "Please, make yourselves comfortable." She gave them a slight smile and went down the hallway.

Both men sat down, Tobias on the sofa and Dante in one of the two armchairs facing it. Nix wandered around the room, hearing the murmur of female voices from down the hallway. She looked at the knickknacks, pictures on the wall, trying to get a sense of the people who lived there. A framed photo of Samantha and Amarinda rested next to a glass prism on a bookshelf. Both women wore wide smiles as they stood in front of a large telescope.

"That was taken about six months ago," a soft voice said from behind her.

Nix turned to see the same young woman from the photo. "Hello, Samantha. Thank you for seeing us. I'm Nix, this is Tobias Caine and Detective MacMillan."

The young woman nodded, her lips trembling in a brief smile. "Hi." She motioned toward the picture. "We had so much fun that day, riding the ski lift on Mt. Lemmon, eating fudge." She paused and gave a little shrug. "Well, I ate fudge. Rinda watched me eat it."

With her mother right behind her, she went over and sat down in the remaining armchair, leaving the only available seating on the couch next to Tobias. Nix drew in a slow breath and sat on the edge, keeping as much space between her and her ex-lover as she could.

Even so, she was acutely aware of him. She cleared her throat and kept her gaze on the young woman sitting across from her, and not on the strong thigh showcased by taut denim next to her.

"How can I help?" Samantha clasped her fingers together in her lap. Her mother placed one hand on her shoulder, her face wearing an expression of concern.

Nix bit back sharp regret that she'd never had that, the loving support of a mother, someone watching out for her. Being there through joy and sorrow. When neither Tobias nor Dante spoke, Nix cleared her throat and asked, "How long had you known Amarinda?"

"Almost two years." Samantha's quick smile brightened her face. "She came into class and sat beside me, and immediately started talking about NEOs and how she wanted to work with the Catalina Sky Survey. Her enthusiasm was contagious. We made an immediate connection, you know? Best friends in a second." Her smile faded. "I miss her."

Nix didn't understand making an instant connection like that, but she did understand loss. She pushed aside her own sadness. Time enough later to deal with that, once they'd caught the bastards who'd killed her friend. There was one thing Samantha had said that Nix didn't understand, though. "Uh, NEOs?" she asked. "You lost me there."

"Near-Earth Objects. Basically the scientists keep an eye on anything that comes within an AU of the planet, give or take a few million miles. Asteroids mostly, some comets." Samantha smiled again, this time a little self-consciously. "Sorry, I forget sometimes that most people don't know the terminology." She rested her head against the back of the chair. "An AU is 'astronomical unit,' equal to roughly ninety-three million miles."

Nix frowned. "And that's considered near?"

"When you consider the vastness of space, yeah, that's pretty near." Samantha sighed. "When she finished her thesis, Rinda wanted to get a job at the University of Arizona's Steward Observatory—where the Catalina Sky Survey project is based—and be part of the team watching the skies." She reached up and wiped the outer corner of one eye. "She loved everything about space. I can't believe..." She broke off and bowed her head.

Tobias leaned forward, resting his elbows on his knees. "Do you know of anyone who might want to hurt her? Or did she ever talk about someone in a way that would lead you to believe she was in danger?" His husky baritone held compassion.

His ability for empathy, to care about the people around him, was one of the things that had surprised Nix about him when they'd first met. A lot of prets, especially vampires, didn't have that ability. Didn't *want* that ability. But Tobias had always seemed to want to hold on to whatever bits of humanity he still had.

Just like Nix did. Yet he hadn't been able to accept that he could have helped her even if only by his example. That they could have helped each other. Remembering how mad he sometimes made her, she figured now that maybe he'd been right. Maybe as good as they'd been together they weren't all that good for each other. They just hadn't been meant to be.

It had broken her heart once, and it wasn't much better five years later.

Now she watched Samantha try to get past her tears. The young woman shook her head. "Everybody liked Rinda, even if most of them were a little scared of her because, well, you know."

"Because she was a vampire," Tobias said, his voice soft and gentle.

The young woman nodded. She swiped beneath her eyes and stared down at her hands, fingers twisting. "She'd been spending a lot of free time down at Mt. Bigelow, at the Steward Observatory. I... I'm pretty sure she was involved with one of the scientists there. Plus it's a great location to watch the part of space where the rift occurs." She looked up, her expression stark with regret. "But she never said anything about someone trying to hurt her. I swear!" She pressed her fingertips to her brow bone. "Oh, God. I should've done something. Asked questions..."

"Why do you say that?" Tobias's gaze remained steady on her. "Did Rinda hint at something? Something you didn't push?"

She shook her head. "No, nothing like that. I just... I think the scientist she was involved with was getting ready to break things off. It was something she said about him being distant with her all of a sudden." She looked at them, her eyes sad and confused. "I assumed it was because he was married. I mean, she never really came out and said he was. It was just a hunch I had. I think he was going to stop the affair." She sighed. "I don't know. Maybe his wife found out."

"Did she ever give you his name?" Dante asked.

Samantha shook her head. "No. She just said he was really cute and mega smart. And he made her laugh."

An irresistible combination for just about any woman.

"Was he human or pret?" Nix asked.

Samantha shook her head. "I don't know," she whispered, and raked her fingers through her hair. "It didn't matter to me, so I never asked." She pressed her lips together. When she looked up at them, her bewildered eyes swam with tears. "What kind of horrible friend was I?"

Nix stood and went over to her, going down on her haunches. She clasped Samantha's hands in hers. "Rinda was a private person, even with her friends. If she didn't tell you, it's because she didn't want you to know. She didn't want *anyone* to know." She squeezed the young woman's fingers gently. "You didn't do anything wrong."

A tear dropped off Samantha's lashes and splashed on the back of Nix's hand. The young woman nodded and pulled one hand free to swipe at her tears.

Tobias leaned forward. "Ms. Smith, I have to ask… Where were you yesterday between two thirty and five thirty?"

Her eyes widened. The fingers clasping Nix's went slack. "You think…you think I killed her?"

"No. I don't." His eyes were as kind as Nix had ever seen them. "But I wouldn't be doing my job if I didn't ask."

The young woman sucked her lower lip between her teeth a moment. "I understand," she whispered. Letting go of Nix's other hand, she wiped her cheeks and then pressed her fingers to her temple. "I got together with some friends for a study session—we have a project due next week." She looked up at Tobias. "We were at the library from about one o'clock until almost seven. I can give you their names."

Tobias stood and walked toward her.

Nix got out of the way and watched as he handed Samantha his small notebook and pen. "Just write them down, and their phone numbers," he said. Once that was done and she gave them back, his lips curved in a gentle smile. He handed the young woman his card. "Thank you for your time, Ms. Smith. If you think of anything else, anything at all, no matter how immaterial you might think it is, please call me."

Samantha nodded.

Tobias looked at her mother. "Thank you for your hospitality, ma'am."

A few minutes later they were back at the SUV. "I highly doubt the wife had anything to do with Rinda's murder," Nix said.

"You don't say." Tobias's voice held snarky sarcasm.

She grimaced. "You know what I mean. If my husband had an affair and I was the kind of person to go after the other woman, I'd do it with a gun, or a knife. But I wouldn't gut her. And if I'm human, I wouldn't have a chance in hell of doing that to a vampire." She huffed out a sigh. "Plus that doesn't explain the other murder, does it?"

"Well, we don't know if the wife's human or not, do we? We don't know anything about her. We don't even know if there *is* a wife." Tobias jerked open the driver's door of the Porsche. "Damn it." He got in the SUV and slammed the door shut.

Dante looked at Nix as they walked around to the other side of the vehicle. "He's, ah, passionate about this, isn't he?"

She gave a one-shouldered shrug. "He and Rinda were friends for a long time. So he's taking it personally."

"Not a good idea." Dante stopped beside the rear passenger door. "Letting your emotions in will cloud your judgment every time."

"Yeah, well, keeping your emotions out of it when you know the victim is easier said than done." Nix reached toward the handle.

Dante put his hand on hers and leaned in. "Wait." When she looked up at him, he curled his fingers over her hand. His dark eyes held concern. "I'm sorry, Nix. I forgot she was a friend of yours, too."

She drew in a shaky breath. "It's okay." The heat from his palm seeped into her hand, warming skin she hadn't realized was cold. She met his gaze. "I deliberately cut her out of my life after Tobias and I split up. What kind of horrible friend does that make *me*?"

He put his hands on her shoulders. "Don't beat yourself up over it, honey."

Nix gave a short nod. "I know you're right. Like I said, easier said than done." She moved away from Dante and opened the back door. "We need to get going." Doing something was better than talking. She wasn't ready to talk. She climbed into the backseat and pulled the door closed behind her. She could feel Tobias's stare and busied herself with arranging her bag at her feet and fastening her seat belt.

Dante opened his door and got in.

"Glad you two could finally join me." Tobias started

the vehicle and put it in gear but didn't take his foot off the brake. "You get all caught up? Or do you need more time for a heart-to-heart?"

"We're just fine, chief." Dante shot him a frown. "Shouldn't we get going?"

She could see in the rearview mirror the way Tobias's lips thinned, but he said nothing.

He seemed...irritated. Maybe even a little jealous. A jolt of excitement shot through her at the thought, but she was careful to not let it show. With a glance at her watch, she said, "We should head down to the observatory. It's early yet. If we leave now we'd get there right around lunchtime."

"I agree." Without waiting for Dante's input, Tobias pulled away from the curb and within minutes they were on the freeway headed south toward Tucson. Nix could tell from Tobias's expression that his mind was hard at work, probably going back over what Samantha had told them, sifting through the bits and pieces to hopefully come up with something since they still pretty much had nothing.

* * *

Tobias tightened his hands on the wheel. He wanted to reach across the seat and thrash MacMillan for...For what? Caring about Nix? Being there for her when he hadn't been?

She'd barely been able to sit on the sofa next to him. He couldn't blame her, but he didn't like feeling like the bad guy. What he'd done he'd done for her. Yet she treated him like she hated him.

He tightened his jaw. Her hatred was a small price to

pay for her sanity. For now, they had about a three-hour drive ahead of them. Three hours for him to collect his thoughts and steel his resolve to be around Nix as little as he needed to be.

For both their sakes.

Chapter Six

So, what's the plan?" MacMillan got out of the SUV and stared at the observatory. Car door still open, he leaned one forearm on the roof of the vehicle and the other along the rim of the door. "Go in and start asking who was having an affair with Amarinda?"

"Yeah, why don't we do that?" Tobias slammed his door shut. "And here I thought you were supposed to be some hotshot detective."

"Oh, I am, Tobester. I am." MacMillan shut his door and started around the front of the Porsche.

Tobias curled his fingers into his palms. This flippant attitude the detective kept sending his way had to stop. And he was just the vampire to take care of it. MacMillan wouldn't even see him coming.

Nix squeezed around MacMillan's left, getting between him and Tobias. She shot the human detective a dark look. "Stop baiting him. We've got a job to do."

As they walked toward the main observatory—a large, round domed building with a catwalk running the circumference about halfway up—Tobias said, "Let's get one thing straight, detective. Don't call me Tobemeister or

Tobester or chief, and there won't be trouble between us. Got it?"

"Sure thing." MacMillan's grin was lopsided. "But you need to loosen up, slick. Being so uptight isn't good for you."

"What? It's going to give me a heart attack or something?" Tobias gave him a dry look. The other man was a pain in the ass, but there was something about him that made Tobias want to laugh.

"Would you two just stop it?" Nix walked ahead of them and yanked open the door. "You're exhausting me." She went into the building with a heavy sigh.

MacMillan grinned, making Tobias unsure whether the detective had been baiting him or Nix. She did bait so easily. And it irritated him that Dante knew her well enough to be aware of that.

They caught up to her just as she stopped a man walking by. "Excuse me," she said, briefly placing her hand on the man's arm. She showed him her ID. "We need to speak to whoever's in charge."

The young man looked startled. "What's this about?"

"Who's in charge?" Tobias asked pointedly as he took off his sunglasses and tucked them into his shirt pocket.

"Ah, Dr. Sahir. Ravi Sahir." The man pointed toward a door. "He's in his office."

"Thank you." Tobias headed that way. Nix and MacMillan followed behind him.

"Guess it takes a vampire to get questions answered around here," Dante muttered. "Your little half-demon ass would've gotten kicked to the curb."

"Shut up, Dante." Nix's voice was tense. Finally her voice held the same note as when she spoke to Tobias.

Tobias felt ridiculously pleased by that. He gave a perfunctory knock on the office door and opened it without waiting for a response. A middle-aged Indian man, a human, looked up from the computer console. His features were symmetrical, his hair ink black and shining in the artificial light. Dark brown eyes framed by thick lashes held curiosity and a slight wariness in their depths. Perhaps this was Amarinda's very good-looking lover?

The man's brow furrowed. "Yes? Can I help you?"

"Dr. Ravi Sahir?" Tobias flashed his ID again.

"Yes. What is this about?"

"My name is Tobias Caine, I'm the vampire liaison to the Council of Preternaturals. These are my colleagues Liaison de la Fuente and Detective MacMillan. We'd like to talk to you about Amarinda Novellus."

Dr. Sahir sat back in his chair. His expression became sorrowful, but behind that Tobias sensed the beginning of desperation. They had yet to ask their first question and already the man was trying to hide something.

The scientist tugged on the cuffs of his long-sleeve shirt. "Um, are all of you vampires?"

"No." Nix didn't offer anything more.

"We're human," MacMillan said, indicating himself and Nix.

"Amarinda?" Tobias reminded the scientist.

"Ah, yes. Amarinda. She was our most promising student." He sighed and looked down at his hands, clasped together in his lap. "It's a terrible thing."

Nix was busy looking at diplomas and award certificates that lined the wall. "How well did you know her?" she asked without turning around.

Tobias watched Sahir closely.

"How well did I know her?" The scientist swallowed. The fingers of his right hand began twisting his wedding ring. "As well as I know any of my student interns, I suppose." His gaze flicked to Nix and then settled on Tobias. "They come here to learn. I'm here to teach. I don't really get that involved in their private lives."

"I see." Tobias picked up a stack of files perched on the only other chair. "Do you mind?" he asked as he sat down.

Sahir shot out of his seat. "Of course not. Sorry." He took the files from Tobias. This close Tobias could see the sweat forming on the other man's forehead. Sahir went back around his desk and sat down, holding the files on his lap.

Tobias drew in a slow breath. The acrid scent of fear clogged the air and pricked at the hunger that always roiled just beneath the surface. He focused his control, fighting back his body's natural responses, and managed to keep his fangs to himself.

"Do we make you nervous, Doctor?" MacMillan leaned one shoulder against the wall, his pen at the ready over his small notebook.

"Not *you. Him.*" The scientist looked at Tobias and swallowed again. "I'm sorry. It's just...I'm not usually around that many EDs. Amarinda was my first. And she made me nervous."

"Why is that?" Tobias leaned back and crossed one leg over the other, ankle resting on the opposite knee, and tried to look as unthreatening as possible.

"You...vampires I mean...have a very penetrating stare, for one thing." A bead of sweat rolled down the side of Sahir's face. He swiped it away with his fingertips, then rubbed his hand against his jeans. "And she was always sniffing. Just like that!" He pointed toward Tobias.

Tobias held the breath he'd just taken and sifted through the assortment of aromas coming off the scientist. Fear, of course. Unease. Building desperation. A little bit of guilt.

Interesting.

He let out his breath. "This makes you nervous?"

"It's like you're reading our minds."

Tobias shook his head. "That's just a myth. We can't really read minds." He leaned forward and held Sahir's gaze. "What we can do is read emotions and reactions. And your emotions are very telling, Dr. Sahir."

Nix came closer. "We heard Amarinda was romantically involved with someone here, Doctor. Was it you?"

"No!" Sahir appeared genuinely shocked. "I am a happily married man." The ring twisted around and around.

"Yes, well, most people who have affairs are married." Nix picked up a paperweight off the desk and hefted it. She put it down and moved on to a nearby bookshelf. Tobias knew what she was doing, taking stock of the surroundings, which told a lot about the person in them, sometimes more than the person knew. "If it wasn't you," she asked, "then who was it?"

"I have no idea." Sahir tugged on the collar of his shirt. "It wasn't me." He cleared his throat and glanced at his watch. "If that's all—"

"It's not." Tobias glanced around the cluttered office. "What exactly did Amarinda do here?"

"She kept an eye to the sky." He smiled when he said it, as if they should get the punch line to a joke they'd never heard. When none of them reacted, his smile faded and he went back to looking uncomfortable. "Do you know what NEOs are?"

"We've had it explained to us," Tobias said.

Sahir nodded and cleared his throat. "Yes, well, we calculate their trajectory so we know how big a threat, if any, they might pose to Earth." A bit of the nervousness left his posture. "Some of them are slow enough they can be visited by exploration craft, and samples taken. It's very exciting."

"And the rift?" Nix asked, turning around with a paperback in her hand. She held it up.

Even from the other side of the desk Tobias could read the title—*What's On the Other Side?* He glanced at the bookshelf and saw what appeared to be a dozen or more books on the subject. He looked at the scientist. "Well, Doctor? Are you investigating the rift here, too?"

"The rift?" Sahir shifted in his chair. "It falls within our mandate, so, yes, we investigate it and the Moore-Creasy-Devon comet that opens it. Or, rather, we will investigate it when it comes along again." His voice took on a defensive tone. "It's a very fascinating phenomenon."

Tobias fought back a grin of triumph. Get the man on the defensive and they'd won half the battle.

"And was that part of what Amarinda was doing here? Was she investigating the rift?" MacMillan turned and rested his back against the wall.

"Not officially, no." The nervousness returned, and Dr. Sahir's gaze darted to Nix, who was still at the bookshelf to his left and a little behind him, then to the two men in front of him.

"But unofficially?" Tobias raised one brow.

"She seemed rather fascinated by it."

"But she wasn't one of the scientists who was charged with observing and documenting it?" Nix moved around to stand at the front corner of his desk.

"Documenting it?" Sahir parroted. He tried and failed to look surprised.

"You know exactly what I'm talking about, Doctor. That's what scientists do. They observe. They measure. They document." She placed her palms on the desk and leaned forward. "What exactly was Amarinda involved with down here?"

Tobias could smell the burned paper scent of demon and knew Nix was getting worked up. He leaned forward and peered at her more closely. She darted a glance his way and he saw the yellow flecks in her irises.

Tobias didn't know if she had called the demon on purpose or if her emotions were eroding her control. He wasn't sure he wanted to know, because he didn't think it was wise of her to do it on purpose. It meant she actively courted the possibility she could lose her grip on it.

But regardless, it had the desired response as Sahir slammed his chair back so it bounced against the wall. "I...I thought you were human."

"Half human. Trust me, you really don't want to see more of the half that's not." Nix straightened. "Answer the question."

The scientist's throat moved with his hard swallow. "Even though she came through the rift centuries ago, she didn't really know anything about it. She wanted to understand it, understand how...you people came from where you were to where you are." His gaze darted from Nix to Tobias and back to Nix again.

"For the record," Nix muttered, crossing her arms and tilting her head to one side, "I didn't come through the rift. I was born here. On Earth. In Glendale, to be specific." She raised her eyebrows. "Was Rinda researching the rift in an official capacity?"

"Officially?" He shook his head. "No. Well, yes as far as it was part of her thesis."

"Is it no or yes?" MacMillan pushed away from his place by the door. He scribbled something in his notebook and looked back up. "You seem a bit confused."

The man rubbed one earlobe between forefinger and thumb. "It wasn't research that we here at the observatory are involved in. Okay?"

"Talk to us, Doctor." Nix braced her hands on the desk, leaning forward again. Tobias could tell she was gearing up for an offensive. He sat back in his chair and let her go. "Just how long were you and Rinda involved?" Nix's eyes narrowed.

"How long were..." He stood and slashed his hands through the air. "I told you—"

"Blah, blah, blah." With one hand she made a talking motion in the air. She straightened and folded her arms over her breasts again. "You weren't her lover or so you say. But you're the man in charge. You know everything that goes on here, I'm sure. So if it wasn't you, who was it?"

"It *wasn't* me." He slowly took his seat again. "You should talk to her friend, Samantha Smith." He lifted his chin. "Those two seemed more than just friends, if you know what I mean." He waggled one hand and then assumed a pious expression. "Not that I care about such things."

"Yes, we'll do that." Tobias wasn't about to let the man know who they had or had not already spoken to. "For the record, where were you yesterday between two thirty and six thirty?"

"You're asking me for an alibi? I had nothing to do with her death!"

"Answer the question." Tobias let a wash of pheromones drift toward the scientist, using the subtle chemicals to influence the man's reaction.

And react he did. He stiffened in his chair. His face paled and Tobias saw his fingers clench around the armrests. As if every word was dragged out of him, he said, "I was with my wife and daughter."

"Doing what?" Nix asked.

He stared at her. "We had lunch around one, then went to the movies, then some shopping at the mall. We didn't get home until close to nine p.m." He turned his pleading gaze onto Tobias. "Please. There's no need to get my wife involved in this, is there?"

Tobias caught the triumphant look Nix sent him. In so many words Sahir had just admitted to being in an affair with Amarinda.

Tobias stood and stared down at the scientist. "We'll take your word for it, for now. We'd like to talk to everyone here."

Dr. Sahir also stood. He looked relieved. "Well, I don't know what they can tell you, but you're welcome to talk to anyone who isn't tied up with telescope operations. You should know that most of the staff isn't in yet. We do our best work after dark."

"So do I." In case the human scientist needed reminding of just what he was dealing with, Tobias curled his lips in a slow smile so that just the tips of his fangs showed. He held out his hand and waited while Sahir slowly reached out to shake it. "Thank you for your cooperation, Doctor." Tobias let go of the man's hand and reached inside his pocket for a business card. He put the card on the desk. "If you think of anything, please call me."

"Yes, of course."

Without a word, MacMillan turned and opened the door. He waited until Nix and Tobias went through, then he left the room and pulled the door closed behind him. "Well, he was lying through his teeth. He's the man your friend was involved with."

"Yeah, I think so, too." Nix stared at the door for a moment. "He's very good looking, and has to be smart to be the leader of this team. Not sure about the sense of humor, because I didn't find anything remotely funny about the man. Though it could just be we intimidated him." She blew out a sigh. "It's too bad we can't smack him around a little."

"To get the truth out of him, you mean?" MacMillan grinned.

"No, just for the hell of it. He's a married man." She lifted her chin. "Vows are sacred. If you're not happy in your marriage, get out of it before you start... spreading the joy." She gave a little growl and looked at Tobias. "How do you want to handle this? Split up and question people separately?"

He studied her for a few seconds. Her eyes were once again her normal lovely dark brown, no sign of the demon present. "Can I talk to you for a second?" He drew her away from MacMillan. In a low voice Tobias asked, "Was that on purpose, in there? Letting the demon show?"

She narrowed her eyes. "What if it was?"

"It's just a question, Nix." He held her gaze. "I worry about you."

"Oh, you do, do you?" Her lips tightened. As he started to speak she held up one hand. "You know what? I don't want to hear it. I'm fine. I can let the demon peek out now and again without any repercussions."

He was skeptical.

"I'm fine," she repeated as she started toward MacMillan. "Now, how do you want to handle the questioning?"

Tobias followed her. He had to take her word for it at this point, but he'd keep a close eye on Nix. He'd take control the second it looked like the demon was on its way. To MacMillan he said, "You take them." He pointed to two human scientists in jeans and polo shirts, one typing away at a keyboard and the other working near the larger of the two telescopes.

"Got it." MacMillan gave a two-fingered salute and headed off. He seemed happy to get off on his own, making Tobias wonder just how much of a lone ranger the detective might be.

Tobias looked at Nix. "I'll question, you listen. Pick up on what they're not saying. You're good at that."

She cocked her head to one side. "So, what exactly are you saying? That I'm sly and sneaky?" Her face was serious but her eyes sparkled with the beginnings of humor.

It gave Tobias hope that maybe, since she could tease him, she'd moved past her hurt and anger. Or would someday be able to. Maybe they could actually get through this case without putting her in jeopardy, and then he could leave again before any real damage was done. He gave her a smile and said, "You're one of the slyest and sneakiest people I know."

She seemed inordinately pleased by that. "Well, then. I'll do my best."

"I know you will." Tobias motioned toward a woman seated in front of a computer console. Nix nodded. Walking beside her, Tobias felt the warmth of her body, smelled her determination enhanced by the mixture of feminine musk and floral perfume. His body tightened.

Focus, Caine. He couldn't allow himself to get distracted. There was too much at stake, not the least of which was Nix's hold on her sanity. He glanced over at her, her curls bouncing as she walked, her breasts...

She was the biggest distraction in his life. She always had been, probably always would be.

Stopping at the workstation, he brought his attention back to the job and said, "Excuse me." When the woman paused and looked up at them, he showed her his ID. "Dr. Sahir said we could talk to you."

She sat back in her chair. "About what?"

"Amarinda Novellus."

Her lips pursed. "I didn't really know her, so I'm not sure what I can tell you. She was here mostly at night and a lot during the week, and I'm usually here on the weekends."

"You never know what you might tell us that ends up being crucial." Tobias watched her closely. "We were told she was involved with someone here. Any idea who that was?"

The woman's eyes flickered but she didn't take her gaze off him. "No idea. She was a very private person." She said this last bit in a hushed tone as if it were a secret she didn't want anyone to overhear.

"I see." He glanced around then leaned forward, keeping his voice low. "So she and Sahir weren't... You know." He wiggled his eyebrows.

"I can't say."

"Can't? Or won't?" Tobias straightened. "There's a big difference."

"I can't." She looked back at her computer and spoke softly. "Some of us still have to work here after you leave."

That told him all he needed to know. He shared a glance with Nix and saw the same knowledge in her eyes. Sahir and Rinda had been involved. This woman had confirmed what they'd concluded in their interview with Sahir.

No big surprise there. One infallible truth he'd learned in his many years of existence—people lied. All the time. About big things and little ones. Sometimes they lied to cover up something, sometimes they lied just because it was easier than telling the truth.

Like him. Telling Nix five years ago that things weren't working out between them rather than telling her he had to leave because he was a negative influence. Instead of being truthful, he took the easy way out and left. Maybe someday they would talk about it. Though he wasn't sure he wanted to.

"One more question," he said. "Do you know where Rinda's research on the rift is?"

She looked at them with a blank expression. "I would assume it's at her home."

"There were a few books there on the subject, but nothing that looked like research."

"I know she typed up her notes and kept them on a

flash drive. But I don't know of any secret hiding place, if that's what you're asking. I don't even know why she'd need one." She looked from Tobias to Nix. "I'm sorry. I can't help you."

Tobias could tell her regret was genuine. But she wasn't going to jeopardize her job for his investigation. He could appreciate that even if it was frustrating as hell. He murmured his thanks and started to turn away.

"Wait!"

Tobias stopped and looked at the scientist.

"There was a guy that came to see her here one night, an ED. I don't know exactly what kind of ED he was." Her brows crinkled in a frown. "He wasn't vampire. Maybe a shape-shifter of some kind? I'm sorry, I just don't know. But Amarinda wasn't happy to see him."

"Do you know his name?" Nix took a few steps forward.

"She called him...oh, it started with an F, I think." The woman's eyes darted down and to the side while she thought. "Fee...Fo...Fi..." She snapped her fingers and brought her eyes back to them. "Finn! That was it. Finn."

"Are you sure?"

Tobias heard the strain in Nix's voice and wondered at it.

"Yes, I'm sure. Does that help?"

"Yes, it does. Thank you." Nix turned and strode toward the door. Tobias followed, checking to see what MacMillan was up to. The detective was talking to the scientist sitting at the computer console. Tobias caught up with Nix before she could head outside. "Nix, wait. Just wait a minute, would you?" He looked back at the woman they'd just talked to. "You want to tell me what the hell that was all about?"

* * *

Dante leaned one hip against the desk and, pen poised over paper, asked, "What was that name again?" He'd already talked to the guy tinkering with the telescope, and for the last few minutes he'd been interviewing an intern who looked about twelve. This kid made him feel old, and he wasn't even forty yet.

"Finn...something. I don't think he ever gave his last name." The young man leaned his forearms on the desk and absently tapped a finger on the edge of the keyboard. "What I do know is that he was one big, intimidating dude."

Dante frowned. "Did he threaten you?"

"No, nothing like that. Not overtly. He just sorta..." He waved his hands around. "Loomed. He was a loomer."

"A loomer?" For a moment Dante reflected on the difference in conducting interviews with humans and EDs. While right now he took a normal stance to make sure his sidearm was on the side angled away from the citizen he was questioning, with EDs he went a little further and usually had his hand fairly close to his weapon, just in case. He had yet, however, to hear anyone refer to a possible ED as a "loomer."

"I said he was big." The guy stood up. The top of his head came to Dante's chin. "You kinda loom, too, you know." There was a hint of accusation in his tone as he looked up into Dante's eyes. He put his hands on his hips, maybe in an unconscious move to appear bigger.

Dante let that one slide. "Anyone else hanging around looking for Ms. Novellus?"

The kid pursed his lips. After a few seconds he shook his head. "Not that I know of."

Dante pulled out a business card and handed it to the other man. "If you think of anything, call me, all right?"

"Yeah, sure." The young man sat back down and slipped the card into the pocket of his shirt. He resumed typing on the keyboard and within seconds Dante could tell he'd been dismissed. Or forgotten. It was hard to be sure which.

Dante tucked his notebook into his pocket and looked around for Nix and Tobias. He saw them waiting at the door and had to fight back a grin when he saw the look on Tobias's face. The vampire seemed a little bemused and a lot befuddled as he gazed down at Nix. Dante knew he'd worn that look before, as had just about every man on the planet. As he walked over to them he heard Nix say, "I'm telling you, he's bad news."

"Who's bad news?" Dante asked.

"Finn Evnissyen." A muscle twitched in Nix's jaw. "He's a demon. A bastard."

"A bastard demon, huh? Well, apparently he's also a loomer," Dante said. At the identical blank looks from his colleagues, he muttered, "Never mind. It was something the kid said." He cleared his throat. "He mentioned a Finn but didn't know his last name. You think it's the same guy?" Nix and Tobias shared a look. "Will someone tell me what's going on?"

* * *

Nix's full lips pressed together a moment before her tongue swept out, leaving them moist and inviting. Tobias found himself staring at her mouth as she continued to speak. "Our lady didn't give a last name either, but if she's talking about who I think she's talking about, it's

Finn Evnissyen. He's the only Finn around here that I know of. He's a demon, don't know which clan. It's rumored he's one of Lucifer's sons, but it's never been proved." She spread her hands. "He's very mysterious."

"Lucifer's son? As in Lucifer Demonicus? The king of demons?" MacMillan paused. "Well, let's hope this Finn knows something, because no one I talked to here seems to know anything."

That tongue came out and slicked across her lips again. "I have no idea why he would want to see Amarinda—he's a loner, much more so than most demons." She stared at Tobias, her slender brows knit in a frown. "But it can't be coincidence that he came looking for Amarinda and then she ended up dead."

Tobias stared at her mouth a second longer, remembering what those lips felt like against his skin, sliding down his abdomen to...He dragged his gaze up to her dark eyes. "Whether or not he killed her, when you're talking about murder there's no such thing as coincidence." He shoved open the door and blinked in the strong sunlight. Yanking his sunglasses out of his pocket, he slipped them on. "Let's put together our next plan of action on the way down the mountain."

* * *

Before Nix could get to the SUV, Dante opened the back door and jumped inside, grinning like a Cheshire cat when she scowled at him.

"Is there a problem?" Tobias asked as he opened his own door. He stared at her from over the roof of the vehicle.

"No, other than with a certain underhanded detective,"

she said, and yanked open the passenger door. She got in and fastened her seat belt. As Tobias started the Porsche, she rolled the window down and leaned her head against the headrest. It smelled fresh and clean up here, the air crisp and cold. As Tobias started driving down the mountain, the air whipped into the car.

"Hey, you trying to freeze us?" Dante rapped the back of her headrest. "Roll up the window, please."

"Wuss." She reached down and pressed the window button, enjoying the whirring sound of the window sliding up. Even that sounded expensive.

"It's gotta only be about forty degrees out there."

She glanced over her shoulder to see him hunched down in his seat. "In about half an hour or so we'll be back down in the valley where it's seventy."

"Yeah, well, then in about half an hour or so you can roll the window back down. Besides, I hit a couple of cold spots in the observatory." He looked from her to Tobias and back again. "Not everyone in this car is a hot-blooded demon or a cold-as-ice vampire, you know."

"Well, not everyone's perfect." Tobias looked in the rearview mirror then put his eyes back on the road. Nix was astonished to see the hint of a crease in his cheek.

She leaned her elbow on the middle armrest and murmured, "You're going to ruin that tall, dark, and scary impression you keep trying to give off by grinning, you know."

His face sobered, though the look he shot her held lingering humor.

"Hey, you think we could stop somewhere and get something to eat?" Dante leaned forward in his seat. "I'm starving."

"After that huge breakfast you had?" Nix twisted around to look at him. He just shrugged and grinned.

"I'll run through a drive-through for you," Tobias said. "Just holler when you see something you like." He slowed to navigate a curve, then accelerated as the road straightened. "Nix, you and I will handle the rest of the interviews with prets, including Finn. Dante, I'd like you to conduct the remaining interviews with any humans who still need talking to." He glanced over his shoulder at the detective. "And seeing how violent these murders have been, I think it would be a good idea for you to take someone with you."

Dante nodded and sat back. "No problem. There are a couple of people in the Phoenix area I need to talk to. Nix, once we do get back to Scottsdale, how 'bout some dinner?"

"You're going to eat lunch and then turn around and eat dinner again in a couple of hours?" She was hungry now, too, but she didn't want to eat lunch and then have dinner as soon as they got back home.

"Well, yeah, I'm sure I could eat again." He flashed a quick grin. "But I meant having dinner at the dinner hour. Around six or so."

She caught the scowl on Tobias's face and wondered at it. Why would he be surly that they were talking about food? It wasn't their fault he couldn't eat. "Sure." She decided to ignore the bad-tempered vampire behind the wheel. "Anywhere in particular?"

"Devil's Domain."

She rolled her eyes. "You're just a glutton for punishment, aren't you? I told you, it can get pretty rough. Besides, I thought you said dinner. Not drinks."

"They have appetizers, don't they?" He grinned. "Come on. What can happen?"

"Oh, I don't know, you could get a troll on a rampage—that happened several years ago. We ended up with twenty dead prets and eleven dead humans," Tobias mused.

"I remember that." Nix shifted in her seat and faced forward again. The incident had happened right before she and Tobias had started seeing each other. She'd been at the bar that night and had been detained for questioning. Even at her worst behavior, though, she'd never been stupid enough to mess with a troll. She smiled at the memory. Catching Tobias's heated gaze, she looked away.

"Yeah, well, nothing's happened recently that I've heard of," Dante said. "If you're so worried, chief, why don't you come along?"

"I don't eat, remember?"

"You drink, don't you?" Dante looked at Nix with raised brows. "I'm sure I've seen vamps drink. And not just blood," he added with a slight frown.

When Tobias didn't respond, Nix said, "They drink, but I'm sure Tobias has other plans." She did *not* want him tagging along.

"Not really," Tobias said.

Nix gritted her teeth.

"Great!" Dante rested one arm along the back of the seat. "It'll be nice to talk over food and drinks instead of over a dead body."

Nix wanted to discourage Tobias from joining them, but she didn't want to appear churlish. "Yeah, sure." Her tone was definitely not enthusiastic. In a cheerful voice she added, "You should come." That was even worse. She pressed her lips together and looked at him out of the corner of her eye.

Tobias shot her a glance. "Actually, that's not a bad idea. We can meet up there and compare notes. I just need to get home at some point so I can..." He paused. "I'll just need to go home first."

Get home and feed was what he'd been about to say. She couldn't help but wonder if someone would be waiting for him, ready to bare her throat.

What he does is none of my business. He could have a harem of willing donors for all she cared. She tried to ignore the pain that knifed through her at the thought of him biting someone else. Maybe even having sex with someone else, because sometimes being a vampire was as much about sex as it was blood.

She drew in a breath and promised herself another round of tai chi just as soon as she could manage it. "Devil's Domain it is."

"After we stop at Mickey D's," Dante said, tapping on the back of Tobias's headrest. "Don't forget."

"I won't." He glanced at Nix, a slight smile tilting one side of his mouth.

It made her want to kiss him. She turned and stared out the window. If she stayed focused on the job, she could make it through this.

Chapter Seven

After they dropped Dante off at his truck, Nix and Tobias went on to find Finn. The demon wasn't at home nor was he at the next half-dozen places they tried, mostly dives and strip clubs. As they walked up to yet another nudie bar with cigarette butts littering the sidewalk in front of the door, Nix took a deep breath. She was getting tired and was way past frustrated. Her gut had started to burn after the fourth stop but she'd managed to keep all evidence of the demon at bay. They needed to find Finn sooner rather than later, because she wasn't sure how much longer she was going to last without intervention of some sort.

Tobias was losing patience, too, if the ramp-up in pheromones was anything to go by. She was learning to cope with them, though she suspected they were beginning to affect her mood. Legwork was a part of the job and she usually had no trouble with it. Certainly she hadn't felt this edgy in a long time. She pulled open the door and entered the dingy club, pausing while her eyes adjusted to the dim interior. A variety of scents wafted her way—werewolves, vamps, a pixie or two and humans, stale beer, and even staler cigarette smoke.

Tobias stood just behind her, a comforting and safe presence at her back. She was completely capable of taking care of herself, but there was something about a tall, dark, and dangerous vamp standing at your elbow that put most people on their best behavior.

Nix took in the entertainment in the center of the room where a large raised stage with a central stripper pole was the main attraction. Tiny white lights clung to the top of the square canopy and four wooden pillars provided support at each corner. It reminded Nix of a large four-poster bed. The exotic dancer swayed and gyrated in thigh-high red latex boots, a skimpy black bra and matching thong, and nothing else. Knowing that pole dancing wasn't easy and feeling like the woman deserved some appreciation above the sexual kind she got from her customers, Nix took a moment to admire the woman's technique, then she moved farther inside the building, eyes scanning for their target.

A werewolf nursing a drink at the bar reached over and pinched her ass as she walked by. "Hey, baby," he growled.

Nix stopped and looked at him. "Do I look like the kind of woman who wants drunken dogs putting their paws on her?"

He just grinned.

She shook her head and started to move on. Before she got two steps away, he reached out a long arm and hauled her backward between his spread legs. The hard ridge behind the fly of his jeans prodded her backside. The arm around her middle shifted and his large palm settled over her left breast. Enraged, she spun and grabbed his arm, wrenching it up between his shoulder blades as she bent him forward onto the bar. “You need to keep your hands and your johnson to yourself.” She ground her teeth against the fire churning in her belly. Her eyes burned as well and she knew her demon was showing.

“Aw, come on, sweetheart. There ain’t nothin’ in the world like werewolf meat. You know you want it.” He grunted when she twisted his arm higher. “I thought demons like you were always... hungry.”

She ignored that. “It’s been a long day. I’m tired. And you’re right. I am hungry. But not for you.” She put her full weight onto him. “Keep. Your hands. To. Yourself.”

“All right, all right.” The werewolf laughed, though it held more pain than any real humor. He was running on pure machismo. He probably had his best buds hanging around close by and didn’t want to lose face with them. He turned his head and gazed at her over his shoulder. “Jeez, honey. How long’s it been since you got laid?” He gave her a once-over, as much as he could with his arm still twisted in the middle of his back. “You need to lighten up.”

“I’ll lighten *you* up,” she croaked, her throat raw, voice hoarse with building rage. Since when did being pretty and having boobs give men permission to touch without asking? Her horn buds burst from beneath her skin. Her vision became awash with yellow. She put one hand at the small of her back, wrapping her fingers around the hilt of her silver dagger. “Werewolves can recover from a lot of wounds, but I bet you can’t grow back a hand. Unless you’re part lizard. Let’s see, shall we?”

“Nix.” Tobias’s voice was low. “That’s enough. Let him go.”

She held on for another few seconds, just to make her point, then let go of the werewolf’s arm and walked away.

The werewolf's muffled "Bitch" almost made her turn back around but she forced her feet to keep moving away from him.

Tobias caught up with her at the end of the bar. "What the hell was that about?" he asked, his voice as hard as the hand he wrapped around her upper arm.

She jerked her arm away and faced him. "What do you mean, what was it about? He put his mangy paws on me."

"It's not the first time you've had unwelcome attention from a drunk, Nix." His mouth thinned. "It's just like before," he murmured as if to himself. "We're together and you're losing control."

"I am *not* losing control," she said even as her eyes burned hotter and her head felt like it was going to explode. She hadn't felt this close to the edge in a long time. "This has nothing to do with you." She wasn't so sure of that anymore, but it helped saying it out loud. Sort of. She drew in a breath and held it for a ten count. It didn't help much. She needed to push the demon back, and fast. "See if Finn is here. I'll be right back." Without waiting for his response, she sprinted to the ladies' room.

The smell of urine in the hallway was abominably strong. The worn carpet wore stains like badges of honor. Stains she was quite sure were more than just urine. Nix grimaced and pushed open the door to the ladies' room, giving a sigh of relief to find it vacant. Locking the door, she leaned against it, eyes closed. She drew in a slow breath through her nose, held it for a few seconds and then exhaled through her mouth. Repeat. And again.

There wasn't time to do much of anything, especially not standing in a less-than-sanitary ladies' room in the back of a strip joint. But she had to do something. Adjusting her purse strap so that it rode across her chest, she lifted her arms above her head and then brought them down in front of her on another long exhale. A slow sideways lunge while waving her hands in the classic cloud movement focused her thoughts. She repeated it to the other side, keeping her attention on her breathing and the technical aspects of tai chi. After a couple of minutes she felt much more in control. Her horn buds receded, her eyes and stomach no longer churned with fire.

She walked to the sink and peered at her image in the water-splashed mirror. Everything was back to normal. Now to go back out and face Tobias and his pheromones.

Was he right? Was it his presence that eroded her emotions, allowing the demon to peek out? Could it be that simple, that heartbreaking?

No! She wouldn't believe it. But even if it were true, he'd at least owed it to her to talk about it instead of just disappearing the way he had. "It's not working out," he'd said, and then nothing. For five years.

And he wondered why she got all stirred up around him.

"Knock it off," she demanded. She'd just restored her control, the last thing she wanted to do was let the past damage that calm.

She pulled open the door and rejoined Tobias who was still at the end of the bar. "What did you find out?" she asked him.

"Finn was here earlier. Bartender said he talked to another demon for about five minutes and then left." Tobias's gaze drifted to the exotic dancer on stage, a different woman from the one who'd been there when they'd first come in.

Nix looked that way, too, in time to see the woman bend over and shake her booty to the catcalls and whistles of the audience. Then she straightened and hooked one arm around the pole, going into a few deep knee bends. As she straightened on the last one, her fingers went to the front clasp of her flimsy bra. She teased the male patrons a couple of seconds, then stripped off the bra and let it fall to the floor.

"Okay, I've seen way too many boobs today," Nix stated.

"I don't think I have." Tobias's eyes flicked to her then right back to the stripper.

"That sounds like something Dante would say." When Tobias's only response was a brief twitch of his lips, she held out her hand. "Fine. Give me the keys. You can stay here as long as you like. Enjoy yourself."

His head swiveled at that. His eyes were appalled. "You're not driving the Porsche."

"Hey!" She frowned. "I'm not a bad driver."

"Yes, you are," he said as he turned and walked the length of the bar. Nix noticed he made sure to stay between her and the werewolf who stared at her with a mixture of humor, disdain, and anger.

Nix stared right back at him, daring him to get off his stool. She didn't need her gun or the dagger to take care of him.

He started to get up, but at a look from Tobias he settled back onto his chair. He glared at Nix and then turned his back on her, muttering into his beer.

She shoved open the door and strode out into the fading sunlight of early evening. "God, I always feel so icky when I come out of one of these places. Why in the hell

Evnissyen finds it necessary to frequent these places is beyond me."

"You're kidding, right?" Tobias slid his sunglasses on and quirked an eyebrow at her.

"No, I'm not. You don't hang out at strip clubs, do you?" She paused at the passenger side of the SUV and looked at him over the hood.

"No. But I'm not a demon."

She scowled. "Oh, give me a freaking break. Not all demons are sex-hungry maniacs who hang out at nudie bars." Then she belatedly heard the teasing note in his voice. "Oh. Sorry."

He just stared at her a moment before replying, "No problem." He used the key remote to open the doors and they climbed into the vehicle. Glancing at his watch, he said, "It'll take us about forty-five minutes from here to get to the Devil's Domain. We need to head there now if we're going to meet Dante on time."

"Okay. Let's go." Nix buckled up and leaned her head against the headrest.

Tobias fastened his seat belt and started the SUV, then pulled out of the parking lot. He reached forward and turned on the radio. The fast beat of a popular alternative rock song came on.

She started drumming her fingers on the armrest, smiling a little when she saw Tobias doing the same on the steering wheel. An eclectic taste in music was just one of the things they shared and in the early days it had helped cement their friendship, then later their love. She glanced out the side window. It was too bad music couldn't save them.

Tobias didn't seem to be in a talkative mood, not that

he usually was, and she used the time to continue her breathing exercises as discreetly as possible. It really didn't matter, though, since with his vampire senses he'd be able to hear her breathing. She finally decided it was all right if he saw what she did to contain the demon. Perhaps he would finally understand that she had more control than he gave her credit for.

They pulled into the lot at the Devil's Domain. As Tobias maneuvered the SUV into a parking space, he asked, "Are you going to be all right in there?"

"Sure. Why wouldn't I?"

"There are probably going to be a lot of vamps in there. Not to mention incubi." He turned his head to look at her, and, as usual, his sunglasses hid his eyes. She couldn't tell what he was thinking.

"Yeah, probably." She scowled. "I'll be fine, Tobias. I'm not the same person you knew five years ago. I've come a long way since we were together." She opened her door and got out, slamming the door behind her. She was proud of how evenly the words came out. Maybe being around him was acting like a catharsis. She wasn't feeling nearly the same level of hurt as she had when she'd first seen him.

God, was that just yesterday? Unbelievable.

"Okay. I... Just know I'm here for you."

She shot him a glance but didn't spout off the words that sprang to her mind. Here for her like he hadn't been in the last five years? And here for her for how long? Instead, she gave a short nod and walked toward the club.

Tobias's cell phone rang. "Give me a minute," he said, and stopped to answer the phone.

Nix went on and met up with Dante who waited for

them near the entrance. He pushed away from the wall he'd been leaning on and they walked to the front door. "Any luck finding your guy?"

"No. How'd you do with the interviews?" she asked.

His shoulders lifted in a shrug. "No one told me anything I didn't already know." He started to reach for the door but stopped when the bulky doorman held out his hand.

Nix looked at him. The ruddy cast to his skin, the bright grass green of his eyes, and the small brown mushroom-shaped birthmark beneath his left ear signified he was one of the nature fairies known as green men. "Reservations?" he asked. The look that passed through his eyes was one Nix had seen before. There were already too many humans inside for comfort, and he wasn't about to let another one in. "This is the first I've heard of needing reservations," she said.

The big man merely stared at her.

"You don't need reservations," Tobias said as he walked up behind them.

"Mr. Caine!" The big doorman cleared his throat. "I'm sorry, sir. I didn't know these two were with you." He glanced at the Glock holstered at Nix's waist. "I'll let you in since you're with Mr. Caine, but weapons aren't allowed."

There was no way in hell they were going to walk into the Devil's Domain without their weapons. "You let vamps and weres and all sorts of prets in there—prets who come equipped with built-in weapons, I might add—and you won't let us inside carrying protection?"

"Club rules. The only exceptions are for members of law enforcement."

"Well, I guess it's our lucky day." Dante flipped his jacket to one side to show the man the badge fastened to his belt.

Without another word the doorman reached out a long arm toward the door. "Have an enjoyable evening." As Tobias walked past him, he said, "It's good to see you again, sir."

When the door swung open Nix was assaulted by loud techno rock and the jumble of voices. Scents of perfumes and colognes drifted in the air, plus the smell of lightly and some not-so-lightly perspiring bodies. There were also plenty of vamp pheromones, just as Tobias had warned.

One thing was sure. Dante was going to get an education about prets.

Just inside the doorway he stopped and took a look around. "Wow."

Nix glanced around the club, trying to see it through his eyes. The place was packed. Out of habit she looked for potential trouble. A gaggle of vamps sat in a large booth in a dimly lit corner; human groupies clustered around offering necks and arms. The dance floor had a mixture of humans and prets, and a few werewolves congregated near the bar, beer in their hands and mischief in their eyes.

"Let's get a seat in the back," Tobias suggested, brushing his way past them to lead the way.

As they followed him, Dante leaned over. "I didn't realize it would be quite so...punkish," he yelled to Nix over the cacophony of sounds.

"Hopefully the drinks will make up for it," she responded.

"What?" He leaned closer.

She shook her head. "Let's get a table," she shouted, and hurried to catch up with Tobias. They walked past the polished mahogany bar which, amid all the modern sights and sounds, was surprisingly Old West looking. Tobias headed straight for the only available booth, one at the end of the row in the corner. He slid onto the bench on the wall side, doing what Nix would have done had she gotten there first. If you were facing the crowd, no one could sneak up on you.

At this point, though, she'd rather get snuck up on than sit next to Tobias. She sat on the seat across from him. To her surprise, Dante stopped next to Tobias.

"You want to shove over, chief?" he asked.

Tobias looked surprised as well. Instead of sliding over, he eased out of the booth and motioned for Dante to get in. Then Tobias took his seat again and lifted a hand to summon a server.

"I've never seen so many EDs in one place," Dante said. Excitement sparkled in his dark eyes. "It's fascinating."

"Easy there, Mr. Spock," she teased. "Just don't be surprised if some sort of mayhem breaks out. It usually does."

"Why?"

"Because most prets, not all, are naturally aggressive. Put a few drinks in them and things get interesting."

"Ah."

A young woman with a pen and pad in her hands stopped at their table. "Mr. Caine. It's nice to see you again."

Tobias's lips curved in a genuine smile. "It's nice to

see you again, too, Gretchen." He looked at Nix. "Know what you want?"

"I'll have a glass of red wine and some mozzarella sticks." Now that she had time to think, Nix realized she was hungry again. The small fries and diet cola she'd gotten at the bottom of Mt. Lemmon hadn't satisfied her for long. "And fried zucchini."

Dante leaned his elbows on the table. "I'll take whatever's on tap. And add some chicken wings to our order, would you?"

"Sure thing, hon," the waitress said as she scribbled on her pad. "How hot do you want 'em?"

Nix shot Dante a look. "Just how much heat can you handle, Detective?"

"Since we're talking about food here, for the moment, I'll admit I don't like my wings very hot. My women, on the other hand—"

"We'll take the chipotle barbecue," Nix said before he could say something to embarrass her.

Dante just grinned and settled back against his seat.

"And for you, Mr. Caine?"

"Red wine with a kick," he replied.

The waitress finished jotting on her notepad. "I'll get those drinks right out to you." She turned and walked away, her gait lithe and sensual.

"Red wine with a kick?" Dante asked, his gaze glued to the waitress.

Nix leaned over the table. "There'll be a little bit of blood in the wine," she explained.

Dante's eyes widened slightly. "No kidding." He glanced at his seatmate. "Maybe I should be on that side of the table," he said, pointing toward Nix.

Tobias smiled, a slow tilt of his lips.

"Give it up, boss. You're not scaring me. Much," he added under his breath. He looked around the club, dark eyes skipping from group to group, person to person. "This isn't so bad," he finally said.

The waitress came back with their drinks. "Your food'll be up shortly." She left as quietly as she'd come.

Nix glanced around, tracking people as they moved around the club. So far no one seemed the least bit interested in their little corner of the world.

"You're always on alert, aren't you?" Dante asked.

"I can't afford not to be around this lot." She picked up her drink. "Especially when alcohol's involved. Besides, it's part of the job, isn't it?"

Dante crossed his arms and leaned on the table. "I guess it is. My sister always gives me a hard time whenever we go out. She says I look for bad guys under every table." He took a sip of beer. "Occupational hazard, I guess." He watched with interest as Tobias picked up his wineglass.

"What?" Tobias asked.

"Just waiting to see if you're going to go all vampy on me," Dante said, shifting his weight toward the wall.

Nix caught the twinkle in his eye and pressed her lips together against a grin.

Tobias scowled, but it was good natured. He took a sip of wine and set the glass back on the table, though his lean fingers played with the stem.

She remembered how those blunt-tipped fingers felt against her skin, stroking, rubbing. She grabbed her own glass and took a long swallow. "So, where are we with the investigation?" she asked, and took a more moderate sip of wine.

"We got nowhere on finding Finn. All we figured out today was where he wasn't," Tobias answered. His eyes grew stormy as he looked at Dante. "How'd you do?"

"Got nowhere, too." The detective pulled out his small notebook and flipped through the pages. "Nothing, nothing, and yet more nothing." He slapped the notebook onto the table.

She looked at them both. "Dr. Sahir down at the observatory knows more than he was saying."

"I agree." Tobias pulled his phone out of his pocket, his long fingers punching in a phone number. Nix forced herself to keep her gaze on his face. When the call was answered, Tobias said, "I have a job for you. There's someone I want you to keep an eye on for me." He went on to describe the astronomer to the person on the other end of the line.

When he hung up, Nix asked him, "Who was that?"

"It's a Tucson PI I know. He owes me one." He took a sip of wine. His pupils had dilated until only the thinnest rim of gray circled them. Emotions or blood, Nix wasn't sure which. Probably a mixture of both. But he was in no danger of going vampy on them, as Dante had joked about. Tobias was much too controlled for that. Tobias went on, "He'll keep an eye on Sahir until we can make it back down to Tucson to question him further."

"So you agree we need to talk to him again." Dante lifted his beer. "This PI, is he human or an ED?" He took a long swallow from the glass.

"Does it matter?" Tobias arched a brow.

"Nope." Dante set his glass down. "Just curious."

"He's as human as you are."

Over the next hour they drank and ate their food when

it came, but around seven thirty the day started to catch up to Nix. She tried to smother a yawn, but Tobias saw it. Despite her protests, he insisted it was time for him to take her home.

Tobias slid out of the booth. He held out a hand to Nix. "Come on, honey." His voice was husky with the same concern that darkened his eyes. "It's been a long day."

For once she wasn't going to get after him for the endearment, nor was she going to fight too hard about leaving. It had been an emotional couple of days. The skin of her forehead tingled. She needed to get home and do a full tai chi routine, something that would help her regain her control.

Dante scooted out of the booth. As they made their way through the crowd, Nix motioned toward the bar. "Just let me get a bottle of wine to go."

Tobias's eyes crinkled at the corners. "You always did like Maldonado's wine."

"He has an excellent winery." She turned and stopped suddenly. Just ahead was a guy who looked familiar, someone who might be able to help them find the elusive Finn Evnissyen. She wasn't sure, though, so she started forward, putting herself on a collision course with him. As she approached, she bumped into him, slipping her fingers into his jacket to relieve him of his wallet.

"Wow. That was smooth." Dante stood close enough to shield her hand and its contents from the guy whose load she'd just lightened. "I knew you'd spent some time on the streets, but I had no idea you had such mad skills."

"Skills she has no business utilizing anymore." Tobias's disapproval fell on her like a sodden blanket.

"I did it for a reason," she muttered. She flipped open

the wallet and pressed her lips together. It wasn't who she'd thought it was. "I thought I knew him, but I was wrong. It's not the guy."

"Well, then, you can give it back." He held out one hand. "Or I will."

She wasn't sure which infuriated her more, when he treated her like some sort of pariah of the preternatural world or as if she were a recalcitrant child. "I'm perfectly capable of giving this back to him and apologizing for taking it," she said with as much dignity as she could muster. Before she could head toward him, though, a hand clamped onto her shoulder.

She smelled vamp and without thinking grabbed the hand and twisted, putting the person on his knees with his arm straight back behind him. She drew his arm higher, exerting pressure on his shoulder. Then she realized who she'd just put on his knees.

It was the bartender. With a bottle of wine in the hand that wasn't being driven between his shoulder blades. Aware that the people around them had become silent, Nix pressed her lips together and let him go with a lame, apologetic smile. "Sorry."

"I figured you wanted one of these. You usually do." He got to his feet and handed her the bottle. His pupils were dilated so that only the faintest bit of green circled them. Elongated fangs peeked out over his bottom lip.

"Uh, yeah. Thanks." She was lucky he hadn't spun out of her grip and ripped her throat out. As he rotated his shoulder, she gave him another tentative smile. "Sorry," she repeated.

He lifted his chin. "I'll put it on your tab." He started to turn away.

Nix stopped him. "Wait." She handed him the wallet. "It belongs to that guy," she said, pointing toward the human man in the navy blue pinstripe.

The bartender rolled his eyes and took the wallet from her. "I'll return it to him, but you really need to stop doing that." He walked toward the man.

Nix turned back and looked at Tobias and Dante. One stared at her with censure and disappointment, the other with humor and a little bit of admiration. She refused to admit how much Tobias's opinion of her mattered and how much it hurt that he thought so little of her.

Chapter Eight

Tobias had thought Nix had outgrown her penchant for pickpocketing, a necessity picked up from living on the streets for a couple of years after her grandmother had died. But without a pause or flicker of forethought, she'd lifted that man's wallet with the ease of a professional.

Some habits died hard, he guessed. He should know. Nix was a tough habit for him to break.

"Let's go," she said now, her cheeks rosy. Whether from anger or embarrassment he didn't know.

He turned and saw Victoria Joseph standing a few feet away from MacMillan. The female werewolf wore a slinky black dress with a neckline that plunged almost to her navel and a hem that ended at midthigh, her makeup more pronounced than he'd ever seen it. She looked sexy, very different from how she looked on the job. She gave him a wink, then checked MacMillan out from behind, lust filling her eyes.

Nix spotted her as well and called out, "Hey, Tori!"

Victoria walked up to them. "Nix. Tobias." She glanced at MacMillan. "Won't you introduce me to your friend?" As always, her voice was calm, in contrast to her appearance that undoubtedly ruined the composure of just about every male in the place.

Tobias was glad Nix was still in her work clothes. He was sure seeing her in something sexy like Tori's dress would erode his calm beyond repair. "This is Detective Dante MacMillan, a member of the Special Case Squad." He motioned toward the female werewolf. "Dante, this is Victoria Joseph, another council liaison."

Victoria held out a fine-boned hand. "It's a pleasure to meet you, Detective."

MacMillan looked like he'd been struck by lightning. He took her hand in his and raised it to his lips. He pressed a slow kiss to her knuckles. "The pleasure's all mine, Ms. Joseph."

"My friends call me Tori." She looked at him from beneath long, silky lashes.

MacMillan drew in a breath. "My friends call me Dante, but you can call me anything you'd like, darlin'." His eyes glittered with carnal interest.

MacMillan's smooth talk seemed to work on Victoria, but Tobias thought he might throw up. "Nix, what do you say we get out of here and let Dante and Tori get acquainted without us."

Nix glanced at him, then her gaze shifted over his shoulder and her eyes narrowed. "What the hell . . . !" She took off at a fast trot.

Tobias saw where she was headed. Finn Evnissyen stood near the door, the expression on his face one that indicated he knew they'd been looking for him. "Damn it," Tobias groaned, and hurried after Nix.

"What the—" he heard MacMillan say.

"Come on," Victoria said before Tobias got completely out of earshot. "They might need help."

Tobias caught up to Nix and took her arm. "Don't do anything rash."

She jerked free and glared at him. "Why do you always assume the worst of me?" The hurt in her eyes was real and sent a pang of regret through him. He admitted to himself it was possible, perhaps even probable, that he still saw her through the filter of the past. She deserved better.

They reached Finn. "I hear you've been looking for me all over town," the demon drawled. He crossed his arms and looked down at them as if to say 'Well, here I am.'

Even though Tobias was six feet tall, Finn towered over him by a good five inches. And probably outweighed him by more than fifty pounds. Not that it mattered; as a vampire Tobias possessed the strength of five humans, easily double the strength that Finn had. Even so, this was one big demon.

Who didn't appear to faze Nix at all. "You bet your ass we've been looking for you." She mimicked his stance, arms folded over her breasts, gaze hard and challenging. "We have questions for you about Amarinda Novellus."

Something flickered through the demon's dark blue eyes but was gone before Tobias could identify the emotion. "Yeah, I heard about that. Bad thing."

"No kidding." Nix took a step closer. "We heard you went looking for her not that long ago. Why?"

He appeared to be as concerned with her getting in his face as he would be with a small dog yipping at his ankles. "That's between Rinda and me."

"You knew her well enough to call her by her nickname?" Tobias asked. The preternatural world was less informal than the human one. You didn't call prets by their pet names unless you were close.

Finn just stood there and didn't answer.

"Listen, you pile of dog shit—" If Nix got any angrier, Tobias was sure she'd start vibrating. And popping her horn buds.

"Maybe," Tobias said, interrupting her and trying to make her back off before he had two pissy demons on his hands, "we should just go to council headquarters and sort this out."

Finn raised eyebrows a few shades darker than the shaggy blond hair on his head. "If you think you can force me down to council HQ, you go right ahead and give it your best shot."

"Be happy to." Nix took another step toward him, unsnapping the safety strap on her holster.

Quick as a flash Finn had her in a headlock, her back to his chest, one brawny forearm across her slender throat, the other behind her neck in a classic choke hold. The wine bottle dropped from her hand and shattered on the floor. Dark red wine splattered on the wall and slowly spread across the floor like the spill of blood.

Tobias stiffened. He started to move forward but stopped when the demon tightened his hold on Nix. "You need to let her go," Tobias demanded. He pushed pheromones Finn's way, trying to influence the demon's behavior. It worked better on humans than prets, but he had to try. From the corner of his eye he saw MacMillan and Victoria stop beside him. The detective had drawn his gun the second Finn had reached for Nix. Tobias filed away the detective's quick reflexes for future notice.

"Tell pretty boy there to stand down before he gets hurt." Finn looked at Victoria. "And you don't scare me either, sweetheart."

"You hurt her, you won't make it out of this club alive." Tobias never took his gaze off Nix, her slim body dwarfed by the big demon who'd dared put his hands on her.

Finn laughed. "You think you can take me, vampire?" he challenged.

"I do." Tobias glanced over his shoulder to see their altercation had drawn attention. Several vampire bouncers were making their way over, fangs out and hands holding cattle prods. He clamped his jaw against the sense of foreboding that began to claw his insides. He had to diffuse this before it got out of control. Nix would be the first to be hurt. Or worse.

"Let go of me." Nix drew her Glock and shoved it into Finn's side.

Tobias admired her spunk, always had, but now was not the time. "Nix, that's not helping." Tobias looked at Finn. "This won't end well for you, Finn. Let her go."

The demon stared at Tobias, his eyes hard and flat, his mouth in a grim line. Finn held Nix a moment longer, then released her and put his hands in the air. Only then did MacMillan holster his weapon.

Nix, however, did not. She put her gun to the middle of Finn's chest. Tobias could smell the demon fire burning inside her, could see the horn buds beneath her bangs. When she shot him a glare, her irises were completely yellow.

"Nix, put it away." Tobias took a few steps closer and

kept his voice gentle. As violent as prets could be, it was still frowned upon to shoot an unarmed man. And if it happened in the Devil's Domain, Maldonado would not be happy. Tobias would be able to smooth things over with his old boss, but it would take some doing and probably end up with him owing Maldonado a favor. Nix was worth it, but he'd prefer not to owe Maldonado if he didn't have to. The old vampire was crafty and just as likely to get Tobias mixed up in something he didn't want to be involved in. He wasn't an enforcer, not anymore. He put a hand out to keep the bouncers at bay. They stopped but remained in an alert line behind MacMillan and Victoria.

"Yeah, little cousin," Finn drawled. "You're not exactly encouraging me to be cooperative."

"You two are related?" MacMillan asked.

"No," Nix bit out. "We are not."

Finn stared at the detective. "We're both demons. So we are related in a way."

Tobias noticed that the demon's eyes remained a normal, human blue without any demon yellow showing at all. This was one cool customer.

"Not in any way that counts." Nix kept the barrel of her gun pressed to his chest. "You demonstrated that just now when you put me in a choke hold."

"And you reciprocated by poking your gun in my side." Finn's stance suggested he was unconcerned about the altercation, and Tobias couldn't pick up any emotions from him, either. "I was just defending myself, little cousin," Finn said.

"Stop calling me that."

"Nix." Tobias put a hand on her shoulder. "Holster your weapon."

She scowled but finally did as he asked.

"Thanks for leashing your little doggy." Finn smirked down at her.

Her jaw tightened and she gave a little growl, hands fisting at her sides, but her gun stayed holstered.

"Well, now that we have that settled," MacMillan said in a low voice, "maybe someone could tell me who the hell this is and what the hell is going on?"

"This is Finn Evnissyen," Victoria offered. Her dulcet tones wore a harsher note than normal. "A smooth operator who's an expert at pissing people off. A living example of an oxymoron, actually."

"Moron is right." Nix hadn't taken her eyes off the big demon.

Finn tsked. "Now, now, little cousin. Don't be mean."

Nix took a step forward, clearly ready to take him on again.

"Enough!" Tobias's voice came out in a low roar. "No more games, Evnissyen. Why were you looking for Rinda?"

The demon gave a careless shrug. "She stood me up and wasn't returning my calls. I wanted to know why."

What a load of... To keep from reaching out and throttling the guy, Tobias shoved his hands deep into his pockets. A dustup between demon and vampire tonight wouldn't solve anything, though he thought he might feel better once he saw blood streaming from the arrogant bastard's nose. He held Finn's gaze. Some other time. "Rinda wouldn't duck your calls. She would've told you to your face why you weren't worth her time. Try again."

"That's all I got for you." Challenge lit Finn's eyes.

"And dragging me in front of the council won't change that."

Tobias studied him. Obviously the pheromones had had no effect. "Fine," he said after a moment. "Get out of here."

"No, Tobias, we can't let him leave!" Nix moved to block the way.

Finn gave a jaunty salute. His deep blues settled on Nix. "The next time we meet, little cousin, I won't be so nice. Now, get out of my way." He grabbed her upper arms and lifted her, setting her none too gently to one side.

Rage rolled over Tobias. He moved with vampire speed and shoved the demon against the wall so hard he broke the drywall. Tobias was vaguely aware of the buzz of voices in the club quieting. His fangs slid down, vision became awash in crimson. Facial bones morphing as they hardened. With his forearm across Finn's throat, Tobias rasped, "You touch her again, you even come near her, and I will kill you." The demon tried to push Tobias away but Tobias didn't budge. Instead he exerted more pressure against Finn's throat. "You read me?"

"Yeah, I read you." The words came out choked but the expression in Finn's eyes was as defiant as ever. "Now lay off."

Tobias released him and backed away.

Finn straightened. Brushing bits of drywall off his shoulders, he cast a glance around the gathered crowd, then turned and walked out of the club.

"You owe me a bottle of wine, you moron!" Nix yelled after him.

Tobias looked at Victoria and jerked his head toward the door. She nodded and followed Finn.

"I, ah, think I'll hang with Tori for a bit," MacMillan said, and sauntered out as well.

Now that the potential danger had passed, the bouncers faded back into the crowd. The club's noise level ratcheted back up to the normal buzz.

Tobias stared at the wall, at the spot where the shape of Finn's body was outlined by a large indent. The bastard had put his hands on Nix, had threatened her. He was lucky all Tobias did was put him into the wall.

"I could've handled him." Nix poked him on the shoulder.

He turned to face her. "How? By putting a bullet into him?"

"Damn right."

He was glad to see the demon had retreated. "That would have bought you nothing but trouble, and you know it."

"I could've handled it." She started toward the door.

Tobias followed her and stepped outside right behind her. The parking lot was well lit, a security step Tobias had recommended when Maldonado had first started opening nightclubs. All sorts of things liked to hang out in the dark. There'd been a lot fewer deaths, and fewer lawsuits, once the lights had been installed. Walking beside Nix, he said, "You would've had the council after you, and Maldonado, and if you didn't kill Finn, he would have come after you too. If you had killed him, then you would have had to deal with Lucifer." He stopped in front of the SUV. "You think you could have handled all that?"

Her slender throat moved with her hard swallow. Like most prets, most demons especially, she was intimidated by Lucifer Demonicus. With good reason. Lucifer was arguably the oldest pret on the planet, which meant he had a lot of power, a lot of influence, a lot of enemies. Also a lot of friends. If he gave the word, there were plenty of people ready and willing to do his bidding.

"Why do you care?" she finally asked. "You didn't care five years ago when you left."

"I care, honey. I've always cared," he said as he stroked her face, his voice husked around the emotion tightening his throat.

* * *

Nix fought back the thrill that shot through her at Tobias's words, the feeling of having those cool fingers caress her face. *Snap out of it*, she chastised. Saying the words didn't automatically make everything all right. So, okay, he cared. That hadn't stopped him from leaving her. He'd been pretty clear she wasn't his priority—the only reason he was back in town was because Amarinda had called him. He had been true to himself, rushing into danger to help his friend. Except he'd been too late. And so now he wanted to save another woman from his past, except Nix was no damsel in distress. She'd been taking care of herself most of her life; she didn't need him.

Instead of engendering anger within her, that thought only filled her with sadness. The same sadness she saw reflected in Tobias's eyes. Mixed with regret, which she found even more unbelievable. Decisive Tobias regretful? No way. Once he'd made up his mind on a specific course of action, he stood by that decision. The look faded, replaced by resolve, and she knew he still believed he'd been right to leave her five years ago.

The more things changed, the more they stayed the same.

Her sadness intensified. Fighting back sudden tears, she pulled on the door handle. The door didn't budge. "Take me home," she told Tobias.

His mouth opened and closed, as if he'd been about to say something and had changed his mind. He pressed the remote and unlocked the door. They climbed into the vehicle in silence, and the ride back to her house was accomplished without speaking. Nix shot him a glance a few times but his expression in the lights of passing cars was inscrutable. When he pulled to a stop in her apartment complex's parking lot, she hopped out. She paused at the open door and looked in at him. "I'll see you tomorrow?" Regardless of how she felt about him, they still had work to do.

He gave a nod and a poor attempt at a smile. "I'll call you."

"Okay." She closed the door and walked toward her apartment, pausing at the corner of the building to look back at the SUV. Tobias lifted a hand in greeting and backed out of the parking spot. Nix went on to her apartment.

Rufus met her at the door with his usual exuberance. "Hey there, sweetie," she said, bending to ruffle his head. He swiped her hand with his tongue. "Wanna go out?"

He pranced, tail wagging, tongue lolling, and she laughed. No matter what kind of day she'd had, he always made her feel better. She dropped her purse on the floor and grabbed his leash. "Let's go for a walk."

Rufus walked her for twenty minutes. As much as she'd tried to teach him to heel, he wouldn't have any of it. There was too much to see and sniff in too little time for him to hang back at her side.

Once they got back inside, Nix dropped onto the sofa and yanked off her shoes, then leaned back with a sigh. Rufus shoved his nose under her hand and she absently stroked him while she played back over the events of the evening.

Tobias and she had connected on a professional level that had been almost friendly. While she couldn't help but regret the loss of love, it said something that she was able finally to move beyond the hurt of the past. She'd grown up, whether she'd wanted to or not.

And he'd said he still cared about her. She wasn't sure how to feel about that. Part of her wanted to believe he cared in the romantic sense of the word and part of her, a large part, shied away from that. Because she knew herself. It wouldn't take much for her to fall right back in love with him. When all was said and done, Tobias was a man of principle, a man who stayed true to what he believed in. There was a lot to admire about that. And whatever the last five years had done to him, she'd still seen enough of the man she'd fallen in love with to know he still existed.

"Keep it professional," she said. When Rufus gave a little whine, she patted him. "Just talking to myself, sweetie." She stood and went into her bedroom. Even though she felt calm enough now, she had lost it at the club when she'd seen Finn. No, more accurately, when he'd acted like such an ass was when she'd lost it. But that demon had called to hers so easily, she knew she needed to regain some balance before she was ready to face another day.

She jumped in the shower and washed away the grime of the day, then got into her pj's and settled into her tai chi routine. This was the only thing standing between her and madness. She had to make it work.

Chapter Nine

The next morning Tobias had just finished his breakfast when his cell phone rang. While he rinsed blood from his glass he looked down at the display, then connected the call, bringing the phone up to his ear. "Yeah, Merle. What's up?"

The council dispatcher didn't waste any time. "There's another dead vamp on Camelback just west of Scottsdale Road." The werebear's low sigh was very close to a growl. "Word I got is it looks like another attack against vamps. Get your rosy butt out there."

Tobias turned off the water and placed the glass in the sink. He walked through the living room and headed down the hallway toward the master bath. "Now, Merle, just what makes you think my ass is rosy?"

Another raspy growl came across the line. "That's for me to know. Now quit dickin' around. You're not the only liaison I gotta dispatch, ya know. I got a little old lady with a pack of coyotes pissin' in her backyard and some damned fairy's been spraying graffiti all over Old Town." He clicked along on his keyboard then said, "You get out there pronto and suss the scene. Or Deoul's gonna be screamin', and I ain't takin' the heat by myself."

"He gives you a hard time," Tobias told the dispatcher, "you tell him to take it up with me."

"Yeah, right. I'll just tell the council president that you said if he don't like it he can kiss my furry little butt. Or, better yet, your rosy-cheeked ass." With that he disconnected the call.

Tobias tucked the phone into its holder at his waist. He brushed his teeth and used mouthwash to eliminate the smell of blood on his breath. Going back into the living room, he grabbed his coat and shrugged into it as he went out the door. He pressed the lock mechanism on his key remote and the black Jaguar chirped. Getting in, he started up the engine and backed the car out of the driveway. Whoever was doing these killings, they weren't wasting any time. Three dead vamps in three days.

What the hell was going on?

He arrived at the crime scene in less than ten minutes. He parked the car and approached the vacant lot that had yellow crime scene tape cordoning it off. Already a crowd of onlookers had gathered. He looked them over as he got closer. They were mostly human, one or two vamps and maybe one of the fey. He caught the eye of one of the criminalists and jerked his head toward the crowd. The woman got his hint and turned to snap pictures of the onlookers.

Tobias stopped and stared at the lot. One thing was glaringly obvious—this was the actual kill scene. Blood covered the area in large pools and long arcs of spatter. As evidenced by the numbered markers littering the scene, pieces of the victim were spread out all over the large lot.

So much blood had been spilled here the air had a metallic tinge to it that he could taste. His eyes burned, muscles grew taut with a hunger that never took much to arouse. He put blue booties over his shoes and as he walked onto the scene he pulled on a pair of latex gloves. Techs were busy finding and marking evidence and photographing the scene. Tobias minded his step, making sure to travel a path already used by the criminalists as he walked toward the body, where the ME recorded his findings into a small recorder.

Tobias stopped a few feet away and waited. There was little left of the body except a gaping torso with one leg to the knee still attached, and a partial head with no face. Christ. Who, or what, had done this?

The ME looked up and turned off the recorder. "Tobias."

"George. What do you have for me?"

He stood. "Male. Mid to late thirties when he became preternatural. But with all the damage..." He motioned toward the head. In addition to the face being removed, the lower jaw was gone as well, and from what Tobias could tell most of the teeth from the upper jaw had been yanked out. "Face is obliterated, no fingers for fingerprints. We only got a couple of teeth, one of which is a fang, so at least we know he was a vampire." He stood. "Other than that there's no way in hell to identify this poor guy."

"Probably what they were going for."

"No doubt. Hell, we found part of his spine in the bike lane." George scratched his chin. "This kind of thing will only further inflame humans against us."

Tobias didn't disagree. He stared at the body a moment longer, then murmured, "Thanks."

"You bet."

Tobias moved to the edge of the site and carefully walked the perimeter. In theory there should be some sort of evidence at the crime scene, this one or the others, to point them toward a suspect or group of suspects. He knew the crime scene techs were working as hard and fast as they could. There was almost always some DNA, some fiber, some plant spore, a tire tread, something to link the murder to the bad guy. The last location hadn't had much since it was a dump site, but this...This was the kill site. He didn't want to obliterate anything of importance so he watched where he put his feet.

While most serial killers were a few points shy of a Mensa invitation, pure dumb luck ended up playing a large part in catching them even with brilliant police work factored in. Tobias didn't care how it happened, he just wanted to find the bastards who were doing this.

At one edge, near an alley between two buildings, he paused. Among all the scents here, those of human, werewolf, and vampire, there was something else. Smoky and dark. Demon. Yet there was an underlying scent of something more. But hell if he could figure out what it was.

Hunkering down, he studied a set of footprints, side by side and facing the crime scene, as if someone had stood here and watched the carnage. This could be the break they needed.

Tobias gave a sharp whistle to get the techs' attention. "I need somebody over here."

A vampire Tobias knew from his days with Maldonado walked over. "Whaddya got?" he asked as he squatted next to Tobias.

"You're a field geek now, Mike?"

The tech grunted. "Can't run around raping and pillaging forever. Gotta make a living somehow."

Tobias grinned at the vampire's dry wit. "Get photos and an impression of this, will you?" Tobias pointed to the footprints.

"Sure thing." Mike opened his field kit and began to rummage through it.

"Thanks." Tobias rose to his feet and moved toward the alley. More parts of the victim rested there, and Tobias called back to Mike, "When you're done with that, print the wall here." Just in case someone had braced his hand on the brick while he watched the victim be torn apart. "Also, there are more body parts back here."

"Got it."

Tobias stared down at the pavement. What had happened here was carnage purely for the sake of carnage. He'd seen prets under the influence of blood frenzy, and their victims ended up scattered like this. The question was, was this third murder a case of some poor sap being in the wrong place at the wrong time, or had he been targeted? Tobias hoped the latter was true, because they had a better chance of finding the people who did this if they could build a profile on the victim. Understand the victim, find out who his enemies were, and you had a much better chance of catching the ones who killed him. If the victims were random, they'd have a much harder time apprehending the suspects.

He caught a fresh scent among the smells of death and knew Nix had arrived on scene. He steeled himself to see her again. Being around all this blood was eroding at his control, and being around her was not going to help. At all.

He hadn't lied to her last night when he'd told her he still cared. But he was under no illusions. Love didn't make the world go round. It just complicated things.

* * *

Nix donned protective gear and ducked under the yellow tape protecting yet another crime scene. Shit. Was that a dismembered hand one of the techs was bagging?

She pressed her lips together. Whoever the victim was, he or she hadn't gone easily. She headed toward the black tarpaulin covering the newest corpse. This scene was so much more gruesome than the others. Various pieces of the victim's body lay tagged as evidence all around the crime scene.

She caught the familiar flow of vamp pheromones and stiffened. She was not going to succumb to Tobias and his damned allure. They were professionals, co-workers. Nothing more.

As she reached the body, Tobias came from around the corner of the nearby building, his face grim. Crimson circled his irises, statement to his agitation. Determined to keep her focus on the scene and not on his delectable face and body, she caught his gaze and lifted her chin in greeting, then squatted next to the largest piece of the victim. She adjusted the shoulder strap of her workbag and pulled back the tarp, exhaling at the carnage before her.

The body was shredded. Barely recognizable as bipedal except for the stub of one partial leg. "What the hell?"

"Whoever's doing this, they're escalating." Tobias hunkered down beside her. This close, the frustration at the lack of leads and the anger at such a senseless crime wafted clearly to her on a wave of lust that always seemed to accompany him.

As did the subtle scent of soap and virile male.

Nix cleared her throat. "For someone to have done all this, the murder had to be personal."

"Maybe." He gestured toward the building from where he'd just come. "We've got his spleen and what looks like part of his pancreas around the corner. One hand was over there"—he pointed toward the east side of the lot where she'd seen the tech putting the hand into an evidence bag—"and the ME says part of the victim's spine was in the street." He grimaced. "I found a pair of footprints over near the alley and had Mike take a cast."

"Great." Nix stared at the body and tried to disassociate herself from all the blood and gore around her. Peering closer at the face, she noticed bone shining through the flayed skin, and one fang protruding from what was left of the open mouth.

Getting to her feet, she drew in a deep breath and held it. She filtered out the scent of humans, pushed past the smell of motor oil on the pavement, and focused her olfactory sense to the smallest degree. There it was again, that smoky scent, the same one from the last crime scene. Only now it was much stronger.

"You smell it too, don't you? Like burned paper." Tobias draped the tarp over the victim, compassion evident in the careful way he did it. He rose and faced her. His expression was hard, his gaze steely. His pupils had completely expanded, obliterating the gray of his irises, and crimson had taken over the whites of his eyes. "Demons were here. It's likely they did this."

As much as Nix wanted to argue, she had nothing

to offer up except her gut feeling. Demons didn't sneak around. "Yes, I can smell demon scent here, too." She looked at him. "Don't you think there's something different about it, though? Something...more than demon?"

He shoved one hand into the front pocket of his jeans. "You're being a little stubborn about this, aren't you?"

She frowned. "You can't tell me you don't smell that extra scent underlying the smell of demon. It's like a mixture of different prets—a little vampire with a dash of werewolf and a twist of..." She paused and drew in another breath, trying to work out the odor that eluded her. She let out a sigh of frustration and propped her hands on her hips. "I dunno. Maybe pixie? Or brownie. They smell a lot alike. I just don't think demons did this." Before he could respond she waved one hand. "I know, I have no evidence to support that supposition. Yet."

"Maybe you should check with your mother." His lips quirked. "Sheena of the Seventh Circle knows everything that goes on with demonkind, and she wouldn't lie to her daughter."

"Shut up, Tobias," she muttered, but the order was delivered without much heat. She knew he was only teasing, plus she knew he was right. If demons were behind this, her mom would know. Nix was less than enthused about going to see her, though. "You know she hates it when you call her that."

His laugh was gravelly, rough, as if he hadn't laughed much in the last five years. The sound stole her breath away. To cover her reaction, she turned to look at the waiting body snatchers. "There's not much to ID the vic. Did the ME at least give a gender?"

"He thinks it's male. But he won't know for sure—"

"Until he gets the body on the table." Nix finished the often-repeated phrase. She started a slow circuit of the crime scene, very aware of Tobias walking next to her. Pools of blood indicated the various places pieces of the body had been found.

She ground her teeth together. They'd already started collecting evidence, which meant that bastard werebear dispatcher had once again delayed the call to her. Damn it. She couldn't worry about that now, it would only distract her from the case. When she got a chance, she was going to show Merle just what the consequences were of messing with her. For now, though, she pushed aside her irritation.

One of the techs photographed some small piece of evidence, then he picked it up with a pair of tweezers and deposited it into a paper bag. As he taped the bag closed, she asked Tobias, "Was this just rage? Or is there some significance to the scattering of body parts? And why kill him here? Why not dump the body like they did with Amarinda?"

A muscle twitched in his jaw. "I don't know." He glanced around the scene. "This could have some significance to the people who did this, but none that I can see at the moment."

"Hey!" The tech motioned them over. "You two need to see this."

Nix and Tobias made their way over to him. He held a scrap of paper about the size of a credit card between the ends of his tweezers. He held it out so they could see it.

"Dimensions... radio..." Tobias read. He shook his head. "The writing's too distorted. Those are the only two words I can make out." He glanced at Nix. "What about you? Can you see anything more?"

The paper was yellowed, ragged around the edges. The writing appeared to be in pencil, written lightly, faded with age. She pointed toward a word taking care not to touch the paper. "This looks like it could be trans...something. T-r-a-n-s...That's an *m* I think..." She pondered a second. "Maybe transmit? Because of the word radio."

Tobias raised his eyebrows. "You could be right." He looked at the tech. "Thanks. Let us know if you find more of this."

The tech nodded and got back to work.

They moved toward the edge of the scene. Nix paused and watched the body snatchers secure the body in its crimson bag onto a stretcher. "I wonder who he is," she mused aloud.

"No idea. Yet." Tobias's voice turned hard. Deadly. Even if Amarinda hadn't been one of the victims, she knew he'd still be taking this personally. Someone was targeting vampires, and Nix and Tobias were no closer to finding out why. The council would not be pleased, and no doubt they'd find a way to lay the blame at her feet.

Tobias blew out a sigh. Lifting a hand, he scrubbed the back of his neck. In a low voice he said, "Look, I know I said I wouldn't tell the council about the demon scent, but you know we can't rule out demons." He shot her a glance. "I wasn't completely joking when I suggested you talk to your mom."

"I know." She pursed her lips. She really had no desire to talk to her mother. At best their conversations were awkward and stilted, at worst they bordered on hostile. It was something she'd be glad to put off as long as she could.

His mouth firmed. "This is the third killing in three days. All the victims are vampires, which on the surface at least leads to the conclusion that someone is targeting us. There appears to be no connection between the first two victims, and until we know who this third one is, we can't tell if there's anything different or new that might connect him to the other two. Go see Sheena." He ignored her glare. "Find out what she knows."

"And you'll go to the council and tell them that we both smell burned paper at the scenes."

"Would that be a lie?" Tobias peeled off his latex gloves and walked to the perimeter of the site. When she followed, he reached out and lifted the yellow tape for her to pass under, then he did the same. They removed the rest of their protective gear and dropped them in the bin. He tipped his chin at the uniformed officer standing guard and walked with Nix to her car half a block down the street.

"It wouldn't be a lie, no. But there wasn't any demon at the first crime scene, just the second two." She glanced at him and brushed her hands together to remove the powder the gloves always left behind. "That has to mean something." Staring up at him Nix saw the anguish he couldn't hide in the way his pupils were still dilated, leaving just a thin line of gray circling them. She was glad to see the crimson had faded, but she knew this crime scene dredged up thoughts of Amarinda's murder. Without thinking she put her hand on his forearm.

Muscles bunched beneath her fingers. He looked down at her. His tongue swept out, leaving his lips moist and inviting. Even the hint of fangs peeping over his bottom lip was sexy. Memories of their time together, of the joining of their bodies twisting on soft, silky sheets swirled in his darkened eyes. Memories she shared. He bent toward her.

"Don't," she whispered, putting her other hand against his chest. She wished she'd sounded more sincere. Wished the hand against his chest was firm and determined instead of soft and giving.

"I have to." He brushed his lips over hers once, twice.

She should tell him no and mean it this time. This was where she should push him away and tell him to go screw himself. He'd walked away from her, he had no right to touch her anymore. She should tell him that, but she couldn't. She was as desperate for a fix as he seemed to be.

His mouth settled over hers, open, seeking, and with a hoarse moan she leaned into him, lips parting to allow him entrance. He stroked his tongue along hers, rolled his hips forward so she could feel his growing erection against her belly.

She'd missed him. Missed his smell, his smoldering intensity when he looked at her with desire darkening his eyes. Missed feeling like she'd finally found her home.

He kissed a path to her ear, gave her lobe a light nip, not hurtful but enough to send a shock of arousal jolting through her. He cupped her breast, thumb rubbing across the tip. Fire raced from her nipple to her core. She let her workbag fall from her shoulder and lifted her arms, twining them around his neck, tangling her fingers in his dark, silky hair.

His mouth, warm from the heat of her body, slid down her neck, planting kisses down the corded tendon. Nix moaned again, head tilting without her permission, giving him unhindered access to her throat.

He felt so good against her, so right. As much as she'd tried to deny her feelings, there was still something here. For both of them, she thought.

"As hot as I remember," Tobias muttered against her skin. His tongue swiped a hot path over the pulse pounding in her throat. "If only you weren't..."

She stiffened and shoved at him. She had a feeling she knew what he'd been about to say, but regardless the fact that she was something he wished she wasn't was enough. Too much. "Get away from me, fang boy." She was half demon. She couldn't change her parentage any more than he could. She bent to grab her purse.

"Nix—"

She shot upright at the same time he bent forward, almost knocking him in the chin with the top of her head. Only his fast reflexes saved him. She tossed the bag through the open window of her car, not caring when it bounced from the passenger seat onto the floor, spilling most of its contents. "What is this, Tobias? Play with Nix week? You come blowing back in town, the big, bad hero riding in to save the day, and what? Just need to get your rocks off a little bit for old times' sake?"

"Honey—"

"Don't call me that!" Her horn buds burst from beneath her skin. She gave a raspy groan at the agony. Pain radiated through her skull, setting up an echo behind her eyes that she knew were now mostly yellow. She doubled up her fists against the desire to beat the hell out of him, but she couldn't lose control of her demon side. She *wouldn't.* The torturous ache rode across her shoulder blades and up the back of her neck as her muscles tightened with tension and rage. She took a deep, calming breath and promised herself an extra long tai chi workout once she got home. "I'm going to make my report to the council, then I'll go see my mother. I'd appreciate it if you'd keep your word and not say anything about the demon scent until after I talk to her."

His lips thinned but he didn't say anything. When she yanked open the car door and nearly nailed him in the gonads, he backed away with a mumbled oath.

She smiled sweetly at him through the pain that now rode around and around her skull. The best thing to do to alleviate the burn was to go completely demon. But every time she did that she ran the risk of losing her humanity, of losing her mind. She'd let Finn bring it out in her at the club, she'd been so frustrated and angry. She wasn't going to let go again. She had to prove that she could be around Tobias without ill effects. Prove that the inherent darkness of his nature didn't call to her, making her already volatile temper and demon tendencies that much harder to control. Prove it to him, to herself.

Nix got in the car, strapped herself in, and drove off. This time she refused to look in the rearview mirror. She didn't care if he was all alone. He deserved it.

She used the ten-minute drive to the council headquarters to rein in her anger, to drive the demon deep inside where it belonged. Making her report was going to be challenging, it always was, and it wouldn't help her to start off by being all hyped up.

For once when she arrived at the council building she was brought in right away. She made the customary greeting to Deoul, Caladh, and Braithwaite.

"Give us your report." As always, Deoul was curt.

"Unknown victim, probably male vampire, was killed

in a vacant lot off of Camelback. He was... Well, the only way to describe it is savaged. Not much of him was left in one piece." Nix kept her gaze steady on the council members.

"That's all you have?" Braithwaite leaned an elbow on the table and propped his chin on his fist. "What about sounds? Scents?"

Her heart pitter-pattered. "As with the other scenes, there was nothing out of the ordinary." That demon scent could have been laid down up to forty-eight hours before the crime occurred. Without proof demons were involved, she didn't feel any obligation to point fingers.

"I see." Braithwaite stared at her. "You're sure of that?"

She kept her face straight with an effort. What was he getting at? Did he know? And, if so, how? "I have nothing more to report about this latest killing."

Caladh spritzed his face with the ever-present spray bottle. "What have you discovered on the other cases?"

This she could answer truthfully. "We've spoken to Pickett's business partner. There's nothing there," she said. "But we're sure one of Amarinda's co-workers—her boss, actually—knows more than he's saying. We're planning on heading back down to Tucson tomorrow to talk to him."

"Why not go today? What if this boss takes off?" Deoul swept his hair behind his ears and turned his glare on Nix.

"Tobias has someone keeping an eye on him. A private investigator." Keeping in mind her body language, she fought the urge to cross her arms. She'd either come off as insecure or as trying to hold in anger. Either way it would shut down any slack the council members might otherwise afford her. "He won't go anywhere without us knowing about it."

"We'd like you to get down there as soon as possible," Caladh said.

"We will." Nix waited for more questions.

"That will be all for now," Deoul said. "You may go."

"As you wish," she said slowly, and turned to leave the room. That had to have been the shortest report she'd ever made. Ever been allowed to make.

As she reached the double doors she glanced over her shoulder to see the three council members in a huddle. When Deoul saw her watching them, he motioned to the guard, who took her by the arm and ushered her out. "I'm going, I'm going," she snarled, shaking him off her.

She went out to her car, knowing there was no way to put off seeing her mother any longer. Best to get it over with. She'd stop by one of Maldonado's clubs on the way and pick up a bottle of wine. That always seemed to put her mother in a good mood. Well, as good a mood as she ever got.

* * *

Tobias stayed in his car and watched Nix drive away from the council building. He'd been instructed to wait until she left and though it didn't sit well with him, orders were orders. He got out of the Jag and walked into the main chamber.

Deoul sat behind the table looking over some paperwork, but Caladh and Braithwaite stood at the far end of the table.

"Tobias!" Caladh walked over and clasped his hands. "Terrible business this is. Another murder."

"Caladh, there are protocols," Deoul called out.

"Protocols-shmotocols." The selkie heaved a sigh and motioned Tobias forward. "No one but you wants our liaisons to do all that bowing and scraping, Deoul." To Tobias he whispered, "I suppose to keep the old elf happy you should go through the motions. We wouldn't want to make his foul mood any worse than it already is." He winked and walked around the table to take his seat.

"Oh, forget it." Deoul looked at Caladh and then Braithwaite, who quickly hid his grin behind his hand. Deoul put his gaze back on Tobias. "What's your report?"

"This latest crime scene was pure carnage." Tobias clasped his hands behind his back. "The victim was ripped into pieces. There was just enough of him left to let us know he was a vampire."

"No ID on the body?" Braithwaite asked.

Tobias shook his head. "The killers have escalated their violence with each kill. But I don't know if that's why this third victim was savaged or if they wanted to obscure his identity."

Braithwaite glanced at the other two members and then leaned forward, resting his elbows on the shiny surface of the mahogany table. "What's your opinion at this point about the suspects? Are they human or pret?"

"With this latest victim I'm positive the killers aren't human. There would have been evidence at the scene if the suspects are human." Remembering the scene, he tightened his lips. "A vampire would have gotten a few strikes in, at the very least. There would have been human blood spilled there, and there wasn't. In my expert opinion, prets are behind these deaths."

Deoul nodded. "That's the conclusion we had come to as well. With that said, there's no reason for us to have a human liaison involved, is there?"

"You want to remove Nix from the case?" Tobias rocked forward and let his hands drop to his sides.

"Do you believe she can still provide value to the investigation?" Caladh asked. His tone suggested he would be amenable to the idea.

"Yes, I do." As much as Tobias thought his being around Nix wasn't good for her, he still had a job to do. She seemed to be better at keeping herself under control and he had to trust that she would tell him if she started having trouble.

"Well, then—" Caladh started, only to be interrupted by the vampire member of the Council of Three.

"What about the demon scent that's been present at the sites?" Braithwaite asked.

Tobias hesitated. There was no way in hell Nix would have told them about that in her report. Not after she'd reamed him a new one over it. "Demon scent?" he asked, stalling for time. Where had they heard about it?

"Word has come to us that there has been a distinct scent of demon at each of the crime scenes." Braithwaite pinned him with a penetrating stare. Or tried to. It might have worked better if Tobias wasn't a vampire. "Are you saying the report isn't true?"

"I wasn't at the first scene, so I can't comment on that. And as far as there being a distinct scent..." Here was a fine line. If the right question was asked he would answer truthfully. But Braithwaite hadn't asked the right question. Tobias said, "There was not a distinct scent of demon, no."

Unfortunately, Braithwaite was smarter than he looked. "But there was a scent of demon there."

Tobias wasn't going to lie. "Yes. But—"

"Then to keep Nix on the case would be irresponsible of us." Deoul's smile reminded Tobias of a Cheshire cat's. "She's part demon. It could be someone she knows."

"All the more reason to remove her." Braithwaite shared a glance with Deoul.

Brown-noser.

"So if we determined that it was a vampire doing these killings, would you also then remove me?" Tobias folded his arms over his chest and waited for their answer.

Of course they had none. Braithwaite sputtered and Deoul narrowed his eyes. Caladh offered, "Perhaps we should wait and see—"

"No!" Deoul stood and planted his hands on the table. "She made no mention of demon scent in her report. She's obviously covering up the fact that some of her people may be involved."

"Her people are also human. Besides, there's no evidence yet that demons are involved." Tobias scowled. "If she'd come in here and told you she smelled demons yet had no evidence, you would've ridden her up one side and down the other."

Deoul slowly straightened, his face rigid. "Watch yourself, Tobias. You, too, can be replaced."

Caladh sighed. "Now, gentlemen, let's get ourselves under control, shall we? I call for a vote. Those in favor of keeping Nix on the case?" He raised his hand.

So did Tobias.

"Those in favor of removing Nix from the case?"

Deoul and Braithwaite raised their hands.

"Unfortunately, Tobias, your vote doesn't count." Caladh seemed genuinely dismayed over the turn of events.

"And you will not say anything to Nix about this," Deoul cautioned Tobias. "We'll tell her."

"For the record, I disagree with this decision." Tobias shoved his hands in his pockets and shot a glance at Caladh, who raised his brawny shoulders in a shrug.

"So noted." Deoul sat back in his chair. "Now, something else." He exchanged glances with the other members of the council. Caladh gave a slow nod, and Deoul said to Tobias, "We have our suspicions that there is an underground movement within the pret community, a group that means at the very least to stir up trouble of some sort." He looked at Caladh and Braithwaite again. "I'm sorry to say we don't know anything more specific than that. We'd like you to keep your ear to the ground and let us know if you hear anything." He paused and then lifted his hand to make a shooing motion. "You may go."

Tobias clenched his jaw. Giving an abrupt bow he left the room. Damn it to hell. He'd known Deoul had a thing about demons, yet he'd hoped Braithwaite would be a voice of reason. But apparently Braithwaite would be nothing more than the council president's puppet.

Nix was going to be furious. And he knew she'd blame him. But he believed in the chain of command, not some musketeers mentality. He wouldn't lie. And she'd be off the case.

Chapter Ten

Early in the afternoon Nix turned into her mother's neighborhood. House after house with Spanish tile roofs lined the street like soldiers standing at attention. Neat, clean, one looking much like another. Before she reached her mom's street she pulled over to the curb. She needed to calm her nerves or she'd end up mouthing off and not getting anywhere. Not that she felt like she owed Betty that much respect, but she did need her mother's cooperation.

As always, whenever she thought of her mom, Nix's thoughts turned to the father she'd never known. Her mother had fallen in love with Arturo de la Fuente, a Mexican American professor at the University of Phoenix. Betty had moved in to Arturo's apartment two months after they met, and nine months after that along came baby Nix. They made a happy home for about six months after Nix's birth. But eventually the trappings of human life and the responsibilities of motherhood had grated on Betty and she'd taken off, leaving her infant daughter behind. Nix's father moved them in with his mother so she could watch the baby while he was at work. For a time they managed to be a cohesive family unit.

Then Betty blew back into town. Seemed she'd missed her husband. And Arturo was so blindly in love with Betty that he'd taken her back. They'd had an intimate reunion that had caused Betty to lose control and siphon off all of his life energy during sex, killing him. Unable to face what she'd done, she left once again, leaving Nix with a bitter old woman who'd lost her only son and was saddled with demon-spawn.

Nix had tried and tried to please her grandmother. She'd studied hard and received straight As in school. She'd comported herself modestly, as a good girl should. She'd even learned to sew so she could make her grandmother pretty things.

Nix had a lot of memories of the hard times of childhood, but one played over and over in her brain now. One night the then ten-year-old Nix had stayed up until two in the morning putting the finishing touches on a dress for her grandmother's sixtieth birthday. She'd presented her grandmother with a perfectly wrapped box, proud of her accomplishments. Her grandmother had looked at Nix, stood up and walked to the trash can where she dumped the unopened box.

Things had continued to go downhill from there. Within three years Nix was spending most of her time hanging out on the streets, being a general nuisance and a youthful hooligan. She'd become an expert pickpocket and shoplifter. She stole sometimes out of necessity because her grandmother was on welfare and there wasn't a lot of money to go around, but sometimes she stole for the thrill of it.

Her grandmother died when Nix was sixteen, and after a short stay with a foster family Nix went back to the streets. Her mother was a stranger who flitted on the outskirts of her life. Puberty had brought out the demon and Nix didn't want to go live with human families who wouldn't understand what she was. Besides, her friends were her family. They would take care of her.

And they had. For a while. But one by one they'd left, either off to better lives, prison, or death. Nix had been alone. Until she'd met Tobias. A dark, lonely life became bright and fulfilling. She'd learned to love without fear of being hurt.

Shortly after Nix and Tobias started dating, her mother couldn't ignore her guilt any longer and had come to Nix, telling her she could help her understand her demon side and what it was capable of. Nix hadn't been interested. She'd gotten along just fine without her mother all those years.

But something inside her had told her to not give up the chance to get to know the woman who'd given birth to her. So she'd pushed back her stubborn pride and allowed Betty back in her life. The two were slowly getting to know each other as people. Maybe someday they actually would relate as a mother and daughter should.

Life had been good. So good that when she let herself think about it she'd gotten scared, waiting for the other shoe to drop. When it did, it dropped with a thud that smashed her heart.

For now...Nix blew out a breath. After Tobias had left her she'd thrown herself into her work, first as a unit clerk in a hospital and then as a dispatcher at the Scottsdale Police Department. Then after prets had been outed she'd landed the job as a liaison to the preternatural council. She'd worked hard to prove she wasn't that light-fingered little thief anymore, tried to demonstrate her professional abilities and show she was more than her demon. Yet it seemed that the council wanted to keep her at the bottom of the pile, letting her be nothing more than the DNA her mother had given her. And if she wanted to solve these killings, if she wanted to be able to go to the council with *something,* she had to talk to Betty.

A couple of deep breaths, and she pulled away from the curb. A few minutes later she sat on the leather sofa in her mother's ultramodern living room and accepted a glass of iced tea. Several candles burned on the console table behind the sofa, permeating the room with the scent of cinnamon and apples.

"Are you sure you don't want wine instead?" Betty asked as she sat down in a matching armchair across from Nix. She crossed her slender legs and idly swung one bare foot in the air. "That bottle you brought me has enough for at least two."

Nix grinned to see Betty's toenails were painted neon green. Flamboyance was her mother's middle name.

"I'm sure, thanks." Nix took a sip and almost winced at the sweetness. "Are you sure there's actually tea in this?"

"It's the only way I can drink it." Betty raised her wineglass to her lips. Her short, bouncy curls reflected the light with a blue black shine. Big, wide dark eyes framed by thick black lashes stared unblinkingly at her. The fact that the Betty Boop cartoon character had been created after her mother met the head of Fleischer Studios at a New Year's Eve party was not a coincidence.

Nix looked at her mom, who stared back without speaking. Tension rode along Nix's shoulders as the silence lengthened.

"So, why are you here?" Betty finally asked.

"How do you know it's not just because I wanted to catch up with you?" Nix caught Betty's slight eye roll. Yeah, right. Neither one of them were exactly full of fluffiness for each other. "Okay, I need your help on a case."

"The vampire slayings?"

"You know about those?" Nix stared at her mom.

Betty fingered her wineglass. "Only what I've heard on the news. The reports have been rather sketchy on details." She paused, circling one finger along the rim of her glass. "I take it from your expression they've been rather gruesome?"

"It was worse than that. The second victim was Amarinda." Nix swallowed as tears threatened.

"Oh." Betty leaned forward, almost as if she meant to reach out to Nix, but seemed to think better of it and slouched further in the chair.

Another awkward silence filled the room while Nix got her grief under control. She glanced around the living room, focusing on the large abstract painting above the fireplace. Slashes of reds, blues, and greens were encased by a stainless steel frame. Pillows of the same colors decorated the sofa and armchairs. She looked at her mother again and cleared her throat. "Yes, well, we've had three vampires killed in three days. The first body was mutilated a little, but Amarinda..." She wet her lips. "She was eviscerated. And her fingers were cut off."

"Most likely in order to get rid of the evidence the killers may have left behind." Betty took another sip of wine.

"That was what I thought, too." Nix set her iced tea on the end table. "This last body was in pieces scattered over a large vacant lot." She stared at her mom while she tried to find the right words to ask what she needed to ask.

"What?" Betty questioned. When Nix didn't respond right away, her mother's mouth twitched into a frown. "Just say it, Nix, whatever it is."

Nix pulled her legs up onto the couch in a lotus position and rested her hands on her calves. "There was a scent of demon at the last two crime scenes. Not strong, but it was there."

"And so... what? You're automatically making the assumption that demons are behind these slayings?" Betty's eyes turned hard. She started tapping her fingers on the padded arm of her chair. "That we're the primitive animals the other prets say we are?"

"No. No, I just..." Nix huffed out a sigh. She met her mother's gaze. "The council is going to hear about it eventually. It won't look good for me if they find out I knew about it and didn't say anything."

"What does your vampire liaison have to say about it? I assume he's smelled it, too."

Nix wasn't going to volunteer that the vampire liaison at the moment was her former lover. "Yeah, he smelled it, too. For the time being he's agreed not to say anything to the council."

Betty shifted in her seat and laid one arm out along the back of the chair. "That doesn't sound like something Knox would do. He's so by the book it's sickening."

Aldis Knox and Betty had once upon a time been friends. Nix had wondered if they'd been lovers, but had never asked. Now, with the disgruntled look on her mother's face, she wondered anew. "People change" was all she said now.

"Not Knox." Betty narrowed her eyes. "So why did he agree to keep mum?"

Nix pressed her lips together. Looked like she was going to have to confess. "It's, ah, not Knox."

"What's not Knox? Nix, you're not making any sense."

"The vamp liaison. It's not Knox." She stared down at her hands. "It's Tobias."

Betty straightened from her slouched position, her eyes wide. "Tobias! As in Tobias Caine? He's back in town?" Her round eyes narrowed to slits. "When did that happen?"

"Two days ago. The first time I saw him was at the crime scene with Amarinda." Nix was proud of how matter-of-fact she sounded. "She'd called him and when the council knew he was here, they appointed him temporary liaison."

"And just knocked Knox off his beat? For the likes of Tobias Caine? Those sons of..." Betty shrugged at Nix's grimace. "You know I'm right. Sanctimonious, arrogant... And they wonder why demons have no interest in having a seat on their precious little council." She gulped down some wine, then pointed a slim finger toward Nix. "If you ask me, you never should have taken that job. It's brought you nothing but trouble."

Nix couldn't help but stare. Betty had abandoned her as a child, had shown no interest in her until Nix had already reached her early twenties. Now all of a sudden she was giving career advice? That was more than Nix was willing to let her get away with. "I didn't ask you."

Betty raised her brows. "No, you didn't," she said in a low voice. She got out of her chair and walked into the kitchen where she poured herself more wine.

Nix turned sideways on the sofa so she could watch her mom. She couldn't tell what Betty was thinking. Was she angry that Nix had sassed her? Or was she sad, regretting the time she'd lost with her daughter?

With her back to Nix her mother said, "Demons didn't do this." She turned. Her expression gave away none of her thoughts, nor did her even tones. "If we had, you wouldn't be here asking the question. You'd *know*."

Which was exactly what Nix had told the council. But she needed to be sure. "So Luc didn't sanction a blood feud?"

Betty swirled the wine in her glass. "As much as most of us hate vampires and might want to see as many of them dead as possible, we're not stupid enough to slaughter them and leave their bodies out in the open."

Nix was well aware that most demons did hate vampires, Betty included. It was something ingrained in them from birth, almost on a genetic level. As a teenager Nix had forced herself to overcome her innate hostility toward vampires. Maybe that was one of the things that drew her to Tobias early on, the chance to prove to herself that she'd mastered her prejudice.

On the few occasions Betty had been around when Nix and Tobias were dating, she hadn't tried to hide her animosity. That Tobias insisted on calling her Sheena of the Seventh Circle didn't help. That he then went on to break her daughter's heart merely solidified her already low opinion of him. The loyalty Betty had shown toward Nix at first had made her feel better regarding her relationship to her mother, until she'd realized Betty was mostly just choosing to side with her own kind rather than with a hated vamp.

Nix realized her mother hadn't answered her question, not really. "So you're telling me Luc hasn't sanctioned an official blood feud?"

Jaw tight, eyes flaring with demon yellow, Betty slammed her wineglass onto the kitchen island. "Don't you dare treat me like one of your suspects. I am your mother."

They'd had versions of this argument before, and Nix wasn't going to back down. "You're my mother because you gave birth to me. Otherwise, look at us. You can barely bring yourself to be affectionate with me, and you want me to treat you like...what? Like we have this wonderful mother-daughter relationship?" Nix stood. She stared for a moment at the flames on the biggest candle and tried to rein in her anger. She looked at her mother again. "We don't. Just where were you when I was being raised by a woman who hated me? Who blamed me for her son's death? Blamed me. Not you, the one who actually killed him." Fire roiled in her gut and burned in her eyes. "Where were you when I was living on the streets, picking money out of wallets and food out of trash cans?"

"You could have stayed in the foster system." Betty crossed her arms and glared. There was no regret, no remorse, absolutely no pity in her voice. "Stop feeling sorry for yourself. Can you honestly tell me you're not stronger for all you've experienced? That it's not made you better at your job? In life? Besides, living among demons was no place for a part human child."

Finally some emotion peeked through that hard demeanor, but not the kind that Nix was looking for. "You were ashamed of me?" Nix asked, hurt etching her words. Why had it taken so long for her to realize that? She'd just thought Betty had been uncaring, not the nurturing type.

It had never crossed her mind until now that her mother had been embarrassed by her own daughter.

"Of course not." Betty turned and picked up her wineglass and took a long swallow, refusing to meet Nix's eyes.

Nix stared at her for a minute while memories dashed over each other like burgeoning waves of the ocean. "When I was five," she said in a soft voice, "I gave my grandmother a birthday card I'd made myself. Do you know what Nana did?" She paused. "She tossed it in the trash. When I was ten, I taught myself to sew and made her a dress. I did a good job, too, spent hours and hours on it. I got the prettiest wrapping paper I could find, scrounged around for a box, and wrapped the package. I was so anxious about how she'd react when she saw the dress. Would this finally be the time she'd be proud of me? Accept a gift I'd made with my own two hands?" Nix drew in a breath and held it. Even after over a decade the memory still had the power to hurt.

"What did she do?" Her mother's voice was as quiet as Nix's had been.

"She didn't even open it. She just went over to the trash can and dumped the wrapped box, then walked out of the room. I gave up on pleasing her after that." Nix shrugged, trying to look nonchalant when the memories sliced her to shreds inside. She picked up her purse. "I guess I went out of my way to prove she was right about me, about everything. I made sure that I was just a good-for-nothing daughter of a filthy whore demon."

Betty's lips firmed. "Is that what she called you?"

"Every damned day. Usually more than once." Nix slung the strap of her purse over her shoulder. She rooted around for her car keys, then looked at her mother. "Would you answer my question, please?"

Betty glanced to one side. "Luc hasn't sanctioned a blood feud, officially or otherwise." A car door slammed in the driveway and she arched an eyebrow. "You can ask him yourself."

Crap. Nix wanted to talk to Lucifer Demonicus, *the* Lucifer, even less than she'd wanted to come see her mother. But while the driveway of Betty's house was long enough for two cars to park, it was narrow, which meant Lucifer had just blocked her exit. She couldn't get out. She was trapped and about to come face-to-face with the devil himself.

Two seconds later the front door swung open. A tall man, slim hipped and broad shouldered with black hair, olive-toned skin, and dimples, strolled in. "Honey, whose car is that out in the drivew—" He caught sight of Nix. "Oh, it's you."

"Yeah. Hi." Nix watched as her mother went up to Lucifer and gave him a long kiss on the mouth.

"You're home early," Betty murmured, leaning against his side.

He had one long arm around her waist, hugging her closer. "I missed you today." His voice was soft, intimate. He placed a kiss on her forehead and then glanced at Nix. His face hardened. "So to what do we owe this pleasure?" His black eyes looked anything but pleased, and his voice was no longer gentle.

"She's here about the slayings," Betty said before Nix could open her mouth. "Can I fix you a drink?"

"Not right now, thanks." He walked with her to the sofa and they sat down. Betty cuddled up against him, her shoulder tucked under his arm and one hand resting on his thigh.

Nix fought back hurt at the tender way her mother dealt with Lucifer. Why couldn't she have ever dealt with her own flesh and blood that way? Of course, Betty was a succubus, so to be placating and gentle with her lover was probably second nature. Maybe that's why she didn't have a mothering bone in her body—all her nurturing instincts were set aside for males.

With a small sigh Nix took a seat in one of the armchairs. "I need to know if you've sanctioned a blood feud against vampires," she said to Lucifer.

His black brows went up. "Don't tell me the council thinks we're behind these deaths."

"They think you're behind everything," Nix said dryly.

He gave a mischievous grin. "So how is it you come to ask me this question?" He crossed his leg and idly swung one Italian loafer in the air.

Nix leaned forward, clasping her hands and resting her elbows on her knees. "At each of the last two scenes I've smelled the scent of demon."

"You mean 'we' have smelled, don't you?" Betty asked. Without waiting for Nix to respond, she turned to Lucifer and said, "You'll never guess who the vampire liaison is on this case."

"Tobias Caine," he responded.

"Or maybe you would." Betty's full lips formed a pout. She lightly smacked his thigh. "How did you know that?"

"I have people." Lucifer smoothed one palm over Betty's springy curls, then looked at Nix again. "You must have a low opinion of your own kind to think we'd be so stupid as to be behind this bloodbath."

"As a matter of fact, I've been saying that demons aren't behind it." Nix sat back and crossed her legs. This guy intimidated the hell out of her, but she wasn't about to let him see it. "Not because demons aren't stupid, because let's face it, you have some pretty dull swords in your arsenal."

He grimaced and lifted one shoulder as if to agree she had a point.

"But I don't think demons are behind it because you'd have no reason to hide it. If things had gotten bad enough to start killing vamps out in the open, everyone would know about it."

"Yet here you are." He rested his arms along the back of the couch. "Questioning us."

Betty turned accusing eyes on her daughter. "Just like we're suspects."

"Quite so." Lucifer stretched his legs out beneath the coffee table.

If she wanted his cooperation, Nix couldn't go off on him like she had with her mother. "I'm sorry, I don't mean to treat you that way. I'm just trying to do my job."

That seemed to placate him, because after a few seconds his lips tilted. It was such a slight movement that she wouldn't exactly call it a smile, but one of his dimples peeped out, softening his face. She'd take what she could get.

Being the dogged investigator she was, she asked the question she'd already asked three times and had yet to get a straight answer to. "Have you sanctioned, officially or otherwise, a blood feud against vampires?"

"I have not." His black gaze pinned her to her seat. "Nor have any of my kind, *your* kind, gone rogue."

Why was it, when it suited people, demons were her kind, and her humanity, something she fought to hold on to every day, was conveniently overlooked? Lucifer looked upon her being a demon as a good thing, the council as bad. She was always in the middle, being pulled in one direction or another. No wonder the possibility of insanity was so great. All hybrids, regardless of their parentage, had a continual struggle to find where they belonged in both the human world and the preternatural one. When neither one wanted you, it could make life excruciating.

She stood. "Okay. Thanks."

"There is something else you should know." He gestured toward her chair and waited until she sat back down before he added, "Word has come to me that there are dissatisfied preternaturals who have made a device that opens a mini rift between the dimensions."

"What?" Nix scooted forward to perch on the edge of her seat and stared at Lucifer in complete stupefaction. She glanced at her mother.

"Why haven't you told me this?" Betty asked him, drawing back slightly from his side.

"I just heard it today, darling," he muttered, giving her a pat on the knee. To Nix he said, "There have been transmissions shared through this rift."

"Transmissions. What kinds of transmissions?" A pulse started thumping fast and hard in her throat.

"Radio transmissions." He lifted one foot and rested it on the coffee table. "Someone here on Earth is talking to someone in the other dimension. And before you ask, I don't know who."

Nix's heart thumped against her ribs, a dull, shocked beat. "Just how do you know this?"

He shifted his position, crossing his legs again. He hesitated as if wondering just how much to tell her. He glanced at Betty then back at Nix. "As I said, I have people." He waved a hand. "How I know isn't important. What's important is that someone here is communicating with someone there."

Nix's mind went back to the scrap of paper they'd found at this last scene. The words "dimension," "radio," and perhaps "transmit" had been written on it. Had it been some sort of note passed between contacts? Or a diary entry? A confession, maybe?

"And the council knows." Lucifer's next words brought her back to the present.

She straightened, once again dumbfounded. "The council knows about the transmissions? You're sure?"

"Some of them at least, yes."

"And?"

"And what?"

Nix raised a hand to the pulse in her throat, pressing down, trying to force it to behave. "Are they doing anything about it?"

"Not that I'm aware of." He gave a shrug. "My network isn't that far reaching. Yet."

Nix felt an urgent need to get out of there, to get home to be alone with her thoughts. She needed time to mull over the facts: first, that someone was actually able to open a rift without a comet in sight and, second, the council was aware of it. "I wonder," she mused out loud, "if any human governments know about it."

"I have no idea," Lucifer replied. "I have contacts at almost every level of the U.S. government, and no one's said anything." He spread his hands. "I don't want to ask questions that are too pointed because then I may let them know something we'd be better off with them not knowing."

She definitely agreed. Humans were agitated enough about the rift that opened every seventy-three years. If they found out that prets could open a rift any time they wanted to, it could mean World War III. She picked up her purse and stood. "Thanks for the information, Luc. I appreciate it."

"No problem."

Nix looked at her mother. "Thanks for the tea… Mom." It was amazing how much trouble she had calling Betty "Mom." It didn't feel natural, but it seemed to help them get along better.

Her mother stayed where she was but murmured, "You're welcome," with a slight dip of her chin.

All righty then. "I guess I'll see you later."

Lucifer stood. "I'll move my car so you can get out."

They walked out together. As Nix opened her car door, Lucifer paused. "I know Betty hasn't been a mother to you in the traditional sense of the word, but she is trying."

From where she stood her mother wasn't trying very hard. But this was not a conversation she was going to get into, especially with the king of the underworld. "Look, I appreciate that you care about her, I really do, but my relationship with my mother is complicated, and not something I really want to talk about."

"Fair enough." He went on toward his car.

Nix waited until he'd backed down the driveway and out of her way before she put her car in reverse. All the way home her thoughts raced, centered on the rift. A way for one dimension to shed themselves of their problem citizenry by exiling them to another realm. Up until now it had been assumed that no one on the other side knew what happened once the entities were sucked through the rift. But this...This! They had to know. Didn't they?

Ordinarily with information like this she'd request an immediate audience with the council to fill them in. But hearing that some of the council members were aware of these transmissions, she didn't know who to trust. The thought flitted through her mind that Lucifer might be playing with her, using her to try to put the council in disarray, but then she dismissed it. If he wanted to mess with the council, he'd use someone with a lot more clout than her.

She knew who she did trust, at least as far as work went. Tobias and Dante. Dante was human with local connections. He probably wouldn't be of much help. Tobias, on the other hand, was a different story. He had connections centuries in the making, and most of the council seemed to respect him, even if he was a vampire. When he'd left town five years ago he'd kept his house. She assumed he'd moved back in. She wished there was someone else she could go to, but there wasn't. With a soft oath she made a U-turn and headed toward his house. Grabbing her cell, she dialed him up.

He answered on the second ring. "Caine."

"What're you doing?"

"Going over my notes, trying to see what we've missed, and getting prepared to go back down to Tucson to talk to Sahir again." His voice deepened. "He knows something, Nix, I'm sure of it."

She wondered if the human scientist was aware of the rift device and the seemingly free flow of communications between the dimensions. They'd find out, one way or another. "I'm on my way to see you. Are you still in the same place?"

"Yes. What's up?"

"Not on the phone. I'll be there..." She glanced at the dashboard clock. "...in about ten minutes."

"All right." His voice held curiosity.

"I'll explain when I get there." Nix disconnected the call and stepped on the gas. This investigation had led them to something big. Maybe bigger than they would be able to survive.

Chapter Eleven

When Tobias answered the door, he wore only jeans, his torso and feet bare, a black T-shirt clasped in one hand. Nix tracked the dark hair across his pectorals and down the flat abdomen to where it disappeared at the waistband of his jeans. The top button was undone. She wanted to finish unbuttoning his fly, wrap her hand around his cock, stroke him, take him inside her body. Ride him until both of them were satiated. The undulating pheromones rolling off him only ramped up the temptation.

She curled her fingers against the urge to touch him.

"Nix." He stepped back to allow her entrance and slipped the T-shirt over his head. The soft cotton molded his hard contours, somehow making him even sexier than when he'd been half naked.

She walked into the living room and looked around while he closed the door behind her. Nothing had changed in five years. Same plain beige furniture, same white walls, same stunning pieces of modern art scattered around the room. He even still had the "magic" mirror she'd given him for his birthday, propped up on a bookshelf. The mirror that, when you turned it toward you as if to look at your reflection, started laughing. Those silly days were long gone. Turning, she said, "I had a talk with Luc tonight, and he told me—"

"Wait a minute." Tobias appeared intrigued as he came closer. "You met with him willingly? How did that happen?"

"He stopped by my mother's house while I was there," Nix said. "From what I know he's there most evenings." Tobias knew she didn't want to have anything more to do with Lucifer than she had to, but this was hardly the time to go into it. She had something important to tell him. "He told me someone has found a way to open a small rift between the dimensions and—"

"What!" He rubbed the back of his neck. "Are you sure? I mean, is *he* sure?"

"Yes. Apparently they're sending radio signals through, communicating wi—"

"What?" His expression went from startled to incredulous. The pheromones streaming from him lightened as if his surprise had cut off the flow.

"Maybe if you'd let me finish, you can just store everything up for one really big 'What!'" She folded her arms and raised her brows.

"Smart-ass." He sat on the sofa and thrust his fingers through his hair. "So?"

There was no easy way to say it, no way to lessen the shock, so she'd give it to him as coldly as she'd gotten it. "At least some of the members of the council know about it."

His pupils dilated in an instant, completely obscuring the gray of his irises. His lips parted, giving her a glimpse of fangs that had elongated.

The reaction at least confirmed that Tobias had been as unaware as she had. But then a wave of pheromones hit her so hard her body immediately tightened in lust. Her heart rate increased, making her breath flutter in her throat.

His gaze fastened on the pulse there, his lips parting further. Nix felt the urge to lean toward him, to turn her head to one side. Give him free access to her life's blood. She forced herself to back away and put the dubious safety of a recliner between them.

Tobias held her gaze. "The last time I met with the council, they told me they had suspicions there was some underground movement within the preternatural community, but they assured me they didn't know anything specific." He cursed under his breath. "They lied to me." His expression was wounded, as if it was one more betrayal he couldn't bear. His eyes were almost completely black, crimson rimming what was left of the gray of his irises. His voice rasped. "I wonder what else they know that they haven't told us?"

Nix knew even though Tobias had lived long enough and had experienced deception more than once, there was something inside him that still managed to be surprised when the good guys weren't so good. It should have saddened her. And to some extent it did. But mostly it just made her mad. It wasn't like he had always been the man in the white hat. When she'd needed help the most, he'd hopped on his horse and ridden off into the proverbial sunset.

"Oh, come on, Tobias." She propped her hands on her hips. "Most of the time people do what's easiest, not what's right. You of all people should know that."

His eyes narrowed. "What the hell does that mean?"

"You know exactly what it means." She hadn't planned on having this argument with him tonight, but it was past time they talked about what had happened five years ago. Her emotions roiling, she tried to tamp down on the fire beginning to churn within her. "You walked out on me because it was easier than staying."

"My leaving had nothing to do with *easy.*" He stood up, his gaze hard and as dark as obsidian. His scowl was just as black. "It had to do with this." He motioned between them.

"*This?*" She mimicked his action. "And this is what, exactly?"

"Take a look at yourself in the mirror," he said, gesturing toward the small hand mirror behind her. The one that laughed.

Nix whirled and grabbed it, holding it up to see for herself what his beef was. She ignored the canned laughter coming from the mirror and focused instead on what she saw. The face that stared back at her was one she hadn't looked at in a long time, one she tried her best not to wear, one that seemed to come forward rather easily whenever Tobias was around. Her eyes were nearly completely demon yellow and her facial features had sharpened. Just a little, probably not all that noticeable unless you were looking for it. At least her horn buds hadn't popped. Yet.

She put the mirror down and turned to face him again. "So my eyes are yellow. It happens when I get angry. Do you honestly expect me to never ever get mad?"

"Of course not." His expression softened. "But that's all I seem to bring out in you, Nix. Anger. No, not anger. Rage."

That stopped her in her tracks. He thought this was his

fault. Maybe it was, to a certain extent, but it was something she had to deal with on a daily basis. Something she had learned to live with. "This is who I am, Tobias. I'm part demon, and it comes out to play when my emotions are aroused. Good or bad," she stressed. "It's not going to go away, and I've learned to deal with it." She hesitated then added, "And anger isn't the only thing you bring out in me."

He grimaced. "Yeah, there's also irritation, frustration, aggravation—"

"Just..." She stared at him. The burning in her gut lessened as she calmed down. "Just tell me why you left."

He moved closer. His eyes had returned to normal, a beautiful stormy gray. "The more we were together, the more violent you got. In attitude and action. I heal quickly, it wasn't that. I was afraid you'd..."

"You thought I'd take a walk on the crazy side and not come back." She sighed and dropped onto the sofa. She linked her fingers and stared at them a moment and then, looking up at him, she asked, "Why didn't you say something?"

He sat beside her and took her hands in his. The feel of his strong fingers curled around hers made her want to weep. "I did, Nix. I warned you over and over about what you were doing. How you were acting."

She cast her mind back over the year they'd spent together. Memories flooded in. She looked at him a bit shamefacedly. "I told you I didn't need a father." In her defense she added, "You were kinda autocratic about it."

"So my manner was a bit off-putting. I was still right." He didn't sound happy about it. He let go of her hands and shifted to slouch against the sofa.

"Maybe you were." And with that statement, much of the anger she'd held on to for so long faded away. If they'd stayed together, would she have come to the conclusion she needed to control the demon? Or would she have continued enjoying the strength of her nonhuman side and allowed herself to slip closer and closer to madness? She just wished he'd gone about it differently. "But that was then. What about now?"

He met her gaze. "What about now?" he asked, his voice gruff. The gruffness didn't fool her. She could see in his eyes that he still wanted her. The pheromones came off him in rich, dark waves that went straight to her head, to her core.

"I'm not asking for forever," she whispered. She unclipped her holster from her belt and set both gun and holster on the end table. Then she moved to straddle him, settling her heat onto his lap. She cupped her hands on either side of his neck, her thumbs stroking across his ear lobes. "We were good together."

"Yes, we were." His eyes searched her face. "Nothing has changed, honey."

"Yes, it has. *I've* changed. I'm not the same girl you left behind five years ago, Tobias. I'm older. Wiser. Better able to deal with my demon half." She leaned forward, thrilling to the feel of the hard ridge beneath his jeans. His hands came up to clasp her hips. "Let me prove it." She dropped her mouth onto his.

His lips parted. Nix took advantage and swept her tongue inside to tangle with his. He tasted like pinot noir with a hint of the tang of copper. He must have just had a glass of wine with a kick. She rubbed gently over his fangs. His aroused gasp and the surge of his hips against her brought an answering dance of arousal down her spine. Pheromones rushed from him in a tide of lust so primal she shivered in response. A wet rush of arousal between her thighs made her moan, the sound swallowed by his mouth.

She kissed her way down his neck, lingering on the strong bump of his Adam's apple and the dip at the base of his throat. With a groan he ripped his T-shirt over his head. "Touch me," he demanded, and she eagerly complied, running her hands over his strong shoulders to grip his biceps, testing his strength with her fingers.

When she swiped her thumbs across his nipples his hips bucked and a throaty growl left him. With one smooth move he lifted and laid her on the sofa, coming down over her, bracing his weight on one elbow while he stared down into her face. "Are you sure about this, honey?" He brushed hair away from her cheek.

"More sure than I've ever been in my life." This would either be a new start for them or it would be the final chapter in the story of their love. A beginning or an ending, it didn't matter. She wanted him. "Trust me, Tobias. I can handle this."

His lips parted. He wet them, his eyes dark, desire and need stark and pleading in their depths. He reared back, just a little, so he could peel off her leather dagger harness, her top and bra, then her boots, socks, and pants. His eyes heated as he stared at her skimpy little panties, then those, too, were dropped on the floor. He slid his long, oh-so-talented fingers up and over her breasts. Her heart slammed against her ribs and she dragged in a breath. The musk of his arousal hung heavy in the air as did the sharp tang of excitement and the softer flood of... love.

She reached for his pants, but he stopped her, his big hands clasping her smaller ones. "Not yet. We're going to take it slow and easy." He dipped his head and pressed a kiss against her mouth. From an inch away he whispered, "I plan to take my time with you."

Nix liked the sound of that. Except... "But I want to touch you, too." She wiggled her fingers, still held captive by his hands.

He groaned. "Oh, God. I want you to touch me again, sweetheart." He lifted her hands to his lips and pressed a kiss to her knuckles. "Just not yet. All right?" He pressed her arms to the arm of the sofa above her head and released her hands. "Just keep your hands right where they are until I say different."

"Bossy." She would be content, for now, to follow his lead.

"Don't you forget it." He bent and tongued her nipples, bringing them to stiffness and sending little electric shocks straight to her core. His fingers delved between her legs, stroking over the fleshy lips of her sex, coming close to her swollen nub but not touching her.

Nix writhed beneath him. "Tobias," she moaned, lifting her hips, swiveling, trying to get his fingers to go where she needed them the most.

The sound that left him was something between a chuckle and a groan. He levered himself to his feet and peeled off his jeans and briefs, leaving his lean, toned body completely naked. His eyes glittered with black and red heat, his fangs glistened wetly. Deep-cut muscles flexed in his neck, his arms.

Her gaze tracked the line of hair on his lower abdomen to the treasure finally bared. His rigid cock curved into his stomach. As she watched a vein began to pulse along the hard flesh, mute testament to the deep arousal that now made his dormant heart beat.

He swept her up into his arms and carried her with effortless ease into his darkened bedroom. Nothing much had changed in here, either. There was still the bold burgundy-and-hunter-green decor, the large king-size bed, the bulky dark wood dressers. He laid her gently on the bed and as he came back down over her she looked into his eyes. There was lust there, but also an underlying tenderness that was mirrored in his touch. Her heart lurched and started to flutter like a mad, trapped thing.

"I've missed you, missed having you in my bed. In my life." Tobias raised her hands over her head. "Keep them there," he reminded her, and then kissed her again, his lips open and searching. He planted his mouth along the angle of her chin, down her throat to skitter over her collarbone. His tongue traced over the slope of one breast. She felt the warmth of his mouth just before he latched onto her nipple and began to suckle. He rolled and tugged her other nipple between fingers and thumb, driving spikes of heat straight to her core.

Nix clenched her fists around the spokes in the headboard. She needed to touch him, to smooth her palms over silken skin covering hard muscles. She closed her eyes and bit her lip, determined to show him she had control of herself, that she was more than the demon fire that burned deep inside.

He moved down her belly, hands feathering over her thighs to part the soft folds of her sex. She tensed in anticipation and when his mouth found her clit her legs fell apart and she bucked up into his touch. He sucked hard, his tongue circling and flicking. She felt the scrape of his fangs and it only heightened her arousal.

Nix moaned and jerked beneath him, her entire being reaching toward ecstasy. The fire within her flared, burning through her eyes, her skin. Then he slid two long fingers deep, thrusting in and out, and she fell over the edge. She bucked beneath him, coming again and again, until the tremors finally stopped and she lay limp beneath him.

He crawled up her body, muscles bunching as he moved. "Now," he said, his voice deep and guttural, his eyes black rimmed in crimson. "Touch me."

She let go of the headboard and one of the spokes dropped to the floor. "I broke your bed," she said, not really caring.

Apparently he didn't care, either, because he just shrugged and rolled to his back. "I'll buy another one."

Whether he meant bed or spoke, she didn't know. Didn't care. He was laid out in front of her like a smorgasbord of delightful flesh. And she was going to feast.

* * *

At the first touch of Nix's soft hands Tobias thought he'd jump out of his skin. Her eyes glowed yellow and the heat in her skin had intensified, but she otherwise appeared to be in control. When she mouthed kisses along the cord in his neck, he moaned and cupped her head to bring her face up to his. She let him control the kiss for a few seconds, then she broke away to swipe her tongue across his throat. "It's my turn," she whispered.

She made her way leisurely over his body, fingers and mouth caressing, stoking the fire of his arousal ever higher.

His cock was as stiff as an iron pike and throbbed like the devil. When her tongue flicked into his navel, he jerked and let out a low curse. She laughed, the sound light and carefree. It was at his expense, but to hear her sounding so happy, he didn't care. If it gave her joy she could tease and torment him all she liked. Her fingers wrapped around his cock, thumb swiping across the tip. He threw his head back and gritted his teeth. His fangs sliced into his lower lip.

He had the fleeting thought that she might kill him. When she took him in her mouth…Christ. He knew she was going to kill him. She sucked him, mouth drawing strongly while her fingers stroked him. After a few seconds she let him go. "I'd forgotten how good you taste," she whispered, holding his gaze. Yellow flecked her irises, her skin was flushed.

"I need you." Tobias reached out and cupped her cheek, amazed that he could still form words, let alone act with any tenderness. Desire was a living, breathing wild thing inside him.

Nix smiled and kissed his palm, then reared back. Bracing herself with palms against his chest, she lowered herself onto his shaft. Inch by agonizing, wonderful inch until her buttocks rested against his thighs. She drew up just as slowly, then slammed back down.

Tobias reached up and cupped her breasts. He swept his thumbs over the hard tips, eliciting a gasp from her. She rode him, her skin covered in a fine sheen of moisture, her eyes shining with carnal excitement.

The snug clasp of her body drove him closer and closer to an orgasm. With a growl he flipped her over and took control of the rhythm. His body hummed with lust as he slammed into her again and again.

"Bite me," she moaned, twisting her head to one side, baring her throat.

He wouldn't. He couldn't. That was what had always driven her demon wild before. Sex she could handle. Being bitten, the drawing of her blood, she could not.

"Tobias, bite me."

Without responding, he leaned down and slanted his mouth over hers, trying to take her mind off the request. He would love her until the day he died, but he would never bite her again.

Her scent made him crazy with need and her touch—soft and hungry and searching—made him ravenous. Leaving her mouth, he worked his way down her throat, stopping at the pulse pounding underneath her soft skin. He rested his lips there for a moment before touching the tip of his tongue to the spot.

He closed his eyes and fought back the instinct that told him to fit his teeth into her, to take her life's blood. Let her nourish him in a rite as old as time itself. But that could tip her over the edge, because his bite would more than double her arousal, which meant in all likelihood she would lose control of her humanity. Letting her demon fully take control could mean also losing her mind.

He would make this good for her but there'd be no drawing of blood. Her tight sheath rippled around him and he shattered into a million pieces. He threw his head back with a loud shout and heard Nix's cry, felt her pulsing around him, milking him, and knew she'd joined him. When he came back to himself he realized he'd collapsed on top of her. She probably couldn't breathe. He shifted to one side, giving a little groan when his sated cock slid from her slick depths.

She moaned, too, and turned into his embrace. Content for the first time in five years, Tobias closed his eyes and rubbed one hand up and down her upper arm.

"I missed this." Her voice was soft and sad.

"What?" he asked, though he had a feeling he knew.

"Cuddling." She rubbed her cheek against his shoulder. "For a vampire, you're a good cuddler."

His eyes popped open. "Cuddler? You're calling me a cuddler?" He turned and slid her beneath him again. "I'm going to enjoy making you take that back."

Her grin was slow and wicked. "And I'm going to enjoy watching you try."

Chapter Twelve

A few hours later, Tobias held Nix, her head resting against his chest while she idly stroked her fingers across his ribs. The sun had set and moonlight filtered in through the sheer curtains. The room was filled with the musk of sex and the lazy sense of satisfaction. "You're different," he said, his voice low. He rubbed his hand up and down her arm. Everywhere her body touched, his skin was warm.

"Hmm. Different how?" Her voice was sleepy.

"Calmer." He raised his hand and combed his fingers through her short curls. She was using the same shampoo he'd always loved, a clean citrus scent with a light overlay of raspberry. She smelled good enough to eat. Not that he was going to. "Much less demon than before." She hadn't even drained off that much energy from him during their lovemaking.

"It's the tai chi." She rubbed her cheek against him like a contented kitten. He was astonished, because when they'd made love before the kitten had had claws. And she'd used them. Had enjoyed using them.

"The what?" He tilted his head to glance down at her.

"Tai chi." Nix rose up a little, a smile curving her lips.

"I tried karate. I tried kickboxing. I even tried yoga." She met his look of surprise with a wider grin. "I know, me and yoga. Can you believe it? With some of the positions I swear I thought I was going to get stuck. Anyway, I finally latched on to tai chi, and that's what worked. It centers me. Calms me. I do it every night before bed to get rid of the stresses of the day."

"Amazing." Tobias couldn't deny it worked. The proof was in his arms. He pondered that and felt a slash of sadness that they hadn't arrived at the solution years ago. He might not have had to leave her.

She cast him a sly glance. "Of course, I think having sex with you might do just as well..."

He cupped her chin and rewarded that observation with a long, slow kiss. When he drew away, she let out a little sigh, her mouth holding a contented smile. She settled back down against his chest. As if she'd read his mind, she asked, "So, what have you been doing with yourself for the last five years?"

He glanced down at her. There was no censure in her tone or her eyes. She appeared calm, serene even. This was such a change from the way she was before. It gave him hope that she finally did have a handle on her demon. Certainly their lovemaking hadn't been as violent as it had in the past. "I'm on Natchook's trail again."

She rose up on one elbow. She stared at him for a few seconds and then said, "I know you didn't look for him at all while we were together. What changed?"

"*We* changed. You and me." He didn't know how else to put it. When he and Nix had been together before, the driving need for revenge had lessened. She had taken over his thoughts and desires so that not much else could find room in his mind. He'd let her distract him from his mission. Willingly. Gladly, even. Because being with her had given his life purpose. Much more than any vow of revenge could do.

He knew eventually his mandate for upholding the law would have taken hold, but for a while he'd been happy and hadn't wanted anything to ruin his serenity. All that had changed when he'd come to realize how detrimental he had been to Nix's mental well-being. "I couldn't take the chance that you'd lose your grip on your humanity, and then your sanity, because of me, honey. It seemed a good time to get back on his trail. I eventually would have started looking for him again, anyway. It's always been my mission to find him and bring him to justice—"

"You mean kill him," she interrupted. When he just stared at her, she gave a little shrug. "Let's not sugarcoat it here, Tobias. You're an executioner. A guilty verdict has been pronounced and you're here to deliver the death sentence."

"That was my directive as an Enforcer of the High Laws." He clenched his jaw. Regardless that Natchook had used him to get to his target, Tobias would still have volunteered to follow him and be the one to bring him to justice. "He murdered the leader of my people, Nix, in full view of hundreds of thousands. He was found guilty; he has no defense."

"I know, I know. It's just..." Nix sighed. Her gaze dropped and she started playing with the hair on his chest. "You're not an enforcer anymore, and you're on Earth now. All that happened a long time ago."

"You think I don't know that?" Tobias put two fingers under her chin and lifted her face to stare into her eyes. "He used me, used our friendship, to get close enough to Kai Vardan to murder him." Even now he still felt the sting of that betrayal, the sadness over losing someone who could have, *would* have, made a difference in the lives of his people. "Kai was a good man, Nix. A noble man in the truest sense. He didn't deserve to be assassinated."

"I'm sure he didn't." Her expression remained gentle, her tone soft. She lay back down, her head next to his on the pillow. "But wouldn't justice be better served here, now, to bring Natchook in alive? To take him to court and try him according to our laws?"

"And what?" Tobias briefly closed his eyes against the memories rolling around in his head. Two men, as close as brothers, or so he'd thought. One betraying the other without remorse. He opened his eyes and stared at the ceiling. "What charges would he be brought up on? Murder in another dimension over two hundred years ago?"

"Why not? There's no statute of limitations on murder."

He shifted to his side, going up on one elbow and propping his head on his hand. "It's been done before, holding a trial for crimes committed before an Influx. The last one was before you were born, about fifty years ago." He pressed his lips together. "Too many prets believe the rift gives everyone a second chance. A clean slate. Not one person brought up on charges was ever convicted. The preternatural council finally stopped doing it."

"Why spin your wheels, I guess."

"Exactly," he said, "It's either make them pay for their crimes or let them get away with it." Her little growl brought a slight grin to his face. She wasn't happy with that last choice. Neither was he. His smile quickly faded.

"Which is why pret laws have evolved to be swift and sometimes brutal." He gave a little growl of his own. "I have no intention of letting Natchook get away."

She looked at him in silence for a few moments. Then she said, "Fine. I'll help you."

"You'll what?" Tobias sat up, the sheet bunching low around his hips. He couldn't have heard right.

"I said I'll help you. As soon as we figure out what's going on with our current case and put it to bed, so to speak, I'll help you catch Natchook." When he continued to stare at her, she raised her brows. "What?"

He narrowed his eyes. Just what was she playing at? "When I find him, I'm going to kill him," he reminded her, just in case she'd already forgotten.

"I know."

"And you're all right with that? What about what you just said?" If he lived five thousand years he'd never understand women.

"For one thing, I don't want you going after him alone. You need someone to watch your back."

Tobias shook his head. "No. No! It's too—"

Nix shot upright, the sheet falling to her waist. "Don't you dare! Don't treat me like I'm some helpless little woman." She pressed her finger to his chest to make her point. "The job I do every day is dangerous, Tobias. I'm not sitting at home baking cookies; I'm a trained professional. I can help you."

His eyes dropped to her bare breasts. His blood heated and he muttered, "I can't have this conversation when you're like that."

Her lips twitched. She yanked the sheet up and held it in front of her breasts. "Better?"

"Yes." What, was he insane? "No."

She didn't stop her grin this time. The sheet dipped, showing off the inner slopes of her breasts. "I thought you were a big, bad enforcer. Dedicated. Focused," she teased. Damned if the little minx wasn't plumping her breasts together a little to enhance her cleavage.

"Oh, believe me, I'm focused. I'm absolutely focused." He dragged his eyes back to her smiling face. "Seriously, though, I don't want you involved with Natchook, honey. He's too slippery. I..." He pressed his lips together, his gut tightening with fear. "I have no doubts about your skills, but he's evil, Nix. You'd be nothing more to him than a pesky little mosquito, a pest to be swatted away." He stared into her eyes. "I don't want to lose you."

Her slender throat moved with her swallow. "Why?" she asked. "You walked away before for my own good."

"But I never stopped loving you, sweetheart. Never." He leaned forward and put his hands on her shoulders. Rubbing his thumbs over her soft skin, he added, "I left *because* I loved you. And now..."

When he didn't go on she prompted, "And now?"

He stared into her eyes. "I don't think I'm strong enough to do it a second time."

* * *

At Tobias's low confession, Nix felt her heart stutter. She searched his eyes and read sincerity in their smoky depths. And such a deep, abiding love; she felt fear grip her. What if she did something and screwed it up? Again. God, she'd have to keep such a tight control over herself she'd be as taut as a rubber band. She saw a hell of a lot of tai chi in her future.

"Whatever you're thinking that's put that look of panic on your face, stop it." His strong hand cradled her cheek. His cool palm immediately began to heat from the warmth of her skin. "This time we'll face things together."

"Swear." She wasn't sure she could take it if he walked away from her again.

He leaned forward and cupped her face with both hands. "I swear it. I'll do everything I can to help you."

"All I need is for you to love me, Tobias." She stroked her fingers down his jaw and then rested her hand on his chest. "Just love me."

"I will. I do." His lips touched hers softly. Once. Twice. He wrapped his arms around her and lay back against the pillows, holding her against his chest. "Nix..." He drew a breath and held it, then blew it out in a long sigh.

"What, Tobias?" She glanced up at him. "What is it?"

"There's something I should tell you." His head moved against the pillow. He stroked his fingers through her hair, setting up a pleasurable tingle in her scalp from the impromptu massage. "Whatever happens—with this case, with our jobs—remember that I love you. That I always have your best interests in mind. But I have a job to do, too."

"O...kay." She frowned a little, wondering where he was going with this and unable to shake the feeling that this wasn't what he'd been planning to say.

"It's just..." His fingers raked through her hair again.

Nix couldn't hold back a little moan at the sensation.

His responding chuckle was filled-with-humor sexy and he dug his fingers in a little harder. "I'll probably be leaving town once this case is solved. Knox will take over again as the vampire liaison in your quadrant, and I'll pick up where I left off with finding Natchook."

She settled more comfortably in the crook of his arm. "Right. And I told you I'd help you."

"It would mean giving up your job, your home."

Nix propped herself up on her elbow. "My home is wherever you are."

His eyes darkened. Pheromones started rolling off of him as the emotions she saw in his eyes manifested themselves. Hope, love, guilt, and satisfaction roiled together to undulate over her skin, seep into her soul. "You'd give up your career?"

He was so sweet. So clueless. "My job is catching bad guys. I won't be giving anything up. I'll be focused on one particular bad guy and I won't be doing it in Scottsdale." She drew in a breath. "I want to be in your life, Tobias."

He stared at her, so much emotion roiling in his eyes it almost brought her to tears. "You're not just in my life, honey. You *are* my life." He drew her down for a long, lingering kiss.

Drawing back slightly, she asked, "So, tell me, if we won't be catching the bad guy here, where will we be?"

His big hand curved over her hip. "My last lead took me to Fairbanks. That's where I was when Amarinda called."

"Alaska?" She snuggled close again. "From desert to snow and back to desert. That was quite a trip for you."

"Alaska was like a barren wasteland because you weren't there." His voice turned gruff. "The last five years have been the worst of my life." His hand tightened on her hip. "I missed you, honey."

She pressed a kiss to his shoulder. "I missed you, too. A couple of days ago if someone had told me you'd come back into town and I'd be happy you were here I would've told 'em they were crazy. Or tried to rip their lungs out." She snickered. "But they would have been right." She paused and traced a random pattern on his chest with her index finger. "When you're young and in love, everything seems perfect." She rubbed her cheek against his shoulder. "Now I know I don't need perfect. I just need you."

Her eyes grew heavy. She was going to fall asleep in the arms of the man she loved, the man who loved her. It was a new beginning for both of them.

Chapter Thirteen

Early the next morning Nix slipped out of bed and went quietly into the living room to gather her clothes. Her muscles protested some of the movement, reminding her that it had been five years since she'd exercised in quite the way she had last night. She smiled and winced as she bent to pick up one of her socks. God, what a night. She and Tobias had never made love in such a deeply intimate way before. Their couplings had always been born out of desperate lust, even with all the love they'd felt.

Maybe it was her newfound maturity, maybe it was Tobias's care in not drawing out the demon. Whatever it was, it had worked. She had felt the tug of her inner demon briefly and not strongly enough that she couldn't fight it back. Thinking of all the time they'd wasted, she pressed her lips together. Had it really been a waste of time? Maybe they were rushing into things too fast now. No, she had to believe that things happened for a reason. Tobias had been meant to go away, to leave her to fend for herself. She really thought that was what had made her finally grow up. There was nothing like a broken heart to mature you.

After taking a quick shower, she started to get dressed.

She held up her panties and grimaced. She really didn't want to put those back on after she'd just cleaned herself up. She tugged on her jeans and fastened them, then wadded up her panties and stuffed them in her pocket. Holding her boots in one hand, she padded in bare feet back into the master bedroom.

"You weren't planning on trying to sneak out, were you?" Tobias's voice was rough with sleep. She looked up to see him leaning on one elbow, eyes blinking, dark hair in a lovely tousled mess. There was just enough sunlight to cast shadows over his chest, defining his toned musculature.

She dragged her eyes back to his face. There wasn't time for any morning nooky, as much as she might like to jump right back in bed. "Sneak out on a vampire? Hardly. I need to get home and change, and grab some breakfast. Unless you have something other than blood in your refrigerator." When he grimaced, she laughed and perched on the edge of the bed to draw on her socks. "Then we need to call Dante and head down to the observatory. When we spoke to Rinda's friend Samantha, she talked about Rinda's affair with a married man, and almost as an aside she'd commented how Mt. Bigelow was a perfect place to study the area of space where the rift occurred."

Tobias lazily scratched his chest. "I'm with you so far."

"Well, when you consider what Luc told me, that there are radio transmissions being sent through a mini rift and that the council is aware of them…" She started pulling on her boots. "We need to go back to Mt. Bigelow and talk to those scientists again, especially that head guy, the good-looker who was so nervous." She twisted around to look at him. "Besides, my poor baby Rufus needs to go outside, and I need to feed him, too."

His eyebrows shot up. "You have a baby? And you named him Rufus?"

She shot him a grimace. "He's my dog. Just what's wrong with his name?"

"For a dog? Not a thing. For a baby?" His eyes darkened and settled low on her belly. "I wouldn't want any son of mine to get saddled with the name Rufus."

A slow smile curved her lips. He might not be thrilled with the name, but he didn't look at all adverse to having a son. She flushed at the thought of carrying his child, of holding the proof of their love in her arms. Before she turned into a maudlin sap, she teased, "Yeah, like Tobias is such a grand name."

He looked hurt for a second but couldn't hold on to the expression. His grin was more carefree than she'd ever seen it. "Yes, well, Tobias Caine was the name of the human I took possession of when I first came through the rift, and I felt it was time to honor him by using his name again. Now that preternaturals are known, I won't have to ever give it up." This time his frown was genuine. "Unless you really don't like it."

She leaned over and kissed him. "It's a fine name, really. You do him proud." She got up and stretched. "Shall I call Dante, then? I can have him meet us at council HQ since it's centrally located for all of us, and we can go to Tucson from there."

"Sure." He lay back down and clasped his hands beneath his head. Biceps bulged and pectorals flexed with his movement. "Just make sure he eats breakfast before we leave. I don't want to sit and watch him stuffing his face again."

Nix laughed. "He sure can put it away, can't he?" She stopped beside the bed and leaned down to kiss him again. He brought one big hand up and cupped the back of her neck, holding her still. When she drew back, her breath came a little faster than before.

"Sure I can't talk you into staying a little longer?" His stormy eyes gleamed with desire.

She groaned. "You are awfully tempting, but I'm sure." She pushed herself away before she could succumb. The spirit was more willing than the flesh, which was too sore. "Don't go back to sleep," she said as she walked toward the bedroom door.

"I just might. You wore me out."

"Hah. That's a good one." If anyone had been in danger of getting worn out, it was her. Most vampires were like the Energizer Bunny—they kept going and going and going.

Or make that coming and coming and coming.

She paused in the doorway and looked back at him. His gaze met hers. "Tobias, I love you."

His slow smile made her heart melt. "I love you, too, honey. I always have. Always will." He looked so delicious lying there, arms bent, showing off the definition in his biceps, the dark green sheet bunched around his hips.

She tracked the happy trail of hair down his belly, below his navel before it was lost to sight. A bulge grew beneath the sheet as she watched. She'd taken three steps back into the room before she caught herself. She held out a hand and let out a small growl. "I'll see you later." She turned on her heel and walked out of the room before she could change her mind. As much as both of them might want to, they couldn't spend all day in bed. But once this case was over... Yeah, all the more reason to solve it, and solve it fast.

She opened the front door and almost tripped over a medium-sized cooler on the welcome mat. "Uh, Tobias?" she called back into the house. "You have a delivery."

"It's my daily blood supply," he yelled. "Put it in the fridge, please."

She bent and grabbed the handle of the cooler and carried it into the kitchen. Setting it down on the counter, she flipped up the lid and saw four bottles of blood in a wire basket. She opened the large refrigerator and shook her head to see it was empty except for one lonely glass of blood. "Well, here now you have four new friends," she murmured, and put the bottles on the shelf. She set the empty basket in the cooler and headed back toward the front door. "See you later," she yelled back to Tobias.

"All right."

On her way home, Nix called Dante. He answered on the first ring. She glanced at her watch. Six a.m. "Oh," she said. "This early I thought I'd get your voice mail."

"I'm always up early to get the horses fed and turned out into the paddock," he said. "Did something happen?"

"No. Tobias and I are heading back down to Tucson this morning, and wanted to see if you're available." She turned into her parking lot and pulled into her spot. Holding the phone between her cheek and shoulder, she shut off the car and hopped out.

"Sure. Do we want to grab some breakfast first?"

Remembering the look on Tobias's face when he'd mentioned making sure they ate first, she grinned. "I'm just gonna fix myself something here. Why don't you meet us at council headquarters around seven thirty?

Does that give you enough time to do what you need to do?"

"Yep. See you then." He ended the call.

Nix dropped her phone into her purse and let herself into her apartment. Rufus was waiting, whining, and pressing against her legs. She went down on her haunches and loved on him for a minute, letting him lick her and doing her best to reassure him he was all right. "Let's go outside," she said, and grabbed his leash.

After he'd taken care of business she put out a scoop of dog food for him and slid a couple of pieces of bread into the toaster. Waiting for the bread to toast she peeled a banana and put it on a small plate, then grabbed a yogurt and took off the lid. The toast popped up. She slathered one slice with peanut butter and the other with orange marmalade.

Nix wandered into the living room and sat on the sofa with feet propped up on the coffee table. Rufus finished his food and sat beside her, his head resting on her shin, his big doggy eyes looking pitiful. She gave him the last bite of her toast, the one with peanut butter, laughing at his antics when the toast stuck to the roof of his mouth. Getting up, she carried her empty plate into the kitchen.

An hour later she was dressed in clean clothes and on her way to the council building. Dante was already there, leaning against the front fender of his truck, and, as she got out of her car, Tobias pulled up in his SUV.

"Well, the gang's all here," Dante said, pushing away from his vehicle. As usual he wore a suit jacket and button-down shirt with blue jeans and sturdy work shoes. When she'd commented to him once that she was surprised he didn't wear cowboy boots, he'd responded that it was too hard to run in boots. Thick-soled work shoes like the beat cops wore were better.

The passenger side window of the SUV rolled down. "Let's go," Tobias called out.

Dante opened the back door, grinning at Nix. This time she was fine with riding up front with Tobias. She just sent the grin back at Dante and opened the front passenger door. Just as she was about to climb in, one of the council guards called her name. She turned to look at him.

"The council wants to see you and Tobias," he said.

"Now?" She frowned and glanced at her watch. It was just now seven thirty. Why in the hell were they in so early?

"Now."

She heard Tobias's aggrieved sigh and closed the door. Dante closed his door, too, and they stepped away from the SUV so Tobias could park it. She looked at Dante. "Do you want to wait for us?"

"May as well." He jerked his head toward the building. "Is there a spare office I can use? I have my laptop with me and can work on some reports while I wait."

She cleared her throat. "They really don't want non-preternaturals in the building unless they're there for a meeting. Sorry."

He shrugged. "No problem. The cab of my truck'll work."

Tobias walked up to them. "So you'll wait for us?"

Dante nodded. "As long as you don't take too long. Some of us do grow old, you know."

"We'll get a message out to you if it looks like it's going to take too long."

"You make it sound like we'll be trying for a prison break," Nix said. "Which, now that I think on that a bit, isn't too far from the truth."

Tobias chuckled. "Are you ready?"

"As ready as I'll ever be." Nix looked at Dante. "We'll be back as soon as we can."

His gaze went from her to Tobias and back again, his expression one she'd seen before—the detective trying to puzzle something out that was bothering him. "I'll be here," he said slowly.

Nix and Tobias went inside and were called straight into the council chambers.

Deoul, Caladh, and Braithwaite were there, in their high-backed seats behind the big table, dressed in their formal white council robes. Caladh looked highly displeased, while Deoul and Braithwaite seemed unusually satisfied. Wondering what was going on, Nix glanced at Tobias, who seemed... ill at ease. "What's going on?" she whispered.

He gave an unconvincing shrug. He knew something was up, she was sure of it. He might not be certain that what he knew was what they wanted to talk about, but he knew *something*.

Deoul sat with folded arms, one leg crossed over the other in indolent grace. "First of all, we have confirmation on the identity of the latest victim. One of our criminalists found a wallet in a nearby Dumpster belonging to Desmond Dumond. The body, what bits of it were recovered, has been positively identified as his."

"Dumond?" Tobias asked. "They're sure?"

"Yes, unfortunately."

"You knew him?" Nix asked Tobias, then said dryly,

"What am I saying? Of course you knew him. You know just about everybody on the planet. And if you don't know a particular person, you know someone who does."

"That is neither here nor there," Deoul said before Tobias could respond to her soft jibe. "We have become aware in the last couple of years that there is a group of preternaturals who may be seeking to undermine this and other councils worldwide." He sent Tobias a look that Nix didn't understand, a shared glance she wasn't a part of. "We had asked Dumond to infiltrate the local group."

"It appears he succeeded. To a point," Tobias responded.

"That's our thought as well." Caladh leaned forward. "We hadn't heard from him in about six months, but we suspected it was because he had managed to infiltrate deep enough that he didn't want to take the chance of blowing his cover."

"It's a bit coincidental that he wound up dead, don't you think?" Tobias clasped his hands behind his back.

The council members nodded. "We think it can be safely surmised," Deoul said, "that Dumond was killed for his involvement in the group. The question is: Were Pickett and Novellus killed for the same reason?"

"It would also be a coincidence if they were killed the way they were and were not involved, don't you think?" Nix asked. Amarinda's murder was tied into her study of the rift. It had nothing to do with an affair with a married man, Nix was sure of it.

"Perhaps." Deoul stared at her a moment. "Which brings me to our next item." He rested his forearms on the table and linked his fingers together. Slyness slid across his face. "Since it has been determined through both evidence and your own statements to this council that humans are not involved in these killings, your services on this case are no longer required."

"Wait! What?" Nix glanced at Tobias, who stood ramrod straight and silent. She looked again at Deoul. "You can't take me off the case." Her heart leaped into her throat. There was too much at stake for her to be removed from this case. They'd just found out about the rift device, for one thing, and now to find out the last victim had infiltrated a group that may very well have a connection to the rift communications? She had to stay involved!

"Of course I can take you off the case. You work for me, remember?" Deoul's tone held sarcasm and irritating condescension. It made her want to smack him. One day, maybe she'd get that chance. Either when there were no repercussions or when she no longer wanted or needed this job.

"Actually, she works for *us*," Caladh muttered. He slouched in his chair and drummed the fingers of one hand on the table. "But unfortunately, Nix, the standard procedure is to remove a liaison when the population he or she represents is not involved in the case. You know that. You're our human liaison, and humans are not involved."

"But exceptions have been made before—"

"Not for you." Deoul slashed a hand through the air. "Not on this case."

She'd always known she wasn't Deoul's favorite, but now he really seemed to have a bug up his butt about her. "Why not this case?"

"You're too close to it. Not only were you a friend of one of the victims, but..." His gaze slid to Tobias. "As we had confirmed yesterday, the scent of demon has been prevalent at each scene."

Her mouth dropped and she turned toward Tobias. The man she loved. The man who'd said he would keep this secret. "You told them?" she whispered.

"I didn't say it was prevalent," he corrected. He looked at her, apology in his eyes. "They already knew, Nix. I merely confirmed their intel."

"Sure they did." She glared at him, having a hard time believing she'd let him do this to her again. But she'd deal with that in a few minutes. For now, she turned back to the council members. She wasn't going to go without a fight. "I can still help. I have contacts—"

"Who may very well be the ones behind the attacks." Deoul shook his head. "No. This is not open for debate. You're off this case." When she didn't move, his voice rose. "You are dismissed, Ms. de la Fuente."

She looked at Tobias, mouth open in shock. He met her gaze and gave a little shrug. She knew he wouldn't go into it with her in front of the council, but, by God, he could do better than shrug at her. Before she could say anything though, the council president spoke again.

"Go. Now." Deoul gave a wave of his hand in perfunctory dismissal.

She didn't budge. Bony-assed fairy. As her anger and outrage mounted, her inner demon began clawing its way to the surface, sending fire to churn in her gut, and slide beneath her skin. She lifted one hand and scratched the skin concealing her horn buds, where the sensation was the worst.

"Nix." Tobias's voice was low. Cautionary. "Just go. I'll see what I can do."

She tightened her lips. "You've probably already done more than enough, thanks." Looking at the council, she dipped her head. Twisting on her heel, she strode out of the room, uncaring that the force of her shove slammed the double doors against the walls as they flew open. She ignored the two guards who hurried to close them behind her. Deoul was a first-rate bastard, and Tobias wasn't far behind him. She even, at this moment, hated him a little bit.

Nix stalked to the far end of the hallway and slammed her fist against the wall. Staring out the window, she tried to calm down and think about this logically. This wasn't the first time she'd been released from a case. As Caladh had said, it was protocol. If neither the victim nor the suspect was human, there was nothing for the human liaison to do.

What had her most concerned was that Tobias had talked to them about the demon scent at the crime scenes and hadn't told her. She felt like all that sweet talk from last night meant nothing. The words were like ash in her mouth now.

She heard the council chamber doors open and turned to see Tobias walk out of the room. He came toward her, his face troubled. "Nix—"

"Did you tell them about the demon scent?" she asked, hands on hips.

"They told me word had come to them. I wasn't going to lie."

"Of course not, because that would be against the rules." She exhaled and shook her head, her emotions going from angry to sad. "You think that living by rules is the only way to go, even when those rules make you a slave. Sometimes rules are made to be broken. Chaos can be good. Sometimes it's even necessary."

"Now you sound like Natchook." His expression hardened. "Can you seriously tell me that if our situations were reversed you would jeopardize your job, your integrity, by lying to them?"

"I might for you," she said. Then she sighed. If Tobias had only confirmed what they already knew, that was different than if he'd volunteered the information without being asked. But, still, he did what he'd always done—made a decision without talking it over with her. Once again he had brushed her aside as if she were too trivial to matter. Maybe she should have paid attention to that little inner voice earlier this morning when it had whispered that perhaps they were rushing into things.

Tobias stared out the window. He wasn't exactly her favorite person right now, but she had to admit if only to herself that she loved his profile—strong and masculine, handsome with just a touch of ruggedness. "There is something else I should tell you, though," he said, his voice low. He kept looking through the glass. "They told me yesterday they were going to kick you off the case."

She blinked. "And you didn't tell me?" She went back to hating him a little. God, he fit right in with these sniveling, sneaky, slick SOBs.

He turned toward her then and put his hands on her shoulders. "They specifically ordered me not to. I almost did last night, before we..."

"Before we took a tumble in the sheets?" she finished for him. "Or after you spun me a fairy tale?" She snorted. "I can't even say we made love now, knowing what I know."

He tightened his fingers. "We did make love, Nix. I meant every word I said last night."

"Right." She shrugged away from him, so angry her vision had taken on shades of yellow. Her forehead felt like thousands of fire ants were biting her skin. A tear rolled down her cheek and she swore, wiping it away with fingers that trembled. "You tell yourself whatever you have to so you can sleep at night, but don't you dare lie to me. Again." She met his eyes. "I spend half of my time thinking about how much I love you," she whispered, not bothering to swipe again at the tears streaming down her cheeks. "And the other half wishing like hell you'd never come back." She started to leave, her only thought to get out of the building before those two tattletale guards blabbed to the council that she'd lost it in the vestibule.

Tobias grabbed her arm and stopped her. Dragging her with him, he walked over to an office and opened the door, then pulled her inside the empty room and pressed her against the closed door. "Don't you dare try to lessen what I feel for you," he said, his voice a fierce rasp. "I walked away from you five years ago because I loved you, because I thought it was for the best—for *you*—and it was a mistake. One I'm not about to repeat by letting you walk away from me now." He gave her a little shake. "Whatever else you may think of me, Nix, you know I've never lied to you. Never."

Nix met his gaze, a little shocked to see his eyes were moist. He was always so strong, so tough. So proud. Yet he was a caring and sympathetic man, one with strong principles and even stronger passions. She shouldn't be so surprised.

He was right. He'd always been honest with her, sometimes brutally so. The fact that he'd thought about disobeying orders on something that wasn't life threatening said a lot. She just wasn't sure it was enough. He knew how much this job meant to her, knew it was the best way she had to prove her worth to herself. After so many years of being rejected by family, this job was all she had. All she was.

The pheromones rolled off him in undulating waves. As a tear dripped off her chin, he muttered a low curse. He brought his hands up and cupped her face, then slanted his mouth over hers.

Her eyes fluttered closed. Lightning traveled from her lips to her core, tightening her nipples along the way. With a moan of surrender, of longing, of desperation, she wrapped her arms around him and held on.

Nix ran her palms across his ribs and over his broad chest, letting her thumbs brush across his nipples. He groaned and pulled her closer, one strong hand just below the small of her back, pressing the knife scabbard into her flesh and her belly against his erection. The kiss deepened, tongues dueling, and she threaded her fingers through his soft hair, holding his head where she wanted it.

She had the hard door behind her and an equally hard man in front of her. She shivered, her arousal climbing another notch. He pulled back a fraction, slid his tongue over her bottom lip and then sucked on it. She moaned again. He nipped her lightly and drew back. "We should get going."

Nix sighed and rested her hands against his chest. The council hadn't fired her. She'd continue to do her job, just not on this case. "Don't you mean *you* should get going?"

"I said what I meant."

Surprise shot through her. "You still want me to go along." The words came out flat, more of a statement than the question she'd intended. "Isn't that against the rules or something?"

"Someone I greatly admire told me not all that long ago that sometimes rules are made to be broken." He pressed a kiss to the tip of her nose. "Something tells me this is all wrapped up with that rift device, Nix. I need you on this. So let's get out of here, okay?"

"Okay." She stared at him, searching his eyes. Maybe he had changed, after all. The old Tobias would never have allowed her to participate in something the council had declared was off limits to her. She swiped the moisture off her face with her fingers, then wiped her hands on her jeans. "Do I look like I've been crying?"

"You look beautiful." He cupped her face between his palms and pressed his lips to hers for a long, lingering kiss. "Let's go."

Chapter Fourteen

As soon as they exited the building, MacMillan hopped out of his truck and sauntered over to them. "You weren't in there as long as I thought you'd be," he said with a glance at his watch. He lifted his hand to shield his eyes from the sun.

"I've been kicked off the case," Nix said.

"Join the club." One edge of MacMillan's mouth kicked up in a wry grin. "Captain told me to take the day off and dig back into my other cases tomorrow." He peered more closely at Nix. "Have you been crying?" He shot a dark look at Tobias. "You been giving her a hard time?" His expression hardened. He looked like he was ready to take Tobias on.

"No." While he appreciated the other man's protective instincts toward Nix, Tobias didn't want to go into details about their personal troubles. As much as he liked the detective, what happened between Tobias and Nix was none of the other man's business. He pulled his sunglasses out of his pocket and slipped them on. "Let's get going."

"Ah, I just told you I'm no longer on the case." Spreading his feet apart, MacMillan hooked his thumbs over his belt.

"And I'll tell you what I told Nix." Tobias gestured toward his SUV. "I need you on this case." At the detective's look of surprise, Tobias said, "You're a seasoned investigator, MacMillan. You're familiar with the case to date. I'm not too proud to say I need help. I'd like your input."

"Well, okay then, chief. My captain told me to take the day off; he didn't tell me what I should do." As they walked toward the vehicle, MacMillan put an arm around Nix's waist. "Are you okay? I've never seen you cry before."

Tobias fought the urge to rip the other man away from her and toss him into a nearby cactus. He should be glad the detective was solicitous of her feelings, but seeing MacMillan with his arm around her brought out all the possessive instincts Tobias had.

"I'm fine, Dante." Nix apparently caught the glare Tobias sent their way, because she scowled at him but then eased away from MacMillan. "I'm just upset at being kicked off the case."

"Uh-huh." MacMillan studied her. "Not buyin' it, sweetheart. What's going on?" He looked at Tobias.

"Nothing." Tobias hit the remote, opened the door, and climbed behind the wheel.

"Right." From his hardening tone, MacMillan wasn't going to let it go. "Somebody tell me what's going on, right now."

"Oh, God, men can be so dense sometimes." Nix's tone was exasperated and a little embarrassed. She opened the front passenger door and paused. "It's personal between Tobias and me, okay?"

MacMillan opened the back door and hopped in as Nix

climbed up into her seat. They both swung their doors closed at the same time. As he fussed with his seat belt, MacMillan said, "Well, you must've gotten something resolved, since you're wanting to sit up front with him."

"Shut up." Nix said it without any real heat, but her cheeks were pink.

"I just want to say, if you hurt her again, you'll answer to me." MacMillan met Tobias's gaze in the rearview mirror, his face set, eyes blazing with determined chivalry.

Tobias turned in his seat to look at the detective. "You and whose army?" he couldn't resist asking. He could take the detective down with the flick of a wrist, and the other man knew it.

"Just me." MacMillan's tone softened. "But only when you're knocked out, tied up, or otherwise helpless."

Nix rolled her eyes with a muffled "Men." She snapped her seat belt together and said, "Dante, I appreciate the sentiment, but I can look after myself. Now, if you two are done, can we get going?"

Tobias twisted the ignition. The SUV purred to a start and he engaged the drive. "Let me fill you in on what we know," he said to MacMillan. By the time they'd merged on to the expressway the detective knew what they did, including the rift device and the interdimensional communications.

MacMillan wore an expression of shock. "So, do you think your friend Amarinda was involved in this mess?"

Nix twisted in her seat to look at him. "You mean . . . *involved?*"

"Well, I don't necessarily mean she sat there with one finger pressed to the on switch, but yeah. Involved. Was she in the middle of what was going on?"

It hadn't occurred to Tobias, but now that he thought about it... "I honestly don't know. Do I think she would have gotten mixed up in this out of malicious intent? No." He glanced at Nix where she sat in the passenger seat next to him, chewing on her lower lip. God, she was so pretty. And he wanted to be the one nibbling on that courtesan mouth. He forced his eyes back to the road. "But could she have gotten involved out of boredom or curiosity? Absolutely."

"You really think so?" Nix stared at him, her lovely eyes dark with so much confusion it made him ache. When this was all over, he'd show her how much he loved her so that she'd never doubt it again.

Tobias cleared the rasp from his throat. "She'd been around a very long time. Lived all over the world. It wouldn't be a stretch to imagine her hooking up with a bunch of hooligans for a break from the monotony."

"I just don't see that. I mean, I know she could be frivolous at times. I actually used to envy her a little for that." Memories of a lonely, hard childhood reflected for a moment on her face. "But she wouldn't be in cahoots with the bastards behind this rift device. Being bored is one thing, but inviting total chaos into the world? Nope. I don't see it."

Tobias stared at her.

"What?" she asked. When he continued to stare, she muttered, "Eyes on the road, Caine. Tobias!"

He growled a curse and corrected the drift of the SUV into the other lane.

"Now, what was that look for?" Nix asked again.

"What you just said. That she wouldn't invite chaos into the world." He glanced into the rearview mirror and saw he had MacMillan's attention as well. "It's something Natchook would do."

"Who's Natchook?" MacMillan asked.

"Tobias, you don't think..." She blinked, horror building in her eyes. "Could it be him behind all of this?"

"I wouldn't put it past him. He's brilliant and charismatic. A deadly combination. And he's very fond of chaos," he added in a dry tone. He tightened his hands on the wheel. It was just Natchook's style to kill his own kind but lay a false trail pointing the authorities toward someone completely innocent of any wrongdoing.

"Who's Natchook?" MacMillan asked again.

"It's the guy Tobias followed through the rift," Nix told him.

"Oh." He leaned forward and braced one forearm on the back of Tobias's seat. "The douche bag who killed your leader."

"You know about that?" Tobias asked, a little surprised.

"Yeah, Nix told me."

"Oh, she did, did she?" He shot her a look. While it wasn't exactly a secret, his story wasn't widely known and he preferred it that way. How he lived his life was nobody's business but his.

"It's not like it was classified or anything. He deserved to know he wasn't going to be working with a criminal." She leaned her head against the headrest.

"Fair enough." Leaning forward, Tobias turned on the audio system. Soon the strains of Vivaldi filled the vehicle. He settled back in his seat and the rest of the drive was accomplished without anyone speaking.

When he started up the road to the observatory, Nix

broke the silence. "How do you want to do this? Should we split up?"

"No. We'll stay together to question Sahir, like before." Tobias wanted to watch her reactions. Sometimes the way she processed information gave him a new direction to move in. MacMillan, too.

He drove through the gate and parked the SUV. They all climbed out and headed toward the observatory. He saw MacMillan turn up the collar of his jacket against the cool air of the mountain. When they walked inside the main building, Tobias took off his sunglasses and stopped the first person he saw. "We'd like to talk to Dr. Sahir."

"Yeah, good luck with that," the young man said. His freckled face turned disgruntled. "He didn't show up for work today."

Tobias raised his brows. "Is that so? Is that normal?"

"No, not at all." He stopped and frowned. Suspicion laden in his voice, he asked, "Hey, just who are you?"

Tobias reached into his pocket and pulled out his ID. "I'm Tobias Caine, this is Nix de la Fuente and Dante MacMillan," he said, motioning toward his colleagues. He replaced his holder in his pocket. "We'd like to ask you a few questions."

"O-kay," the other man said slowly, looking unsure and more than a little nervous. It could be because he was young and being approached by law enforcement for the first time, or it could be because he had something to hide. It was time to find out.

"Did you know Amarinda Novellus?"

The young man gave a nod. "Amarinda? Yeah, sure. I knew her." He stared down at the clipboard in his hand.

"It's a damned shame, what happened to her." He looked up at Tobias. "You found out who did it yet?"

"That's why we're here." Nix had pulled out her notebook and held pen poised to page. She peered at his name badge and scribbled something down.

"Uh, what're you doing?" The young man's nervousness increased. His eyes drifted from her notebook to the gun at her side and back to the notebook, neck craning as he tried to see what she was writing.

"Just noting your name for now. Charles." She stared at him with raised brows. "Is that a problem?"

"Oh, no. Of course not." He gave a sheepish grin. "My friends call me Charlie." One eyelid dropped in a wink.

Even in an uncertain situation here the guy was flirting with her. Tobias curbed his inclination to smash his fist into the little numb nut's face.

Charlie went on. "I'm just not used to... This is my first interrogation." He looked equal measure scared and excited.

Tobias sighed. There were just too many damned cop shows on television these days. "This isn't an interrogation. It's an interview. There's a difference."

"Really?" Charlie gave Tobias a wide-eyed stare.

Tobias leaned forward as if imparting some deep dark secret. He waited until Charlie moved closer a few steps. "If this were an interrogation, you'd be at council headquarters in handcuffs. Surrounded by vampires and shape-shifters and all sorts of things that go bump in the night." His voice came out more gruffly than he'd intended, and it clearly startled Charlie because he quickly put space between them, eyes even wider and youthful face a couple of shades paler than before.

"Tobias, behave." Nix rolled her eyes and turned to Charlie. "What do you know about what Rinda was working on?" When the young man's attention stayed glued to Tobias, she prompted, "Charlie?"

He gave a start and looked her way. "Oh, uh, not much. She was studying the rift, but I don't know anything more specific than that." He snapped his fingers. "You know who you should talk to? Dr. Sahir." He gave a definitive nod.

"You said he's not here today." Nix tipped her head to one side, her expression conveying much more patience than Tobias had with the little nimrod.

"Yeah." Charlie's face fell. "No, he's not."

"Do you know where he could be?" She brushed a wayward curl from the side of her face. It popped right back where it had been.

Tobias clenched his hands against the instinct to tuck it behind her ear. If he touched her, even just her hair, he wouldn't want to stop there. He was more professional than that, and so was she.

He saw Charlie give Nix another flirty grin. "No, I'm just a grad student. He doesn't tell us much, so I really don't know where the great and powerful Oz is. Sorry."

"He treats you pretty bad, huh?" Nix's voice held commiseration. Of the three of them, she would have the most empathy for the kid based on her experiences with the council.

Charlie snorted. "OMG, he can be such a prick. Pardon my French. As long as whatever you're doing will reflect well on him, he's like your best friend. As soon as you move on to something else, he drop kicks you to the curb."

"Is that what happened with Rinda?" she asked.

"OMG?" Tobias asked as an aside to MacMillan.

"Oh, my God." MacMillan shot him a sidelong glance. "Text speak. You need to get with the times, boss. Maybe you should start tweeting or something."

"I dunno," Charlie said to Nix. "I mean, they seemed kinda tight, you know? But like I said, I'm just a grad student."

Tobias restrained a growl of irritation. This kid was getting them nowhere. His gut told him the youngster didn't know anything, and his gut was rarely wrong. "Who *would* know where Sahir is?"

Charlie's mouth opened and then shut. "I was gonna say Amarinda would know, but..." He sighed.

Tobias glanced at Nix. She pulled a face and shrugged. Looking back at Charlie, she asked, "Is there anyone else here that can tell us what Rinda was working on?"

"Um..." Charlie glanced around. "She pretty much kept to herself, but maybe..." He paused. "Clarissa, uh, I mean Dr. Busham might know." He pointed to a curvaceous blonde standing next to the large telescope. "She's worked with Sahir more than any of the rest of us. And she helped Amarinda with some of her rift research."

"Thanks," Nix said with a soft smile.

A blush fired up Charlie's freckles as he stuttered a response.

Tobias shook his head and walked toward the blonde scientist, fishing out his ID as he went. "Dr. Busham?"

She looked up, her ponytail bouncing against her nape. "Yes?"

He showed her his ID and introduced himself and then Nix and MacMillan. He saw interest flare in her eyes when she looked at the detective. "Dr. Busham?" he said, drawing her attention back to him. "We'd like to talk to you about Dr. Sahir."

Her lips thinned and blue eyes flared with anger. "Before you ask, I don't have any clue where he is. We have a report due to NASA in a week, and he up and disappears?" She gave a derisive snort. "Bastard. I should have known he'd leave me to finish up the work."

"Why is that?" Nix jotted down a few notes.

"Because he's not a serious scientist. He's in it for the glamour of working in conjunction with NASA, with getting his face in the news." Dr. Busham huffed. "And it looks like he took off with some of our equipment, too, which will slow our progress even more. Damn it!"

"What kind of equipment?" Tobias asked.

"A couple of laptops, a radio transceiver and transmitter, and our only broad-bandwidth videotape recorder." She shook her head. "I can't imagine why he would want them, but since they disappeared at the same time he did, I can only presume he took them."

Tobias shared a look with Nix. They needed to find Sahir. He would lead them to the one behind the transmissions.

Natchook.

"Thank you," he murmured to Dr. Busham. To Nix and MacMillan he said, "You two go talk to the other staff we missed the last time we were here. I'm going to call my PI friend." Knowing they would do their jobs, Tobias walked back outside, his phone in hand. He hit the speed dial. While he waited for Percival to pick up, he sniffed the air to make sure there wasn't anyone around. The only things he smelled were natural animals and trees. No prets or humans were near enough for him to smell, and, therefore, they weren't near enough to listen in on his conversation.

The PI answered on the fourth ring. "What the hell kind of weird shit did you get me into here, Caine?"

"What're you talking about?" Tobias walked toward the edge of the drive, head up as he scanned his surroundings.

"I left you a voice mail. Didn't you get it?" Percival's voice sounded strained. "Your scientist met up with a couple of vamps last night, which, okay, is not that big a deal. Humans hook up with vamps all the time, right? Afterwards he made a call to a prepaid cell in Scottsdale. The person he called paid in cash, I already checked. No way to trace who the phone belongs to." His voice dropped a notch. "Early this morning, around dawn, your guy comes out of the house and throws a couple of suitcases in the trunk of his car. Before he can take off, though, these same vamps jump him." The PI paused and then said, "Sahir's dead, Caine."

"Damn it." Tobias scrubbed the back of his neck with his hand. He hadn't gotten the voice mail. Sometimes he hated modern technology. "Did they know you were there?"

"I don't think so." Percival sighed. "I had the windows up and stayed real still. Didn't move until I knew for sure they were gone."

"What did they do with the body?"

"Tossed it in the trunk with the suitcases and drove off in his car." Tobias heard the rasp of whiskers and pictured the grizzled PI rubbing his fingers against his chin, a habitual move he did when he was thinking. Percival said, "By now he's out in the desert somewhere getting picked over by coyotes. Since he'd packed those suitcases, law enforcement will assume he just took off of his own volition."

"And it's fine to let them keep assuming that for now. This is big, Perce." And the less the PI knew, the safer it was for him. Tobias warned, "You keep your head down."

"No kidding. Those vamps were some scary freaks, man. No way I'm letting them know I saw what I saw." He cleared his throat. "Consider us even now, Caine. I don't owe you any more favors." It took a lot to shake Percival, but it was obvious seeing a bunch of vamps kill a human was more than enough to do the job.

Tobias agreed and ended the call. He stood for a moment, listening to the birds and the wind blowing through the evergreens. The air up here was crisp and clean, chilling his already cool skin. He didn't feel the discomfort of it, but he could sense the coldness of the temperature.

At least four deaths now in conjunction with the rift device. Three vamps, one human. This was going to blow up in their faces if they didn't track Natchook down soon.

He heard the door to the observatory open and turned to see Nix and MacMillan headed his way. The detective turned up his jacket collar again and folded his arms, tucking his hands in his armpits for warmth. Nix had a slight smile on her face that faded as she got closer. "What happened? What did your PI friend have to say?"

Tobias glanced around one more time to make sure they didn't have any eavesdroppers. "Sahir's dead. Killed by vampires early this morning."

MacMillan let out a low whistle. "Well, that jibes with what we just learned."

"Which is?"

Nix glanced down at her notes. "One of the scientists

said Sahir met someone at the base of the mountain a few days ago. He saw them pulled over on one of the side roads as he drove by on his way home." She closed up her notebook and slipped it into her bag. "He said the other guy looked like a vampire."

"He could tell that as he passed by going fifty miles an hour?" Tobias couldn't help but be skeptical.

"That's what I said," MacMillan replied. "It was at an intersection, so he had to stop and check for clearance before he kept going. They weren't that far away, and apparently the vamp was showing quite a bit of fang."

"Would he recognize him if he saw him again?" Tobias would borrow a police sketch artist and get him up here if that were the case.

MacMillan shook his head. "Nope. Said once he caught a glimpse of fangs that was all he saw. He couldn't even say if the vamp was blond or brunet. Just that he was male." He grimaced. "I have a feeling we're lucky he managed to notice that much."

"Shit." Tobias looked at Nix. "Did you get anything more?"

"No." Her eyes held sparks of demon fire. "It looks like our best lead to Natchook has hit a dead end. Literally."

Chapter Fifteen

It was nearing five o'clock by the time they got back on the road heading out of Tucson. MacMillan wanted to stop for dinner, Tobias made a concession and went through a fast-food drive through. Nix ordered a single cheeseburger and a side salad, while the detective ordered a triple beef burger with bacon and three kinds of cheese, large fries, and a regular cola.

"Your arteries are probably screaming for help," Nix said before biting into her burger.

"Nah. I get lots of exercise with the horses," MacMillan said. "That and running around after my little sister."

"Your sister?" Tobias asked. "How old is she?"

"Thirty." He grinned at Tobias's roll of the eyes. "She just separated from her husband." His grin faded and sadness flitted across his face. "I told her she could move in with me while she gets back on her feet."

"That was nice of you," Nix said.

Tobias glanced in the rearview mirror and caught the detective's modest shrug.

"It was the right thing to do," MacMillan said. "Anyway, it helps me, too, because she's there during the day to keep an eye on things, and when I have a long day like this she can work the horses a bit for me."

"He has a quarter horse and an Appaloosa," Nix volunteered, her face alight with interest. "Our schedules haven't jelled enough for me to get over there for a ride, but one of these days I will."

"You bet." MacMillan met Tobias's gaze in the mirror. "You're invited, too, chief, but the horses probably won't let you near 'em."

"It's all right." Tobias knew from experience he'd have a hard time with horses. They sensed he was a predator and wouldn't settle down until they could no longer see or smell him. He'd told MacMillan before that he'd had horses when he'd first moved to Arizona a century and a half ago. It had taken long months of working with them, a few minutes each day, to get the horses to the point where they trusted him. But eventually they had and he'd been able to get around a little more easily. He missed that. His phone rang and he pulled it out of his pocket and frowned. "It's Braithwaite. I'm going to put him on speakerphone, don't let him know you're here." He connected the call. "Caine here."

"Tobias, it's Will Braithwaite." He paused. "Am I on speaker?"

"Yes, so I can be hands-free. I'm driving back up from Tucson." Tobias shot a glance at Nix, who raised her hands, clearly baffled as to why the vampire council member was calling. "What can I do for you, Councilor?" Tobias asked.

"Things are happening, getting out of control..." He paused.

When he didn't go on, Tobias thought maybe the call had been dropped. "Will?" he asked. "You still there?"

"Yes. Yes, I'm still here. I just...I really didn't want to go over this on the phone. It's not secure."

"Well, I won't be back in town for another..." Tobias glanced at the dashboard clock. "It'll be at least an hour and a half before I hit the 202."

"Maybe I can meet you somewhere."

"Will, what is this all about?" Tobias frowned and glanced at Nix.

MacMillan slid forward and leaned his arm against the back of Tobias's seat without making a sound.

"Are you alone?" Braithwaite asked him. "Is anyone in the car with you?"

"You're free to speak, Will." Tobias waited. As long as Braithwaite didn't realize he hadn't actually answered the question, he'd be all right.

"I've made some poor choices lately, Tobias," Braithwaite said. "Decisions made in a misguided attempt to garner more power for myself on the council. And they've come home to roost. People are dead, our own people and now a human. The council hasn't been completely forthcoming with you."

He saw Nix mouth the words "That's a surprise" and grimaced in agreement. "Forthcoming about what?" Tobias asked.

The other vampire cleared his throat. "You know we sent Dumond undercover to infiltrate a group of dissenters. What you don't know is that this group has been opening a small rift between dimensions and sending radio transmissions through. We wanted Dumond to find out who the leader is so we could deal with him."

Nix's hand came out and gripped his thigh. Braithwaite had just confirmed what Lucifer had told her.

"And you didn't feel this had any bearing on our current investigation? Especially after Dumond's identity was confirmed?" Tobias clenched his jaw. Damn, but the council was made up of slippery bastards.

"Some of us felt you should know. But the majority ruled."

"Majority meaning how many?" Tobias checked his mirrors, keeping an eye on traffic around him and trying to process what Braithwaite was telling him.

"Eight. Five of us voted to let you know about the transmissions. We were uncomfortable with keeping it hidden."

"You were one of the five?" Tobias asked.

"Yes. For all the good it did."

"Did Dumond find out who the leader is?"

"Not to our knowledge. On that I'm sure," he added hurriedly as if he were afraid Tobias would question his truthfulness.

"Okay. Let's say I believe you," Tobias said, partly to keep the councilor off balance and partly because he wasn't sure he did believe that Braithwaite had been in the minority. The vampire council member was clearly a minion of Deoul, and Deoul had never bothered to hide his disdain for humans. Tobias had no problem believing that the wily elf was in this up to his eyeballs. Where Deoul went, Braithwaite usually wasn't far behind. "Why did the others want to keep it a secret?"

"I can't say."

"Can't? Or won't?" Tobias couldn't keep the distrust from his voice.

"Can't." Braithwaite sounded sincere. It was difficult to tell when someone was lying over the phone because you couldn't pick up visual clues. There was no opportunity to sense elevated blood pressure, increased heart rate or sweating. It was even more difficult to tell when vampires lied because they had no physical changes at all to give themselves away. For the time being, Tobias would believe him. Braithwaite went on. "The first two murders seemed unrelated. They still seem unrelated from what I can tell. But Novellus and Dumond had a commonality, as frail as it might be."

"The rift," Tobias murmured.

"Exactly. But I'm the newest one on the council. I'm not included in a lot of discussions that go on behind closed doors. There are machinations behind the scenes to which I'm not privy."

Tobias pondered that for a moment, then asked, "Do you suspect that any of the council are involved with the group of dissenters?"

Braithwaite's sigh was heavy. "All I know is that powerful people are involved in this, Tobias. I don't know who, but I know they have influence. If they find out we know about it, our lives won't be worth spit. You know there's a tenuous peace between humans and prets right now. There are those who believe true peace only comes through chaos."

That shot a chill through Tobias. What Braithwaite just said had a familiar ring to it. "Will, who—"

"Look, I've said all I have to say. Good luck." He disconnected the call.

Tobias hit the end button on his phone. "Well, hell. This just keeps getting better and better."

"You're talking about the council being aware of the transmissions?" MacMillan asked.

"That, and what he said about chaos." Tobias clenched his jaw. "Someone I once knew used to say 'Righteous men live in peace and think they're free; only the enlightened can know true peace through anarchy and chaos.'" He clenched his jaw as memories seared him. The betrayal of a friend. The murder of a good man.

The never-ending guilt over the failure to protect.

Nix stared at him a moment, then turned to MacMillan and whispered, "Natchook."

Tobias swallowed back the rage at the mention of his enemy's name. The man who'd pretended to be his friend with the intent of gaining access to their people's leader, whom Tobias had sworn to protect with his own life if necessary.

Natchook had in reality been quite mad and a revolutionary intent on plunging their people into anarchy. He'd used Tobias for years and, when the time was right, had killed their leader before Tobias could stop him. Then he'd bribed a few officials, gone through the process to be stripped of his physical body, and escaped through the rift with the rest of the undesirables.

It was only after the fact that Tobias had learned that the name Natchook was an alias, though he hadn't had time to suss out the man's real identity. He did discover, though, that the bastard wasn't even from Tobias's planet. He had a parent who was of Tobias's species, but the other parent had been from another planet, another species entirely. Why Natchook had fixated on Kai Vardan was beyond him. But he had, and Vardan had lost his life as a result.

Tobias had chased Natchook from one dimension to another. He had no idea what his nemesis looked like in this world, but he knew he'd recognize him by his scent once he found him. And he would find him if it took the rest of time.

"This is just further proof that Natchook is behind this rift thing," Nix said. "Otherwise, how could Braithwaite have known that saying?"

"You forget, Braithwaite is the same species as me." Tobias glanced at her. "It's not out of the realm of possibility that he heard Natchook say that before his Influx."

"Did he come through the rift at the same time?" MacMillan slid back in his seat.

"I don't know. Hmph." Tobias thought it over, but couldn't ever remember anyone discussing Influx dates in the same breath as Braithwaite. But he was pretty certain Braithwaite had come through the rift centuries before Tobias and Natchook had.

"Wait." Nix gripped his thigh again. "Braithwaite said vampires and 'now a human' have been killed. How would he know that? We just found out ourselves."

The three of them fell silent, each lost in their own thoughts. As the sun began to set, Tobias turned on the headlights. Within an hour he pulled up behind MacMillan's truck, parked at the curb in front of council headquarters.

MacMillan opened his door but didn't get out. "You know, if someone in there"—he jerked his head toward the building—"knows something, there might be a file that's worth taking a look at." He hopped out of the SUV. "Just sayin'." His cell phone buzzed. He frowned and pulled it out of his pocket. "It's my sister. Excuse me," he said, and got out of the vehicle, closing the door behind him. "What's up?" Tobias overheard him say as he walked a few steps away from the SUV.

Nix twisted in her seat and faced Tobias. "There's a pretty big storage room in there," she said. "With files that go back decades."

"You really think they'd keep something like that in a paper file and not on a computer? Or, better yet, as an encrypted file on a flash drive?" Tobias asked.

"If that's the case, Dante's our man. He can look into that for us." Nix unfastened her seat belt. "But I don't want to miss the chance to find out if there's something on site. Do you?" She opened her door but waited to get out, looking at him expectantly.

He stared at the darkened building. "Close your door."

"Tobias, I know you have this whole we-need-to-abide-by-the-rules thing going on here, but I really think we need to do this."

Tobias turned his head and stared at her. "With my SUV parked right in front of the building?" He lifted one brow. "I want to move my car."

Before she could pull the door closed, MacMillan poked his head in. "I'm afraid I'm gonna have to leave you two kids to all the fun. I've gotta go."

"Is everything all right?" Nix asked.

The detective gave a shrug. "Yeah. It's just my sister. She's having some trouble at home." He glanced at the building. "You two watch yourselves in there." His hand came up in a gesture of good-bye and he turned and walked to his truck.

Nix leaned down and fished around in her purse, pulling out a small flashlight. Brandishing it with a triumphant air, she closed her door. "All right, let's do this thing."

Tobias drove the SUV around the block, parking a few side streets away from the building. As Nix opened her door, Tobias wrapped his fingers around her upper arm. "A few ground rules first." He waited until she looked at him, then he said, "If we run into anyone, let me do the talking."

"No problem. I'm off the case, remember?"

"That's what I mean." He couldn't keep his hand from drifting up to cup the back of her neck. He pulled her in for a lingering kiss. "If anyone asks," he murmured, his lips a breath away from hers, "I'll tell them I needed to pick something up."

"Pick what up?" She pressed her lips to the corner of his mouth. Once, twice, the light caresses encouraging him to slant his mouth over hers for a longer, hungrier taste of her mouth.

He swallowed her moan and lifted his mouth reluctantly. "I'll think of something." He rasped his thumb across her lips. "Ready?"

"For anything," Nix said with a slow upward tilt of her mouth.

It was a sultry smile, one full of promise, and Tobias wanted to do nothing more than take her right then and there in the darkened confines of the SUV. But they had a job to do. *After,* he assured himself. Once they were safely out of here and back home, he'd get her in bed and take his time with her. "Let's go," he said, stepping out of the vehicle.

A couple of minutes later he unlocked the back door of the council headquarters and peered in. "It's clear," he whispered, and went inside.

"I've worked here for three years. Nobody ever gave me a key to the damn building." Nix's quiet voice held a distinct note of malcontent. "Aren't you special?"

That last bit was much more sarcastic than disgruntled. He glanced over his shoulder to see her eyes twinkling with good humor. "You're just now figuring that out?" he asked softly.

She patted his rear. "Nope. I've known that for a long time. Sometimes the definition changed now and then, that's all. For the past five years, you've been really special," she said, making quote marks in the air.

Tobias shook his head at her, then stopped and held up a hand. One of the ever-present guards was coming their way. He tried the nearest door and found it unlocked. Pushing it open, he shoved Nix inside, then crowded into the tiny utility closet behind her. Her lips parted and she took a breath. He clamped his hand over her mouth. "Quiet," he mouthed.

The tip of her tongue tickled his palm. He narrowed his eyes. She licked his hand again, her eyes glittering with dancing sparks of yellow demon fire.

With his free hand Tobias grabbed a bottle of glass cleaner and sprayed it in the air. The strong ammonia smell should cover their scent long enough for them to be undetected by the guard making his rounds. He heard the shapeshifter as he went past the closet, whistling an off-key tune.

Tobias silently counted to ten, making sure he couldn't hear any movement before he eased open the door and peered around the edge. "Clear," he whispered, and started down the hallway, Nix right behind him. They ducked into the file room. Tobias closed the door with a soft click and then turned on the light in the windowless room. He stared at the two-dozen file cabinets lining the walls like victims awaiting a firing squad.

"Oh, my God. Just shoot me now," Nix muttered. She tucked the small flashlight into the front pocket of her jeans.

"This is part of the job," he rejoined, his eyes still affixed to the cabinets. Some of these files probably contained information that went back hundreds of years. He wondered if they had a file on him and Nix, then figured they most likely did. Maybe someday he'd see what was in his...

"Yeah, a part I don't really care for." She sighed. "Okay. I'll take this side of the room, you take that side."

They split up and quietly got to work. About thirty minutes into it, Nix said, "Tobias, come look at this."

He walked over to her. She had opened a drawer marked "Vampires A-C." He looked down at the file she held. His name was written on the tab, the manila file worn with age. "Looks like this has been looked at more than once."

"No kidding." She flipped it open.

Tobias grabbed it from her before she could begin reading. He'd done things in his past that he'd rather she not know about, things that he wasn't proud of. Things that still haunted his dreams. If she insisted on knowing what the council had on him, he'd tell her, but it would be better coming from him than from the pages of this file. He returned it to the drawer.

"Hey!" She stared at him. "Aren't you the least bit curious about what's in there?"

"I know what I've done, honey. There's nothing in that file that would surprise me."

"Not even if they know something you thought was a deep, dark secret?"

He shook his head. "Secrets have a way of coming out, no matter how hard you try to keep them." He tapped the top of the filing cabinet. "Let's get back to it, shall we?"

Nix grimaced but obligingly started going through the rest of the drawer. "All right, but someday you're going to have to tell me what's in that file that you don't want me to see."

"It's a deal." Tobias went back to the other side of the narrow room and started back on his search. After several minutes of going through paperwork on various shape-shifters, he pulled out a drawer marked "Demons." Several familiar names leaped out at him, including Lucifer Demonicus, Betty de la Fuente, and Finn Evnissyen. Knowing he and Nix had limited time, he resisted the urge to pull out their files.

"There's a file here on Dumond," Nix said, her voice hushed. "But I don't see anything about the rift or him going undercover."

"We may be on a fool's errand," Tobias answered. "But we had to try."

Over the next few hours they continued plowing through files until Tobias got done with his last row and went to help Nix finish up her side of the room.

"This is creepy, the amount of information they have in this room." Nix met his gaze. "Do they have files on humans over there?"

"Of course. Mostly politicians, police and fire departments, that sort of thing. Nothing on you," he said before she could ask.

"What, I don't rate a top-secret file?" She scowled.

"All the dirt on you is probably in your personnel file."

"Oh, right." She went to her knees and pulled open the last drawer, flipping quickly along the tabbed files. "There's nothing here," she said, her voice defeated. She turned her head just as Tobias hunkered down beside her.

Lips inches apart, their eyes met. Hers darkened to deep, dark chocolate lit by small yellow sparks. His own eyes began to burn. He couldn't very well berate her for letting her demon out when he knew his vampire was showing as well. Yet it still gave him pause, that he drew this reaction from her time and time again.

His hesitation vanished when she closed the distance between them, her soft mouth pressing against his, her tongue sliding between his lips. His need immediate and absolute, he cradled her head in his hands and deepened the kiss. His cock hardened, his fangs elongated. She drew back slightly. "I've never made out in a filing room before," she whispered.

"It's a first for me, too." He kissed the smile from her lips, then pulled away. "But we've got sharp-eared shape-shifters out there," he reminded her in a low voice. "Now is not the time. Or the place."

"Anytime. Anywhere. It's always the right time and place. With you." Nix traced her index finger across his lower lip. She leaned forward and paused, her eyes capturing Tobias's in a sensual snare. "Let me show you." As she dropped her mouth on his, her eyes fluttered closed.

Tobias wrapped his hands around her upper arms and stood, hauling her to her feet and into his arms. Without taking his lips from hers, he walked her backward until she was stopped by the outer wall. Hands on her hips, he angled her lower body and pressed against her softness.

She moaned into his mouth and lifted one leg, tilting her pelvis further, fitting the ridge of his erection into the V of her thighs.

He slid his hand from her hip, down her thigh, and cupped the back of her knee. He ate at her mouth like a starving man at a banquet. Greedy. Gluttonous.

She tugged his shirt out of his pants and ran her palms across the contours of his back. Then she slipped them around to the front of his waistband and started to unfasten his belt. "This is the challenge," she whispered against his mouth. "Can we be quiet enough to not attract the attention of the guards?"

Tobias unbuttoned her shirt. "You're quite the daredevil, aren't you?" Her warm hand wrapped around his cock, bringing him to full hardness. Keeping his voice low, he said, "Even if they don't hear us, they're going to smell us."

"If they haven't already. You're putting off a lot of pheromones there, Tobester." With a wicked grin Nix stroked his shaft, her thumb swiping over the sensitive tip. "I'm so ready for you." Her dark gaze met his, yellow sparks glittering with carnal fever.

He sucked in a reflexive breath. With a soft oath he unzipped her jeans and yanked them down to her ankles, then did the same with her panties. He spun her around, one hand on the small of her back urging her to bend. She braced her palms against the wall and arched her back, spreading her legs to open herself to him.

Tobias tested her readiness, trapping a growl in his throat at the slick heat he found between her thighs. He thrust home with one smooth, hard jab of his hips. Nix gasped and shoved against him, taking him even deeper.

Their joining was fast, furious, and wild. She muffled a moan against her forearm as he hammered into her again and again. Her core tightened around him like a fist as she met him thrust for thrust. Then her entire body stiffened, her sheath clenching around him with her climax.

Stifling his own shout, he gave himself over to his release. He threw back his head against the urge to bend forward and sink his fangs into her soft, giving throat. One more lunge of his hips and he held her against him, feeling her quaking around his cock in another orgasm. When it was over, and his brain started working again, he turned her around and drew up her panties and jeans. Looking up at her face he saw that blood smeared one corner of her mouth. With a low curse Tobias leaned down and swiped his tongue over the rich liquid, growling at the salty tang on his taste buds. That little taste only made him want more, but he couldn't go there. "We need to get out of here," he muttered, tucking his penis back into his pants and zipping them up.

"I'm ready to go as soon as my legs stop shaking." Nix smiled and raked her fingers through her hair, making her curls even wilder. She glanced around the room. "I really can't believe we just did that."

He shot her a quick look. "You're not disappointed, I hope."

Her eyes widened. "God, no. That was...was..." She shook her head. "There are no words."

"Well, that's a first," he whispered, and swooped in to press a quick, hard kiss on her mouth. "Nix de la Fuente is speechless."

"Yeah, well, enjoy it while it lasts, Tobester." She gave him a wink.

He put one finger to his lips and then eased open the door. He took a quick look around, listened intently for a couple of seconds, then motioned for her to follow him. A few minutes later they were back in his SUV. Nix was a little breathless, though he wasn't sure if it was from running or because she was now laughing so hard.

"Oh, my God. I feel like a teenager again, sneaking around and making out in the principal's office." She looked at him with sparkling eyes.

He raised a brow. "You made out in the principal's office?" He started the SUV and pulled away from the curb.

"Just one time." She grinned and pulled her seat belt across her body, fastening it with a quick click.

"Hmm. Something new I just learned about you." Before he could say more, his phone rang. Tobias answered it, hitting the speakerphone button so Nix could hear as well.

Braithwaite's voice, tense and low, came across the line. "I have more information but...can you come to my house?"

"Sure. When?" Tobias shared a glance with Nix.

"Now." Braithwaite's voice became even more strained. "Right now. I'm afraid. I'm not sure how long...Just get here." He hung up the phone.

Tobias disconnected the call and slipped his phone back into his pocket. "Well?" he asked, looking at Nix. "Are you coming with me?"

"Try and keep me away," Nix said.

He nodded. "Call Dante. Tell him we'll meet up with him at your place and go to Braithwaite's from there."

* * *

"It's a trap." Nix couldn't keep the worry from her voice.

"Maybe." Tobias held out his hand. When she laced her fingers through his, he whispered, "Good thing I have you to watch my back."

"You don't think it'll be too dangerous for me?" She sent him a challenging look.

"Not for you."

From the backseat came a low snort. "Oh, I get it." Dante leaned forward. "You two kissed and made up."

Nix caught the glitter of carnal memories glinting in Tobias's eyes. "Something like that," he said as he changed lanes. "Braithwaite lives in Avondale. Whether I take the 202 and loop around or get off and go the other direction, it's still going to take some time to get there."

In fact, it was almost an hour before they pulled up in front of his house, a two-story Californian territorial on the north side of town. Nix got out of the SUV and stood by the open door for a moment, studying her surroundings. Just about every room in the house was lit up, and the outside was illuminated by outdoor security spots that shone fully upon the open front door. The slight tang of copper hung in the air. Blood. All of her instincts kicked into overdrive. "Something's wrong," she murmured with a glance toward Tobias.

He carefully closed his door, the sound of it latching into place barely audible. "I agree." He glanced at her. "Eyes open," he cautioned.

She nodded and closed her car door just as carefully as he had done his. Dante did the same and joined her. She drew her gun but kept her hand at her side as they walked toward the front door.

As they reached the house, the scent of copper became

stronger, especially when Tobias eased the door all the way open. He shot her a cautionary look and drew his weapon. One hand wrapped around the grip, the other hand supported his wrist, just above groin level. It brought to mind all sorts of images of him holding his other weapon and how well he used it.

Nix cleared her head and followed him into the house, deliberately keeping her gaze off his delectable derriere. She needed to stay focused on the job, not be distracted by admiring his assets.

She drew in a slow breath and focused all of her attention on the house. As far as she could tell, she, Tobias, and Dante were the only ones in the house, but she couldn't smell or hear nearly as well as Tobias could, so she'd wait for his all clear before she'd relax.

Tobias stopped, his stance alert, his nostrils flaring as he smelled the air. After a few seconds he holstered his gun. "We're the only ones here," he said. He blew out a breath and headed toward the back of the house. "The only ones alive and kicking, that is."

"Though at least one of us is more undead than alive, really. Right?" Dante glanced around the foyer.

Nix slid her weapon back in its holster but didn't snap the safety strap in place. She wanted to be able to draw—fast—if she needed to.

Dante kept his weapon drawn. "I'll check upstairs and let you know if I find anything."

She watched him go up the stairs, then turned back toward Tobias. "I smell blood."

"Yeah." He peered around the edge of the room at the end of the hallway. "The smell is coming from in here." He entered the room cautiously.

Nix followed him and looked around the room. Wealth screamed from every corner—expensive paintings, all askew, on the walls, built-in bookshelves with their contents mostly on the floor, and large, dark mahogany furniture including an antique pedestal desk with ornate carvings on the sides set in the center of the room. The thing was four feet deep and easily weighed at least three hundred pounds. She paused in front of it, glancing around the room. "There was a struggle here." Squatting down, she looked over the floor lamp lying on its side, the glass globe in shatters. The base of the lamp was dented as if it had smashed into something.

Tobias walked around to the other side of the desk and stopped. "Yeah, and Will lost."

"What?" She joined him and saw Braithwaite on the floor. Death had already begun to glaze his wide-open eyes. Blood had pooled around him on the wood-planked floor. Through the mess of his throat she caught a glimpse of bone and realized he'd nearly been decapitated.

"If we'd gotten here earlier..." Tobias scrubbed the back of his neck with his hand.

"His blood loss would have been too much for either of us to make any difference." She put one hand on his arm. "He's been nearly decapitated. It would have taken gallons of blood administered seconds after he sustained that wound for him to recover. I'm not even sure that would have done it, either."

Tobias remained silent but she felt a slight push of pheromones her way. She looked away from Braithwaite and tried not to feel guilty for being so suspicious of him. Perhaps he really had been trying to do the right thing. "Well, it's probably not a coincidence that Braithwaite called you, wanting to give you more information, and then ended up dead before he could."

"Where murder's involved, there's no such thing as coincidence." He squatted down beside the body, touching Braithwaite's jaw, then sweeping his fingers over the vampire's eyes to close them. "Rigor hasn't even set in yet." He glanced up at Nix. "He was most likely killed within the last hour." He stood again and headed toward a corner of the room.

Nix could hear him sniffing as he moved. "What is it? What do you smell?" She started his way only to stop when he raised one hand.

He pointed to blood splatter on one of the bookshelves. "This is not Will's blood." Leaning closer, he inhaled. He stiffened and rage emanated from him in waves. "It's *him.*"

"Him? Him who?" Nix caught her breath. "You mean…Natchook?" Her heart did a quick rat-a-tat behind her ribs. They'd suspected he was involved, but to actually end up with proof made it all seem surreal for a moment.

"I'd recognize that stench anywhere." When Tobias glanced at Nix, she saw his pupils were completely dilated, giving his eyes that eerie, otherworldly look. "He's been injured." His jaw tightened, the muscles twitching. "I can't tell how badly."

She glanced at the desk. The drawers were open, the contents clearly rifled through. "He didn't come here just to kill Braithwaite. He was looking for something."

Tobias started toward the door. "I have to go after him. Now." He pointed at the splatter he'd identified as Natchook's blood. "That's still fresh."

"No. Tobias, stop!" When he paused at the door, looking over his shoulder at her, his entire stance one of supreme impatience, she hurried up to him. "We don't know how many people Natchook had with him. You go off half-cocked, by yourself..." She looked away. "We have to see if there's anything they missed here."

Dante walked up to them, holstering his gun. "Upstairs is clear. So is the rest of the downstairs." He looked back and forth between them. "If anybody cares."

"You two can look through the house for evidence," Tobias said, his voice a hard rasp. "I'm not going to let the bastard get away, not when I'm this close."

"Looks like they went out the back door," Dante said as he eased past Tobias. "There's a blood smear on the kitchen island and a few drops leading out the back."

"One of us should go with you," Nix said.

"No." Tobias held up one hand when she started to argue. "This is my fight. Not yours." He walked up to her and put his fingers under her chin. He tipped her face up and planted a gentle kiss on her mouth. A good-bye kiss? Without giving her a chance to respond he left the room at a run.

She heard the back door slam and scowled. Was that it? The way he acted, their relationship might be over as soon as it had begun. And to chase after him now would mean potentially losing valuable evidence. She had a job to do and had to trust, for the moment, that he could take care of himself. If they lived through this, she was going to kick his butt later for ditching her. "What did the rest of the house look like?" she asked Dante, trying to ignore the way her lips still tingled from that brief kiss.

"Pristine." He walked into the room and surveyed the

damage. "Maybe they already found what they were looking for."

"Maybe." She studied the desk. From the power cord lying on the desk, it appeared a computer had been hooked up on there. "Looks like they took his laptop. It seems to me if he had something he really wanted to hide, he wouldn't have kept it on his computer or in a drawer." The council certainly hadn't kept any important, incriminating evidence in that file room. She grew warm just thinking about their tryst at headquarters.

"What're you thinking?"

She hoped he wasn't asking what had made her face flush. Pointing to the desk, she said, "I'm thinking that Braithwaite was a vampire with vampire strength. He could lift a three-hundred-pound desk with no effort at all. If he wanted to keep something secret, what better place to hide it? Help me with this." She went to one edge of the desk. When Dante positioned himself at the other edge, she said, "Flip it on its front."

Dante managed his side but Nix struggled with hers. "Set it down," she told him.

"I guess Tobias should've stuck around."

"We can do this. Just give me a minute." Nix closed her eyes and took a deep breath. She hadn't called up the full power of her demon on purpose in almost five years, not since Tobias had left her. It easily bubbled to the surface whenever her emotions were high and she spent countless hours fighting it back down. But now, now she needed the additional strength that going demon would bring.

She reached deep inside and searched out the burning that was a constant part of her. She relaxed her control and gave a moan as the fire overtook her. Her skin felt aflame, her gut churned and roiled. Her horn buds erupted from her forehead. With a flex of her fingers she opened her eyes. "Let's try again," she said.

"Wow."

She gave Dante a second to adjust to her new image, then said, "Come on, let's do this."

They flipped the desk to its front, the remaining items on the top spilling to the floor, and she gave a cry of elation. Reaching over, she pulled a taped manila envelope from beneath the base of the desk. "See?"

"Well, aren't you the clever one?" Dante leaned his hip against the desk. "So was Braithwaite, apparently."

She opened the envelope and peered inside, then held it over the bottom of one of the desk's pedestals. Several folded papers and a flash drive fell out. She picked up the small drive and looked at Dante. Already she could feel the demon receding. "Do you suppose this is Rinda's?"

He took it and slipped it into his jeans pocket. "We'll find out as soon as we can get to a computer."

"Yeah, you can do your computer mojo magic." She unfolded one of the papers. "These look like blueprints of some sort."

"Schematics," Dante said. "May I?" He held out his hand. She gave him the drawing, and he studied it more closely. "I'm no engineer, but this looks like a radio transmitter." He pointed to one specific area.

"How do you know?" She leaned in to get a better look.

"I've done some messing around with ham radios." He didn't look up from the schematics. "This here, it kind of looks like a variable frequency oscillator, this might be whatever they've constructed to open a mini rift." He handed the paper back to Nix.

She looked at the other documents. "More of the same," she murmured. She folded them all up, smaller than before, and tucked them into the back pocket of her jeans. "We'll need to get these to an expert. Someone we can trust."

Dante nodded.

She blew out a breath. "All right, then. Let's go after Tobias." And if he knew what was good for him, he'd better be all right.

Chapter Sixteen

As Nix and Dante went through the back gate of the property, they both drew their weapons. Dante pulled a small flashlight from his jacket pocket and flicked it on. He shone it on the ground, lighting their way.

Even though he was no longer in sight, Tobias wasn't hard to track. He'd left a wake of pheromones a smell-impaired hound dog could follow. But more disturbing, the blood trail left by Natchook was equally easy to follow.

Within fifteen minutes Dante had taken off his jacket and had it slung over one arm. Neither one of them was dressed for a hike, but they couldn't let Tobias go off on his own to face his enemy. For one thing, Tobias wasn't thinking clearly and so was at a disadvantage. For another, from what she'd heard, Natchook tended to surround himself with people willing to martyr themselves for the cause, whatever it might be.

Tobias, as strong as he was, could very well be outmanned.

She pressed her lips together and picked up the pace. Already she might be too late. If anything happened to him…

"Nix?" Dante kept pace with her, his gaze darting

around their surroundings. His eyes reflected his concern that they were fast approaching the outskirts of town and soon would be heading up the White Tank Mountains. "Something wrong?"

"Natchook rarely travels alone" was all she said.

"Damn it." Dante's voice was low, his epithet heartfelt. He was quick; she knew he realized the danger Tobias was in. The peril they *all* were in.

Another twenty minutes and they had left civilization behind. There wasn't much of anything except sand and scrub. The lights of town were far behind them, only Dante's small flashlight and a sky full of stars lighted their way. The moon provided some light but kept ducking behind clouds.

They reached a rocky area and scrambled over it, taking care where they placed their hands and feet. Rattlers could be sleeping among the rocks. Neither one of them wanted or could afford to be bitten.

Nix stopped, taking a deep breath. She'd lost the blood trail. And Tobias's pheromone scent. Her heart, already pounding from exertion, began banging against her ribs. "Damn it!"

Dante looked at her. "What?"

"I've lost the scent."

"What?" He glanced around. "How could you lose the scent?"

She scowled. "It's not like I'm a hound dog, Dante. My nose isn't nearly as good as a werewolf's, or a vampire's for that matter." She spread her hands. "The blood trail ends here. And Tobias must have scaled his pheromones back so far I can't smell them anymore."

"He can do that?"

"When he wants to." She remembered the waves of pheromones he'd given off at that first crime scene and how she'd told him to ramp it down. He hadn't paid her any attention then. Now when she wanted him to be putting off a chemical trail he didn't. A coyote howled, the sound lonely and sad. It seeped into her soul, heightening her fear. She couldn't stop the shiver that sliced down her spine.

"Somebody just walk over your grave?" Dante asked.

"Don't say that." Nix had to pick up the trail again. Tobias needed them. "Give me a minute." She walked in an ever-widening circle, bending now and then to look at the rocks, but mostly sniffing the air, trying to grab on to something, anything. After a few minutes she paused. "Oh, hell. I don't know what I'm doing." She looked at Dante. In the darkness she could only see the outline of his body. "I'm not a tracker. I have no idea which way to go."

"Let's split up." He walked over to her. "You go that way, I'll go this way," he said with a gesture. "One of us at least might stumble on to Tobias and be some help."

"We don't even..." She broke off and held up one hand.

"What?"

"I thought I heard something." When he started to talk again she shushed him. Male voices drifted to her on the wind.

"Well?" Dante leaned close and whispered. "What is it?"

She turned her head to one side, then the other, trying to gauge where the voices came from. It was only because of her demon abilities that she could hear them. From what she could tell they were at least a quarter of a mile away. "Men talking," she said just as quietly. She pointed to the right. "From that direction. I think."

"You need to be sure, Nix. If we head off in the wrong direction..."

"I know. We'd be too far away to help Tobias...if we aren't already too late." She took a few steps toward the sound but the voices faded away. She stopped. After a few seconds they began talking so she started up again, Dante right beside her. She glanced at him.

"What?" he asked.

"It's just...Thank you for treating me like a professional, Dante."

His brows dipped. "How else would I treat you, Nix? You're not some little woman who needs to be tucked up safe at home." His expression was that of the serious warrior she knew he could be. "There's no one else I would want watching my back."

It was a good thing he felt that way, because her demon tendencies were about to be let out to whoop some vampire ass and he was going to have front row seats.

A scream pierced the air. Dante swore. "Even I heard that."

"This way," Nix said, and took off at a run.

She heard Dante's pounding footsteps behind her. The beam from his flashlight bounced over the rocky ground as he ran. They went down the side of a narrow wash, their feet sliding on the loose dirt. Once they'd scrambled up the other side, they slowed. A slight breeze lifted Nix's hair off her neck and brought with it the scent of vampires.

Not one or two. Several.

Her pulse quickened. She brought her gun up, clasping her left hand around her right to support the weapon, and adjusted her stance to be able to deal with the recoil when she pulled the trigger. Bullets might not kill a vamp, but they could sure as hell slow one down long enough for her to finish him off with her blade. She moved forward cautiously, staying alert to where Dante was so she wouldn't shoot him by accident.

Another few steps and she caught movement out of the corner of her eye. She spun to face the threat, her pulse taking off like a rocket engine. One of the largest vampires she'd ever seen barreled toward her, fangs bared, hands outstretched. She fired three rounds, each catching him in the upper chest. He flinched, blood streaming from his wounds, but kept right on coming.

She heard more gunshots coming from the direction where she'd last seen Dante. She hoped he had better luck than she'd had with her weapon.

Tobias was nowhere in sight, but she could hear him now, his voice low but urgent. She focused on the vamp heading her way and told herself that if Tobias was gabbing with someone he was in no immediate jeopardy. Not like she was. A quick glance showed her Dante was holding his own, so for the moment she forced the worry about him out of her mind.

Another vampire headed toward her. She fired until she was out of bullets. He fell to the ground, groaning. The first vamp, shirt front bloodied, came toward her, arms outstretched, reaching, grasping. Holstering her gun, she prepared herself for close combat. She slid her knife from its scabbard and held it at her side. Her breath came quick between parted lips. Adrenaline raced through her bloodstream, her vision yellowed as her inner demon began making itself known. She backed up and then took a few running steps forward, launching herself feetfirst at the vamp.

She caught him in the chest, her feet thudding against the bullet wounds. He roared with pain as he went down, Nix on top of him. She slashed across his throat, then rolled out of his reach and bounced to her feet. The trick now was to *stay* out of his reach while he bled out.

She took a breath. *Damn it.* She recognized that smell! This was the bastard that had been leaving a demon scent at each of the crime scenes. Which meant…Either he'd been making out with a demon right before they'd happened on him, which she thought pretty unlikely, or else the son of a bitch had been dining on demons. That would explain why there'd been a demon scent at each scene, familiar but somehow different. The demon blood having mingled with his own had for a short time subtly altered his scent.

The second vamp rose to his feet and lunged for her. She ducked under his arm and shoved him as she went behind him. With a quick glance she saw Dante straight behind her vamp, fighting his own battle. He had wounded the vampire he fought, but he was still at a disadvantage.

As much as she'd like to help him, she had her own six-and-a-half-foot problem to take care of. And he was coming at her again. This time, as she tried to dodge him, he latched his fingers onto her hair and held fast. She couldn't contain a yelp of pain. He laughed and hauled her back against him, wrapping his free arm around her waist. "Looks like I got you now, girly. Game's over."

When they had their fangs on display some vampires could talk and sound menacing, and others...not so much. This guy's lisp was so pronounced he sounded like a girly-man. He was the pot calling the kettle black. And she was tired of it. No more Ms. Nice Guy from her.

"Don't call me girly," she ground out. Knowing she needed an edge, she actively summoned her demon side, letting it burst into a full, glorious explosion of strength. Everything became tinged in yellow, her insides burned with rage. Her horn buds popped, and for once she welcomed the pain that accompanied the stretching of the skin on her forehead.

She slumped against his arm, pulling him off balance. Then she reared up, slamming the back of her head into his face. He grunted, his hold loosening enough for her to pull free. As she left what felt like half her hair in his fist, she growled and spun her leg up, ramming it into his gut.

He staggered back. His eyes completely black, he stared at her for a second, rage turning his face red. Blood from his bullet wounds covered the front of his white T-shirt, making it stick to his chest, and now also dripped from his nose. His tongue swept out, licking it off his lips. "You're gonna pay for that one, girly." His hands fisted. "You'll die screaming for mercy."

Nix shot a quick glance over his shoulder. Tobias appeared at the top of a rise, heading her way at top speed, when he was tackled by yet another vamp. He rolled to his feet, going into a fighter's stance as yet another vamp ran up to help his buddy. He appeared to be holding his own against the two vampires he fought—though all three showed signs of battle with blood and dirt covering them—and Dante had managed to stay out of the grasp of his vamp. She put her attention back on the bloodsucker in front of her. "You really think you can take me, *akĥ khantu*?"

He bristled at being called a carrion eater. She hoped her false disdain based on a long-lived prejudice would keep his outrage amped up and hopefully cause him to make a fatal mistake.

He came at her again and caught hold of her jacket. She twisted out of it, leaving it hanging in his grip, and slammed her foot into his knee. His leg crumpled beneath him with a satisfying crunch of bone and he went down.

He yelled and lurched forward, reaching for her. She dodged him, but he managed to grab hold of the hem of her jeans. Her momentum carried her forward then to the ground. She braced her fall with her hands, her eyes widening as her momentum almost face-planted her into a small barrel cactus. With a lithe twist, she turned onto her back and kicked the vamp as he pulled himself up her body.

One knee caught him in the chin. His head rocked back but he kept coming. She slammed her fist into his jaw, grimacing at the hard smack of bone on bone, and wincing again when he turned his head, catching her knuckle with the tip of one fang.

He caught her wrists in his hands and held her arms at her sides. His tongue did a slow lick over his fang, and his eyes narrowed. "Less than human but more than demon." His slow grin was malevolent. "I've never done a half-breed before." He licked his lips, the action bringing an image to her mind of Princess Leia facing Jabba the Hutt. Disgusting vermin.

"And you're not going to have one now." Tobias's voice was hard. He yanked the vampire off her and tossed him several feet away. Then Tobias pulled Nix to her feet. "You all right?"

"Fine. I had him." She watched the vamp pick himself up and turn toward them. Glancing over her shoulder, she saw two more heading their way. "We got more company," she said with a lift of her chin.

He turned his head. "Damn it." He looked at her again, indecision in his stance, written on his face.

"I've got this one," she insisted. Without waiting for his response, she turned to meet her foe's attack with a fist to his gut.

Tobias hesitated long enough to watch the vamp double over. Nix's knife made two quick slashes and the vamp's neck was sliced from ear to ear. She let him fall to the desert floor.

* * *

Tobias turned toward the two vamps coming at him, knowing the one she'd just dropped would be too busy bleeding out now to be any further threat. From the corner of his eye he saw Nix head toward MacMillan. Tobias was amazed that the detective was still standing, though he was bloody from being punched in the face. His vamp was toying with him, like a devil with a saint.

Nix would take care of that.

Tobias bent his knees in a fighter's stance. "Just what game are you playing?" he asked, looking at the vampire on his left. He was small of stature and thin, stronger than he looked, even for a vamp. Dark hair and eyes, swarthy skin. A stranger to look at, but familiar to Tobias even with the new face and body.

Natchook slowed and stopped. He wore a satchel at his side, the strap crossed over his body. He kept one hand on the top of the bag. "The same game I've always played. Anarchy is the only effective law of the land. Lasting peace can only be achieved through chaos." He shook his head, his lips curling into a sneer. "You never could see that though, could you, my friend?"

"We are not friends. We never were." Tobias clenched his fists. He could hear the sounds of fighting from behind him and resisted the urge to look. To let himself be distracted at this moment could prove to be a fatal mistake. He had to trust Nix's skills and ability to take care of herself. And now that she'd gone demon, he'd have to worry about her sanity.

God above, he hoped she could come back from this. If she went insane because of him and his obsession, if Natchook took away the one person on this planet who mattered the most to him...

Natchook clasped his hands behind his back. "You don't understand. You never could." He leaned forward slightly, the light of fanaticism brightening his eyes. "Sacrifices have to be made. Leader Vardan was one of many, with many more to come."

"Like Braithwaite? And Dumond and Amarinda? Pickett?"

Natchook gave a slight incline of his head. "They all served their purpose in their own way. Amarinda was...collateral damage. She wasn't involved, though I would have welcomed her to the cause. But she was getting too close and I am not about to let anyone ruin my plans. Not now."

Tobias held back the relief he felt at hearing Rinda hadn't been mixed up with this insane bastard.

Natchook went on. "And Braithwaite... Well, he was useful, since he was a member of the council. But his loyalty wavered. He outlived that usefulness." He paused. "You're on the list of sacrifices to be made. No surprise there, I think."

On one hand it was gratifying to know he'd made that much of an impact on the other man, but on the other hand... not so great to be on someone's hit list. "Yeah, I figured that out when you stopped and waited for me to catch up to you." Tobias shifted his gaze to Natchook's crony who was starting to inch his way to Tobias's right. "Just what was at Braithwaite's that you had to kill him for it?"

"What, you expect me to tell you all my plans?" Natchook rolled his eyes. "The villain spilling his guts only happens in the movies, my friend." He lifted his chin. "Not that I'm admitting to being a villain. I do what's necessary and nothing more."

"Humor me." Tobias crossed his arms, striving for an indifferent attitude toward the crony who was now behind him. In truth he was less concerned about an attack from the rear than he was with the bad guy leaving Nix and MacMillan alone. He needed to keep these two vampires' focus on him.

Natchook reached into the pocket of his jacket and pulled out a black box roughly the size of a cell phone. It had several small dials and what looked to be a couple of retractable antennae. "Braithwaite was holding on to the research Amarinda had done on the rift and the schematics for this little thing, but we couldn't find them at his house. He said he'd hidden them off-site and wouldn't say where, even when I started skinning him." His eyes reflected his enjoyment of the act. "But no matter. I have this"—he waggled the device—"and can reverse engineer another one."

"That's what you're using to open a mini rift?" Tobias frowned. It seemed such a simplistic machine. And a hell of a lot smaller than he'd thought it would be.

"It doesn't look like much, does it?" Natchook stroked his hand across the top. "It's amazing how such a little gadget can do such a wondrous thing." His eyes glittered, lips stretching in a broad grin. "Ain't technology grand?"

"Just what is it you hope to achieve?" Tobias knew Natchook's goal on their home planet had been to overthrow the government and ensconce himself as some sort of dictator. The assassination attempt had succeeded, but instead of the people rallying around Natchook they had cried for his death. So he'd fled, Tobias on his heels.

"I told you. It's about what I've always wanted to achieve. It doesn't matter where we are, my goals have never changed." Disdain flattened his mouth. "Humans are weak and easily distracted. They're so concerned about the politics of things they aren't keeping their eyes on the ball. I'll have my chance to run things the way they should be. The way I want them to be."

"You couldn't screw up our world, so you thought you'd try this one?" Tobias dropped his hands to his sides, hyper aware of the vamp behind him inching his way closer. Another few seconds and he'd be back in a fight to the death with these two. "You've got balls, I'll give you that."

He heard MacMillan groan and glanced around in time to see Nix pull the vamp off the detective. Blood streamed down MacMillan's shoulder from a bite but he was steady on his feet. The vamp hadn't been able to take enough blood—MacMillan would be fine. Well, fine as long as he and Nix could take care of the guy. Tobias put his attention back on Natchook.

"You just can't ever leave well enough alone, can you?" Natchook paused, his eyes narrowing. "What name is it you go by these days? Tobias?" He smirked. "That's rather a girly-man name, isn't it?"

"And what's *your* name now?" Tobias paused for effect. "Sally Sunshine?"

Instead of getting a rise out of him, Natchook only laughed.

Tobias shook his head. "This is a new world, Natchook. We're guests here. You have no right to—"

"Don't stand there, drowning me with your two-bit morality." Natchook scowled. He slipped the small rift device back into the pocket of his jacket. "I have the right to do whatever I feel is necessary. It was my birthright to lead."

"Just because you have royal ancestors doesn't mean squat. If you look hard enough, I'll just bet you find that a lot of our people have ties at some level or another to the royal family. Hell, I think I had an eighth cousin twice removed who was the son of a grand duke. But we chose democracy over monarchy centuries ago." Before Tobias could say anything more, the vamp behind him attacked. Tobias staggered forward. Expecting Natchook to take advantage, he was surprised when the other man took several steps away from him. And as teeth sank into the side of his neck, Tobias had to turn his attention to the vampire on his back. He punched his fist into the vamp's face, but couldn't get any real power behind the blows.

Without hesitation he straightened his index and middle fingers and jabbed backward as hard as he could, right in the vamp's eyes. The vampire shrieked in pain and dropped off Tobias's back. Tobias whirled around and with a quick twist of his wrists broke the vamp's neck. He let the body drop to the ground, knowing the vampire would die within seconds without a fresh infusion of blood to help him heal.

He lunged at Natchook and slammed him to the desert floor. Before he could sink his fangs into his old foe's throat, Natchook got his feet between them and catapulted Tobias into the air. Tobias hit the ground, hard, several yards away. He rolled to his feet and charged forward, catching Natchook in the midsection and knocking him down again.

Tobias managed to get in a couple of blows before Natchook twisted, getting on top of Tobias to straddle him. His fist to Tobias's jaw twisted his head to the side. As fangs slid deep into the side of his neck, Tobias growled and tried to buck Natchook off him.

Natchook raised his head, holding Tobias in place with one arm across his throat, and opened his mouth wide to bare fangs stained by Tobias's blood. "You're a pathetic weakling, Tobias. This is what comes..." He leaned close. "...from not drinking live," he whispered. "You. Are. Nothing." He leaned back slightly, his laugh low, full of disdain. He bent forward again, his black eyes reflecting Tobias's image.

"Hey!" Nix stood a few feet away, blood dripping

down her right arm, a long gash across her left cheek. Her eyes glowed with demon fire, horn buds parted her bangs, and the structure of her face was harder. Alien.

Tobias felt dread ice through him. She was as fully demon as he'd ever seen her. Would she be able to return to her humanity with her mind intact?

"Get off him, you son of a bitch." Her slender hands clenched at her sides.

"You just wait your turn, girly. I'll be right with you." Natchook turned his attention back to Tobias.

"Get out of here," Tobias told Nix. "Go."

"I got your back, remember?" Her breasts rose with her deep breath, then she ran full tilt at Natchook, spreading her arms and diving through the air like a linebacker sacking the quarterback.

With a growl Natchook caught her and tossed her aside as if she were weightless. She slammed into the unforgiving bulk of a large boulder. She grunted with the impact and groaned as she hit the ground.

Natchook bent to Tobias again, drawing on him strongly. Tobias felt himself growing weaker, even as he continued to struggle. Finally Natchook stopped and got to his feet. He stood a moment, looking down at Tobias. "You're as weak as you ever were," he said. Incredibly his voice seemed to hold a note of regret. "We could have done great things together if you just had more stones."

Tobias tried to rise, managed to get himself up on one elbow before the blood loss made everything go black. As he succumbed he heard Nix's low cry.

Stirring, he wasn't sure how long he had been out, but felt someone patting his cheek, hard, then heard MacMillan's voice. "Come on, sleeping beauty, wake up. Damn it, Tobias. Wake up!" Another smack, this one even harder.

Tobias opened his eyes and grabbed MacMillan's wrist as he prepared to slap him again. "How long have I been out?" he asked as he struggled to sit up.

MacMillan helped him. "Less than a minute, I think." He glanced around. "I don't know where he is." He looked at Tobias, fear darkening his eyes. "He took Nix."

Tobias braced his hands on the ground and tried to push himself up, cursing when in his weakness he fell back to the ground.

MacMillan muttered a string of cuss words and rolled up his sleeve. He thrust his wrist under Tobias's nose. "Here."

Tobias looked up at him.

"You need blood, right? Otherwise..." He shook his head. "We're all done for."

Tobias met the detective's eyes. "You may need to stop me."

"Right." MacMillan's jaw tightened. "Just do it."

Tobias grasped his wrist in both hands and sank his fangs in deep. Within seconds he felt strength returning, oxygen rushing to his organs, his muscles. He let go of MacMillan. "You all right?"

"Dandy," he said with a slight grimace. "Find Nix."

Tobias got to his feet.

"I'm here." Nix's voice came from behind him and he whirled around to see her standing several feet away. She looked frail, human, even with the demon peeking out of yellow eyes.

Natchook had one hand wrapped around her waist, the other cupped her chin. Blood smeared her throat, stained the front of her shirt. The same blood that rimmed Natchook's mouth.

Tobias went cold. Then hot. He took a step forward but stopped when Natchook *tsked* him. "Be very careful what you do next, Tobias."

Tobias froze and focused on Nix. She blinked slowly, her head lolling, clearly only upright because of Natchook's hand on her chin. Tobias could ascertain her heartbeat, but it was faint.

And growing fainter with each passing second.

She might be greatly weakened, but she was still scrappy. "Is this what he was like before? Hiding behind a woman?" She scoffed, the sound faint and dry. "No wonder he botched things up."

Natchook's hand moved to her throat, choking off her words. "I really don't care to hear the prey trash talking the hunter." His gaze never left Tobias. "You can save the girl or you can chase me. Which is more important—her life or your revenge?" He quirked his brows. "Your choice. Seems you never can protect the ones you're supposed to." With a low laugh, Natchook let go of Nix. As she collapsed to the ground like a marionette whose strings had abruptly been cut, he spun on his heel and ran.

There were no choices here. There was only one thing to do. Tobias ran to Nix and dropped to his knees, single-minded attention on the woman he loved. He drew her carefully into his arms and cradled her against his chest. With a trembling hand he brushed sweat-dampened hair away from her soft cheek.

Her eyes fluttered open. Her eyes were once again the chocolate brown he loved, all trace of the demon gone. "You all right?" she whispered.

He gave a choked laugh. She lay dying in his arms and her concern was for him? He leaned down and pressed a kiss to her dry lips. "I'm fine, sweetheart." He swallowed. "God, I'm sorry. So sorry. I should've been watching out for you."

MacMillan knelt beside him, though Tobias was barely aware of anything outside of the woman in his arms. For once the detective had nothing frivolous to say. Tobias spared him a glance and saw the devastated expression on MacMillan's face. He truly cared about Nix. Tobias actually felt a bit comforted that the other man joined him in his misery.

"It's not your fault." Nix's voice rasped from her ravaged throat. "You couldn't have known he'd go after me."

He shook his head. "I *should* have known."

"Where is he?"

Tobias shoved aside the guilt for the moment. Nothing would be achieved by letting his culpability distract him from the situation at hand. Nix needed him. Now more than ever. He nodded in answer to her question. "Don't worry about him, sweetheart." He spared a quick look at their surroundings. The other vamps were all dead and of no further threat. "You're safe now."

"*We're* safe." Her unfocused glance traveled to MacMillan. "You okay?" Her attention focused on his wrist. Her fine brows knit in a frown. "You're bleeding."

"Don't worry about me, darlin'." When her gaze went to the blood on his shoulder, he gave a lopsided grin. "My first, and second, vampire bite."

Tobias felt her tense in his arms. "He'll be all right, sweetheart."

"You're sure?"

"I'm sure." He leaned down and pressed a kiss to her forehead. "He would have had to have been drained in order for the vampire essence released in the bite to have any effect."

"Well, that's good to know," MacMillan muttered. "But you need to do something about *this*," he added, motioning toward Nix. "Now."

Tobias stared down at Nix. Her skin was as pale and thin as paper. She labored to breathe, the air rasping in her throat. She was cool to the touch, and he knew she didn't have long to live. A few minutes at best.

Pain clawed at his insides, churning his gut with regret. To save her life he'd have to take her humanity away from her. Take away the one thing she valued the most. He couldn't do that to her. He briefly closed his eyes. He could turn her, or let her die.

God in heaven. The only choices he had were bad. One day, and one day very soon if Tobias had anything to do with it, Natchook would die for what he'd done here today. He had to ignore, for now, his own culpability in this fiasco.

Her breath rattled in her throat and she gasped, her mouth open as she tried to drag in air.

"Damn it, Caine. *Do* something." MacMillan's anguished voice came at him through a fog of sorrow.

"I...can't." Tobias looked at MacMillan. "Don't you understand? If I take away her humanity, the one thing that's kept her centered, allowed her to keep control over her demon, she could..."

"I could go insane," Nix whispered, finishing his sentence when he trailed off. He looked back down at her to see her gaze darken. The demon was now nowhere to be seen, and the knowledge of her upcoming death was clear in her brown eyes. "It was only a matter of time anyway, right?" Her lips trembled in a smile.

She could be just fine... or not. He stared down at her. "You're sure about this? It's not like I can undo it."

"Yeah, well, you can't undo it if I die either." She swallowed and then winced at the pain. "I don't want to die." Emotion sparkled her gaze with tears. "Please, Tobias. Please don't let me die."

Chapter Seventeen

Nix stared up at Tobias through eyes rapidly losing the battle to stay open. She was so tired. And her body hurt all over. Damn. Even her eyelashes hurt. And she was pretty sure she had cacti needles in her behind.

All she wanted to do was close her eyes and sleep. But she knew it would be the Big Sleep and she wasn't ready for that. She wasn't sure she was ready to live forever, either, but between the two she'd take life every time.

"Please," she whispered again. She hated that she'd put Tobias in this position. If he turned her and she went insane, he'd feel it was his duty to end her. She knew him well enough to know he'd never forgive himself.

He'd also never forgive himself if he let her die.

While she still had the strength to form words, she said, "I'm sorry I screwed things up. If I hadn't tried to jump him, maybe you would have been able to fend him off and finally finish him."

He shook his head. "Don't. None of this is your fault." His throat moved with his hard swallow. The self-recriminating look in his eyes clearly proclaimed who he thought was responsible.

"It's not your..." She closed her eyes. So tired. Even

with the solid feel of Tobias's arms around her, his chest and legs supporting her weight, she felt as if she were lighter than air. If she opened her eyes, would she see a bright light beckoning her to enter?

"Nix!" Tobias gave her a little shake.

She forced her eyes open, relieved when all she saw was his dear face. Lifting her hand, which felt oddly heavy, she stroked his cheek. "Don't look so worried."

He cupped her fingers against his face, then pressed a kiss into her palm and held her hand against his chest. "You're sure about this?" he asked again.

She nodded. But she had to tell him something, just in case. "If… if this doesn't work—"

"Don't." His lips firmed. "Don't talk like that."

Nix gave a slight shake of her head. "Let me finish. If this doesn't work, you remember I love you. I never stopped loving you, even when I hated you." A tear slid from the corner of her eye, leaving a heated trail down her cold cheek.

Tobias stared at her, unspeaking, but his heart was in his eyes. He swallowed again and she caught the slight tremble of his lower lip before he regained control. His pupils dilated completely, swallowing up the stormy gray of his irises. He parted his lips, baring his fangs.

Feeling the need to say something, and with her uncertainty and fear came sarcasm, she whispered, "Do it on the other side. You don't know where his fangs have been."

Tobias sighed. With his hand at her chin, he gently turned her face toward him. She felt his tongue at her throat and the fleeting pain of his bite. Then ecstasy flooded her as his mouth drew on her flesh, the natural euphoria produced by the effect of his bite ramping up her arousal even as her body began to die.

She tried to stay focused on Tobias, tried to hold on to consciousness as long as she could, but all too soon her eyes closed and she lost the battle.

* * *

Tobias felt Nix slump in his arms and knew his timing was critical. If he released too much of his essence into her bloodstream too early, it would be ineffective. Release too little, same result. Release it too late...

He would lose her forever.

Her heartbeat was almost nonexistent. One more beat. Then another.

It was now or never.

Tobias closed his eyes and willed part of his other-dimensional being into Nix's bloodstream. With its release came a feeling of dizziness, his neck the only thing keeping his head from floating away. After a few seconds, he pulled away, licking across the wound to aid in its healing, and straightened.

"What happens now?" MacMillan's voice was hushed.

"Now we wait."

Tobias felt his fangs slide back into his gums and ran his tongue across his teeth. He stroked his hand down her cheek. Waiting would be agony. Especially at the moment when...

There it was. Her breath stuttered and then stopped.

MacMillan leaned into him, peering down at her face. "She's not breathing!"

"It's part of the process." Tobias hunched his shoulder and gave the detective a slight shove. "In case you hadn't noticed, I don't breathe except to talk or smell something."

"Oh. Right." MacMillan moved around to the other side of Nix. As he lowered himself to the ground, he gave a grunt of pain and then groaned when he sat down, resting his forearms on his bent knees. He wore the expression of a man racked with pain and tortured by his thoughts. By his worries. "When will we know?" he asked, his voice deep and soft.

"It will be a while." Tobias was just as quiet.

"Hey." When Tobias looked up at him, MacMillan met his gaze. "I get how bad a guy that...Natchook, is it?" Tobias nodded and MacMillan went on. "I'll stay with Nix if you want to—"

"No." Tobias looked down at her face, so pale and still. "I won't leave her." Never again. He should have responded when she'd told him she loved him. He should have let her know with words that she was so much a part of him he'd never be the same, whether she lived or died. And if she died...

He would never recover from his loss. With a quick glance at MacMillan, he said, "I appreciate the offer. But I'm not leaving Nix."

The other man nodded. "I understand. I've known since you hit that first crime scene that she was still in love with you." He gave a crooked grin. He stared at Nix a moment and then stood, brushing the seat of his jeans free of dirt. "I'll call dispatch and have them get in touch with the council to send a, ah, cleaning crew out for these guys." He waved toward the bodies of the fallen vampires.

"Thanks." Tobias at the moment didn't care about anything but Nix. He looked down at her as the detective moved away, his cell phone to his ear. In the two hundred years he'd been on this planet, Tobias had never before turned someone into a vampire. And he hated the fact that his first was Nix.

He stroked one hand through her hair, not caring that his fingers shook. And for the first time in a very long time, he prayed. *Let Nix survive. Let her be all right.*

Because, God help him, he didn't think he had the strength to kill her if she went insane. He would let her drink him dry before he harmed her.

Long minutes passed while he held her, his gaze never leaving her for long as he waited for some sign that the turning was successful. He was just about to give up hope when her eyes flew open and she gave a little gasp.

Already he could see the changes taking place in her body—her pupils were dilated, and the little bit of iris he could still see was the yellow of her demon. Elongated canines protruded over her lower lip.

A panic-stricken look covered her face as her brain directed her body to take breath it didn't need. He remembered those first few minutes so long ago when he'd woken up in a strange body, and figured that this moment wasn't much different for Nix. "Easy, honey," he soothed, cupping her cheek. "Look at me. Look at me," he coaxed.

Her eyes connected with his.

"Don't fight it, sweetheart. You don't need to breathe but your brain doesn't realize that yet. It hasn't reset. It's trying to run the autonomic systems. Just let it." As her struggles and panic lessened, he kept crooning to her. "That's it. Easy. Easy."

He was aware that MacMillan had approached and

stood nearby, close enough to jump in and help if needed but far enough away to still give them some privacy. Tobias felt a grudging respect for the other man's strength of character. He could almost like the guy.

"Tobias?" Nix reached up and gripped the front of his shirt.

He knew what she was feeling, he'd been there before. She was a creature of instinct right now—bewildered, scared, and *hungry*. He lifted her to a sitting position, keeping his arm behind her back to support her, and tipped his head to one side. "Go ahead, honey," he murmured. "Take what you need."

Her teeth sank into his throat with the fierce single-mindedness of a starving tiger cub. Or a mindless revenant. He would soon find out which.

The pull of her lips against his flesh fired up his libido. His penis hardened, and he groaned, closing his eyes. He felt her hand curl over him and he thrust his hips into her touch. Then he remembered they had an audience, so he grabbed her hand and held it against his chest. She pulled away from him and he stared at her, waiting to see how she'd react to her first feeding as a vampire.

Her tongue swept across her lips, removing the traces of his blood, leaving her mouth shiny. Her eyes were slumberous, the yellow of her irises fading to the human looking brown he was used to. "That was amazing." She lightly touched the tip of his chin with two fingers. Her fangs hadn't retracted completely, giving her a sexy kittenish look he couldn't resist.

Tobias held her gaze. "How're you doing?" The next couple of minutes were critical. The fact that she'd stopped feeding on her own accord was promising. But how she acted now that she had blood in her belly would tell the tale.

"I'm a little tired. Kinda lethargic." Her head rolled to one side. "It's different."

"What is?" Tobias was aware of MacMillan hovering in the background, the detective clearly wanting to be included in the action surrounding a newly turned vampire yet at the same time savvy enough to keep his distance and not become potential prey.

"Drinking blood. I thought it would bring the demon out, but..." She looked sad for a moment, then frowned and closed her eyes.

When she didn't continue, he prompted, "What?" He couldn't keep from touching her, sliding his hand through her hair, stroking across her soft cheek. The gash on her face was beginning to heal. In another few seconds there wouldn't even be a scar.

She looked at him, her gaze perplexed yet relieved. "I don't feel that inner burning that I just about always have." Her brows dipped in a frown. "That's odd." She blinked. "You know what else is odd? Wouldn't adding a vampire to a demon make the bloodlust stronger?"

"Does it feel like it has?" He brushed her hair away from her face, tucking thick strands behind her ear, and let his hand linger on her face.

She nuzzled him like a sleepy kitten. "No, Dr. Phil." Her expression turned teasing. "Answering my questions with more questions. That would be why I said it was *odd*," she stressed with her eyebrows raised.

Little smart-ass.

But her light-hearted response took away any remaining fear he'd had. If she were going to be a raving lunatic—which had always been the fear because of her being a hybrid—the madness would already be evident. Bloodlust only heightened the insanity.

MacMillan came closer. "Maybe it's because she's not human anymore."

Tobias looked at him, aware that Nix had done the same. "What do you mean?"

The detective gave a one-shouldered shrug. "Maybe her humanity at odds with the demon part of her was what would have driven her mad. Now that that's been changed..." He shrugged again. "I'm just thinkin' out loud."

"No, that makes sense." Nix sat upright.

Tobias was sorry to realize she didn't need his physical support anymore. Would she remember what she'd said when she had been about to die? Had she even meant it?

"It was the demon fighting against my humanity that caused the problem." Her expression was concerned. "But..."

Tobias waited, but MacMillan wasn't as patient. "But what?" the detective asked as he came closer.

Nix looked up at him. "That would explain why I don't burn inside anymore."

"So, no more tai chi, is that what you're saying?" One corner of MacMillan's mouth tilted up.

Her smile came full and bright. "Well, maybe, but just because I want to, not because I have to."

Tobias caught MacMillan's eye. The detective seemed about to say something but then stopped himself. "What?" Tobias asked.

"Nothing. Well, not *nothing*." He shook his head. "Sorry about your guy getting away."

Nix jumped to her feet. "You let Natchook get away?"

Tobias stood. "It was either that or let you die." He tried but couldn't joke about it. "I couldn't let you go." His voice rasped from a throat tight with the emotion of what might have been. "I'll find him again."

"But he took the rift device, too." MacMillan hooked his thumbs over his belt. "He can just go into hiding and keep right on doing what he's been doing."

Nix reached into her back pocket and pulled out a black box the size of a cell phone. "You mean this rift device?" She waggled it back and forth. Her grin widened as the two men stared at her in disbelief. "I managed to slide this out of his jacket when he first bit me." She scowled and rubbed the side of her neck, the wounds already nearly healed. "Bastard."

Tobias gave a shout and hauled her into his arms. He planted a hard kiss on her lips and hugged her tight, lifting her off her feet. She laughed and hugged him back, her newfound vampire strength evident in the fierceness of her embrace.

"So," MacMillan said, "we have the schematics and the device?"

Tobias reluctantly let go of Nix. "What?" He looked from one to the other. "You have the schematics?"

"Oh, yeah, we haven't had a chance to tell you yet." MacMillan cocked a thumb toward Nix. "She had the brainy idea of looking on the bottom of the desk. We found an envelope with schematics and a flash drive." He reached into his pocket and pulled out the small plastic drive.

Nix did the same with the schematics, holding the folded papers up for Tobias to see. "It sounded like he doesn't have a copy of these. If that's the case, it'll take him a while to get another one built." She appeared highly pleased with herself as she tucked the papers back into her pocket. The look was ruined by a face-splitting yawn.

"I need to get you home." Tobias put an arm around her shoulder and drew her close. "You need to rest."

"Go." MacMillan leaned against the rock outcropping. "I'll stick around to wait for the cleanup crew."

"We can't leave him alone," Nix said, though her droopy eyes spoke of her need to get horizontal. Tobias felt his flesh quicken at the thought of sliding her beneath him, and inwardly cursed his unwieldy libido. She needed to sleep, not go through a round of bedroom gymnastics with him.

"I'll be fine." MacMillan lifted his chin toward the vampire he'd killed. "I took care of him, didn't I? He wasn't so tough."

"He was injured." Tobias lifted a brow.

"So?" MacMillan folded his arms. "I'm the one who hurt him. Besides, *someone* has to fight the wounded." His grin was as cocky as they came. "That could be my niche."

Tobias rolled his eyes. MacMillan could be ridiculous, but it was hard not to like the guy. He gave him a nod. "You called dispatch about half an hour ago, so they should be here soon."

"Yeah, as long as my directions were good."

Tobias shook his head. "Most teams have at least one shape-shifter on them."

MacMillan looked a bit shamefaced. "Oh, yeah. Right." He tapped his nose, indicating they'd smell their way along just as Tobias and Nix had been able to do. He looked at

Nix, his expression growing more concerned. "She looks dead on her feet." He pressed his lips together, no doubt fighting a grin.

"Hey!" She frowned at him.

"Sorry."

Tobias didn't think he looked very sorry. He couldn't resist joining in the teasing. "He has a point." Tobias bit back a grin when she tossed a scowl his way. "You can't deny it. You are dead on your feet."

"Isn't the term 'undead,' fang boy?" she muttered.

Before she could get any testier—Tobias remembered what she was like when she was really tired—he urged her forward. "Come on, honey. Let's go home."

"Home." She sighed and leaned her head on his shoulder. Her feet scuffed in the dirt as she walked. She yawned again, her body still not having figured out she no longer needed to breathe. "I like the sound of that."

He couldn't help but wonder if she'd feel differently after she'd rested. After she got used to the new sensations her changed body offered. She'd need him even less than she had before—and she'd never really needed him then, either. She was one of the most independent, competent women he knew. Something more for him to love about her.

They had resolved a lot of the past hurts, but it remained to be seen if they would be able to build on that foundation. A kiss, soft words, and hot sex didn't make the pain go away. After she'd gotten some rest, he supposed he would find one thing out: Would she stay with him? Or was he destined to live the rest of his life alone?

* * *

Dante watched Nix and Tobias until they went out of sight. He blew out a sigh and scrubbed the back of his neck, and surveyed the scene. Blood-soaked sand and five dead vampires pretty much told the story. It was too damned bad that the ringleader had gotten away, and not just because it was someone Tobias had been hunting for so long. Some payback would've been nice. Dante prodded his wound and winced. That bite had hurt like hell when it happened, but it hurt even more now. The sooner the crime scene specialists got here the sooner he could take off and get it seen to.

He walked over to the nearest corpse and stared down at him. The vampire's eyes were open, his bloodied fangs still in evidence. This was the bastard that had bitten him. Dante drew his weapon and prodded the body with the toe of his boot. No reaction. He backed up until he was stopped by a large rock, then leaned against it and kept his pistol at the ready. From what he knew, blood loss was just as devastating to a vamp as it was to a human. And these guys had lost a hell of a lot of blood. They all seemed dead, but with vampires you never could tell. He'd just have to trust that Tobias and Nix wouldn't have left him here alone to fend off a horde of vamps coming back to life.

After about half an hour or so he heard voices calling his name. "Up here," he shouted.

Roughly a dozen criminalists came over the rise. Knox, the former vampire liaison of his quadrant, walked over to him. "You just can't stay out of trouble, can you, MacMillan?"

Dante lifted his shoulders. "Trouble seems to find me in spite of my best efforts." He clapped Knox on the shoulder. "So, you're on the case now?"

He grimaced, flashing a fang. "I get to clean up your mess."

"Not mine. Caine's."

"Uh-huh." Knox stopped and gestured toward Dante's arm. "You all right?"

"It's just a scratch." Dante figured he needed to keep the whole rift device thing out of the realm of common knowledge, so he made sure the conversation stayed on point. He nodded at the dead vamps. "These guys were buddies of the vampire that Tobias chased through the rift."

"Natchook? No kidding." Knox made a circuit of the scene, looking at each vampire. He stopped at the spot where Tobias had turned Nix and stared at the few smears of blood on the rock. Going down on his haunches, he drew in a breath and then shot a sharp glance up at Dante.

"She's fine, now," Dante said. "Natchook got to her, forcing Tobias to turn her."

"And?" Knox sniffed again, his eyes going vampire black. "How did the transformation go?" He seemed wary, his voice sounding tight.

"Fine, I guess. I've never seen one before, so I don't have anything to compare it with."

"Believe me, if it had gone badly, you'd know. Actually, you'd probably be dead." Knox stood. "She seemed all right?"

"Yeah. She seemed...normal." Dante tucked his thumbs in his belt. "Still a little smart aleck."

Knox relaxed his stance. "That's good. Real good." He looked around the scene. "I'd better start directing these boys or they'll just wander around in circles." He began to walk away and then stopped. "You go get that looked at," he said, pointing at Dante's shoulder.

"Planning on doing that right now." Dante hesitated, watching the techs working away, and knew he was one lucky SOB. Five vampires and he managed to come out the other side alive. He'd take that kind of win any day.

Chapter Eighteen

By the time Tobias pulled the car into the parking lot of Nix's apartment complex, she was asleep. He turned off the car and watched her, so full of emotion he felt...hesitant. It was something he hadn't felt in a long time—not since he'd first come through the rift and found himself in such an alien place.

It wasn't a feeling he particularly enjoyed, so he did what he usually did. He pushed it aside and went into action. He opened his door and walked around to the passenger side. Leaning over, he eased Nix out of the car and into his arms. Before he straightened he snagged the strap of the huge tote she called a purse. He went up the sidewalk and, once at her front door, he knelt on one knee, balancing her on the thigh of his other leg while he rooted around for her keys.

She didn't stir as he opened the door and went inside. Rufus was at the entryway, his whine loud. Before Tobias could stop him, the dog raced through the open door. Tobias didn't wait around or try to catch the damned thing. He held a precious burden in his arms. The dog would come back.

Tobias carried Nix to her bedroom. As much as he'd

like to let her keep sleeping, she needed to get cleaned up. She'd sleep better after the grime was washed away. *He'd* sleep better, knowing she was comfortable and safe. He went into the bathroom and set her gently on her feet, keeping one arm around her waist to support her weight. "Nix," he coaxed, patting her on the cheek. "Wake up, honey."

Her head lolled on his shoulder but he felt the amount of weight leaning into him lessen, so he knew she was standing on her own. With her eyes still closed she replied, "No. Not time to get up yet." She sounded like a disgruntled kid being told it was time for school.

He would have laughed had the situation been different. As it was, there wasn't much humor to be found under the circumstances. Nix was no longer human, at all, and it was his fault. He clenched his jaw. He'd deal with that later. Always later. "We're going to take a shower, sweetheart." He guided her to the toilet and helped her sit on the closed lid. Kneeling at her feet, he unzipped and removed her boots, then gently peeled her socks off her feet.

"Oh. Sh-shower's good." Her voice was so slurred she sounded drunk. She scooted forward so abruptly that her knee caught him in the face and knocked him on his ass. She stood and looked down at him with a frown. Her fingers went to the buttons on her blouse. "Why are you just sitting there?"

He got to his feet, rubbing the sting out of his cheek. He shook his head. "I don't know what I was thinking." In her fatigued stupor she had only managed to get one button undone. He brushed her hands away and finished the job, easing the material over her shoulders and letting it drop to the floor. He unbuckled her belt, noticing for the first time that both her gun and knife holsters were empty, and pushed her jeans to her ankles, supporting her as she lifted first one foot and then the other. Trying to ignore the enticing picture she made standing there in lacy bra and panties, he focused instead on the dried blood smeared on her neck and upper chest, scowling when he caught sight of the bruises on her shoulders, ribs, arms and thighs.

Damn. He was a bastard for lusting after her in the shape she was in. He should be wrapping her in cotton, not thinking about sliding her beneath him, less so of sliding himself into her.

He undid her bra and removed it. When he reached for her panties, she wrapped her fingers around his wrists. He could feel the new strength in her hands. "Thank you."

He stared down at her. "For what?"

"For saving my life." She leaned forward and pressed her mouth to his shoulder.

"Any time, sweetheart." Tobias finished undressing her, then stripped off his own clothes. He reached in and turned on the shower. The water warmed up within a few seconds. Grabbing a clean washcloth from the shelf above the toilet, he guided Nix into the stall and closed the frosted glass door behind them.

He stood behind her, bracing her against him, and gently cleaned the blood, sweat, and dirt off her. Every once in a while she'd shift against him, her soft buttocks rubbing against his cock. He couldn't stop his natural reaction any more than he could make his heart start beating again.

She turned and looped her arms around his neck. Her eyes were still sleepy but more alert than before, and there was a spark of sensual awareness that hadn't been there. "This is amazing. My senses are so much more alert. It's like I can feel every drop of water as it hits my skin." Her gaze fell to his chest. "I can see every drop of water on *your* skin." She bent her head.

Tobias jerked at the feel of her tongue swiping across his nipple. His cock twitched, too, ready for more. He put his hands on her shoulders and moved her away from him. "I don't think this is a good idea, Nix."

Her brows lifted. "Don't you?" She glanced down. "Mr. Happy there seems to think it's a very good idea."

When she tried to get close again he straightened his arms, keeping her at bay. Even while he knew he was doing the right thing, part of him was yelling at him to cut it out. He wanted to be inside her, now. But his Southern gentleman half won out. "My cock doesn't do my thinking for me."

"Since when?" She blinked like a sleepy, sultry kitten. "You're a guy. I thought guys always led with their cocks."

She might be right, but... "Not this time," he muttered. He leaned forward to shut off the water. Nix took advantage and put her mouth on his shoulder, licking a trail across the sharp ridge of his collarbone before she bit down on his shoulder. Hard enough to draw blood, which she drew on with a hungry, sexy little moan.

God, she never made things easy for him, did she? "Knock it off." He sounded a bit angry, and he was. Here he was trying to be a gentleman, trying not to take advantage of her vulnerability, and she kept teasing him.

She pulled away with an aggrieved sigh and opened the door of the stall. Stepping out onto the mat, she grabbed a towel and began drying herself. As soon as she moved off the mat, Tobias came out of the shower and dried off as well. He wrapped the towel around his hips as he walked into the master bedroom. He grabbed a T-shirt and a pair of shorts off the end of her bed. Turning, he saw Nix standing in the doorway, still completely nude and seemingly oblivious to it. He walked over to her, holding out her clothes. "Here," he said, his voice gruff.

She slipped her arms into the sleeves of the shirt and dropped it over her head. The soft cotton draped her to midthigh, covering her curves yet somehow enhancing her femaleness. He stooped and held the shorts out for her, appreciating the dainty femininity of the act of her putting first one foot and then the other through the legs. He pulled them up as he stood.

She looked like a forlorn waif, and it brought out every protective instinct he had even though now, as a vampire-demon hybrid, she really didn't need his protection in the least. He moved away from her, going to the bed to turn down the covers. "In you get." He motioned to the crimson-sheeted mattress.

She held up one finger and padded back into the bathroom. When she came back out, she held the rift device in her hand. In his rush to get her home, he'd forgotten the thing was tucked in the pocket of her jeans.

Just as she reached the bed, she exclaimed, "Rufus!"

Tobias turned to see the dog standing at the open doorway. "Guess I can close the front door now," Tobias stated, and left the room. He closed and locked the front door of the apartment and then went back toward the bedroom. He paused in the doorway and watched Nix with her dog.

Rufus had gotten closer to her, but backed away from every overture she made. His tail tucked between his legs, he whined and whimpered, confusion evident in the way his ears twitched and his head tilted from one side to the other.

She looked at Tobias. Tears made her eyes shine. "He... he's afraid of me."

Tobias shook his head. "No, sweetheart. He's uncertain of you, that's all. You're different and he hasn't figured it out yet." Tobias walked into the room and stooped down beside the dog, who whined again and leaned against Tobias's hip. "Give him time. See? He likes me, remember? And you're part of me now."

Pleasure ripped through him at that thought. No matter what their future held—whether they faced it together or apart—Nix was now and always would have part of him inside her.

She pressed her lips together and gave a small nod. With a slight sniff she climbed up onto the bed and sat cross-legged, her back resting on the pillows leaning against the headboard. She glanced at Rufus, who went closer to the bed and lay down, his gaze steady on her. "That's right, baby," she murmured. "I'm still me."

The dog's tail thumped once against the floor and then he rested his head on his paws.

A small smile curved Nix's mouth, then she looked down at the small box in her hands, turning it over and over. "How do you suppose this works?" She glanced up at Tobias.

He sat on the edge of the mattress and took the device from her. "We can figure that out later." When she started to reach for it, he leaned over and placed it on the end table, out of her reach. He took her hands in his. "The last thing we need to do is just start turning dials to see what happens."

Pink swept over her cheeks. "I-I wasn't thinking of doing that."

"Uh-huh." He reached out and chucked her lightly under the chin. "You need some rest, honey." He stood and started to move away, only to be stopped by her grabbing his hand.

"Don't go."

"Nix..." There was no way in hell he could stay in this bedroom with her and not put his hands on her. She was naked under that thin cotton, and he wasn't gentleman enough to continue to resist her allure.

* * *

Nix stared at him, holding her breath. She started to respond to him and then realized something. That inner burning and itching sensation she usually got when she was ramped up, the same one that had allowed her to go demon on the vamps in the desert, was gone. Her demon rested quietly. She recalled saying something about that earlier, but she'd been so exhausted, her body transitioning from human to vampire, that she couldn't remember exactly what conclusion she'd come to. Something about it being her humanity that had caused all the trouble.

Nix reached forward and took Tobias's hands in hers. "I don't have a clear memory of everything that happened after Natchook bit me, but I remember this. I told you that I love you. And I do." She squeezed his fingers.

His pupils dilated and those vamp pheromones rolled off him in undulating waves. Knowing he was helpless to stop his reaction to her, she welcomed them. Reveled in them and the answering emotions they drew from her, like love. And a healthy dose of lust. And, now that she was part vampire, she could send some of her own.

He leaned down and kissed her lips, tongue seeking, using a gentleness she neither needed nor wanted. Nix planted her hands against his chest and pushed him onto his back. She shimmied out of her shorts and top and then yanked the towel away from him, watching with greedy eyes as his shaft thrust upward, a clear drop of liquid already lubricating the fat head.

She wrapped her fingers around him, stroking from base to tip. As she leaned forward, Tobias stopped her with his hands on her shoulders. "Not that I don't appreciate what you're about to do," he said, his eyes serious but a little anxious. "But can we wait on that until you get used to those?" He motioned toward her mouth.

Nix ran the tip of her tongue across her fangs, wincing when they cut into her own flesh. "Good idea." She came up over him and lowered herself onto his hard shaft, inch by slow inch, until her buttocks were cradled by his upraised thighs.

She lifted herself and slammed down on top of him. Again. And again. She didn't want slow and sweet. Not this time. She wanted the heat of primal mating. Every thrust made her writhe. Every time his black eyes met hers she burned inside, but not with the fire of the demon.

With the fire of lust. No, it was more than sex. It was love. Pure, unadulterated, love. "I love you," she gasped, bracing herself with her hands against his hard chest, her nails digging into his muscles as she came.

He gave that little smile of his before he climaxed with

a throaty growl. "And I love you." He held her in place until the pulses within her quieted, then he shifted to one side, still inside her, and tugged her close. "Forever."

Forever. That had a nice ring to it, especially since he meant it literally. Or as close to literal as anyone could get.

"And that?" she asked, looking at the rift device.

"That," he said, placing a soft kiss on her mouth and then getting off the bed, "we'll get to Victoria tomorrow." He picked it up and padded over to her dresser. He studied the device a moment, resisting the urge to turn it on, then tucked it beneath a pile of silken bras in her top drawer. As he turned back toward the bed, he said, "If we can dismantle it without activating it, we need to put the pieces in various places so it can't be reassembled easily. And the council can't know we know about it, let alone that we have one."

"Don't forget the schematics and the flash drive." She leaned up on her elbows. "Do you think Victoria will agree to keep it secret?"

"I think so. We'll have to trust her." He got back in bed and pressed a kiss against the swell of her breast. "Until we know whether these are the only plans and that's the only device, we need to keep everything under wraps."

"Until we know who all is involved." Her gaze darkened. "I can't believe that everyone on the council knows about this."

"That would be...unthinkable." He turned onto his back and drew her into his arms.

"We need to do something about Natchook." She bared her fangs. "I can help you catch him."

Tobias raised up on one elbow. "Don't even think

about taking him on, honey. He hasn't survived as long as he has by fighting fair. Just look what he did to you!"

"I can play dirty, too." She poked him in the chest. "I am part demon, after all. And now I'm part vampire, too. We can't just let him run off into the sunset."

"We won't." He settled against the pillows. "But we have obligations here. We need to find out who on the council knows about the device, and find out what their plans are." He drew her down against his chest. "We'll be in Scottsdale for a while. You'll move in with me?" He sounded oddly hesitant.

She put one fist on top of the other on his chest and propped her chin on her fists. "Only if you marry me." At his startled look she added, "I let you get away from me once, buster. Never again."

He closed his eyes. "I can live with that." And with that he fell asleep. She wasn't quite sure how she knew it, because it wasn't like his breathing had changed or anything. But she was sure he was dead to the world.

She lay down and rested her head on his shoulder. She knew she had a long road ahead of her, getting used to being a vampire, but she also knew Tobias would be right there with her, helping her. Together they could do anything.

Werewolf Tori Joseph, Council Liaison, knows more about a recent spate of attacks on humans than she can ever let on.

But as she gets closer to her human colleague, Detective Dante Fabrizio, her attraction to him becomes the secret she must hide . . .

Please turn this page for a preview of

Secret of the Wolf.

Chapter One

Hard muscles rippled beneath skin and fur. Sharp teeth re-formed themselves. Bones crunched, shifted. Realigned. Glossy brown fur receded, leaving behind only silken, tanned skin as the wolf became human.

Became a woman.

Hugging her knees to her chest, Victoria Joseph took several shuddering breaths, fighting her way back from the mind of the wolf. Perspiration dotted her skin. Her bones ached, muscles flexed and quivered, recovering from the shock and pain of transformation. As the last of the wolf retreated inside, giving her one final slash of pain through her midsection, a soft moan escaped her. She took another deep breath, the humidity of the August morning traveling deep into her lungs. The rain overnight had cleared out, but not before it had tamped down the pollen and dust that ordinarily floated in the air. It was monsoon season in the Sonoran desert. Even with the rise in humidity, unbearable with the hundred-degree temperatures, she loved this time of year. Monsoon storms were wild, swift, and could be deadly. They spoke to her soul.

She skirted a saguaro and, with arms that still trembled, shoved aside a large rock to retrieve the plastic bag she'd stashed there earlier. She pulled out a bottle of water and took a long drink, then another and another until she'd downed it all. She'd learned a long time ago to rehydrate as soon as possible after a shift. Otherwise she'd be in real danger of passing out from the strain of the metamorphosis.

Dropping the bottle back into the bag, Tori drew out clean clothing and shoes. Once dressed, she tucked her cell phone into the front pocket of her jeans and plaited her long hair in a French braid. She hiked the mile back through the desert to the trailhead where she'd left her car. Whenever she went wolf, she wanted to go to a place where she'd have some degree of solitude, and the McDowell Sonoran Preserve afforded that, especially when it was still dark.

As she steered the little Mini Cooper into her driveway, the sun was just coming up over the eastern mountains, sending alternating shafts of light and shadow across the valley floor. She shut off the engine and sat there a moment, wondering if her brother was up yet. Randall had shown up four days ago without warning. The last time she'd seen him had been just before they'd been stripped of their bodies. Their souls had then been sent through a rift between dimensions. As incorporeal entities they'd been drawn to Earth, to the bounty of human bodies available for the taking, for instinctively they'd known if they didn't take a host they'd die. She'd ended up in London in the body of a woman making her living on the streets of the East End.

Randall, she'd found out just recently, had gone into a man in Leeds. Less than two hundred miles away from her at the time, but it may as well have been the other side of the world. In 1866 it had been impossible to even begin to try to find him. She'd been alone, a stranger in a borrowed body, overcoming the guilt at displacing the rightful owner, finding a way to stay alive in a primitive world.

She and her brother hadn't seen each other in nearly a hundred and fifty years until he'd shown up on her doorstep, a familiar spirit in a stranger's body. She'd known him instantly. He was the same sweet brother she remembered, yet he was different in some ways. More withdrawn. But even with the newfound secrecy she would take what she could get. He was her family. The only relative she had in this world. She was willing to overlook a few eccentricities to have her family with her again.

Tori just wished she knew what to do to make him more at ease. He'd had some predisposition toward obsessive-compulsive behavior before the Influx of 1866, but those tendencies seemed to be exacerbated here. Perhaps the human he'd ended up inhabiting, Randall Langston, had also had such predilections.

With a sigh she got out of the car and let herself into her small two-bedroom rental. Smells of lavender and vanilla assailed her from the various bowls of potpourri she had around the house. Her job as werewolf liaison to the council was more often than not dark and full of violence, and as a werewolf she was predisposed to be more aggressive in nature than an ordinary human woman. So when she came home she wanted calm and tranquillity. She needed it in order to slough off the stress of the day.

Tori drew in a breath and held it a moment, letting the tranquil setting of her home seep into her spirit. Neutral beige and cream furniture was piled with blue and green pillows, and the same color scheme played out on the walls. The wooden wind chimes on the back patio clinked, the sound coming to her as clearly as if she were standing beside them.

She didn't need to use her keen werewolf hearing to pick up the snores coming from Randall's bedroom. He rarely arose much before noon, preferring to stay up until the wee hours of morning and run as a wolf as much as possible.

She kept trying to not let it bother her that he chose to run alone instead of with her. After all, he'd been on his own just like she had, and he was much more of a loner than she'd ever been. But bother her it did. Why had he gone to the trouble of locating her if he didn't want to spend any wolf time together? It was as natural for werewolves to run as a pack, even a pack of two, as it was to breathe.

Shaking off the feelings, Tori moved quietly through the house, not wanting to wake him. She undressed in her bedroom, putting her cell phone on the nightstand. After she took a quick shower, she slipped into a robe and padded barefoot into the kitchen. She was starving, which wasn't unusual after a shift. She pulled some raw hamburger meat out of the fridge and gulped down a couple of handfuls—just enough to satisfy her inner wolf. She'd long ago gotten over the gross factor of eating raw meat.

She remembered her first time as if it were only yesterday. She'd been half asleep and had come wide awake when she realized she was chowing down on raw liver. Repulsed by her need for flesh, she'd soon discovered that the longer she denied the wolf its meal, the more violent it became when it finally got out. As long as she fed regularly, she could shift without worrying that she'd brutally murder someone.

Tori dumped some granola into a bowl and added a few diced strawberries. She poured herself a cup of coffee and went into her bedroom, closing the door with a soft click behind her. She placed the cup and bowl on the end table and went over to her bookshelf. Reaching for a well-worn paperback, she pulled it off the shelf and went back to her queen-size bed. She perched on the edge and opened the book in the middle, staring down at the pages before her.

She spooned cereal into her mouth and slipped a finger inside the book to retrieve the small black device nestled into the area she'd cut out. The size of a cell phone, it was about half an inch thick with a couple of small knobs and two retractable antennae at one end. Tobias Caine, former vampire liaison to the Council of Preternaturals and now a member of the same, had given it to her two weeks prior. Apparently he and his wife, Nix, had acquired it months ago but had held on to it in secret, waiting for a safe opportunity to hand it off to her.

As Tobias had put it, he'd chosen Tori because she had a background in radio communications and the ability to keep her mouth shut. The two things he needed most. She'd been honored that he trusted her with such a task.

He'd also given her the schematics, which hadn't been very useful in making the thing work. Oh, she'd managed to turn it on, but within minutes a voice had spoken in the standard language of the other dimension, asking for a password. Worried she would set off some kind of alarm by not responding, she'd quickly turned the device off. Now, as she studied the thing, rolling it around in her hands, she tried to figure out how to activate the device without having someone on the other side know about it. The schematics didn't indicate that. Perhaps it wasn't possible.

Tori wouldn't know until she tried. Her assignment, as given by Tobias, was to determine how the device worked as quickly as possible, without letting anyone know she had it. As far as she was aware, only three other people knew about the little doohickey—Tobias, Nix, and Dante MacMillan, a human detective who'd been right in the middle of the action when the device had been confiscated.

Tori finished her cereal and set the bowl back down on the nightstand. Grabbing her coffee, she took a sip and carried the cup as she went to her dresser. She opened her lingerie drawer and lifted her panties out of the way so she could pick up the folded schematics. She shoved the drawer closed with her hip. Going back to the bed, she spread out the plans and stared down at them while she sipped the hot liquid.

There were drawings of gears and lines and sections for a first amplifier and a second amplifier, R-F output, a resonator and at least two doublers. Mostly though it was a lot of letters and numbers that must have meant something to the person who'd drawn them up, but she couldn't decipher it. Not yet, anyway.

She placed her empty cup on the table and folded the paper up again. Sitting on the edge of the bed, she slid the schematics under her pillow for the time being and stared down at the device. It was hard to believe that something this size could open up a rift—a mini one, but still, a rift nonetheless. The thought chilled her to the bone. What was the purpose? Oh, she knew enough to figure that right now this was used to communicate from one dimension to the other. But there had to be more to it than that. What nefarious plans were being hatched, and by whom? Tobias hadn't told her from whom he'd gotten the device, just that the person had been mad with ambition.

Tori picked up the apparatus and brought it closer to inspect the small knobs. She couldn't discern any labels or hatch marks on the casing, nothing to indicate what function each knob had. She needed to get a magnifying glass to tell for sure.

The more she studied the device, the more intrigued she became. It really was an ingenious contraption created by an imaginative and clever inventor. What had been his intention behind building it? Had he meant to make mischief? Or had his plans been more altruistic than that?

A quick rap on her bedroom door was followed by Randall poking his head inside. "Good morning." He paused, looking at the device, then glanced back at her. "Did you go out early or come in late?" His head tipped to one side as if he were considering a complicated brainteaser. "Oh, well, no matter. What's that?" he asked, his gaze returning to the device in her hands. Pushing the door open, he came into the room wearing jeans only, his chest and feet bare.

"Rand!" Tori closed her fist around the object in question and fought the urge to hide it behind her back. She wanted to deflect him from the rift device, not call attention to it.

Lifting a hand, he lazily scratched his chest. His mouth opened wide in a huge yawn.

"You can't just barge in here. You need to wait for me to tell you to come in." She scowled at him. "What if I'd been getting dressed?"

"Then I'd have seen bits of you I don't necessarily want to see," he said. Tori had lost her East End accent long ago, but even after all these decades, Randall's tones still held the flavor of his British human host. He stuck his fingers into the front pockets of his jeans and hunched his shoulders. "I dare say I'd have recovered from the shock eventually." He offered a smile, then glanced back at the device. "So, what *is* that?"

Though she was certain she could trust her brother, she was duty-bound not to divulge the secret. She liked Tobias. More than that, she admired him and wouldn't betray his trust in her. As nonchalantly as she could, she replied, "It's just an MP3 player a friend asked me to try to fix for him."

Randall raised his brows. Skepticism shadowed his eyes. "And why would he think you could fix it?"

"I was a radio communications technician back in the day. I've kept up with all the new gadgets as a hobby," was all she offered. She didn't want to talk to him about serving as a communications officer in the American army doing World War II. If he was as passive as he'd been before their Influx, he wouldn't approve. She was sure he'd felt right at home during the sixties. Hell, he probably started the whole "Make Love Not War" movement. He would overlook the nobility of the cause, and right now she didn't want to get into an argument with him. Not when they'd just found each other again.

It was time to change the subject. "So, what do you think of Arizona?" She kept her eyes on him and her hand wrapped around the rift device. It wouldn't do for him to get too close a look, or he'd see it wasn't an MP3 player as she'd previously told him. She kept her voice cheery, hoping she could distract him. "I mean, I know you've only been here a few days, but how do you like it so far?"

Her brother looked like he wanted to pursue the other topic, but for now he let it drop, for which she was grateful. While ordinarily she had no problems not discussing her job or, in this case, a special assignment, this was different. He was her brother, and she didn't like being deceitful with him. She wanted him to feel like he could trust her because maybe, just maybe, he'd be more inclined to stay. But if he thought she was being disingenuous with him, it could be all the encouragement he needed to leave.

"I don't know," Randall said. His shoulders hunched further. "I like it well enough, I suppose. I don't believe I'll be staying here for the long term, though." He grimaced. "It's hotter than hell, for one thing. I mean, who the hell lives where it's a hundred and ten degrees, for crying out loud?"

"Right now it's hot, yeah. But it's perfect in the winter months." Tori bit back her disappointment. Randall didn't have to stay in Scottsdale with her, but she'd like him to be close. "And of course I want you to stay here, but wherever you end up, we have to stay in touch."

"Absolutely." He walked over to her dresser, making her stiffen for a moment. Not that there was anything he could get into—the schematics to the device were under her pillow. When all he did was stick a finger into the glass bowl of potpourri, she relaxed. He stirred the fragrant mixture around, making the scent of lavender and vanilla permeate the room. "It's been great to finally find you," he said without glancing her way, his tone one of a stranger making small talk with her. They might as well go back to discussing the weather.

He sounded less enthused about being with her than she'd like. It befuddled her. What was going on beneath that brush cut? She'd thought they had been on their way toward rebuilding the relationship that had been put on hold by their trip through the rift all those years ago, yet he seemed remarkably disinterested.

Before she could delve into it further, her cell phone rang. With a murmured apology, she slipped the rift device under her pillow and then grabbed her phone from the nightstand. She noticed her brother's sharp eyes hadn't missed the fact that she'd hidden the alleged MP3 player. She'd have to make sure to find a better hiding place than her underwear drawer. She answered her phone on the second ring. "Hello?"

"Got a brouhaha over on Chaparral, just east of Hayden," the council dispatcher said without any formal greeting. He was an irascible werebear who didn't put up with a lot of crap, though he sure could dish it out. "Local LEOs have things in hand at the moment, but you need to get your furry self over there now."

"What happened?" All business, she rose from the bed and headed toward her closet. For the time being the Scottsdale police had things under control. She paused as she reached for a blouse and wondered if Dante MacMillan was already at the scene. A sensual shiver worked its way through her. Though he was human, there was something about the man that called to everything feminine and primal within her.

"Some kind of skirmish between a werewolf and a vamp," the dispatcher answered her, drawing her back to the conversation, "with a human bystander caught between 'em. Think the human's okay, though. Well, mostly okay." The werebear gave a little growl. "As okay as one of 'em can be in the middle of a fight between two prets, I suppose. But you need to get over there pronto."

"Ten-four." She grinned at the dispatcher's disgruntled snarl. He really hated it when she used police codes. Tori hung up and looked at her brother. She shoved her phone into the pocket of her robe. As she pulled the blouse from its hanger, she started, "Rand, I—"

"Let me guess," Randall said. His voice held a hint of sarcasm that dismayed her. "You have to go."

She nodded and went to her dresser to pull out a clean pair of jeans. "Rand, we really—"

He slashed a hand through the air, his face darkening, glittering eyes meeting hers. "Just forget it, Tori. It's always been this way with you. Job first, family second." He sounded like a sulky child.

She felt the need to defend herself, her choices. "That's not true!" She dropped her clothing on the bed and went over to him. She put her hand on his shoulder and gave it a squeeze. "I love you, you know that. And I love having you here. It's just like old times. With you around, it makes this place, this planet, feel like home."

She was surprised to see a film of tears make his blue eyes shine.

"It's not that I don't like being here with you," he said, his voice low, a little hoarse. "It's just..." He shook his head with a sigh. "I've always felt like I existed in your shadow. 'Why can't you be more like your sister?'" he mimicked in an excellent approximation of their father's bellicose tones. "'Your sister never disappoints us.'" He went back to his normal voice. "I knew he was disappointed in me. Always disappointed. And I'm just not sure that, if I stay, things will be any different. I'll be known as Tori's brother, the inept one. The loser."

"That's not true." Tori felt much more compelled to build up Randall's self-esteem than to defend her father. He had been strict, demanding perfection from a son who was too emotionally fragile to withstand the pressure. She squeezed her brother's shoulder again. "You're not inept. And Father loved you. You know he did."

"Did he?" Randall gave a shrug. His fingers started tapping against his thigh. "Whatever." He wore the same churlish expression he had when he'd been a teen. She felt momentary dismay that he could still be so immature. Hadn't he learned anything from his trip through the rift? Had he not grown at all in the century and a half they'd been on Earth? He seemed to shake his mood, because a slight smile tilted his lips. He lifted his hands, spreading them in a sheepish gesture. "Listen, I'm just being..." He shook his head. "Don't pay any attention to me. Go. Get to work. Save the day," he said in an approximation of a superhero's voice.

Tori returned his smile, though she couldn't get rid of the worry that niggled at the back of her mind. He was lost, and alone, resisting her attempts to make him a part of her life again. On impulse, she hugged him tightly. He was thin, but firm. Anyone who made the mistake of thinking he'd be physically weak might make the last mistake of their lives. She pressed a kiss to his cheek. "I'll see you later, all right? We'll have dinner together.

Think about what you'd like, and I'll stop by the store on my way home." She searched his eyes, looking for a sign, any sign, of what he was thinking, what he was feeling. "We'll talk. Catch up some more."

"Yeah. Sure." He gave another smile, though this one was definitely forced. With a nod he left the room, pulling the door closed behind him.

Tori quickly dressed. Being a werewolf was so much a part of what she was, she needed to find ways, even if it was just in what she wore, to feel like a woman. To be feminine. To be more than the beast inside of her. The jeans she pulled on were form-fitting, the blouse was frothy in various shades of turquoise. Her sneakers were serviceable but with the bright pink along the edge of the sole they were clearly women's shoes.

She brushed her still-damp hair and braided it, then slipped her brush into the fanny pack she usually wore instead of carrying a purse. After shrugging into her shoulder holster, she retrieved her Magnum from the gun safe. It was a requirement of the council that all liaisons, in essence law enforcement officers for preternaturals, had to carry guns. Tori didn't usually mind, but sometimes the gun was the least favorite part of her job. While it sometimes made her feel sexy, it rarely made her feel feminine.

Besides, when it came to defending herself or running down a suspect, all she really needed were her claws and fangs.

THE DISH

Where authors give you the inside scoop!

From the desk of Jennifer Haymore

Dear Reader,

When Olivia Donovan, the heroine of SECRETS OF AN ACCIDENTAL DUCHESS (on sale now), entered my office for the first time, she stared at the place (and me) wide-eyed, as if she'd never seen an office—or a romance writer—before.

Bemused, I offered her a chair and asked her why she'd come. I was surprised when she got straight to the point; honestly, from the way she looked, I'd expected her to be far more reluctant.

"I want you to write my story."

I leaned forward. "Well, just about everyone who comes through my door wants me to write their story. To get me to do it, however, requires . . . more."

She carried a reticule looped around her wrist, and at this point she began to riffle around in it. "How much more?" she asked. "I haven't got much, but whatever I have—"

"Oh, no. I didn't mean 'more' in the sense of payment."

She frowned. "Well then, it what sense *did* you mean?"

"Well, I write about love . . . the development of relationships, the ups and downs, the ultimate happily ever after."

She gave a wistful sigh. "That's exactly what I want.

But"—she clutched her reticule so hard, her knuckles went white—"I fear I shall never have it."

I raised my eyebrows at her. "Why not? You're a lovely young woman. Obviously well bred, and from the looks of that silk and those pearls you're wearing, you're not lacking in the dowry department."

She gave me a wry smile. "I believe there's more to it than that."

"Look, I'm pretty familiar with your time period, Miss Donovan. In the late Regency period in England, looks, breeding, and financial status were everything."

She shook her head. "It's partially him...well, the man I'm thinking about, the one I'm hoping..." She hesitated, then the words rushed out: "Well, he's going to be a *duke* someday."

I blew that off. "In one of my books, a duke married a *housemaid*." (And this lady was no housemaid, that was for sure!) "Honestly, I can't see why any future duke wouldn't want to pursue a lady like you. You'd make a lovely duchess."

She licked her lips, hesitated, then whispered, "There's where you're wrong. I fear I'd make a terrible duchess. You see, I'm... ill."

I looked at her up and down, then down and up. She was a little thin, and pale, but ladies of this era kept themselves pale on purpose, after all. Otherwise, she looked healthy to me.

She stared at me for a moment, blinking back tears, then stood up abruptly. "I think I should go. This is hopeless."

She wasn't lying. She really believed she'd never have a happy ending of her own. Poor woman.

"No, please stay, Miss Donovan. Please tell me your

story. I promise, if there's anyone who can give you a happy ending, I can."

"Really?" she whispered.

I raised three fingers. "Scout's honor."

She frowned, clearly having no idea what I was talking about, but she was too polite and gently bred to question me. Slowly, she lowered herself back into her seat, still clutching that little green silk reticule.

I flipped up my laptop and opened a new document. "Tell me everything, Miss Donovan. From the beginning."

I truly hope you enjoy reading Olivia Donovan's story! Please come visit me at my website, www.jenniferhaymore.com, where you can share your thoughts about my books, sign up for some fun freebies and contests, and read more about the characters from SECRETS OF AN ACCIDENTAL DUCHESS.

Sincerely,

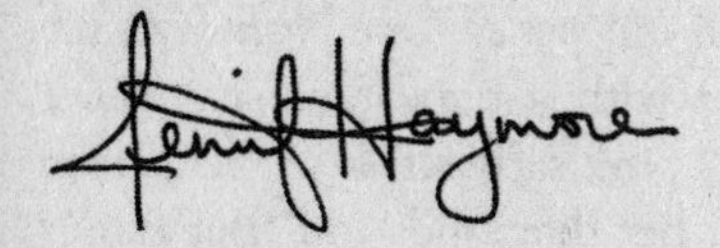

♥ ♥ ♥ ♥ ♥ ♥ ♥ ♥ ♥ ♥ ♥ ♥ ♥ ♥ ♥

From the desk of Kristen Callihan

Dear Reader,

I fell in love with classic movies at an early age. While other kids were watching MTV, I was sighing over Cary Grant or laughing at the antics of William Powell and Myrna Loy.

There was a fairytale aspect about these films—from the impeccable clothes and elegant manners to the gorgeous décor—that took me out of my own world and into a place of dreams. Much like a good romance novel, if you think about it.

Watching old Fred Astaire movies had me dreaming of living in New York City in an apartment done up in elegant shades of white. *It Happened One Night* had me yearning for a road caper with a handsome stranger. I coveted Marilyn Monroe's pink satin dress in *Gentlemen Prefer Blondes*...all right, her diamonds too! But hands down, my favorite aspect of classic movies was the dialogue.

Back in the 1930s and 40s, the tight rein of censorship turned scriptwriters into masters of innuendo. Dialogue back then wasn't merely conversation; it was banter, the double entendre, a back-and-forth duel of words and wit. It was foreplay.

Therefore, it wasn't any surprise to me that when I started writing my own stories, dialogue would play a key part in my characters' relationships. Before the touches, there are the words.

In my novel FIRELIGHT, the verbal foreplay between my hero, Lord Benjamin Archer, and my heroine, Miranda Ellis, is particularly important. Archer hides his appearance behind masks, determined not to let Miranda see what lies beneath. In turn, Miranda hides her true nature behind the mask of her beauty. With so much hidden, they must rely on verbal communication to slip past their physical walls.

And so we have a dance of words. Words that say one thing but mean another. Words that test and tease. Words that make the sexual tension between Archer and Miranda burn hotter and hotter, until it can do nothing less than combust.

Hope you enjoy the heat,

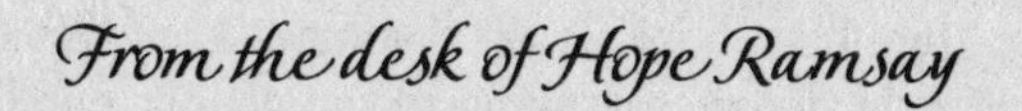

From the desk of Hope Ramsay

Dear Reader,

Among the things I love best about small, rural towns are the events they hold. Some of these events commemorate national holidays, others celebrate civic pride. And still others, like festivals and county fairs, seem to be mostly about having a real good time.

You can find small-town events everywhere. Even in the suburban landscape around Washington, DC, small towns maintain their sense of identity through their festivals, fairs, and special days. Alexandria, Virginia, where I currently live, throws an annual birthday party for its hometown hero, George Washington. Imagine parading through the streets in the February cold and snow. Seems strange, but it's a big annual event. It's fun. And my kids have fond memories of marching in that parade as members of their scout troops.

So it should come as no surprise that, when creating the world of Last Chance, I made sure to give it a festival complete with a parade, a barbecue, dancing, games of chance, and carnival rides. What better place to turn the matchmaking church ladies of Last Chance loose? The fact that they set up a kissing booth to raise money for a good cause should come as no surprise to anyone. Of course, I couldn't let the women have all the fun, so I also gave the local men a demolition derby where they could wreck cars to their hearts' content.

It was a lot of fun to send a member of the British aristocracy off to attend Last Chance's Watermelon Festival. Since my hero comes from a small village in the UK where they light bonfires on Samhain, Lord Woolham surprises the locals by taking to my county fair like a duck to water.

His Lordship enjoys his visit to Last Chance so much that he decides to stay. I hope you enjoy your visit too.

Hope Ramsay

♥ ♥ ♥ ♥ ♥ ♥ ♥ ♥ ♥ ♥ ♥ ♥ ♥ ♥ ♥

From the desk of Cynthia Garner

Dear Reader,

I have been a fan of the paranormal since I was a kid. My teenaged years were spent watching re-runs of Christopher Lee and Peter Cushing in those wonderful Hammer horror films. When Frank Langella played Dracula and later on Gerard Butler... whoa! Tall, dark, and sexy won the day, except... those Draculas were evil. While I don't mind an evil vampire every now and again (they keep us on our toes, right?), I highly prefer them to be one of the good guys. Or at least a reforming bad guy who's struggling against his inner big bad.

When I first came up with the concept of an interdimensional rift being the origin of Earth's creatures of lore, excitement at the wonder and unlimited potential of such a world made me giddy. And it takes a lot to make me giddy. But a lonely, hot-bodied vampire named Tobias was my first indication that my gleefulness wasn't going to end anytime soon.

Add a feisty heroine who's part demon, part human, and full-on furious with this yummy vamp, and you have all sorts of fun as each of them fights their feelings for the other, determined to keep their relationship on a professional level while they investigate a string of murders.

Yeah. Like that ever works—in fiction, at least. We want our characters to be heroic, but flawed. And you can't get much more flawed than when you fall in love and completely complicate your life.

My website has some extras from KISS OF THE VAMPIRE: a deleted scene, a map showing where the bodies were found as well as an X-marks-the-spot where the final battle took place, a page of Nix's investigative notes, and a brief interview with Tobias Caine.

Look for Dante and Tori's story in my upcoming *Secret of the Wolf.*

Thanks for coming along for the ride!

Happy Reading!

Cynthia Garner

cynthiagarnerbooks@gmail.com

Find out more about Forever Romance!

Visit us at
www.hachettebookgroup.com/publishing_forever.aspx

Find us on Facebook
http://www.facebook.com/ForeverRomance

Follow us on Twitter
http://twitter.com/ForeverRomance

NEW AND UPCOMING TITLES

Each month we feature our new titles
and reader favorites.

CONTESTS AND GIVEAWAYS

We give away galleys, autographed copies,
and all kinds of exclusive items.

AUTHOR INFO

You'll find bios, articles, and links to personal websites
for all your favorite authors—and so much more.

GET SOCIAL

Connect with your favorite authors, editors, and
other Forever fans, and share what's important to you.

THE BUZZ

Sign up for our monthly romance newsletter,
and be the first to read all about it.